I0685941

Praise for A Hero's Promise

"Rich with intrigue and suspense, Carter's story of love and family will enthrall readers. A HERO'S PROMISE weaves together threads that solve the murder and blend two families." FOUR STARS!

—*Robin Taylor, for Romantic Times Book Club*

"Again, Anne Carter has not only surprised this reviewer at her brilliancy in creating a sequel to her hit novel STARCROSSED HEARTS but has actually made it heart-felt and a keeper. [Jessica and Dane are] two characters that are unforgettable as ever. I will definitely be on the lookout for the next book in this wonderful saga!"

—*Melinda Barerra for LoveRomances.com*

"A HERO'S PROMISE is one of those well-crafted books that leaves you thinking about the characters long after you've finished. Anne Carter is a master at creating rich, believable characters. I look forward to more books from this talented writer."

—*Cheryl Norman, Award-winning author of LAST RESORT and RESTORE MY HEART, Medallion Press*

"...Dane has mellowed, but... he's still the most amazing, vital, appealing hero I have had the pleasure of curling up between the covers with in a very long time!"

—*Roberta Olsen Major, author of BOUND*

A Hero's Promise

A Contemporary Romance

Anne Carter

Beacon Street Books

A Hero's Promise

by Anne Carter

Edited by J.R. Turner

Cover © by All Kinds of Covers

ISBN 978-0615628714

Previously Published ISBN 1-59088-834-0

February 2022

Beacon Street Books

Santa Clarita, CA 91355-2026

http://www.beaconstreetbooks.com

Printed in the United States of America

To all the Celluloid Heroes of
The Silver Screen...
Thank you for the inspiration, gentlemen.
May your stars always shine brightly.

Prologue

I swore I would never again put my thoughts on paper after that last disastrous go at keeping a journal. Perhaps here, in the sanctity of personal cyberspace—like what is that? — I can release a few of the demons that still haunt me after all this time.

It's been three years, give or take a heartbeat, since I left L.A. and the woman of my soul behind. I guess I've seen her a couple of times since, but they were faux meetings; she might as well have been a stranger on the street, an acquaintance, the wife of my new business partner. A partner, and friend, to whom I made an impossible promise. Why do we do such foolish things? In my case it was because it was the only way out alive.

Wyoming has been good for me. Ghosts have trouble breathing here, the air is so crisp and clean. Sometimes I have trouble breathing here, but it is not because of the air.

I know it was crazy to think that distance would be enough. But the physical separation from temptation has, at least, afforded me my dignity and some minor relief from the madness that pervades in her presence.

MacKendall has asked me to come back, to work on a new film with him. I haven't made a picture for a year or so, haven't done a decent one since the last one I did with her, and this is an excellent opportunity to get back into the dance. Reading the script, I could feel the heat of the lights, hear the crackle of electric excitement when the cameras begin to roll. I didn't even realize I was already making notes in the margin.

It is the picture that could turn my career around. Still, it will mean that I will see her; worse, her and him, together. Damnation.

I might be crazy if I think this keyboard will remain my ally, and my disk space a safe, password-protected harbor for my restless thoughts.

The old journal is in the corner of my closet shelf, dusty, dark, forbidden. Chapters of my life that are closed.

Can I do this? Can I wear the face of smiling deceit, playing the greatest role of my life, that of a caring but distant friend? She can never know of the turmoil, the torturous love that lives on inside me, of the indefinable need or of the monumental promise I made.

I guess I will call him back.

Filmmaking is in my blood.

One

Trade Off

"Is that him?" the little boy asked, his small finger arrowed toward the tiny twinkle of light in the distant sky.

"Maybe," the woman answered, leaning down to lift the toddler and support him on her hip. "It should be. Daddy's not usually this late."

"It looks like his plane!"

Despite her anxiety, the woman chuckled. At this distance, the speck in the northern sky could be any type of aircraft, including Mac's single engine Cessna.

"Let's hope so, sweetheart. My, you're getting heavy!"

Jessica MacKendall shifted her son to the other hip, and then pulled a wisp of hair away from her lips. Mac had never been so late before, and at last check, her friends in the tower had not heard from him. It was a short flight from Monterey to L.A., but she didn't know exactly what time he had lifted off. Still, it was getting dark, and a fog was creeping in. Although Mac was licensed to fly by instruments, he disliked doing so.

Weary, she put the boy back down and stretched her muscles.

"Maybe he crashed!"

"Devon! Don't ever say that!" Alarmed, Jessica squatted down and took her son by the shoulders, peering into his soulful brown eyes. "Daddy is a really, really good pilot. He is very careful when he flies, so don't worry, okay?"

Devon nodded solemnly and wrapped his arms around his mother's neck. Over his shoulder, Jessica squinted at the single headlight, hoping with all her being that it was Mac's plane.

What would I do without him?

They were rarely apart. In the three years since Devon's birth, their marriage had grown steadily stronger, their lives fuller. Sure, the spotlights made it difficult; the media and the couple's notoriety often threatened to diminish their intimacy, taking every opportunity to invade their privacy. Even now, standing on the tarmac at the small, community airport nearest their home, Jessica could see fans gawking from the terminal window.

How could I go on?

Mac put up with the fans better, she thought. So patient, and genuinely friendly to everyone he met. *If he were here right now, he'd be waving at those gawkers*

Those rude people. They have no idea how worried I am.

He said he'd be home in time for dinner. They were going to pick up barbequed beef sandwiches. Dinnertime, to Mac, was over an hour ago. Around the time Devon had turned two, Mac had instituted a set mealtime, telling Jessica how important it was to have routines. Especially for Hollywood kids.

"That's him, Mommy. He's hungry for dinner."

Jessica cupped her young son's cheek in her hand.

If he ever shows up, I'll have to tell him to never do this to me again.

There was a time when he left her. Worse, he had left her in anger, and had traveled halfway around the world to get away from her. Years ago, now, and the jealousy that had surfaced into rage was all but gone. And so was the man triggering that jealousy. The other man.

"I never want us to be apart again," Mac had said, when, at last, they reconciled.

And we won't. Ever.

They usually flew together, Jessica sometimes taking control of the plane while Mac patiently taught her the ropes. Like most pilots, he was fascinated by aircraft, passionate about flying. But she had never met a more cautious man.

Jessica turned her face into the wind, letting the brisk breeze pull the hair away from her face. The craft in the northern sky banked, correcting its path, then straightened out again.

He'd had all new gauges installed. New tires put on. The vertical stabilizer was next for maintenance, but there was really nothing wrong with it, Mac had assured her. Still, there was that annoying rattle on their last trip to Santa Barbara.

"Probably just the passenger side door," Mac had assured her. The door was damaged in a windstorm several years earlier.

Jessica nibbled at her thumbnail. What if it wasn't the door?

"Mommy, I'm tired."

"I know, darling. He'll be here soon."

Soon. Please, God. I know I'm being unreasonable. I know I begged you for a baby just last night. But please, I'd rather have Mac. I'd rather—

"Mrs. MacKendall?"

Jessica jerked to attention as a man wearing a baseball cap tapped her on the shoulder.

"Thought you'd like to know, that's your husband on approach," he said, waving a finger toward the headlight beam descending at the north end of the runway.

Jessica let out the deep breath she had been holding. "Yes," she said, "I know. My son told me."

"How can she not know who the father is?" Jessica asked, looking up for the third time from the open screenplay in her lap.

"She knows. She's just not saying," Mac murmured. Leaning over a one-inch-thick document neatly stacked on the desk before him, he raked his fingers through his shaggy locks. "Dane must be nuts to let these guys put all this crap in here. There's got to be a simpler way to form a corporation. Oh, by the way, is this our weekend to have Megan?"

"No. She called and said her mother is taking her to Catalina as a belated birthday gift. I swear, your daughter sounds more like seventeen than ten." Jessica paused, then returned to their previous discussion. "I thought Charlene had really cleaned up her act."

Mac stopped reading and twisted around to gaze at his wife.

"She has. You know my sister. She gets bored."

"Bored? Is that any reason to get pregnant?"

Mac turned off the desk lamp and stood up. "Okay. What's eating you?"

Sullen, Jessica looked back at the script. "Nothing."

"Right." He sat on the couch beside her, throwing his arm across the back as he turned to face her. "Look, I'm sorry I was so late. I should have called you when I put the plane down in Santa Barbara. I just got so hung up on trying to find out what was wrong with that damned oil gauge—"

Jessica lifted her eyes slowly to meet his, her annoyed expression softening to one of sadness tinged with fear. "Of course, you had to land. What if—what if you had really been out of oil? I was just so... worried," she said, her eyes glistening with unshed tears. "And Dev was getting freaked out, too. You should talk to him."

"I will." Mac took her into his arms and gently rocked her. It was enough of an apology for Jessica.

"I didn't mean to be critical of Charlene," she said later as they prepared for bed.

"You were right, though. It was a dumb thing to do. I'm thinking of asking her to come out."

"Here? When? Isn't the baby almost due?"

"Yeah. I think she should be here when it comes." Mac paused, toothbrush in hand, watching for his wife's reaction.

Jessica stopped brushing her hair and returned his gaze. "Well, if you think that's best, of course she can stay here."

Mac sighed and tilted his head, giving her a look she adored. "She's never been through this, you know. I'd hate for her to be alone."

"That can be scary," Jessica agreed, looking down in memory at her own abdomen, now slender and flat.

"Hey, I got here in time!" he reminded her with a smile.

"Barely. Just barely, husband dear."

"As I recall, you were in good hands."

"Dane, good hands? Ha! Who are you kidding?" Jessica pulled her knees up and wrapped her arms around them, her eyes now glazed in memory of the night their son was born.

"Well, with any luck, I'll be here the whole time for the next one."

"If we ever get a next one."

Mac dried his face, then sat on the bed beside her and grasped her chin in his fist. "We will. Soon." Pressing her back against the pillow, he brought his lips against hers with such gentle purpose that Jessica was filled with new affection for her husband. He pulled away only long enough to turn out the light, and then recommenced his amorous demonstration of love. "Who knows, maybe tonight's the night," he whispered in the dark, prompting giggles from Jessica.

"Maybe," she whispered back, her frivolity waning as she remembered her prayers for another child and the trade-off she had opted for that day on the runway.

It was silly, she decided. She hadn't made any deals with God, either way. He alone decided when and where babies were conceived, and airplanes crashed. One woman's hysterical plea in a world of billions would not have caught His ear.

Two

Wrongful Death

Dane Pierce left the front door opened wide and stepped out onto the broad, wooden plank porch. Fixated on the sunset before him, he slowly lowered himself into the Adirondack chair and slouched into his usual comfort zone. Dusk signaled the end of another peaceful Wyoming day, but Dane did not absorb the tranquility to which he had grown accustomed.

He barely saw the dramatic reds softly become magenta and pale pink, as the sun dipped lower above the prairie's farthest point. His ear, normally keen to every sound, every nuance to the tiniest degree, could not discern the horses' cranky discourse or the onset of the crickets' evening song.

Peering out through slightly squinted eyes, he pulled at the moustache adorning his lip, seeing not the palette of colors before him but instead the woman who colored his soul more brilliantly than any sunset tinted sky.

Mac would be calling soon. Dane recalled the text of the e-mail waiting for him this morning, chastising him for his failure to respond to the offer. The script was a good one, and just the right vehicle to re-establish Dane Pierce as a top box office moneymaker. But if he went back, it would not be for this deal or that. There was any number of outstanding screenplays stacked on his own desk.

No, he would have to examine his motives very carefully; for should he stumble, the consequences were hefty.

How could he go back? Back to Hollywood, back in close proximity to the one thing he could not have?

Unbidden, his fingers moved upward to the bridge of his nose, sliding downward and tracing its shape thoughtfully. It was too big, had always been too big. She had called it distinguished. A smile curled his lips at the memory, and he shook his head slowly.

She would never willfully hurt anyone. Not knowingly. But she didn't know, did she? She had never really believed him, never trusted him, never thought his interest in her was anything more than unadulterated lust.

And why should she.

The smile faded from his lips and fingertips now felt their way across them and down to his chin, bearing the stubble of two lazy days.

No, Jessica didn't know the depths of his love. And his task, his ultimate challenge, was to get in and out of Hollywood once again without her finding out.

As expected, the shrill ring of the telephone interrupted his meditation, and he reached for the cordless on the table beside him.

"So, what's holding this up?" Mac wanted to know. "You could be here in the morning."

"I don't know."

"This is it, pal. Think about it. Another year off and all those sweet young girls will tear your posters out of their school lockers."

"All right. You've convinced me."

"No lie? You're coming then? I can get my wife off my back?"

Dane paused. Mac's reference to Jessica grew a small mound in his throat. He stood and walked to the opposite end of the porch. "I... have a few loose ends to tie up here. Gimme a week."

"Hallelujah. I can set up a meeting with Access a week from Monday?"

"Access?"

"Michelhenny's new group. They're the guys that spun from Paramount, I told you about them. Can we count on you?"

"Yeah, sure." Dane paced as he talked, his anticipation building. "Jessie in on this?"

"You're kidding, right? You want to say hi? She's right here."

"No, that's—" Dane cut himself off as he heard the muffled

sounds of the phone already being handled. Like an ornery horse wary of being saddled, he filled his lungs and held his breath. He didn't want to talk to her; he couldn't wait to hear her voice.

"Hi, stranger." Jessica's words drifted into his head like the sweet notes of a familiar love song. "Do say you're heading south."

"Looks that way."

"Well, it's about time. How've you been? And what's so important in Wyoming?"

Dane blew his breath out through pursed lips. "Oh, clear skies, good whiskey, rugged women and the like..."

"Ah. Women. Of course. There are women down here, too, you might recall."

"Last L.A. woman I hooked up with almost killed me."

"Good point," Jessica agreed with a small giggle. There was a pause, and Dane sensed she was moving about. Muffled, indistinguishable sounds filled the space until she spoke again. "I miss you," she said at last.

"Like a disease," he murmured, stuffing his fingers into the hip pocket of his jeans. "How's everything?"

"Couldn't be better." Her voice was confident, and Dane closed his eyes. He'd hoped for worse. "Devon's going to preschool now."

"You don't have another one yet, do you?"

"No, no such luck. Did you hear about Char?"

"Can't hang that one on me." For the fourth time, Dane walked the length of the porch and turned around.

"Too bad you two couldn't make a go of it," she said with a wistfulness he hated.

"We're better off friends. I haven't seen her much since we got back from East Asia. I call her occasionally."

"So, you don't know who the father is?"

"You don't seriously think she'd tell me, do you?"

"I don't know. You have a way of extracting confessions from unsuspecting women."

"You got one?" Dane grinned.

"A confession? I already gave it to you. I miss you."

The grin remained static, his throat again swelling painfully. When he could speak again, his voice was soft, too soft for his intention. "I miss you, too, sweetie. You take care."

Dane pushed the "off" button on the phone and stared at it for a moment. This small black device had put her voice inside his head, her face inside his mind. The vision brought him both joy and misery.

"Damn it," he muttered, and pitched the phone as hard as he could in the direction of the Grand Tetons.

·♥·♥·♥·♥·♥·

"Did Dane sound different to you?" Jessica asked, returning to the house from the back patio, the telephone still in her hand.

"Different, how? He always sounds a bubble or two out of plumb to me."

"Oh, I don't know. Just a little... melancholy, perhaps."

Mac shrugged, took the phone from her, and started punching in a new number. "He's probably been alone too long. That ranch is pretty isolated up there."

"If you're right, it's a good thing he's coming back. It worries me."

Mac looked about to contradict her when his party answered, and he turned away to begin his conversation. Jessica went back to the patio and the warmth of the late spring sun. Soon, Mac returned, walking slowly along the edge of the pool, obviously troubled.

Jessica felt compelled to reopen their conversation. "Do you think he'll ever be... really happy?"

"Dane? No."

"Why do you say that?"

"He doesn't know how. I mean, it's like every time he gets a shot at something good, he blows it. He... he sabotages his own happiness."

Jessica stood from the chaise lounge on which she had been lying. "Surely you don't think he created the problems with Jackie?"

"I'm not talking about Jackie. But since you mentioned it, what happened there, anyway? Why would a guy, a guy who could have any woman eating at his feet, propose to a woman psychopathic enough to put a bullet into his chest?"

"He didn't know that about her when they met."

"No, but you can't tell me that he loved her. He didn't love her then, you knew it, I knew it and he knew it. Why would he do that?" Mac squatted down and dipped two fingers into the pool water. "Yeah, well, I know why he did it," he finally murmured.

Jessica was taken aback at the tone of his voice. "If I didn't know better, I'd think you have unresolved issues with Dane."

"No. I don't."

"You're really upset about this. Is there something we need to talk about, because I happen to know Dane thinks the world of you."

"Yeah, I know. Look, we're going to be late, so could we just table this discussion?"

"Mac... I thought everything was great between you guys."

"It is, okay? I just feel bad for him. I want to shake him sometimes. He hangs on to things that he shouldn't."

"Well, it sounds to me like you're the one hanging on to things. I, for one, can't wait to see him."

Mac stood and turned to peer at his wife. His face bore a mask of indignation, and his eyes were those of a stranger. Jessica raised her eyebrows, tilting her head in confusion. Her expression moved him somehow, and his look softened as he reached for her.

"I'm sorry. Don't worry about this, okay?" He gave her a brief, preoccupied hug, then released her. "Have you called the sitter? I've got to get my hair cut if I expect anyone to recognize me at that dinner tonight."

Jessica stared after her husband as he strode purposefully toward the house. She would assess Dane's demeanor when he arrived.

The ringing of their bedside telephone at 3 a.m. brought Mac to startled consciousness, his heart pounding from the unexpected shock. The fundraiser had lasted well beyond midnight, and he had slept a scant hour. His sister's thin, distressed voice further alarmed him.

"What's the matter? Are you okay? Are you in pain?"

"I'm scared, Core. I can hardly believe it myself, but I'm scared shitless. What if I can't do this? What if I can't take the pain? I'm afraid I'll, you know, self-medicate with coke or something."

"Calm down. Take a deep breath."

Beside him Jessica sat up, her eyes wide. Mac brushed the hair from his eyes and moved the phone to his other ear.

"I told you you're welcome to come out here. Why don't you hop a jet tomorrow and come on out? No sense in being alone."

"I called the airline today. They say I'm too far along to fly."

"Bullshit. Look, I'll fly out there and get you. What do you say?"

"You'd really do that? For me?"

"Naw, I really just want to put some more mileage on my plane. But you can hitch a ride if you want."

"Oh, man, that would be sweet. I'll get someone to fill in for me for a couple of weeks or so. When will you be here?"

"Day after tomorrow. So get packing."

"Yeah, like I got a lot of stuff. You don't worry, I'll be ready." The joy in Charlene's voice satisfied Mac, and he fell back into his pillow with a resigned sigh.

"She's coming."

Jessica, too, collapsed back into bed. "You're flying all the way to Minneapolis?"

"It'll be easy. Don't worry."

·♥·♥·♥·♥·♥·

Dane methodically checked over his saddle and bags before hoisting himself up onto Big Barley's back. Even though Greg had taken great care in preparing for the ride, Dane was obsessive when it came to horsemanship. Leaning close, he slid his hand down Barley's neck, delighting in the silken mane and taut muscles beneath.

"I might be out a day or two," Dane called to his groom, who nodded. "Make sure you lock up when you take off."

Greg offered a salute and a grin. "Happy trails, boss."

Giving his Stetson a little tug, Dane was off, heading for the familiar trail leading away from Jackson. His trek would take him not only away from his ranch, but also away from the world at large and his latest dilemma.

Ah, who was he kidding?

He had not expected last night's phone call from Minneapolis; Mac was giving off mixed messages. Worse than mixed—he'd been downright asinine. And it was more than just a change of heart. His on-again, off-again "best friend" was apparently off-again. *I should have known better.*

No, Dane's little field trip would not separate him from the fact that his future was up for grabs. But the fresh air might afford him some clearer perspective.

·♥·♥·♥·♥·♥·

"He still has a little cough, but he's not contagious," Jessica assured the preschool director while tugging off her son's jacket. "I'll be at home if you need me."

"I'm sure he'll be fine. Today we're making sea animals out of clay."

Jessica smiled and squatted down. "Mommy will see you later. You have a good time with Miss Sue."

Satisfied with Devon's toothy grin, Jessica took her leave before either of them reconsidered. Although she knew it was good for her son to be away from her and exposed to other children, she missed his presence at home.

Maybe I do need to get back to work.

While driving back to the sprawling ranch estate she shared with Mac, Devon, and occasionally, Mac's ten-year-old daughter Megan, Jessica thought about the film project her husband was trying to put together. Romantic comedies were always popular, but it would be a first for the action-oriented MacKendall and for Dane Pierce. Mac insisted that Dane should direct Mr. Romance and possibly even star. Jessica shook her head, smiling at the prospect of Dane Pierce starring as a romance novel cover model.

Dane, romantic? Funny? Of course. And it was just off-kilter enough to thrill his fans.

Early on, Mac had subtly suggested that she consider the role of the heroine, a tough non-believer type reporter who is covering the Mr. Romance competition. His offer surprised her; she would never forget the fury Mac had displayed in times past, the ugly—and needless—jealousy over her friendship with Dane. Still, he was a determined man, and had taken great pains to keep that jealousy under wraps.

It was a long time ago. Things had changed, and Mac had resolved those differences, come to terms with Dane's presence in their lives. Or had he?

As she drove, Jessica pondered the emotions she had seen crossing her husband's face after their poolside conversation about Dane. Yet, Mac had initiated the contact. Mac had coerced Dane into forming the partnership, the new production company that would make *Mr. Romance.*

Jessica turned the Lexus convertible onto the long gravel driveway, instantly aware that someone was already waving to her from the front porch. Frowning, Jessica didn't bother to put the car into the garage, instead leaving it near the steps and hurrying to join

Gretchen at the front door. The housekeeper was dabbing at her cheeks with a tissue, unable to speak but beckoning for Jessica to follow her inside.

The large screen television in the family room was on, and Gretchen turned her stricken eyes back to the picture being broadcast. The words "breaking news" appeared in the corner of the screen, and the scene being transmitted by a helicopter cam was of a sparse, hilly landscape.

"What is it? What's happening?" Jessica asked, looking from the television to Gretchen's face and then back again.

The older woman merely shook her head. The sound of the helicopter was muted slightly as the newscaster's voiceover began.

"Once again, we're looking at the terrain around Pike Lake Regional Park where it is believed the small craft may have crashed, that plane belonging to movie and television entertainer Cory MacKendall..."

"Rescue teams are on the move, as you can see, they have several aircraft scanning the area and ground crews are already on the scene. We're told the single engine Cessna left the Minneapolis area just minutes ago bound for Los Angeles, with MacKendall and one passenger on board. It is unclear if a mayday call was picked up or not, but we'll bring you that information as soon as it becomes available. Again, a small aircraft being piloted by Cory "Mac" MacKendall is thought to have gone down just moments after taking off from Crystal Airport, just north of the Twin Cities..."

"MacKendall is best known for his long-running television series, Dr. Jim, and for his much-publicized marriage to Academy Award nominee Jessica Taylor. The couple has a four-year-old son and resides in Los Angeles, California, for which, according to a flight plan filed by MacKendall, his plane was bound this afternoon."

Jessica stared at the television screen, her face an emotionless mask. She made no movement, no effort to answer the phone that had been ringing since she had walked through the front door.

THREE

The Role of a Widow

Thomas Jarrick was one of those indispensable friends no one should be without. Calm and methodical, he went about the business of making essential arrangements for Mac's remains to be transported to Los Angeles for burial while dealing with the many people all wanting to help somehow. His wife Roxanne remained her best friend's protector, keeping all but those closest to Jessica at bay.

At the MacKendall home, mourners began to gather on the fringes of the property, and well-meaning friends called and dropped by at will. Mac's ex-wife telephoned to share her own heartbreak with Jessica, sadly informing her that young Megan had to be sedated when she was told of her father's passing. Jessica was newly devastated at this news; Megan was barely ten years old.

Feeling primarily cold and numb, Jessica went through the motions of preparing for a funeral, avoiding a massive attempt by the media for interviews and glimpses of her grief. Every television station and newspaper carried Mac's picture and photos of the crash site. In Minneapolis, fans camped on the steps of the hospital where Charlene MacKendall lay holding a tenuous thread to life. Dr. Jim's sister was loved by default.

Devon cried when his mother told him that his daddy would not be coming home anymore, but he would be with them in their hearts forever. Unable to get the answer he wanted from his mother, he cloistered himself in his room.

"Have you heard from Dane?" Christine asked, watching with trepidation as her twin sister's hand shook visibly while pouring out two cups of coffee.

"No. His antiquated answering machine is no longer picking up. No one knows where he is." Jessica's tone was low with disenchantment. "I can't believe he hasn't called."

"Maybe he doesn't know."

"I don't know how he could not know. It's everywhere. The media won't let it rest." She paused and briefly covered her eyes. "Tom even sent him an e-mail."

Christine didn't reply.

"I got another call from the hospital. They've decided to leave Charlene on life support for the baby's sake. They want me—they want me to come back there and make some decisions. Next week. After the... the funeral."

"Why you?"

"I'm the closest thing to next-of-kin. The airlines made her fill out some kind of emergency info due to her condition naming Mac and me... for the baby in case anything happened to her. She was really freaked out about having that baby."

Christine nodded. "So, the baby's okay?"

"I guess so. They think so."

"Do you want me to go with you?"

Jessica offered what she knew was a bleak smile. "You've done so much already, Sis. If you could just keep Devon for a while, that would be the best thing. He loves to play with Angel. He calls her his cousin-girl." She took a tentative sip of the coffee. "Someone, possibly Tom, will go to Minneapolis with me."

They could not stop the phone from ringing, but a rotating staff of aides answered the queries and screened the calls.

"Mrs. MacKendall? The man on the phone says he's Mr. Pierce."

Jessica wasted no time in picking up the kitchen receiver. "Dane?"

"Mrs. MacKendall. This is Bob Pearce with WSBA News. I was wondering what you thought about the FAA's statement this morning. I'm sure you know we're being told that your husband radioed about a loss in oil pressure. Is it possible that your husband would fly without checking the oil level on the plane?"

Jessica left the phone dangling from the wall and crossed the family room to the back glass doors. She stepped outside to the patio, leaning heavily on the roof support post. "Oh Dane, where are you?" she whispered desperately. "I need you."

•❤•❤•❤•❤•❤•

Jessica was only dimly aware that the chapel behind her was filled beyond capacity. Her eyes drifted from the minister's face to the smooth, glossy finish on the mahogany casket, then to the forest of floral arrangements surrounding the alter. The sounds in her head would not let her hear the clergyman's words, his praise for Mac's so worthy lifetime, his regret that it was over too soon.

"Damn, she cut it so short this time," Mac was saying, his right hand smoothing the golden strands on the back of his head down to his collar. "I hate it."

"You always hate it at first. It will grow back, darling. It always does." Jessica smiled; she also preferred it longish, but she was careful to hide her opinion.

"I hope it doesn't diminish my virility," he said with a playfully wicked grin, slipping his hands around Jessica's waist and pulling her near.

"Not possible."

"When will we know?" he asked, nuzzling her ear as she twisted her head away from his plundering lips.

"Maybe Monday," she said with a giggle.

"We did everything right this time." His voice had lowered to a seductive whisper, sending chills down Jessica's back. "But perhaps we should try some more, just in case."

Jessica laughed and pushed him away. "You have to pack. We don't have time for this nonsense."

Still fussing with his hair, Mac turned to peer into the dresser mirror. "You didn't used to call it nonsense," he teased, watching his wife's reflection as she straightened the comforter on their bed.

"It is when you have a plane to fly. You'll thank me when you get on that 405 freeway."

People were standing and filing out of the church. Low murmurs floated about her, words like "graveside" and "hearse," words that meant nothing. Nothing but nonsense.

The minister ushered the last mourners out the door, asking that the widow be given a private visitation. Jessica stood and approached the open coffin, pausing several times in the aisle.

I have to do this. I must see him. It's the only way I will ever believe it.

For a moment, she was back at Jackie Spencer's funeral four years before. Sitting in the back of the chapel with her husband and their closest friends, she had stayed behind while Mac paid his last respects. Her eyes wide and brimming with tears, Jessica had trembled at the sight of Mac kneeling at the alter and crossing himself before standing to peer into Jackie's white lacquered coffin. As hard as she tried, she could not muster the will to join him. She could not look into the dead woman's face.

She had regretted it since.

Barely breathing, Jessica now peered into the ornate coffin at Mac's still form. She tried desperately to relate the words she had heard the others utter; those euphemistic, useless adjectives people always use to describe the departed.

But Mac looked neither serene nor peaceful. He did not look "good," or "at rest." The man in the casket was not Mac at all. An imposter perhaps, lying very still, with make-up on his face and Mac's blue silk shirt on his body.

Slowly, Jessica drew her hand up from where it dangled at her side, moving it inch by inch toward the man before her, her fingers not quite steady in their quest. They hovered an eternity over his chest, moving even more slowly now until her fingertips finally touched the fine silk fabric above his breast pocket. Gently she rested her hand there.

Waiting for a beat.

Waiting for a movement.

Waiting for his eyes to flutter open and adore her one more time.

Sensing someone beside her, Jessica withdrew her hand and turned. The minister was taking her by the elbow. She paused, gazing over the empty pews, the nearly spent, dripping candles and the stained-glass windows. Someone was sitting in the very back, someone sitting very still and unrecognizable in the shadows. Jessica had barely noticed his presence when she forgot it and glanced back to the casket.

"It's not him," she murmured, allowing the minister to gently steer her out the side door and toward the black limousine at the curb.

Henry was waiting, sweating in the late morning sun. Perhaps it wasn't perspiration, Jessica decided. No, those were tears wetting the big man's cheeks as he opened the rear door for his longtime employer's widow.

Tears. They were everywhere. The paper was sure to read that there was not a dry eye in the place. None, except for hers.

She paused before climbing into the backseat, aware that her friends were watching from beside the limo ahead of hers. She could not see their faces in the bright sunlight. They were probably crying, too, behind their dark sunglasses.

In the cemetery, she stood alone, away from the others. Again, Jessica ignored the sermon, lost in her own thoughts, caught between the web of the past and the dark emptiness of the future.

He had cried at his mother's funeral. It was not the first time Jessica had seen her husband cry, but certainly the first time she had witnessed such grief.

"I can't believe she's gone," he said, swiping at the tears that plummeted down his cheeks. "She was always so strong."

Jessica watched, dry-eyed, as they lowered Mac's casket into the ground. "He was always so strong," she murmured. And then she was back in the limousine.

"Mr. Jarrick's house, Mrs. MacKendall?"

"No, Henry. Take me home, please."

She pushed her key into the bolt, only remotely realizing she had left the front door unlocked.

"I'll wait," Henry said from somewhere behind her.

"No need, you go ahead. You were part of Mac's family; you go on over."

"But Mrs. MacKendall, I think—"

"Don't worry about me, Henry. I'll be okay."

With a regretful tilt of his head, Henry got back into the car and maneuvered the long vehicle around the circle driveway. Jessica did not look back.

Easels bearing wreathes lined the entryway of the house, the frame of one catching the delicate ecru gauze of her skirt. She paused, half-heartedly attempting to disengage the material from the stand but failing before finally giving the arrangement a hearty kick. Gardenia petals rained over the foyer.

Walking straight to the bar, Jessica perused the rack for something to drink. Something that would be fast. Scotch.

She slipped out of her pumps and started to sit on the couch, but instead stood staring at it from the middle of the room. She sat down on the floor, took a sip and grimaced, still focused on the massive sectional sofa she and Mac bought on their first wedding anniversary.

It was comfortable.

"Remember when I got so mad at you for flying to San Diego without telling me?" she asked aloud. She smiled and took another slug of scotch, then leaned forward to stroke the heavy tweed upholstery.

"Cushy, huh?" The salesman hovered nearby. "You folks want to talk it over?"

"Naw. We'll take it," Mac said, folding his arms behind his neck and stretching his long legs to the end of the couch. "If she likes it, I'm happy."

"I didn't like it that much, Mac," Jessica whispered. "It wasn't quite wide enough for both of us."

Looking around the room, her eyes trailed along the bookcases, the fireplace mantel, the corner shelves. Every surface held him, displayed him, identified him. His awards, his trophies, his photos —his model cars, his toys. And more, they identified her. For everything he was, so was she.

And without him, she was—

She was nothing.

The burning in her stomach couldn't match the searing pain that seeped into her eyes. Setting the glass beside her on the floor, she drew her knees up to her chest and lowered her face against them. The floodgate was finally open.

"You should have taken me with you," she cried, her voice a desperate whisper. "I can't be here without you."

She got up and went to the fireplace, still weeping, and reached for the Emmy statuette. It was cold and heavy in her hands. She carried it back to where she had been sitting and resumed her position, taking another sip of the scotch and cradling the trophy in her arms.

"Oh, God, he can't be gone..." she wailed, rocking back and forth on the floor. "You promised! You promised you would never leave me again!"

The sobbing escalated. Jessica could no longer control the deep spasms originating from within, the heart-rending cries of terror borne of the ultimate loneliness. Oblivious to her surroundings, she relinquished all hold on time and space. Reality faded away, was lost to her... lost until she was temporarily delivered from grief.

Startled, she struggled to glimpse the face of the man who held her so tightly, who cooed into her ear with assurances and love. But even before her swollen eyes could focus in the ebbing afternoon light, she knew the name of her savior.

There was distinction in the way he embraced her; a scent that was entirely his own, right now a comforting potion of tequila and expensive cologne. There was familiarity in his tone, a voice not deep, but deceivingly youthful.

"Shh... it's okay, sweetie. It's okay. He didn't want to leave you, baby."

He gathered her into his arms and lifted her to the couch, where she immediately curled against him, her face dampening his chest. Ever so gently he stroked her back, his lips brushing across the top of her hair as still she wept. It was some time before her breathing returned to normal; the room was nearly dark.

"Dane, is it true what they say about your hair still growing even after you die?" she asked.

"I don't know, Jess." Dane closed his eyes tightly and turned them slightly away. "It probably is."

·♥·♥·♥·♥·♥·

Every head in the room turned when Dane Pierce ushered Jessica MacKendall through the doorway into Tom and Roxanne's home; the reception was nearly over.

A band of mourners immediately surrounded her, many of whom she did not recognize.

"He was one helluva guy, Jessica."

He never liked you, Fred.

"He was always so kind and generous."

Not as generous as you were, with his money.

"I'm just devastated by what happened."

Of course you are. Now, please move on.

"I'll never forget working with him in The Senator."

Funny, he had already forgotten you. What was your name again?

"He was so cute in Dr. Jim!"

Get away from me!

Roxanne hovered nearby, taking the opportunity to pull her aside when Jessica was momentarily alone.

"Honey, are you okay? I've been so worried."

"Is there coffee, Rox?"

"Sure."

Roxanne herded a wobbly Jessica into the kitchen while Dane parked himself in the corner of the living room, allowing Tom to fill him a glass.

"When did he show up?" Roxanne wanted to know, handing Jessica a steaming mug of fresh coffee.

"He was there, at the... chapel, he was sitting in the back, he said. He came by the house after I went home."

"Why didn't you come over here after?"

"I wasn't ready to face all these awful... people."

"They're your friends, Jess. And Mac's friends. They're grieving."

Jessica put her cup down. "And I'm not?"

Roxanne turned an incredulous face her way. "I sure didn't mean that, Jessica. I only meant..."

"That as the widow of the hour, I should be hugging strangers and shaking hands and smiling and saying how I'm going to be okay?"

"Are you drunk?"

Roxanne's question, aimed right between the eyes, hit its mark.

"I'm not so very drunk, Mac, just hurting."

"I know, baby. I know."

It was the premiere of Bellerive, her film debut. Dane had snubbed her. Mac had rescued her. A lifetime ago.

"I'm sorry, Rox." Jessica lowered herself slowly into a kitchen chair. Looking up, she forced a dim smile. "It's a role I've never played. I'll get better at it, I promise." She held up the mug in salute, and Roxanne gave her a pitying look.

"You don't have to get better at it. You just have to get through today. And then tomorrow. One day at a time."

•♥•♥•♥•♥•♥•

Jessica collapsed on the sofa beside Tom. In the corner recliner, Dane lay back with his eyes closed. Roxanne joined them after seeing the last guest to the door.

"Nice of you to join us," she said in Dane's direction as she bent to pick up a collection of empty glasses from the coffee table.

"Don't bother with that stuff. We have people to do that. You sit down," Tom directed his wife. Without another word, Roxanne dropped onto the couch between Jessica and Tom.

Jessica fell over to the side cushion, throwing an arm across her eyes in exhaustion and despair.

"How you holding up?" Tom asked, his usual sincerity even more evident tonight. Reaching across his wife, Tom grasped Jessica's free hand and squeezed it.

"Barely."

"You want to stay here tonight?"

Jessica had not had time to answer when Christine emerged from the hallway. "The kids are asleep."

Jessica frowned, looking around dizzily. "Where's Mom?"

"Nick took her back to the hotel. She's a wreck."

She's a wreck! That her mother had recently come to love Mac was irrelevant; Jessica had never forgiven her for the days when Wesley Elliot, her psychopathic ex-husband, had meant more to Janet Taylor than her own daughter.

"Don't be so critical, Jess. Everybody has their cross to bear. People don't always say what they really mean."

"I know... it's just that..."

Mac looked up from where he squatted, inspecting the rear tire of his motorcycle, and flashed that dazzling smile.

"Just what?"

Just that you're not supposed to be dead.

Four

Changing Gears

Jessica stared out the first-class window of the wide-bodied jet at what she supposed was the Rocky Mountains. It was impossible to look at the landscape heading to Minneapolis with anything but painful despair, for although it was not the same terrain that claimed her husband's life, it represented the same. She slid the window shade down and eclipsed her view.

Taking a deep breath, she reached up and opened the nozzle on the air conditioner blower, and then turned to her companion. "How long a flight is it again?"

"A couple more hours," Dane said, squeezing her hand briefly. "Why don't you just take a nap?"

Jessica smiled and retrieved his hand for a return gesture. "Thanks. Maybe I will."

But she was unable to sleep. Indeed, the only sleep she was getting these days was involuntary, and fraught with horrendous nightmares. She couldn't even keep her eyes closed.

"I really appreciate your going with me," she said at last.

"I had to go anyway. To check things out at the House. Char did such a good job running it, I never had to do anything. I won't know where to begin."

"Surely your business manager could handle this for you?"

"Woody? Probably. But I want to see for myself what's going on there. When Charlene told me about her dream of a halfway house for potheads and junkies, I was skeptical. It was a touchy subject for me, after what happened to my folks. But she just kept on about it, saying things like, maybe someone else can be saved if we do this."

Jessica remembered well Dane's tormented retelling of his parents' deaths due to a drugged-out train engineer. The Marian Pierce House was a dream-come-true for both him and Charlene. Without her, the House's future was uncertain. It made perfect sense that Dane would want to see it through personally.

"You shaved your mustache."

Dane nodded. "I've been told it doesn't do anything for me."

"I told you that, didn't I?"

"It might have been you."

Jessica smiled briefly. She had complained to him... once upon a time. "I've been meaning to ask, how's your son? Is he still away at camp?"

"At his own request, yes. I'm bringing him home at the end of summer to live with me on the ranch. Alex is a cool kid—he's got his own agenda. We're getting along pretty well these days."

"Devon's been asking to visit your place ever since you sent us that postcard."

"Bring him up. It would be good for him. Good to get away from all that shit going on in L.A."

"Well, I don't want to bounce him around too much. He's already in Utah."

"It's a short hop to Wyoming."

"Maybe."

Seeming satisfied with her answer, Dane leaned back in his seat.

Jessica's breath caught in her throat at the site of her sister-in-law. Abrasions covered one side of her face, and a myriad of tubes snaked in and out of her body. Her swollen belly seemed unbelievably oversized.

"She's in a coma," the doctor was saying. "And we need to take the baby. Today."

Jessica nodded dumbly, a barely audible sob escaping her lungs. Dane slipped a comforting arm around her shoulders.

"Do whatever you have to do," Jessica murmured. "I'll sign the papers."

The baby was delivered that afternoon. Benjamin Cory MacKendall weighed in at eight pounds and was guardedly assessed as healthy; his mother remained on life support.

"There's nothing you can do at the moment," a nurse advised. "We have a chapel on the third floor." Dane led Jessica to the elevator and then into the small, non-denominational chapel. They sat down in the back of the empty room.

"I can't get her face out of my mind," Jessica said. "At least Mac died instantly, his neck... you know... but she looked so banged up."

"Maybe it was a tradeoff, her being thrown from the plane. It may have saved the baby's life."

"There's no such thing as a tradeoff." Jessica looked up at the religious images above the small pulpit. "Mac's dead and I'm not pregnant."

Dane looked up in confusion.

"It doesn't matter," Jessica said softly. "Never mind."

After a time, she turned to Dane, tears brimming in her eyes. "I don't know what to do," she confessed, her voice breaking.

"Neither do I. I quit praying when my mother died. Just... just close your eyes and say you love her."

"I haven't been very nice to her."

"Nonsense. She thinks you're the best." And she did, he reminded himself. As tough as she was, Charlene had a soft side not many had seen. He counted himself lucky to have known her.

Jessica squeezed her eyes tightly closed and stifled her sobs. "I'm sorry," she offered quietly.

He kept his arm around her as they approached the nursery window.

"You up to this?"

"Yes. I want to see him. He's family."

Dane nodded, keeping his own thoughts well buried. Focus on the miracle, not the tragedy.

Benjamin was sleeping.

"He's beautiful," Jessica breathed, admiring the tiny boy with the whisper of almost colorless hair. The nursery attendant smiled and adjusted the blanket around the infant. Jessica's chin quivered slightly. "It's awful that he won't be nursed."

"A lot of babies have grown up fine without being breast fed, Jess. He's lucky to be alive."

"Lucky? With no father, almost no mother? I'm not so sure. He needs family." Jessica beckoned for the nurse. "I need to come in. I want to hold him."

The neo-natal nurse looked uncertain, but a warm smile from Dane dashed her concerns and she allowed Jessica to take the sleeping infant from his bassinet.

"Ohh..." Jessica lowered her cheek against the baby's downy-soft head and closed her eyes. "That baby smell. It's like a tonic."

"The smell I remember the most is poopy diapers," Dane quipped, but he caressed Benjamin's chin with the back of his finger. "Something tells me he'll do fine. Comes from good stock, right? At least half of him."

"I hope you're right."

"You need to not worry so much." But Dane knew she would worry. He sensed a plan was forming in her head, and unlike Jessica, he hoped he was wrong.

The following morning Jessica accompanied Dane on a tour of the Marian Pierce facility. He took careful notes as they walked, asking several questions of the young woman who had been appointed manager in Charlene's absence.

"I never thought it would be any more than a couple of weeks. Until she had the baby," Paula Reed said. "We're all shaken up.

"Anyway, we have six bedrooms on this side. Three are private, three are shared. As you saw, the middle is the community room, and the dining room, and the office in the front. And in the back is barracks."

"Barracks?"

"We call it that. A big sleeping room for over-nighters. A place to crash. There are seventeen cots in there."

Dane nodded. "So, you can keep nine people in residence at any one time?"

"Well, nine or more if they squeeze. But each person can only stay up to ninety days at a time. There're just so many people who need a place to stay while they clean up. That's why we're getting the new wing."

They walked to the far side of the building where construction was underway.

"This side will add ten shared bedrooms. It's a major deal," Paula explained. "She was so excited about it."

"She mentioned it to me, but this is bigger than I thought."

"We got some great donations."

"Obviously," Dane murmured.

Jessica remained quiet throughout the tour.

Sporting a Minnesota Vikings cap and sunglasses, Dane accompanied Jessica to her gate at Minneapolis-St. Paul International Airport. Her flight to Salt Lake City would leave twenty minutes before his to Los Angeles.

"God, I hate airports," he told her, looking around at the crowded terminal. "I hate flying, for that matter."

"You hate not being in control."

"True enough." He started to comment further about her perception when the gate attendant announced Jessica's flight. First class would board after the pre-boarding passengers.

He picked up her carry-on bag. "You take care."

"Of course. You, too."

"A little different than the airport in Amande, huh?"

Jessica turned at his reference to the day he'd sent her home from the Caribbean after the completion of their epic film, Lost Season. After his confession of love, and a night of lovemaking on the sand.

She swallowed hard. "Oh yes. Different."

Dane knew her smile was forced; he wished her hopelessly sweet brown eyes were not so red.

"Then there was Cambodia," she added with an obviously faux cough.

Dane shook his head. "That doesn't count. I was on a stretcher." A melancholy chuckle emanated from his chest, and he grasped Jessica's forearms as they called First Class passengers. "You think about what I said. About coming up to the ranch."

"I will. I have a lot to do before I can even begin to—"

"I know. Just... just remember I'm around."

He kissed her on the forehead and took a couple of steps backward, then turned and walked briskly in the direction of the gate collecting Los Angeles-bound passengers.

Dane's thoughts continued to be jumbled, had been that way since he'd returned from his three-day ride to multiple messages conveying horrifying news.

He had many questions but avoided the most important one; how he felt about Mac's death was still off-limits. A spot too sore to touch, a knotted chain too tangled to unravel. His feigned comfort with Jessica was easy enough; he was, after all, an actor.

Irma Carvey could well have won a role as the mouse that roared. Barely four feet six inches tall and wearing a suit Barbie might have found tight, she perched herself on the edge of Jessica's living room couch, clipboard on her lap.

"Social Services is a difficult job, Mrs. MacKendall. While some action may seem perfectly normal to you, it may be quite complicated on my side."

"I just don't understand why this can't be simpler. I am family, after all."

"Not blood-related, however."

"You don't need to be blood-related to love a child."

"Of course not. But the fact remains, we have not ascertained if this child has other blood relatives still living. So, our decision is to keep him in foster care for an additional sixty days while we publicize our search for his natural father."

"And if he doesn't come forward?"

"Well, the courts must decide. If his mother is still alive... you may or may not bother to initiate adoption proceedings. It's out of my hands."

"And I can't be his foster parent in the meantime?"

"We feel it's best to keep him in Minnesota at this time."

Jessica stood. "Miss Carvey, I don't mean to be... antagonistic. But this is a waste of time. Charlene... my sister-in-law's accident was well publicized, especially in the Minneapolis area. Benjie's story has been carried by every major news agency in the country. It's already been a month, if the father were going to come forth, he would have by now. I don't see the point in dragging this out further. I can provide a good home for him. And... I love him."

"As I said before, that's not for me to decide."

The social worker now stood also, clutching the clipboard tightly to her chest. She walked to the fireplace, lifting her hand and slowly dragging her fingers down the gold Emmy statuette on the mantel. Then she turned abruptly, rocking her head back until her nose was unnaturally higher than ear level.

"I'm sorry, Mrs. MacKendall. If you want the child badly enough, you'll have to be willing to wait the necessary time."

What a waste. And to think that I paid her way out here just so she could insult me.

Setting her jaw, Jessica walked the woman to the front door, closing it behind her with a little more force than necessary. In the hall, she clicked the thermostat down a notch and then collapsed on the couch.

She had not been able to forget about the sweet, practically orphaned baby left behind in Minnesota. The realization, after Mac's death, that she would never again be pregnant had enhanced her mourning. It was a cruel turn of events. But seeing the blue-eyed infant born to a nearly dead mother had sparked a glimmer of hope in her heart. While Benjamin was not Mac's son, he was genetically similar in some way.

And if Charlene did not recover, Jessica would raise that boy as her own.

Back in the kitchen, she poured a glass of lemonade and picked up the phone, retrieving a business card from the counter.

Her attorney was in.

"Funny you should call. I'm just reviewing the papers Dane dropped off."

"What papers?"

"Dissolving StarCrossed Productions. The new corporation."

"Oh..." The production company Mac had recently formed. "It seems like we just got it all set up. Office space, furniture, computers... Is he just dumping it altogether?"

"Yes. But what did you call about?"

Jessica relayed the latest information concerning Benjamin MacKendall. "Can they do that?"

Phillip Stern grunted. "Unfortunately, yes. I'm afraid you're going to have to sit tight, Jess. I've started a file on this deal, but until they give a little, we're kind of stuck."

"I just want him so bad."

"I know. But I think you should take some time to examine your own needs right now."

Fatherly advice was Phillip's specialty, and Jessica sighed. "You're right, of course." She rubbed her forehead, peering out the back glass doors to check on Devon, who was playing in the yard. Something else was needling her mind. "Phillip, do me a favor? Hold off a few days on dismantling the company. I want to talk to Dane."

"Sure. There's no real rush. One of you give me a call when you're decided."

Thoughtful, Jessica hung up the phone. Perhaps it was time to contact Dane.

•♥•♥•♥•♥•♥•

What was I thinking?

Dane ran his fingers through his ashen hair, pulling the near-straight locks away from his face as he peered into his bedroom mirror. Accusing green eyes peered back at him, reminding him of the complete idiot he turned into when it came to Jessica Taylor. MacKendall, he chastised himself. MacKendall! Mac's wife.

But it was too late to worry about his motives now. He had invited her to come, and coming she was.

He's only two months in the grave.

Dane turned on the bathroom faucet, splashing cold water on his face.

She called me. She wants to talk about StarCrossed.

The beach house had belonged to Tom and Roxanne Jarrick, but Dane had bought it from them for the periods he would be in L.A. Now, looking around, he saw the mess he'd made of it during his most recent, short stay. Quickly he began gathering up dirty glasses, paper plates and pizza boxes and hustling them into the small kitchen.

Stuffing the debris into the trashcan, he began running hot water into the sink, squirting in a healthy dose of dishwashing liquid. Water splashed onto the kitchen window and the floor as Dane shook off his hands and reached for a paper towel, unrolling several in the process.

"Damn," he muttered, bounding on to the bedroom where he swept up an armload of dirty laundry and threw it onto the closet floor.

What am I doing? She won't be coming in here.

Glancing around the bedroom, he closed the door and returned to the living room. It looked better. But why should he care? Trying to impress Jessica would only make her suspicious. He'd never been neat.

So he sat down on the couch. He didn't wait long.

"I wasn't sure if it was a left or a right back there," she said, breezing into the room like a walking bouquet of spring flowers.

"Where's Dev?"

"I left him with Lydia. My new nanny. I wanted us to have time to talk, you know?"

"Something to drink?"

"I can get it," she said, brushing past him. "I trust they didn't move the kitchen."

Dane grimaced behind her back despite his prior self-admonition.

"Want to sit outside?" she called over her shoulder.

"Sure."

She didn't seem to notice the two or three empty beer cans he'd missed on the patio deck as she made herself comfortable facing the sea.

"How's the deal coming with, uh, Benjamin?" he asked.

"It's taking time. I won't know anything for a while."

Dane nodded and pried the cap off a bottle of Corona. "How're you doing otherwise?"

Jessica seemed to focus on the crashing waves for a moment, as if deciding just how she was doing. "I miss him. I miss him every minute of every day. Some days are worse than others... but I keep reminding myself that he hated people to whine around."

"You, uh, wanted to talk about the company?"

"Yes." Blinking a few times, she created a smile and turned back to Dane. "I want to assume Mac's position in the corporation, whatever that was."

Dane cleared his throat and put down his bottle. "You what?"

"Let's keep StarCrossed intact. I think we should go ahead with *Mr. Romance*. He would have wanted it that way."

Dane broke his gaze and took a long draught of the beer, wiping his lips on the back of his hand. He stood, walked to the railing on the deck, and then turned to face her. "I don't think so."

"And why not?"

"Because I can't do it without him. It was a joint effort."

"We can do it together. He already had a crew in place. Come on, it will be a tribute."

"No."

Jessica rose and stood face to face with Dane, her eyes now defiant. "Is that it, then? You're certain?"

Dane tossed the beer bottle into the trash, planting his hands on his hips. "Yup."

"Then I'll find someone else to do it. Thanks for the Coke."

She was at the front door before he was able to comprehend that she was leaving. "Jess, wait."

"I'll call Phillip and let him know you want out. You were my first choice, of course, but I think I can get Kyle. He did *Bedroom Wars*, last year, remember? Now that was a funny movie... anyway, I'll call you."

"Jess—"

"Sorry, darling, I'm on a tight schedule today. Thanks for seeing me," she trotted a couple of steps back to give him the requisite peck on the cheek, and then was behind the wheel.

Dane stood on the porch shaking his head.

Damn that woman. She doesn't have a clue.

FIVE

Wanted: Mr. Romance

"Jessica! Great to hear from you! How are you doing?"

"I'm well, Kyle. I can't believe I have you on the phone. I've been trying for days."

"Well, sweetheart, the sun is just too good here, and I've threatened death to anyone who comes within twenty feet of me with a cell phone. Had I known it was you, I would have hit the ground running. In your direction, of course..."

Jessica drummed her fingers lightly on the desktop, looking at her office ceiling with a slight grin. "You needn't flatter me. This is a business call, I'm afraid. It's about a film I'm trying to put together. You may have heard about it already; Mac was shopping the deal when ... last spring."

"Oh... gee, I wanted to tell you how sorry I was to hear about Mac. I just couldn't get to the funeral, Jess."

"It's okay, really. I'm... fine." Jessica took a deep breath and looked into the mahogany framed mirror on the opposite wall. Fine had to be the most inadequate word in the book.

"Anyway, it's right up your alley. I was wondering if you'd like to take a look at it."

"Take a look?" There was a pause while Kyle negotiated a drink from a waitress. "Tell you what. Come on out and pitch it to me. I have all weekend off."

"To Maui? Are you kidding?" Jessica could not help a giggle. He expected her to drop everything and fly to Hawaii to pitch a story.

"And why not? I'm telling you, sugar, the wine is fine, the sun is fun, the spot is hot. I got a condo that don't quit, private beach, tons of island hospitality. Just what you need, I guarantee."

"Sounds tempting."

"And it is. And you should. Call me from Kahului Airport and I'll send a driver. What have you got to lose? Your pallor?"

Again, Jessica glanced at her reflection. She was pale. Drawn. Pinched! She looked like a ghost.

"I'll let you know. Thanks for the offer."

·♥·♥·♥·♥·♥·

"You'll be staying with Aunt Linda for a few days, darling. Megan is so excited that you're coming."

"Why can't I stay with Lyddy?"

"Lydia has to go to Argentina to visit her Mommy."

"But I won't go to school?"

"No, but Aunt Linda will take you with her to pick up Megan at her school every day, and she's going to take you both to the pizza place, and maybe the zoo on Saturday."

Devon considered the plan carefully, his brown eyes seriously panning his mother's hopefully convincing face.

"Okay. Will you bring me something from Hawaii?"

"You bet. Something cool."

"They have volcanoes there, Daddy said."

"Yes, but they are all sleeping right now." Sort of.

Jessica tucked the blankets around her small son and retreated to her own bedroom, climbing tiredly into the big bed and exhaling loudly.

"Oh Mac, this bed is so big without you. I might as well trade it for a twin." She reached over as she often did and pulled the extra pillow, his pillow, against her chest and curled herself against it.

"We always meant to go to Hawaii together. We had so much time to do that, someday."

It didn't bother her to speak her thoughts aloud. Like embracing the pillow, talking to Mac had become a nightly habit.

"I hope you don't mind me leaving Dev with Linda. Even if she is your ex-wife, she's been wonderful to me, you know? And anyway, he adores Meggie.

"Kyle's a nice guy, really. Still sounds a little immature, but maybe it was just that day. Could've been just me." She thought about the days in tropical Amande, during the filming of *Lost*

Season, when she first met Kyle Wagner. He was a cock-sure understudy, a stand-in for the hero. Hired as a double for Dane, Kyle equaled the leading man's height and coloring; but he was no match for the seasoned actor's savoir-faire. Jessica blushed at the memory of an incident in the local cantina, when Dane had all but taken Kyle apart for teaching her to "dance dirty." Afterward, they had barely made eye contact.

The four years since had seen Kyle Wagner snag a leading part in a "B" horror flick, and then a pivotal supporting spot in an Oscar contender. He was suddenly one of Hollywood's "golden boys," seeing offers from a couple of major studios and finally landing a plumb role in a Neil Simon-esque black comedy.

He would make a great Mr. Romance, Jessica told herself. At least as good as Dane.

Possibly.

Tossing, Jessica took the pillow with her and pulled her comforter up to her chin.

It was almost Labor Day. Too late to be starting a film she had hoped to release next summer. Still, with the right cast, the right director, it could happen.

The next-best director, she reminded herself. The next-best hero.

Mac would have lost his patience by now. "I don't know what happened. You had him all talked into it," she murmured. "He can be so unreasonable sometimes."

Dane was being stubborn, and for no good reason. But she would show him. She could, and would, do this picture without his help. She would start by heading for Maui in the morning.

•♥•♥•♥•♥•♥•

The humidity hit her like a warm, wet blanket as she stepped from the terminal. The driver spoke little, ushering her into a brand-new sports car, a model she did not recognize.

"Guess I've been out of touch," she murmured, gliding her fingertips over the tiny chrome logo imbedded in the abbreviated dashboard.

They took a wild ride to the west side of the island, slowing as they entered the beehive of Ka'anapali Beach condominiums. The man carried her bags ahead of her, entering a beachfront unit and motioning for her to follow.

"He's out front," he said, gesturing toward a wide expanse of sand accessed through sliding glass doors. "Drinks in the kitchen. It's warm out there."

"Thanks," Jessica said, but the man had disappeared.

She took a moment to look around the downstairs area, noting the modern design and décor. A broad, sweeping bar separated the kitchen from the living and dining area, and a wide, curving staircase with white iron railing led to the second floor. The carpeting was cream-colored Berber, and a massive, volcanic rock fireplace filled one entire living room wall.

The sub-zero refrigerator was well stocked, for a bachelor, she decided. Row upon row of beer bottles lined the shelves, an assortment of cheeses and summer sausages filled one drawer, pineapple and mangoes packed another. On the counter were bags of "Maui" potato chips, boxes of gourmet crackers and cans of party mixed nuts.

Re-opening the fridge, she selected a soft drink and popped it open. It was time to meet the young lord.

·♥·♥·♥·♥·♥·

"So, I ended up cutting the whole scene. Sometimes you just can't make it work." Kyle leaned forward slightly, pushing his dinner plate away and folding his arms against the table's edge. The candle danced exotic ribbons of light across his features, and Jessica smiled, fully enjoying his exuberant spirit.

"I do know," she said. "What was it like working with John Lauder? I've heard he can be... difficult."

"Difficult? Johnnie? It was a walk in the park after working with Pierce." Kyle took a sip of wine. "At least I still had some dignity left."

Jessica could not help the slight lift her eyebrows executed, but she was able to close her open mouth quickly before jumping to Dane's defense. It would not do to piss off her potential lead.

"So how is old Dane, anyway? Heard he got run out of Hollywood a few years ago. Hermited away in Montana or something?"

"Wyoming," Jessica said. "I think he got a little disenchanted with the scene in L.A."

"More like L.A. got disenchanted with him," Kyle said with a chuckle. "Aw, I shouldn't be so critical. He taught me a thing or two. Like how to drink shooters, for example."

"Getting back to the film, what are you thinking? Does it sound like something you'd like to do?"

Kyle looked at her solemnly, a slow smile just turning the corners of his lips. His hazel eyes, slightly reddened, seemed glazed for a moment as he peered into hers. At last, he pulled back with a sigh.

"Let me read it. I'd have to push back another project to do it. But maybe it's worth it, we'll see. I'll have an answer for you... soon. By the time you go home."

Satisfied, Jessica leaned back in her wicker chair. S*o far, so good.* Bemused, she watched as he ordered dessert for them both. He was cute, in a boyish way. The evening had begun with his hair combed straight back, but his busy antics had it falling into his face repeatedly. And despite his egocentric manner, there was an underlying sweetness about him that Jessica found charming.

Once dwarfed by Dane's aura, Kyle had grown into celebrity on his own. His enthusiasm for cinematography reminded her of the man Dane once was.

"You going to eat that or just watch it melt?" he was asking her.

Jessica gave him a smile and picked up her spoon.

Back in the condo, she found her bags had been unpacked and her bed turned down. Huge, wooden louvered doors were parted, revealing a balcony that opened above the beach.

In her bathroom, a basket containing bubble bath, shampoos, conditioners and lotions had been left on the side of the oval tub. Hanging on the door was a thick, velour-terry robe, on the floor, terrycloth mules.

"This is just too tempting," she whispered, quickly running the water and stripping down.

Drowsy from the wine, she nearly fell asleep in the tub before finally dragging herself to the too-soft bed. The sound of the crashing surf below carried her away.

Kyle Wagner kept himself busy at doing nothing, a practice that both satisfied and annoyed Jessica over the next two days. Away from the media, the children, the endless stack of mail and of course, the house where every turn reminded her of the man who would not come home, Jessica felt her tension begin to dissipate.

The private beach became her sanctuary. She had reading material not bradded together – she had left anything even resembling a screenplay at home – and no one's face to keep clean but her own. Kyle evaded her attempts to ask about his decision, but Jessica kept her patience in check. She was beginning to feel alive again after months of numbing cold.

"Wanna go for a drive?"

Jessica looked up from her book, shading her eyes from the sun as she peered at Kyle's smiling face. He held out his hand, helping her stand from the sand chair.

"Ever been to Hana?" he asked from behind the wheel of the black Mercedes Kompressor moments later. "Oh, that's right, you've never been here before."

"I've heard it's beautiful."

"Six-hundred seventeen curves on the road to Hana. Soft, black sandy beaches. There's even a red sand beach! Rains there nearly every day, and if it's raining when you get halfway, you're supposed to turn around and go back because the road is so treacherous in the rain."

"That's nice," Jessica murmured.

"There's a little winery if it's open."

"You're quite the expert. Ever plan on going home?"

"The mainland? Never plan on it. But I suppose I'll run out of money eventually."

Jessica laughed at his revelation. Kyle was refreshing, if naïve.

She delighted in the Seven Sacred Pools, giggled at dipping her bare feet into the turquoise waters at Hana Beach Park. He bought her a woven straw hat in the little town, and after a lazy lunch, they were on the way back to Ka'anapali.

"I'm serious about staying here," he said suddenly, rounding one of the last bends in the road. "I even have a Hawaiian driver's license." He wrestled his wallet from his pocket and flipped it open in proof. Jessica took it from him. She was surprised to discover they were the same age. He seemed so much younger.

Or she felt so much older.

Back at the condo, she couldn't wait to get into the shower and hurried up the stairs toward her room.

"I have plans for your dinner, woman. Don't get too comfortable up there," Kyle called after her.

"Oh, yeah?" she said over her shoulder in surprise. He merely grinned and waved her along.

It was dusk, and the small fishing boats were returning to shore, many of them lit with small lanterns. The old whaling port of Lahaina was the charming antithesis of modern, upscale Ka'anapali, and its romantic atmosphere impressed Jessica.

"This place used to be The Blue Max. They have awesome pizza, salads, and the best damned Mai Tais you could ever hope to suck down."

"Okay," Jessica said, tearing her eyes away from the sublime sunset to meet Kyle's gaze. She was only halfway through her first drink when Kyle ordered a third.

Jessica stayed his hand.

"You'd better save some room for pizza," she cautioned with a smile.

"Don't worry. I won't go horizontal on you anytime soon." He lowered his eyes slightly, adding, "Not unless you want me to."

Unsure of his meaning, Jessica felt herself blush, hoping the dim light hid the fact. She straightened slightly.

"So, tell me about you and Dane in Amande," she suggested, immediately sorry she had brought up Dane's name.

Kyle straightened a little also, clearing his throat and tightening his grip on the Mai Tai glass. "Aw, Pierce isn't such a bad guy. He wasn't at his best, you know, with you around, and I guess I can relate."

Jessica tilted her head in question. Kyle did not look her in the eye but continued with a little chuckle. "Matter of fact, now that your husband isn't around, forgive me for saying so, I'm mighty surprised Dane hasn't... well, I wouldn't be shocked if he stormed in here right now and tossed me into the breakers." He took a moment during Jessica's stunned silence to swirl his drink. "But we're on even ground, now, I'd say. After all, you're here, I'm here, he's not..."

"I don't know what you're talking about," Jessica finally managed. The waiter swooped past and exchanged her near empty glass for a full one.

"That's what I love about you. You can be so damned innocent of everything, and sincerely, too. You could miss a freight train heading right for you."

At this comment, Jessica laughed nervously, her eyes still wide in surprise. "Whatever you say," she murmured finally, dismissing his statement as the ramblings of an inebriated man-child. They were both saved by the delivery of the pizza.

"That's Moloka'i, Lana'i, and Kaho'olawe over there."

"Ever been to any of those islands?" Jessica asked as they strolled along Launiupoko Wayside Park after dinner.

"Moloka'i. Like everyone else, I just thought it was all about leper colonies. It's nothing like that. Just beauty, everywhere you look." Kyle sighed and directed Jessica to a nearby bench where they sat down. "I want to talk to you about the film."

Jessica drew in a breath and waited. Kyle slipped his arm around her and leaned close.

"I want to do it, but I'm afraid."

"Afraid? Why?"

He ran his hand slowly up and down her arm, his embrace becoming more intimate as he pushed her hair aside with his chin and then pressed his lips against her ear. Jessica shuddered.

"I don't want what happened to Dane to happen to me," he whispered. "But I know you won't understand that."

Jessica turned, confused and feeling indignant. "If you think I had anything to do with Dane disappearing from the scene, you're wrong. Dane and I are friends, good friends, and he was good friends with Mac, too."

"Shhh. Never mind. Forget I said anything."

"No, I—"

"I said forget it." Kyle brought his other arm around to fully encircle her, pressing his forehead gently against hers. "Let's go back."

The next several minutes were hazy for Jessica as she tried to decipher Kyle's cryptic suggestions and recover from his intimate touch. The brief ride back to the condo was spent in silence, and once inside, Kyle excused himself while she sat on the couch decompressing. The cocktails had been stronger than she'd realized, and her mind became increasingly foggy. She was about to retire to her bedroom when Kyle returned from his and joined her. From an envelope stashed in his breast pocket, he removed a small cigarette.

He lit it with a lighter, drawing in a deep drag before handing it to Jessica.

Alarms went off in her head and she held up her hand.

"Suit yourself," he mumbled, coughing as he let the smoke escape his throat. "Just a couple of hits to take the edge off."

Jessica nodded, but her face reflected her dismay that Kyle felt the need for further chemically induced relaxation in her presence. He sensed her disappointment and cleared away the contraband.

"Don't partake, do you?"

"No. A drink now and then is about all I can handle. Especially since Devon was born," she replied. "Tonight was an exception."

"I'm sorry if I made you uncomfortable. Forgive me?" His smile was appealing, and he again took the liberty of sliding his fingers across her back to draw her closer.

"It's okay." Jessica stiffened slightly but let him take her into his arms. She was tired, emotionally spent, and suddenly very lonely. The fact that Kyle was being anything but affectionate did not cross her mind.

Until his lips were hovering so close to hers that his true intention was apparent. He asked no permission before plundering her mouth, pressing her slowly backward on the couch while stretching his long legs out alongside hers as they reclined. She started to protest but became caught up in the kiss and instead grasped him around the neck. The little voice that would have normally told her to stop was overpowered by larger effect of the alcohol.

The kiss became kisses, hot, hungry kisses lasting an eternity of mindlessness Jessica would later question. It felt so good, so completely enthralling to be loved, caressed, and cherished once more...

Cherished? It was a word she would have applied to her late husband; it definitely did not describe the wanton, frantic way Kyle was now tearing at her clothes. She squirmed beneath him, clawing her way back from the abyss into which she had briefly fallen, struggling to locate his wrists and pull his hands away from her breasts.

"Kyle, no."

Still, he wrestled in passion, unwittingly pushing her harder, driven by her denial.

"I can't do this!" Speaking with force directly into his ear, Jessica managed to disengage herself from his lustful attack and sit up.

Clearly perplexed, Kyle pushed the hair from his glistening brow and stared at her as she hastened to re-button her blouse.

"I'm sorry. I should never have come here. I didn't think—"

"You didn't think what? That I would come on to you? Well, there you go." He stood up and strode to the refrigerator. "That's just what I was talking about," he called to her. Visibly shaken, he twisted the cap off a bottle of beer. "I'm the one who's sorry. I saw it coming."

Jessica stood up, tucking in her blouse and taking a deep breath. "Well, I guess I have my answer. Thank you for your hospitality. Don't bother your driver, I'll get a cab to the airport in the morning."

He smiled then, a sad smile, and held up his bottle in a mock toast.

Six

Foul Play

"She's back," the voice on the phone said. "No deal."

"You're sure?"

"Not yet anyway."

Dane hung up the replacement phone and carefully seated it back on the base. It had been his first purchase upon returning to Wyoming, another painful reminder of the days just prior to Mac's death. But this phone call was a good omen. Slumping back against the brown leather couch, he contemplated this latest development.

"So, no deal." He smiled to himself and stood up. "The kid didn't make the mark." This was reason to celebrate.

In the kitchen, he found a near-empty bottle of vodka and poured the last of it into a glass, topping it off with orange juice. He threw the bottle toward the over-full wastebasket, where it rolled off the heap and crashed to the floor, sending broken glass skittering across the terra cotta. Unthinking, he took a step toward the mess and immediately set his bare heel down upon a jagged shard.

"God damn it!"

Backing quickly away, he left a trail of blood mixed with remnants of vodka on the tile floor, splashing his screwdriver as he hopped.

"Damn." Dane leaned back against the sink counter, surveying the mess he had made, and took a big gulp of his drink. Then, reaching over his opposite shoulder, he put down his glass and whipped a dishtowel from the counter, squatting to remove the fragment before wrapping his bleeding heel.

"This really sucks," he murmured, hobbling out of the kitchen and in the general direction of his bedroom. The stairs were not easy to negotiate, but Dane managed to make it to the master bathroom where he pawed through the medicine cabinet in search of a bandage. Exasperated, he stared at the bottles of sleeping pills and pain relievers, antacids and eye drops.

"Not even one stinking Band-Aid? Jesus!"

Hopping to the bedroom phone, he pushed the button marked "intercom," hoping he could raise someone in the barn.

"Greg? You wouldn't happen to have a first aid kit down there, would you?"

"Be right there, Boss."

Fifteen minutes later, Dane grimaced as Greg snapped the lid shut on the medic kit.

"You really could use some help up here," Greg said, shaking his head. "Especially if you don't plan to be around this winter. There's stuff that needs to be done when it's freezing outside. This ain't L.A."

While pulling on a fresh pair of white socks, Dane frowned at his groom. Greg ignored the look, his eyes panning the bedroom and its various disasters borne of deferred housekeeping.

"When's that cleaning gal coming back, anyway? Have you seen the kitchen—"

"Yes. I have seen the kitchen."

"I mean, excuse me for saying so, but it's not like you can't afford to hire a few people to help out. Over't the Perons' ranch, they got servants all over the place."

Dane's frown became a glare. "Now that you mention it, why don't you just get a broom and dustpan and take care of that little accident in the kitchen?"

Greg grinned, backing out the bedroom door. "I actually have to get back. I think Whiskey threw a shoe."

Dane gritted his teeth. Whiskey had not thrown a shoe, but he could not be mad at Greg. Greg's responsibility was the horses, not the kitchen floor.

In search of his drink, Dane went back to the bathroom and retrieved the last sip. Bringing it to his mouth, he caught sight of himself in the mirror. What he saw caused him to put the glass down and lean closer.

"Pierce, you look like absolute crap."

He picked up a comb and hastily began running it through his unkempt locks, combing them away from his face. But it wasn't just his hair, or the stubble on his chin. It was more the dark circles below his eyes; the lines in his forehead; the tell-tale bulge above his waistband.

Hastily, he pulled up his t-shirt and gave his belly a critical eye, turning a profile and sucking in the shapelessness that was beginning to form.

"Damnation," he murmured.

Returning to the great room downstairs, he sat down, newly dismayed. Greg had left today's mail on the coffee table, and he reached for the magazine at the bottom of the stack, thumbing through it in avoidance of thought.

On page thirty-six was a photo that all but stopped his heart. How did they get it so quickly? He groaned in disgust.

The man in the photo with her could have been himself, ten years ago. Youthful, shining, poised. Where had that little punk gained such confidence? How dare he. How dare he touch her, a woman of integrity, a woman of such... quality.

Dane slapped the magazine closed and tossed it onto the table, only to pick it up again moments later and return to page thirty-six.

It was only an arm, an arm around a woman, a smiling woman. What did it mean?

The magazine was unceremoniously dropped back onto the table.

It meant he was going back to Los Angeles.

•♥•♥•♥•♥•♥•

It took him almost a full day to clean up the beach house. He didn't want to hire someone to do it; he trusted no one in this town. His beer cans could end up on page thirty-seven.

A commotion at the front screened door made him turn around.

"Where can a poor fellow get a pint around here?" The man's voice, a just-outside-London dialect, brought a smile to Dane's lips.

"Pete! What the hell?"

Holding the door open for his former personal assistant, Dane clapped Peter Welles on the back as he strode into the small living room.

"So, it's come to this, eh? A small house on the beach? Finally living where you want! I'm duly impressed. Now, where's that drink?"

"I've got Evian, Diet Coke and ginger ale. Name your poison."

Peter reached up to take the taller man's face between his hands. "No booze?" Quickly he pressed the back of his hand against Dane's forehead. "You taken ill, man?"

Dane chuckled. "Nope. Just cleaning up a little. But there's a pub down the way if you want a brew. Just let me change."

Thirty minutes later, Dane faced Peter across a booth at the corner saloon. He casually assessed his old friend while sipping iced tea. Peter had worry lines that were not a part of his features when he'd left the United States four years before. Still a bit on the portly side, his brown hair thinner but held in his characteristic ponytail.

"So whatcha been up to, my man?"

"No good, I'm sure," Peter answered, lifting a mug of dark ale to his lips. "I won't bullshit you, Dane. I've had a bit of trouble of late."

"And what kind of trouble would that be? Money? Female? Scotland Yard?"

"Two of the three, I'm afraid."

"Well, you don't seem to be looking over your shoulder, so it must be the first two. Is there something I can do to help?" Dane leaned back in the booth, his eyes slightly narrowed as he watched Peter squirm. "I thought you were pretty well set when you left here."

"I'm truly embarrassed to even be here. Your generosity was not taken lightly, my friend. When I went home, I took one-half of the money you gave me and started a small publishing company. I, uh, invested the other half."

Dane nodded slowly.

"I lost it all."

"Do you have debts? How much do you need?"

"No, no debts, thank the good Lord. I paid off everybody and closed the business. Took me last pound and a bit o' begging to get here." Peter cleared his throat and took another swig. Dane waited.

"No, all I need is for you to point me in the direction of some stable employment. A job. You're aware of my skills; you have a lot of contacts..."

Dane wet his lips and shifted positions. "And where does the woman fit in?"

Peter drew in a deep breath that culminated in a sigh. "She was part of the publishing deal."

"Ah. I take it she found all kinds of ways to spend your money."

"Something like that. Anyway, she's now waitin' tables in Southend. East of London."

"Okay. When can you start?"

"You have something in mind?"

"Ever been to Wyoming?"

"You don't have any women living up there, do you?"

Dane grinned, opening the door to the second bedroom in the house on the beach. "Nope. A girl comes around to clean up sometimes. You can stash your stuff here for a few days, then I'll ship you off."

"Thanks, mate. Couldn't have asked for a better arrangement. Anything you want me to do right away?"

"Yeah. A couple of things." Dane rubbed his fingers across his lips in thought. "First, get me a personal trainer. Female, preferably. Somebody that will come here and help me get rid of this." He slapped his stomach in demonstration. "You might want to go shopping, buy a bunch of healthy crap."

"And?"

"And... call Jessie. Tell her you're back."

"Jessica? And how is our lady doing these days? Awful thing about Mac, eh?"

"She's doing okay. It's been tough for a while."

"That's it? Just say I'm back?"

"Get her to invite you to lunch or something."

Peter turned his head to the side, peering at Dane in suspicion. "And the purpose of this meeting would be?"

"No real purpose, she's just lonely these days, and I thought she'd like to see an old friend."

"If that's the case, why don't you just invite her over here for dinner? I can still cook."

"Look. It's complicated. She's a little annoyed with me right now, and..."

"And you want me to find out if she's really peeved or not?"

"Find me a trainer."

•♥•♥•♥•♥•♥•

Trina Vidal was right on time and brought her own music. She wasted no time in getting Dane onto the floor.

"You realize," he said, breathless between sets, "this deal has to remain an absolute secret."

"Don't worry. No loose lips here. And I don't talk in my sleep, either." Her shining red hair tied up on top of her head, the trainer was a picture of female fitness without being muscular. Her measurements surely defined standards for the "perfect woman."

"You have a special event you're working for? A role, maybe? I helped Matt Damon get ready for *Unlawful Demands.*"

"I thought you said you didn't talk," Dane panted.

"If people tell me not to, I don't. Matt doesn't care. There wasn't much to do anyways, he was already in great shape."

"Hmmm." Dane groaned to himself.

"I want you to think about something else," she said, walking around him as he worked. "Consider this a change in lifestyle, not just a 'get fit quick' routine. You need to make better decisions about your life."

"Whatever you say."

"No, really. It's about doing all things differently, not just the eating and exercising. If you want to improve things, you have to work on all areas."

Dane ignored her sage advice, choosing to focus on his breathing, which was becoming labored.

"So, what is it? A film, or just health?" Trina asked.

"I'm going to model for the cover of a romance novel."

She gave him a skeptical look. "Yeah, right. You're favoring your left leg. What's up with that?"

"Old injury."

"Sports? War? Trip over a crosswalk?"

"Confrontation with a gang."

"That's a good one. I was sure you were going to say a woman did that to you."

"That, too."

Before she left, Trina made him an agenda that included daily routines of exercise, tankards of water and a vegetable-rich diet.

"The water will help clear out the toxins, and from the look of you, I'd say—"

"Did I ask your opinion?"

"As a matter of fact, it's part of what you're paying for. So, as I was saying, you're in seriously bad—"

"I'll see you Tuesday. Bye."

Trina Vidal found herself on the porch, bag in hand.

Peter arrived just as the red Corvette tore away from the curb. "Broccoli, carrots, Brussels sprouts, all standard fare," he said, perusing the list.

"So, what did she say?"

"Who?"

"Damn you, man. Jessica. What's up?"

"She's even more beautiful than I remember. She's tougher now. Has very definite ideas about what she wants."

Dane grunted and resumed his sit-ups. Sweating, straining, cursing, he finally lay back, staring at the ceiling, his mind far from the number of sets he had just completed. Hoisting himself up, he went to the kitchen for another bottle of water.

"So, she didn't ask about me," he murmured to himself, downing the water and tossing the empty into the new recycle barrel under the sink.

Peter followed from the living room. "She asked about you," he said, opening the refrigerator. "You have nothing on this list, y'know."

"What did she say about me?"

"Just asked how you were. I told her you were pining your damned life away."

Dane glared at him, but was pleased, nonetheless. She had asked. That was something.

He continued to work out until he nearly collapsed from exhaustion. The following day found Peter chasing down exercise equipment of every variety, directing deliverymen to the upstairs third bedroom. A treadmill, stair-climber and multi-purpose weight machine barely fit into the formerly empty room.

Dane looked around in satisfaction as the installers connected the parts. He picked up the ringing phone in the bedroom.

"Dane, it's Tom. Wanted you to know, Rox and I are throwing a Halloween party, if you're going to be in town, we'd love you to come."

"Not in costume..."

"Yeah, in costume."

"Shit. Like I haven't been in costume half my damned life." Dane smiled to himself. "I could probably manage something."

"It's a fund-raiser for Make-a-Wish Foundation. A very worthy cause. Only a few weeks away, so don't forget now. Jess is coming," Tom added.

As if I wouldn't know that, Dane thought in amusement.

Once again stealing a glimpse of himself in the mirror, he pressed his palm against his abdomen.

"Three weeks."

·♥·♥·♥·♥·♥·

Jessica sat in the waiting room, glancing nervously around at the others, like herself, who were sitting on hard wooden chairs.

When at last they called her name, Jessica expected some recognition to pass across a face or two, but no one seemed to notice. She wondered if they, too, had received fear-instilling phone calls early this morning.

"Mrs. MacKendall, I'm sorry to have kept you waiting. We didn't want to discuss this matter on the phone, for obvious reasons."

Larry Boston was the local head of the Federal Aviation Administration's investigation bureau. He beckoned for her to lean closer to the desk.

"These are photos of your husband's plane."

Jessica swallowed hard and looked closely at the photos. Try as she might, she could not comprehend the investigator's suggestion.

"I know this is difficult. It's hard enough to see, being it's so mangled and all, but these marks here are holes. Bullet holes. Made by a high-powered assault rifle."

"Bullet holes? You mean, someone... someone shot him down?" Her words came out as barely more than a whisper.

"That's right. We're not sure, of course, but we think someone may have intended the plane to blow up. It didn't. Instead, it appears that he lost oil pressure. We don't know if his oil gauge malfunctioned, or what, but he should have had time to return to the field. We don't know why he didn't."

"His gauge did malfunction just a couple of weeks ago. It read... it read empty when it wasn't—and he landed immediately to check it out... oh God..."

Overcome with new grief, Jessica bowed her head and covered her face. Scenes returned to her mind, pictures of Mac at the controls of the small plane, his voice explaining each dial, gauge and knob to her as they hung suspended in the sky. His words just after his last flight home, when he'd complained about having to set down due to a bad oil gauge.

"Normally, he might have been able to turn around and get back to the airstrip. But it looks like the engine froze up... I'm sorry."

For months, the question had hung suspended: equipment malfunction, or pilot error? Now, a new revelation had reared its ugly head, answering one question and raising others.

Cory MacKendall had been murdered. But by whom, and why?

Her hands cramped into painful fists, Jessica vowed to find the answers.

Seven

Next of Kin

She had been driving around for what seemed like hours, once nearly arriving home before turning the car around and getting on the freeway heading west. It was after dark when she arrived in the upscale beach community of Malibu. The porch light was on, and she rang the doorbell.

Jessica was about to retreat to her car when Dane answered the door.

He leaned against the doorjamb, wearing only sweat shorts, a t-shirt in his hand. His skin glistened with a fine layer of perspiration, and his face was flushed.

"What's up?" he queried, pulling the shirt over his head and dragging it down, then smoothing his damp hair away from his face. Before she could reply, music started playing from somewhere inside and Jessica looked past him into the house.

It only took a moment to put it all together. Jessica felt her face flush in embarrassment and took a step back.

"Oh... you're not alone. I am so sorry! I should have called first." She turned to go.

"Wait. Is something the matter? Has something happened?"

"It can wait," she said over her shoulder as she hurried toward her car in the driveway. Dane took a step, as if thinking he would try to stop her, but Jessica turned her face away, throwing the Lexus into reverse.

Why didn't I notice that red convertible parked at the curb? And why does it bother me so much...

"Finish your cereal, sweetheart. We don't want to be late for school." Jessica steeled herself against the sound of the phone, which was ringing again in another part of the house; the kitchen unit had been turned off, and she opted to let the call go to voicemail. She made a mental note to cancel the number.

"Do we hafta go today?" Devon whined. "I wanna stay home with you."

Jessica started to protest but held her tongue. Instead, she reached across the table to stroke her son's cheek fondly. News of the FAA's findings would rub new salt into their wounds.

"Okay, darling. We can stay home together today."

Devon immediately brightened and resumed eating. The telephone began ringing again, startling Jessica so that she stiffened. She was reluctant to answer but the caller's I.D. changed her mind.

Dane's voice was rough from sleep, and Jessica sighed.

"I guess you heard," she said matter-of-factly.

"That's why you came by last night."

"Actually, yes. I'm sorry if I disturbed you."

"Is there any more than they're telling the media?"

"And what are they telling the media?"

"That some asshole son of a bitch shot at his plane. Is it true?"

Jessica sighed. "I thought you'd risen above that schoolyard language."

"Well, is it?"

"That's what they told me. Someone shot him down." Calmer now, the misery of the night before locked away, Jessica presented the strongest front she could muster. "Although why anyone would want to kill Mac is... is beyond me. And you'd think with all the security around airports these days..."

Dane murmured something Jessica could not understand.

"I'm sorry?"

"I said we'll get the bastards that did it. I promise you."

"That's a big promise," she replied tiredly. "I've been contacted by a number of private investigators. I hired them all. I don't know where else to start." She was already more than weary of the whole affair. "I saw Peter last week."

"Yeah, I heard."

"It was good to see him. He told me he's going to manage the ranch for you. Does that mean you'll be staying in L.A.?"

"For a while. I'm looking at a couple of options. How's... how are things going with your deal?"

"*Mr. Romance?* Oh, all right, I guess. I'm meeting with Johnnie Lauder next week."

"He's going to direct?"

"He's interested. Why?"

"No reason. So, you take care."

"Sure. You too."

John Lauder had attained moderate success in the past five years. While his last film had not taken home the Academy's coveted Oscar, it had garnered a Golden Globe award for best direction. It was no secret in Hollywood that Lauder was primed and ready for the former's gold statuette. He only needed the right material. Jessica MacKendall hoped to be carrying that material in her briefcase this morning as she walked into Lauder's Beverly Hills office.

"Awful sorry to hear about Mac," he began before he had even released her hand. "So, you're developing this on your own?"

Jessica slowed her movements as she withdrew the script from the valise, wondering if she had really detected some skepticism.

"StarCrossed Productions is developing this project."

"Right. Okay, I'm ready. Give me the pitch."

"Are you going to time me?" she asked with a flirtatious grin.

"Not if you answer one question for me."

"I will if I can."

"Why isn't your partner directing this film?"

Momentarily taken aback by the term "partner," Jessica's smile faded slightly, and she crossed her legs.

"I guess that's one I can't answer. Perhaps you can ask him yourself."

"Okay. That's fair. Go."

"Michael Harris hates his father's mortuary business and all he can think about is moving to Hollywood to become a big star. He's already past the youngster roles, being near thirty, but he goes anyway. Of course, he has to do odd jobs to pay his way, and he rooms with another wanna-be actor, a kid ten years younger, and one day the kid gets a big break so the guy, Michael, is coerced into filling in for the kid, Jason, we'll call him, on his day job as a bagboy at the local market.

"When Michael goes to get his clean clothes from the dry-cleaning bag, he's shocked to find a costume there instead, this being Hollywood and all. The costume is a medieval nobleman's outfit, so he's forced to wear it to the market.

"Of course, people just kind of accept him, after all, it's HOLLYWOOD, and he sees this beautiful woman shopping in a similar era costume, with a low-cut gown—"

"Now we're talking. Go on," the director said.

"She's leaving the store and her trailing dress gets caught on a rack of dime-store romance novels and he's the only one who sees it, so he rushes to help her, and they both fall together into a heap of paperback books. Naturally, someone takes their picture, and it appears in *The Star*."

"So far, so good."

"So, the next thing he knows, he's being sought out by Harlequin or someone as a model for their covers. He absolutely hates the idea, but needs the money, so goes along with it. And keeps going along with it, and one day finds out he's a contender for Mr. Romance, a contest for all the cover models."

"So of course, he goes to the contest and wins," Lauder said, nodding.

"Right. Shoulder to shoulder with all these Fabio-types. And there he meets the heroine, a tough reporter who thinks the whole deal is ludicrous and rigged—"

"Julia Roberts. Maybe Sandra Bullock. Go on."

"He finds himself fighting to defend the industry and falling in love at the same time."

"So, he changes, becomes a proponent of the romance novel business? That's good."

"Yeah. I thought so."

"And who you got to play Michael?"

Jessica pressed her palms together.

"Dane won't do that either?" Lauder frowned.

Coloring, Jessica shook her head briefly and then straightened. "I was hoping you had someone else in mind."

Lauder uttered a short cough and then offered her a melancholy grin. "Let me get back to you on this."

Her heart heavy, Jessica forced a meek smile and took her leave.

Driving back to the office, mortification swept over her. Damn that John Lauder. If Mac had been the one to bring the deal, Lauder would have snatched it up. If Dane had warmed to the film, they would have been in production by now.

Even egotistical Kyle Wagner had bailed out on her.

It wasn't fair. There were certainly other women producing films in Hollywood, but they were women with more power, more history, more friends. Friends that didn't treat them with condescension and pity.

Why did it matter? She certainly had better things to do than to tramp all over L.A. looking for someone with good taste willing to take a little risk.

Better things to do. Like trying to figure out who murdered her husband?

The StarCrossed Production offices were empty when she arrived. Dane's desk was neat and obviously not a place he frequented; Mac's office was a working model of a successful producer's workplace. A box akin to an "in" basket was stacked high with scripts, some thick, some thin, some shoddily constructed, and others letter perfect. Sticky notes identified some as "promising," color-indicated in yellow. The "rejected" notes were blue.

Jessica looked in wonder at Mac's careful lettering, and a sample rejection letter he had prepared on the computer. Respectful, apologetic, encouraging. Nothing like Lauder's "don't call us, we'll call you" game.

Pulling open the lap drawer, she perused the contents and discovered a small address book.

"Hmmm." Jessica smiled, remembering Mac's disdain for smartphones, tablets, and any kind of device with an ON button. She thumbed through a few pages, then tossed the book into her purse.

She took one more look into Dane's darkened office as she walked toward the door.

•♥•♥•♥•♥•♥•

Roxanne Boudreau had closed the small dress shop on Sunset Boulevard; she now sold her gowns by appointment only and from the large manor house she shared with her husband. Tom Jarrick optioned an occasional screenplay, but mostly dabbled at golf, home remodeling and fund-raisers. He was also a widely sought-after film critic.

Now, while pinning fabric together on her living model and best friend, Roxanne glanced quickly out the window at the broad expanse of lawn across the rear of the estate where Tom tossed a toy football to young Devon MacKendall. She immediately turned her attention back to Jessica.

"So, are you going to tell me about Hawaii or not?"

"It was fun."

"Fun. Now that's an all-encompassing term. Fun."

"Well, up to a point... Ouch!"

"Sorry. How did Kyle treat you?"

"Don't ask."

Roxanne rose from where she had been kneeling, her eyes delving. "Well that's telling," she uttered.

Jessica sighed. "Oh, it wasn't really his fault. It was mine. Being an idiot, as usual. Just like the other night at Dane's. I just can't seem to make anything go right."

After a decided pause, Roxanne began removing the pieced-together garment from Jessica's frame and draping it over a mannequin. Jessica picked up her discarded cover-up and put it on over her bodysuit.

"Let's take a break." Roxanne led Jessica to a kitchen chair and told her to sit. After pouring them each a cup of coffee, Roxanne joined her friend at the table. "Now, talk."

"There's nothing to talk about. It's just—just that I'm tired. I'm tired of trying so hard, every day, and nothing happens. Nothing's happening with the film. Nothing's happening with Charlene or the baby. And now I have this murder investigation to deal with, and I am so tired of thinking about that, too... and I'm worried about Devon, and Dane's mad at me, and—"

"Whoa, whoa. Time out. What do you mean, Dane's mad at you?"

Jessica jammed her fingers into her hair, now chagrined at the tangled mess it was. "I don't know," she murmured. "I screwed up with him, again. First, I pressured him about doing *Mr. Romance* when he didn't want to, then the other night I stopped by his house and damn if he didn't have a girl in there. I felt like a complete imbecile, he got out of bed to answer the door! I don't even know why I went there."

"You went there because you're friends and you needed some support. I'm sure he wasn't mad at you. Probably just a little red-faced."

Jessica looked at her lap. "She drives a red Corvette."

Roxanne chuckled. "Of course you would notice that." Then, reaching across the table, she squeezed Jessica's hand. "You need a little vacation. Why don't you and Dev go back up to your sister's lodge for a while? Just drop out for a month or so. It would do you good."

"Christine and Nick are going into their busy season next month."

"Perfect. You can help out."

"It's hard to be there without Mac."

"Ughhh! Would you just knock it off? Can you get any more down-trodden?" Roxanne's eyes were wide with exasperation. "I'm sorry, honey, but you need to get off this train. You were doing fine until the murder thing came up. You need to focus on one thing at a time here."

Jessica was oblivious to Roxanne's admonitions. "Kyle won't do the film. Dane won't do the film. Lauder won't do the film unless I can bring in a big name."

"So don't do the film! Is that so hard?"

"The adoption people won't let me adopt Benjie because Charlene is still alive, and Charlene is not going to come out of the coma, and no one is authorized to pull the plug on her."

"Table that one. It's out of your hands. And I might ask you, what the hell would you do with a little baby right now?"

"We wanted another baby so bad..."

"We, as in you and Mac. Sorry to be blunt, but you have no father for a baby right now."

"You've never had a problem being blunt," Jessica observed, sipping her coffee.

"No offense, dear," Roxanne said lightly.

"None taken." Jessica peered out the window, her eyes growing misty. "Do you think Dane's serious about her?"

"Her, who?

"The woman he was all sweated up about."

"Red Corvette?"

"Mmm."

Roxanne looked at her closely. "What do you care?"

"I just... worry about him, that's all. Mac says... said... Dane sabotages his own happiness over and over again."

"Your husband was a very perceptive guy. I'd say he was on the mark with that one."

Jessica put down her mug and stood up. "You've never been fond of Dane, have you?"

"Let's just say I've come a long way from the days when I couldn't stand the sight of him. He broke your heart more than once, as I recall."

"Only because I handed it to him on a platter."

"Well, I don't think we need to dredge up that old stuff now. I still believe you should take a vacation."

"Maybe so," Jessica mused. "I'll think about it."

She was still ruminating it when the call came from the hospital in Minneapolis. An ethics panel had convened, and after much deliberation, had deemed Jessica MacKendall the authorized party in Charlene MacKendall's medical proxy case.

"It's your decision, Mrs. MacKendall, as her only living relative."

A cold chill passed over her body and her hand trembled as she held the phone to her ear. "I'll come right away."

Her plans had been made for her. A higher power was intervening.

Forty-eight hours later, Charlene Raylin MacKendall was removed from the devices that pumped prolonged, artificial life into her otherwise lifeless form; she slipped away minutes later, peaceful and unaware of the heaving sobs of the sister-by-marriage at her bedside.

It was a brief trip, over practically before it began. Jessica was on her way home by the following night. Choosing not to put herself through another funeral, she had arranged for Charlene's remains to be buried alongside her father's. It was fitting, she decided. Mac had been laid to rest beside his mother.

She made one half-hearted attempt to visit her young nephew but knew his foster family had been warned against allowing her to see the infant. It was unfair, more than unfair, but she hadn't the strength to fight the system after listening to the exhaustive process described by her attorney; the hearings, depositions and yes, even witnesses she would have to find. Such a fight. So much trouble – when all she wanted to do was cuddle Benjamin, bring him home to the sweet and playful nursery she'd already designed in her mind.

Still, she left a voicemail message for Irma Carvey, demanding an update of her adoption application, now that the baby's mother was officially dead. It took all her effort to sound strong and confident in the message.

The flight home was long and incredibly lonely. Guilt washed over her like a summer rain, warm and sticky, permeating her mind. I should have stayed. Mac would be so disappointed in me.

Charlene's friends and co-workers had planned a ceremony and had graciously invited Jessica to join them. Now, lying back in her reclined seat, she fought more tears. Indeed, she had cried so long and hard after Charlene's death she felt she could never cry again.

I am so tired of all this grief, she thought miserably. Roxanne was right. She was due for a change.

The following afternoon found her helping the Jarricks with the arrangements for their first annual Make-a-Wish Masquerade Ball. The guest list had grown so long, the party had to be moved to the banquet hall at the Elysian Country Club.

"I don't know what I'll wear," she mumbled, absently checking off names as Roxanne called them out to her.

"Not a problem. I've already started your gown."

Jessica looked up. "My gown? You're making something for me?"

"Let's just say Cinderella would scratch your eyes out for this dress. And hopefully, lend you her glass slippers."

"I always wondered how you could possibly dance in glass shoes." Jessica commented.

"Plexiglas. Discovered in 1680."

"What's it like?"

"Supposed to be tougher than glass, flexible, scratches though..."

"The dress! What's it made of?"

"Forest green velvet. Faux fur-trimmed. The squeeziest waist you'll ever wear. Whale-bone stays. Hooped shoulders..."

"Cleavage?"

"Oh ho ho, built-in boob builders. He won't be able to take his eyes off you."

"Who?"

"Prince Charming, of course."

"Is he coming?" Jessica asked with a giggle.

"Could be," Roxanne replied, her smile mysterious. "Could be."

Jessica sighed and tried to envision the fabulous gown Roxanne had in mind. Unbidden, her thought took a turn. "Is Dane coming?" she asked suddenly.

"Actually, he is. Paid for two tickets. I can't wait to see what he shows up in. And with whommm..."

"Hmm." Jessica put down her pencil. "I'd better call these last two people. Could you hand me the phone?"

Eight

Masked Man

"Now I know how Scarlett O'Hara felt when she was getting ready for the barbecue at Twelve Oaks." Jessica groaned as Roxanne pulled the costume tighter to fasten the small pearl buttons down her back.

"Suck it in, girl! You can't have put on any weight this year. You've always been a perfect—"

"Not anymore," Jessica complained, peering down her lowered chin at the promised cleavage. "God, if I could only breathe, I'd be fine."

"You don't need to breathe, or eat, for that matter. Just flit around and look gorgeous. There. And here's your mask."

"Do I have to?"

"Yes! Everyone has to wear a mask, that's the rule. They can come stark naked if they want, but they must wear a mask. Until midnight, when we pull them off."

Jessica picked up the understated, green satin mask and carefully stretched the elastic band over her perfectly curled coiffure.

"How does it look? Stupid?"

"Very sexy, actually," her friend admired. "And your hair turned out great. I love the blonde streaks. I can see your dance card will be filled immediately."

"You can't be serious. Dance card?"

"Just kidding. Hey, I've got to get ready myself. Oh, this is going to be so much fun! You know we've raised fifty thousand in tickets alone? That doesn't include the silent auction or the donations."

"Wonderful. I'm really thrilled. And you've never told me what you're wearing."

"It's a surprise. Let's just say I'll be packing my superpowers tonight. Now where are your Plexiglas slippers?"

Jessica gazed at herself in the guest room mirror as her friend left. She barely recognized the young widow she had arrived as; staring back at her was a vision of a fairy-tale princess.

Whimsy captured her momentarily, and she made a deep curtsey, then stood and practiced a repertoire of facial expressions, finally succumbing to a fit of giggles.

"You would love this," she murmured when her laughter subsided. "You always liked me in green." Reaching into her overnight bag, she withdrew a small velvet case. Soon it would be time to go downstairs and join her friends in the limousine.

•♥•♥•♥•♥•♥•

"Just stand around and help people who need... help," Roxanne directed.

"You. Look. Smashing!" Jessica shook her head slowly. "I've often thought of you as Wonder Woman, you know. Your costume is absolutely perfect."

Roxanne adjusted the strapless, gold trimmed, red bustier above her royal blue satin skirt. "It was harder to make than your gown," she confessed. "Especially these arm thingies."

Still amazed, Jessica made her way across the ballroom toward the punchbowl. The room couldn't have been more elegant; the twelve tables set for eight each were beautifully appointed with intricate rose and candle centerpieces. A large dance floor was central, and a band was tuning up at one end of the great room.

Every few minutes she attempted a deep breath, hoping her breasts would not lift right out of the low cut, V-necked gown. The emerald and diamond necklace Mac had given her went perfectly with the dress, and she adjusted it in nervous anticipation.

Smiling and nodding, Jessica was happy to encounter several old friends with whom she had lost touch. She made a conscious effort to shed her problems, at least for this one special night. She was due for some light-hearted fun.

Soon, Roxanne joined her for a brief respite from her hostess duties. "How ya holding up?"

"I'm really enjoying this. The band is awesome. Where did you find them?"

"They found me. They heard about the ball and called us."

The two women stood together, perusing the room, each with her own thoughts.

"This is where you and Mac had my birthday party. He proposed in the ladies' restroom." Jessica grasped Roxanne's hand, turning toward her with a smile.

"I know. I was worried that it might bother you."

"It doesn't. It's kinda nice, actually."

"I noticed you aren't wearing your rings."

"Oh! I caught one of the prongs on the gate at home. I had to leave it to be repaired." She held up her bare left hand. "Wearing just one felt weird."

Roxanne nodded, and Jessica turned her eyes back toward the growing crowd. "I'd better get back," Roxanne said, but Jessica detained her.

"Wait. Who is that? That guy just walking in?"

Roxanne followed Jessica's gaze to rest on the tall man entering the ballroom. He was wearing a white, high collared shirt, a burgundy velvet waistcoat, black silk pants and cape, and over-the-knee black boots. His thick, chestnut brown hair was pulled into a ponytail at the nape of his neck and hung to the middle of his back. A narrow, black satin mask was tied around his head.

He carried himself like a nobleman.

"Don't have a clue," Roxanne uttered. "Despite my vast popularity, I don't know everyone on the list. But it looks like he's headed this way. I'm outta here."

"Rox!" Jessica whispered urgently, but her panic was wasted on Roxanne's retreating bustle. The man meandered but was making his way toward the empty corner where Jessica stood.

As he passed the dining table closest to her, he leaned across it and plucked a small, deep red rose from the arrangement and brought it to her. Coming close, he offered her the bloom with a slight bow.

Speechless, Jessica took the rose and unconsciously held it to her nose. The man held out his hand, and she gave up hers; he brought it to his lips with great ceremony.

It was as if a spell had been cast. Despite the dim lighting, and the mesmerizing aura that surrounded him, Jessica was suddenly aware that his appearance was, in part, a deception. The green eyes that fixed on hers from behind the mask could not be disguised.

"Dance?" he asked softly, still holding her hand in question.

Wordlessly she allowed him to guide her to the dance floor, the rose still held delicately in her hand as she slipped her arm around his neck. Pulling her firmly against him, his hand sliding across her back was comforting and, most certainly, welcome.

"I didn't recognize you at first," Jessica told him, her smile filled with relief and amusement.

"Well, that's the whole point, isn't it? The essence of a masquerade? I'm not him, you're not her, and we can each be someone else for a couple of hours. Live different lives, be people we'd rather be... but just for a couple of hours."

"Okay," she replied, closing her eyes and relishing the feel of the contact between her forehead and Dane's cheek. She could almost slip away... dance her way into a fairy tale and never come back.

Indeed, the slow, romantic melody, the lyrics recounting the joy of rekindled love washed over her as they danced. For a moment or two, she could make believe that things were different; that she was a woman in love, a woman without pain, without grief.

She could be a woman with a man, a real hero, so steady and true that he would lay down his life for her in the blink of an eye.

Involuntarily, she tightened her embrace on her dance partner; he responded by doing the same. The song ended, but they remained frozen in time, in place, eyes closed, hearts beating in harmony.

For a moment, nothing else existed. Dane's arms around her gave Jessica a feeling she had missed; a sensation she so desperately needed in her life, a sense of protection and all-encompassing security. It was a place from which she did not want to come back.

The band had other plans, striking up their rendition of "Copa Cabana."

Embarrassed now, the spell broken, Jessica pulled away, hoping to hide her confusion. "I need to get some air," she mumbled, and Dane followed her through the throngs of costumed disco dancers.

"Mind if I join you?"

"Not at all," she said over her shoulder, pushing open a heavy side door leading to a wide veranda.

Turning her back to him as if admiring the view, she quickly tugged at the neckline of her dress, attempting to conceal some of the creamy white flesh that now seemed vulgar. He was watching her though, and she waited for his expected, lewd, comment. Instead, he turned his eyes away.

Perplexed, Jessica stole a glance at Dane as he leaned casually against the ornate concrete railing at the balcony's edge. He looked different, and it was more than just the wig that altered his appearance.

"Great hair," she teased.

"Took a truckload of Rogaine," he replied with a smile. Reaching behind his head, he loosened and removed the mask, stuffing it into his trouser pocket. "Hate these damned things."

"Me too," Jessica said, removing her own mask and slipping it over her wrist.

The smile faded from Dane's lips as he regarded her. "You look..." he began, but he ended by shaking his head slowly.

Possessed by powers she would never understand, Jessica stood before him, peering up into his face in unabashed affection. "I look... what?"

He stared at her for several moments, his thoughts unreadable. Finally, sighing, he reached out to her as though he would stroke her hair. Jessica closed her eyes, only to have them flutter open again as he tweaked her nose.

"Cute. You look really cute."

He walked to the door and grasped the handle. Still stunned by her off-target expectations, Jessica did not move from her position, her emotions a mixed bag of hurt and relief.

"I, uh, think my date might be here," he said, clearing his throat and pulling the mask from his pocket. "Better put this back on, huh? Roxanne will have my ass."

Jessica nodded. "You go on. I'll be in in a minute."

"Suit yourself. Don't get cold."

He was gone then, and Jessica stared after him in disbelief and disappointment. Disappointment in herself. She stared at the rose, still in her hand, and without further reflection, tossed it over the side.

Through the windows she watched as Dane greeted a petite redhead with a seductive smile and an honest D-cup.

She was crazy if she thought that for a couple of hours, she could be someone else, he could be someone else. That, even for a few minutes—the time it took to dance a slow dance—she could forget.

But then, she had always considered herself a little bit crazy.

Trina Vidal was well cast, Dane decided, as a warrior princess, albeit a small one. Looking like a three-quarter version of Xena, Trina made up for her lack of mass with an in-your-face demeanor.

Physically, she was a knock-out.

Personally, Dane could do without her. She was nice enough, but not his type; his conscience suggested that he may be, once again, flirting with disaster.

So why had he invited her? Watching as she chatted up the "A" list attendees at their table – and no doubt lauded her services – Dane wished he had not brought her, or anyone else, for that matter. In contrast, Jessica sat one table away, demurely listening while the matronly actress sitting beside her imparted late-breaking Hollywood news. She looked regal, yet vulnerable... or was it only his imagination?

The blonde tresses, swept up into the intricate coiffure, intrigued him. He wondered, fleetingly, what it would look like hanging down around her face, her beautiful face, flushed with passion...

"Centime for your thoughts?" Trina asked, bursting into his vision like a buffalo leaping onto a cloud.

"I'm sorry?"

"You know, I don't usually date clients," she said, taking a sip of her Perrier and avoiding his eyes.

"That's what I like about you. You're a woman of principal," Dane said dryly. "I'm ready to go. How about you?"

"Certainly not! We have to stay for the unmasking."

Before Dane could protest, a waiter appeared, offering a selection of desserts.

"Nothing for me," Trina said with a little flip of her hand.

Watching her, Dane became newly annoyed. "No, but I'll take a shot of Southern Comfort," he asserted, and the nodding waiter backed away. Dane looked around the room while waiting for his drink, trying not to focus on the exquisite woman in the green velvet gown. Trina chattered incessantly, and Dane caught only a word or two of her dissertation. Checking his watch, he sighed in impatience, pressing his fingertips together.

"I need to walk around," he said at last. "Will you excuse me?"

"Do I have a choice?"

Dane gave her a genuine smile, then turned to survey the room. It was nearing midnight, and he decided to take a short tour of the auction items in the adjoining ballroom.

He snickered to himself at the items some believed to be treasures. "Should have offered my toothbrush," he muttered in amazement while examining a child's lunchbox autographed by Zachary Slade.

Not all the items were so ostentatious. Travel packages, wardrobe items, personal appearances were offered to the adoring public, allowed into this room but not the other. Bid sheets were mostly filled, many outbidding the stated value of the item. Dane shook his head. Surely there was something here he could stand to bid on.

A ski trip to Vale. Season Dodger tickets. A Newport Beach yacht excursion. Yawn.

It was more amusing to look at the donor's names. In addition to his so tasteful lunchbox offering, Zach Slade had ponied up an autographed copy of the *Bellerive* script.

Bellerive. Dane chewed on his upper lip as he thumbed through the script, pausing for a moment to peruse the page bearing the dialog between the rogue pirate captain and the young lady in waiting. It was the first time he had laid eyes on the woman that would come to change his life forever.

Spunky, she was. She didn't like him much, but he'd eventually won her over. For about ten minutes in time.

Dane put down the script.

The next item was a weekend for two at a bed and breakfast in Northern California, donated by Jessica MacKendall and Brian Winslow.

Puzzled, Dane stared at the names on the auction card. Who was Brian Winslow? He made a mental note to check it out later. They were calling him back to the party.

In the main ballroom, he took a moment to scan the crowd. Everyone was standing, making it next to impossible to locate Trina until he heard her too-loud laughter coming from the area adjacent to the bar. Zachary Slade had apparently proffered some amusing anecdote; one Dane was certain he was happy to have missed.

"Dane! Dane, come over here. Have you met Zach?"

"Yes, I believe so," Dane said, extending a handshake. "By the way, I signed your script in there, it's now worth twice as much."

Zachary gave him a sour smile, then chugged the rest of his drink. Dane grinned, taking a small sip of his own. "Some asshole wrote your name on a rusty lunchbox, so I threw it out. Can you imagine someone doing that? What lousy taste." He took Trina by the elbow and gently urged her away from the bar. "Not that I really care, but you'd do better to stay away from that guy," he said close to her ear.

"I can take care of myself."

"I'm sure you can. My mistake."

"You didn't really, did you?" she asked, turning to look up at him expectantly when they were out of earshot.

"What, get rid of his trash? I didn't lay a finger on his crap. He can be a loser without my help."

Before he could comment further, Dane was interrupted by the feedback of a microphone on stage. Tom Jarrick was adjusting the sound.

"Just a brief announcement... thanks to the generous efforts of all the folks here tonight, I'm extremely happy to report that current tally puts us at nearly one-hundred thousand dollars in donations for the Los Angeles Chapter of the Make-a-Wish Foundation."

A general shout of joy emanated from the crowd.

"The silent auction is now closed, and the final figures will be announced in about an hour. If you purchased something at the auction, you'll have to stay until the sale is finalized... but even more importantly it's now time to remove your masks. And..." Tom was forced to raise his hands to quiet the group. "If you'll be so kind, there are markers at each table, if you will please autograph your mask and leave it behind, the masks are also being donated to the Foundation for their further fund-raising efforts."

Dane chuckled. "I think we should all just sign Zach's name. What do you think?" he called out.

Tom returned the laugh. "Why not?" Beside him, his wife was scowling, her eyes traveling from Tom to Dane and back. As masks were stripped off, laughter grew and the noise in the room ramped up. Batman kissed Wonder Woman to diffuse her ire. On cue, the band resumed their classic rock repertoire, and Dane realized Trina had again slipped away. Stopping at the nearest table, he picked up a silver paint roller point and signed his name on the black silk mask, leaving it beside the centerpiece.

He wandered about the room, looking for Trina, wishing he could just sneak away without her. Perhaps some emergency could arise, and, unable to find her, he might just... he stopped at the edge of the stage, watching with interest as Jessica swept onto the dance floor with a man he didn't recognize. A man wearing green tights and a feathered hat.

"Okay. Let's go." Trina appeared out of nowhere, tugging on his shirtsleeve with a yawn.

"In a minute," he said. "We should dance."

"Huh?"

He dragged Trina into the throngs of waltzers, smoothly guiding her across the floor, avoiding collisions as he neatly maneuvered her nearer Jessica and her partner.

"If you get any closer, you'll tread on her dress," Trina was saying.

"Who?"

"Is her name Pavlov? You've been drooling over her all evening. Tell me, did her Mammy make her that gown out of her mother's good drapes?"

"What the hell are you talking about?" Dane asked, frowning down at the undersized dynamo in his arms.

"You're worthless, you know that?"

"At least that's something I can understand," he answered with a grin, finally catching Jessica's eye. "Actually, worthless is a generous description."

Trina just shook her head as Dane's eyes were again fixed on the vision in green velvet.

"Did you say your name was Robin?" Jessica asked, tearing her eyes away from Dane and back to the blushing man leading her around the floor. "As in, Hood?"

"Only for tonight. Usually, it's Quill. I'm just down from B.C. Looking for a niche. It's hard to get work here."

"How did you get in? I mean, no offense, but the guest list was ... exclusive."

"Batman's my mentor. I'm somehow related to his ex-wife, I think, I don't know, anyway, I'm an actor, or will be one, I hope, someday, I'm sorry, I'm just rattling on..."

Jessica laughed. "That's okay. I run off at the mouth quite regularly." She really looked at the man now, noticing his curly, golden-brown hair and eyes that nearly matched.

"So Tom invited you. What kind of part are you looking for?"

"What am I not looking for? I just did a commercial for flea collars, and I'm supposed to do another one for some exercise device —just missed getting a shot on a thirty second Toyota ad."

Jessica grimaced. "I know how you feel. It's terribly hard to break in. I only got into it by accident." She paused, noticing the perpetual color in Robin's cheeks. "Hasn't Tom been able to help you out at all?"

"I think he would if he could."

"But you've never done feature film work."

"Nope. I did some modeling when I first came here."

"Modeling? What kind?"

"Beachwear. Me, in some skimpy little Speedo or something, and a surfboard. Funny, because I can barely swim."

Jessica giggled. There was something so charming about this young stranger that made her like him instantly.

"I'm going to give you a card. I want you to call these people and tell them I said to give you a screen test." She dipped into the small handbag on her wrist and produced a business card.

Robin looked at her in sheer disbelief. "You're kidding, right?"

"Why should I joke about something that important? I know the owner of Casting One personally, so be sure to tell them Jessica MacKendall told you to call."

He stepped on the edge of her gown then, causing her to trip and fall against him; he broke her fall with his arms. "Oh, I am so sorry! I am such a klutz..."

"It's okay, really." The song was ending anyway, and Jessica took a deep breath and was immediately sorry. Robin could not keep his eyes from her neckline, her tight bodice threatening to expose all.

"You, uh, just make that call," she repeated, backing away. "And good luck! It was nice meeting you."

"Oh, the pleasure was all mine..."

The light was red, and Dane applied the brake. The Corvette came to a smooth, firm stop. The car was certainly responsive, if Dane wasn't.

"You're tense," Trina said, but she seemed unconcerned about Dane's tight grip on the steering wheel.

"No, not at all." Do things differently, he reminded himself again. Change. That was his new by-word. "Nice automobile," he said, staring hard at the red light on the corner. Should have taken the limo.

"Well, I've gotta hand it to you, I didn't think you could do it, but you look fabulous. You had every girl in that room wanting to take you home."

"That so," he mused, now drumming his fingertips on the steering wheel. "Every one of them?" Only one mattered. And that one was no longer wearing a wedding ring. But it was too soon. Too soon!

Change. In the past, he might have suggested they get together on a more intimate level. And although Jessica seemed comfortable... hell, dare he think affectionate? He knew pushing her was exactly the wrong thing to do. No, he had to be patient.

In the meantime, he had the she-warrior to keep him company.

Nine

Confessions

Jessica checked her purse for the tickets. Still there, zippered in, just where she'd placed them the night before. She was nearly hyperventilating at the prospect of getting on another airplane, this one bound for Seattle.

Tom and Roxanne had insisted upon seeing them off.

"Really, I could take the limo," she argued half-heartedly as Tom loaded their bags into his trunk.

"S'pose you could," he muttered, with a bemused expression. "But then you wouldn't owe us a trip to the airport."

Devon was quiet. Jessica prayed he wasn't worrying about the flight, his third since his father's death in an airplane.

"Excited about seeing Gramma?" she asked, squatting down to give him a little hug.

"Yeah," he said in a voice so small it broke her heart.

At the terminal, Roxanne hugged her girlfriend. "Have a great Thanksgiving, hear?"

"We will. It sure will be different being with my family," Jessica said with a courage she didn't really feel. "You, too."

Devon fell asleep soon after take-off and Jessica was immensely grateful. At least she could relax while he napped. She even dozed off and on before the final descent into Seattle-Tacoma International Airport. How long had it been since she had seen Paul and Terry?

Jessica was fond of her younger brother but never close to him. He had failed to come to her wedding and had met Mac only once when they had traveled to Seattle for a visit. Now he was opening his home to her, Chrissie and their mother for the long-planned family reunion.

Paul was waiting at the gate.

"Hey, stranger!" he called, wrapping her in a bear hug that would not quit. "And the little slugger, what's up, my man?"

Devon stared at his Uncle Paul, his eyes like saucers.

"Mom's already got the turkey thawed. She's choppin' away like a banshee, there's celery and onions flyin' all over the place," Paul told them as they picked up the luggage and hustled through the terminal. "She can't wait to see you guys. Especially you, Damon."

"It's Devon. Thanks so much for picking us up, Paul."

"No problem. It's the silver van over there," her brother said, pointing out a more-gray-than-silver minivan with hazy windows. "Never get the chance to clean the darn thing."

"Oh." Jessica looked with dismay into the center seat of the van. "I thought you said you had a car seat."

"Built in. Right in the middle there."

Relieved, Jessica belted her son into the center seat and joined her brother in the front. This was going to be an interesting weekend.

Looking around the dinner table Jessica felt oddly out of place. Here was her mother, Jan; her sister and Nick, and their daughter Angel; her brother and his wife Teresa. And of course, little Devon. It had been so many years, and so many changes had occurred in her life that she no longer fit her piece of the family puzzle. Chrissie was the only one to whom she felt close, and even then, it was a remote sort of closeness.

Chrissie was pregnant again, and while she was thrilled for her twin sister, she couldn't help feeling a sad emptiness inside. She herself would be six months pregnant right now, if only... She dashed the thought before it could hurt her again.

When it came time to say grace before the meal, the only meal of the year when it truly seemed appropriate to Jessica, she listened to all the blessings counted by those around her. Good health, food on the table, friends and family. All the usual things people give thanks for on the last Thursday in November. She dreaded taking her turn, for no matter what she said, she knew what the others would be thinking.

A year ago, she had everything in the world to be thankful for. This year, most of that everything was gone.

"So, what's it like, living among the gods?" Paul asked, scooping an enormous portion of mashed potatoes onto his plate. "Feel like royalty?"

Jessica took a deep breath to keep from sniping back at her brother. She had to remember how far removed the Microsoft engineer was from the reality—or non-reality—of Hollywood.

"It's different," she said at last.

"Lonely at the top?" he prompted, his tone not as friendly as it might have been.

"Not at all." Jessica whipped back. "I have a lot of friends. And I don't consider myself to be at the top of anything."

"I'd say you're on top of a good pile of cash."

Jessica tilted her head slightly, and Christine reddened.

"I don't think Jessica's financial situation is any of your concern," Jan pointed out. "She's still just your sister, my daughter, and Devon's mother."

Paul smiled whimsically. "Right. Having several million dollars in the bank doesn't change a thing."

Jessica smiled back. "Well, you're right of course. And to think that I turned down offers from your boss, the President, and Buckingham Palace all to have dinner with you low-lifers."

At her comment, Nick Reeves burst into laughter, and everyone else followed suit. The tension was broken, but Jessica was reminded of why she did not visit her brother more often.

With Nick and Paul firmly rooted before the television and the afternoon football games, the women crammed into the small kitchen to clean up and talk. Much of the buzz was over Christine's baby. Everyone was excited at the prospect of a new baby in the family, especially since it was generally known that Terry and Paul had decided against having children. Of course, Jessica was not expected to have more, not now, and it would be inappropriate to bring up her plans to adopt Benjamin.

Devon reluctantly trudged off to play with Angelica in the den. Jessica watched him go with mixed feelings. There was a part of her that wanted to scoop him up and catch the next plane home. But the doctor had warned her not to go out of her way to shield him from the world. Grieving is a natural process, he advised, and she should refrain from being overly protective. He would need to develop coping strategies of his own.

That night, uncomfortably full from the abundant meal, Jessica lay awake with Devon curled up at her side. Letting her mind wander, she revisited the last few weeks of her life, wondering about the logic in signing Robin Quill as Mr. Romance. Lauder was willing to take a chance on the guy if they could attract a plausible female lead. Josie d'Angelo wanted the part, but they were waiting on a response from Kate France.

The details made her head hurt. She was beginning to wish she had waited until the spring to start such a project. She had lost the admittedly inexplicable obsession to make the film and while she didn't want to openly acknowledge it, she knew it was Dane's refusal to participate that had thrown water onto her fire.

She turned over, wrapping a protective arm around her young son. Soon it would be his fourth birthday, just before New Year's. Try as he might, he could not understand why his father had to go away. And Jessica was unable to explain.

He was no longer excited about preschool. He was easily frustrated with his normal activities, often resorting to scribbling rather than detailing the bright colored pictures he once drew. Many times, he was downright unresponsive to his mother's directives. She'd hoped coming to Seattle might ignite a spark in him. It hadn't.

Now, lying in bed with Devon deeply asleep beside her, Jessica became aware of a new problem. The sheet beneath them was wet.

"It's okay. Really." Terry's face was only slightly pinched as she helped Jessica strip the bed.

"I'll be happy to pay to have it cleaned, or for a new mattress if you'd like," Jessica offered, hoping Chrissie had gotten Devon away from the room before he could witness their activities. The last thing he needed was more stress.

"No, really. Don't worry about it."

Leaving Devon in her sister's care, Jessica took her mother to lunch, hoping to reconnect with her if only for an afternoon. She looked older now, but still managed to stay current with world affairs.

"How are you feeling, dear?" Jan asked, closing her menu.

"Not too bad, I guess. I'm more worried about Dev than anything else. He wet his pants a few days ago while he was outside, but I figured it was just a fluke. He potty trained so easily when he was only two. He'll be four in a month."

"He misses his daddy. He's probably just going through a difficult time."

"It's weird, Mom, but sometimes I get the feeling he blames me for Mac's death."

"That's absurd. He couldn't possibly."

"I hope you're right. I need to call the doctor when we get home."

"You haven't brought anyone new home, have you? Men, I mean."

"Mom, what do you think? Absolutely not. I haven't even seen anyone, really. I'm not ready to see anyone."

"I read about your trip to Hawaii. What was that all about?" Her mother lifted an accusing eyebrow.

"Business. Kyle and I were evaluating a script. He invited me for a little vacation, nothing more. I was stressed out; I just needed to get away. Mom, we had separate rooms! It was nothing. I don't even like him."

Her mother nodded. "How about that other man, what is his name? The actor you did that big picture with."

"Dane?"

"That's it. You see him much?"

"Dane is always around... when I need him. He's a good friend." To her mother's questioning look, she added, "nothing more."

"Okay. Well, I think you need to spend a little time with that wee one of yours. He just needs a little one-on-one attention."

"Are you saying I don't take good care of my son?"

"Not at all. Just that you are all each other's got right now, and you need to take care of your priorities."

"I do take care of my priorities. Devon is always first."

"Of course."

As soon as they returned to Paul's house, Jessica packed her bags.

"Hold it steady while I tighten the bolts," Jessica directed.

"The pine needles are perforating my face! Hurry!" Roxanne yelled as she held the broad Christmas tree upright. Below her, Jessica was crawling under the lowest branches.

"You'll survive," she called back. "A little more toward the wall, please."

"I'm not into acupuncture, here."

Soon, they stood back to examine their handiwork. "Looks better than ours," Roxanne lamented.

"I want it to be special for Devon. I'm so glad you guys will be here to decorate it with us tonight."

"Tom is looking forward to it. He gets such a bang out of Dev."

"It's good for him to see Tom. I wish they were closer."

Roxanne smiled. "I think Tom regrets not having more kids. Devon reminds him of when Robbie was little."

Jessica nodded, remembering that Roxanne had a grown stepson raised by his mother. She could understand Tom's regret. "Maybe Tom can help me. I'm, uh, having some problems with Devon. He's not using the bathroom at night."

"Post trauma syndrome. I wanted to mention that he seems depressed. Should you see a kid-shrink?"

Jessica turned away, heading toward the kitchen to wash her hands. *My child doesn't need a psychiatrist. He just needs time.*

Roxanne followed. "Really. Is he wetting the bed every night?"

Jessica felt her teeth beginning to grind. "I shouldn't have said anything. I should have known you'd have an opinion."

"I'm not supposed to have an opinion? Are you nuts? You're the one who brought it up."

Jessica turned off the faucet with more force than necessary and turned to face Roxanne. "Let it rest, Rox. Devon will be fine. He just needs a little time, that's all. And so do I."

"Suit yourself. Don't say I didn't warn you."

That evening, Jessica watched closely as her son hung ornaments on the Noble fir in the family room. Preoccupied, careful, Devon selected only certain items to hang and then quietly sat on the couch watching the others. Jessica's heart cried for him.

Usually the happiest time of year for her, Christmas was a particular strain for Jessica. She wanted so badly to make it exciting and happy for Devon, while knowing that the hole in their lives could never be filled with material gifts; they painfully joined the masses of bereaved survivors for whom the holidays brought only sadness.

As the month progressed, she became obsessive in her quest for holiday magic, buying lavish gifts for her family and friends and streaming a different Christmas video every night of the week. With Devon standing on a chair at the kitchen counter, they baked every kind of cookie imaginable and packaged them for the L.A. Mission shelter.

By Christmas Eve, Jessica was beyond exhaustion. Fighting a cold, she huddled with her son before the great tree, a meager fire in the fireplace behind them.

"Isn't it beautiful, Dev?"

"Yeah."

"Sometimes I squint my eyes real tiny, and the twinkle lights get so blurry and pretty."

"Me too."

"We still need to put the plate out for Santa."

"Okay."

They went to the kitchen and Jessica helped Devon put cookies, milk and a carrot on the special Santa plate. Solemnly the little boy carried the plate to the hearth.

"Does Santa see Daddy?" he asked suddenly.

"Maybe."

"If we leave him a letter, do you think he could tell it to Daddy?"

Jessica's throat swelled so that she couldn't speak for a moment. "We can, but I think Daddy would just like us to send our thoughts in a prayer. He doesn't need us to write them down, sweetheart."

"Okay."

Later that night, after carefully nibbling most of the cookie, drinking the milk and breaking away all but the end of the carrot, Jessica made good her promise to pray.

"I need some help here, God. Nothing fancy, not necessarily tonight, but soon, please? Send me some kind of help. I'm not particularly good at steering this ship all alone."

She paused to blow her nose and wipe her eyes once again.

"And Mac darling, if you're listening in, don't be too disappointed in me. I'll get better. You'll see. I remembered the Santa plate."

"Christmas ain't what it used to be, that's for sure," Trina said, refilling Dane's coffee mug a second time. "My family's all the way the hell down in Florida. Damned if I'm gonna pay for airfare when they never come to California. You got any family?"

"Nope."

Dane took a sip and reached for the newspaper on the kitchen table. Skipping to the entertainment section, he perused the page for anything of interest.

"No brothers, sisters? You surely have an ex-wife."

"A fact I'd rather forget."

"Kids? You really ought to call them on Christmas."

"Why did you ask if you already knew?"

"Why don't you just tell me about them, you big galoot?"

Dane put the paper down, trying to decide if she was worth the annoyance. She was, at least, a great tumble.

"Galoot? Really? Okay. Two girls, one boy, one bitchy woman who gets a sizable chunk of my bank account. Girls are about seven and twelve, the boy is eleven and he's mostly mine."

"Now we're talking," Trina encouraged, carefully poking her toes into the leggings gathered by her fingers. "Go on. Tell me about the green velvet doll at the party."

Dane's teeth began to grind involuntarily.

"Aw, c'mon. What have you got to lose? I'll just bet there isn't another person on earth you can really talk to. I'm not so bad, really. Might do ya good. Do me good to know who it is you're thinking about while we're doing the deed."

Her frankness bothered him, and yet he was unable to keep a smile from his lips. "Okay. As if you don't already know, her name is Jessica and I met her... maybe four years ago. We did a couple of pictures together. We're still friends. She just lost her husband."

"And she's still holding your ticket. So, what's keeping you?"

"He was a friend of mine. She was... completely devoted to him. She may never get over it."

"Does she know?"

"Know what?" Dane shifted in his chair.

"Know you've got the screaming hots for her?"

"I don't."

"You lyin' bastard. Bad enough lyin' to me, but don't lie to yourself, Dane Pierce. And don't lie to her. She's better'n that."

Dane looked away from his companion, hating the words that were coming from her now.

"You want me to talk to her?"

He turned back toward her so abruptly that she jumped. "No. Don't even think about it."

"Well, all right! Cripes, you scared me. I don't even know the broad."

"I'm sorry. I'm a little touchy, I guess. A few years ago," he paused, knowing he should keep his mouth shut, but also knowing that Trina was right; he had no one to talk to about his private issues. He had to hope he could trust her. "There was this woman. Beautiful girl, crazy as a dervish, and I dated her for a while. She wanted me to marry her, and she was willing to go to... great lengths to assure an engagement. She secretly harassed Jessie and Mac, then tried to pin it on me—"

"She found out you were in love with Jessica, didn't she?"

Dane hesitated, hating the scenes that were forming in his mind. "Something like that. Anyway, she tried to blackmail me. And when it was obvious it wouldn't work, she... she shot herself."

"Oooh. Bad."

"Worse than bad."

"Did she find out?"

"Who?"

"Your lady. Does she know what happened?"

"Not everything. It was never brought to light." Dane issued a heavy sigh. "Come on. I'll drive you home."

He was sorry he had said so much. The less people that knew the story, the better. And until he had run off at the mouth this morning, everyone who had known his secret was dead. Jackie Spencer had died at the scene, by her own hand. Charlene MacKendall, intuitive as she was, had picked up on the truth almost instantly. That left only one other person who had stumbled onto the sordid mess. And that person had died in a questionable plane crash.

Ten

Twenty Questions

New Year's. A time for change, new goals, new spirit.

Jessica launched headlong into January, more determined than ever to rise above her misfortunes and move forward. With rehearsals for *Mr. Romance* underway, perhaps her life would finally even out.

Filling in as the film director was terribly exciting. It was only for a few weeks, but Jessica was hungry to absorb the knowledge and experience her late husband had so enjoyed. She packed a small bag of toys, snacks and spare clothes and took Devon with her to the studio. Watching from the director's chair, Jessica crossed her legs and tried to keep from bouncing her foot as she scrutinized Robin's walk.

"A little more swagger," she called.

"What's swagger?"

"Sauce. But it's forced. You don't believe you're a sex symbol, but you must act the part. So, you act like you're acting."

Robin looked doubtful but practiced swinging his hips slightly as he crossed the soundstage. Josie D'Angelo sighed, but smiled.

"Be saucy! Like this." Jessica stood and dropped her script into her chair. "Like, I'm cool. I'm God's gift to womankind. I hate this, but I gotta walk-the-walk." She gave her impression of the hero's gait, and Robin nodded, following her lead.

"Much better. Let's do that line again."

Jessica sat back down and forced herself not to rub her eyes. It was going to be a long day, and she wondered if Devon was okay in the dressing room with the set hair stylist.

"And you wanted me to do that?" Dane asked, sauntering up from somewhere behind her. "What did you call it? Sauce?"

Jessica lifted her chin. "What do you want? I'm busy."

"Thought you might want some lunch. Unless you've adopted the Dane Pierce Film Fast."

"Pretty much."

"Suit yourself. Cute kid. Who is he?"

"Robin Quill. He's perfect, don't you think?"

Dane grinned down at her. "What I think doesn't matter, remember?"

"Then go away."

"Where's Lauder?"

"He'll be here next week."

"How was your Christmas?"

Jessica stared straight ahead, pretending to be engrossed in the action. "It was awful," she murmured at last.

Dane's expression turned serious, but he remained rooted to the spot, his hands clasped behind his back.

"I'm sorry to hear that. Devon okay?"

"No."

"Boy, you're just a mass of good news." Dane licked his lips and looked around. "Anything I can do?"

Jessica finally stood and faced him. "Look, I really don't have time to chit-chat right now. I'll call you next week. I'm not feeling real sociable."

"Coulda fooled me," he muttered, and took his leave.

Now Jessica did rub her eyes. She had an enormous headache brewing, and Dane's visit had further unnerved her. She didn't have time to analyze why he'd come or why she felt so unsteady in his presence.

She called it a day around 5:30. The woman who watched Devon complained that he was overly sensitive, and that Jessica should find someone better equipped to deal with his moods. She salved her own hurt feelings by driving through McDonald's on the way home. Devon seemed relieved for the day to be over.

"I don't like that lady, Mommy. She wasn't nice."

"It's okay, darling. We won't stay with her anymore."

Later, swallowing what little pride she had left, Jessica made the phone call she had been dreading.

"Rox, you know I wouldn't ask if it wasn't really important to me. It's just for a few days, until I can find someone regular. I'm having a terrible time since Lydia left. I can't wait for her to get back; it's going to be a while. Her mother is terribly sick."

Roxanne was quiet for a moment, and Jessica held her breath. Their friendship was already on shaky ground. No matter what Jessica wanted to do, Roxanne was against it. She had always been opinionated, and Jessica had never let it bother her before. But in recent weeks Roxanne had become almost adversarial.

"Sure. A couple of days is fine."

She was holding back, it was obvious; still, Jessica was immensely relieved. Devon was completely comfortable at Tom and Roxanne's.

She barely slept three hours before it was time to get up again. Warming a cup of yesterday's coffee in the microwave, she scrambled around the kitchen, grabbing a boxed drink and a granola bar for Devon to eat in the car.

"Can you find your own shoes, sweetie?" she called.

"I lost them," Devon called back.

"Arrrrghh!" Jessica put down her cup and raced to the family room, digging the boy's sneakers out from under the couch cushions.

"We gotta hurry. We're late. Aunt Roxanne will make you a real breakfast later."

She kissed him goodbye three times at Roxanne's door.

"He'll be fine."

"I know."

"But what about you? Are you going to survive this madness?" Roxanne asked, leaning into the doorjamb.

Jessica forced a smile she didn't begin to feel. "Of course. Things are great. The film is going... well. I'll see you around six."

Roxanne nodded slowly. The skepticism was not lost on Jessica, who turned and scurried down the driveway to her car.

Such was the routine for the next two weeks. Roxanne was tight-lipped, nurturing to Devon but cool to his mother. Jessica was unable to find what she considered suitable day care. She had to be painstakingly careful; everyone and their mother wanted to take care of the late Dr. Jim's son. Plus, she had only had a day to even explore the options; she was in the director's chair. Things were happening fast.

John Lauder would be taking over as soon as his other picture wrapped, which would be any day now. Then, perhaps, she could take a day off.

Robin was becoming increasingly fussy and argumentative, and Jessica could not understand why. It was nearing the end of January, and he wasn't close to being ready to go before cameras. She took him to lunch.

"So how do you like being a star? So far, I mean?" she asked, stirring sweetener into her iced tea.

Robin shrugged and gave her a silly smile. "Not what I expected. I thought it would be easier."

"Ha! That's a good one. We only make it look easy. So, tell me about your hometown. You said you were living in British Columbia?"

"For a while. I was living in Vancouver with a friend. But I'm really from Ohio."

Vancouver. It struck a negative chord in her mind. Wesley Elliot had lived in Vancouver just before his reign of terror on her life. But her ex-husband was now serving time and no longer a threat.

"And right now, you live in..."

"West Hollywood."

"That's convenient. You have family here?"

"No... is this twenty questions, or what?"

"Just trying to get to know you. I'm curious to know if there are any women in your life. Do you live alone?"

Robin chuckled. "No. No women, but I do have a roommate. A close friend."

"Well, that's good. This can be a lonely town."

"We do a lot of things together."

Jessica nodded. "Probably better not to be going with someone right now. Making a movie is hard work, your social life would have to take a backseat, if there was a backseat."

"I didn't say I wasn't in a committed relationship."

"Oh." Jessica tried not to look confused, instead focusing on the tines of her fork as she jabbed at her salad. "Well, I think you'll like John Lauder. He's finishing up another film, coincidentally up in

Vancouver. He'll be on the set in a day or two. He really liked your screen test."

"That's cool," Robin said. "That Josie chick is a little weird."

"Josie? She's a fine actress. You look good together."

"I don't feel any chemistry."

"Sometimes you don't. A good acting team can pull it off, though. Sometimes it helps to envision someone you do have chemistry with."

Robin didn't respond. His eyes were focused on a young man just entering the commissary. "You know that guy?" he asked suddenly.

Jessica followed Robin's gaze, then shook her head. "I've seen him around, but his name escapes me, if I even knew it. Why do you ask?"

"No reason. He sure is buff." Robin shook his head, then mumbled something about chemistry.

Jessica looked again, and then back to her lunch companion. Something, some unformed thought was niggling at her. She hoped she was wrong.

Robin was dead-on about having no chemistry with the leading lady in *Mr. Romance*. The actress was more than accommodating, good-naturedly trying to play upon the young actor's sensitivities. Jessica, however, grew more nervous by the hour.

"I have a good coach in mind," she told him after a particularly trying afternoon. "I'll ask him to see you this weekend, if that's okay with you."

"No, it's not okay. I need my weekends, Jessica. I do have another life, you know."

"No, I didn't know. When you work in this business, this business is your whole life. Where did you hear otherwise?" Her annoyance was hard to keep a lid on. "His name is Russell Powers and he'll be at your house Saturday morning."

"Forget it. And forget the whole damned movie. I'm sick of being told how to do what I do. This script is crap, this role is for shit, and I'm outta here."

He stormed away, lifting a dressy black leather jacket from the back of his chair, leaving Jessica to stare after him in complete shock.

"You can't!" she screamed, stomping her foot. "You have a contract!"

"Screw the contract," he called over his shoulder just before the stage door slammed.

Jessica was unable to move for several moments while she considered the repercussions of what had just transpired.

What the hell do I do now?

After dismissing her whispering crew, she sat in her car for twenty-five minutes. There was more on the line than just Robin's breach of contract. John Lauder would be livid. Access and the other investors would cry foul. But worst of all, Dane and Roxanne would have the last laugh.

She couldn't cry. She could barely think. Eventually shaking herself loose, she found her cell phone and called Roxanne.

"Tell him I'll be there in twenty minutes."

"Jess, we have to talk about this arrangement."

"Don't worry. I won't be bringing him back."

Once home, Jessica started a bath for Devon and laid out his pajamas, then poured herself a glass of wine. Pawing through the freezer, she rejoiced at finding a frozen lasagna and promptly pushed it into the oven. While it cooked, she went to her room to change.

She stripped down to her underwear and succumbed to the desire to lie back on her bed for a few moments, trying to coax a little relaxation. Closing her eyes, she forced the picture of Robin's dramatic exit from her mind, replacing it with thoughts of spending more quality time with her son.

Forget Robin. Forget Lauder. Forget Roxanne, and for that matter, forget the whole damned world.

"If only I could," she moaned. Roxanne had been short with her at the door. And in retrospect, it was more than just distancing herself from Jessica; Roxanne looked pale and despondent.

The ringing of her phone on the nightstand jolted her upright.

"Mrs. MacKendall, this is Irma Carvey. I've been trying to reach you all day. I'm afraid I have some rather bad news."

Surely the digital counter on the treadmill was malfunctioning. He must have logged at least three miles by now, yet the red numbers said differently. Dane grabbed a towel and mopped his forehead but continued running.

He was down twenty-eight pounds and two inches off his waist. His stomach muscles weren't exactly rock-hard, but he now had a respectable profile, and he fought to go the last two pounds.

Dane glanced at the large wall clock. He was picking up Alex from the airport in two hours and needed to shower. Slapping the "cool down" button, he slowed his pace for a minute or two before finally stepping off the treadmill. Again, he wiped his face.

In the bathroom he reached inside the shower stall and flipped on the hot water. He was pleased with his progress. Not only did he look and feel better, but his breathing also wasn't as labored. Back in the bedroom, he stripped off his t-shirt and sat down to untie his shoes. He was about to return to the bathroom when the phone rang.

"Mr. Dane Pierce?"

"Who wants to know?"

"Sgt. Denehy, L.A.P.D. Got a minute, Mr. Pierce?"

"I might have. What's it about?"

"It's about Cory MacKendall."

Dane asked the investigator to hold on while he shut off the shower. Now his respiration did elevate.

"As you might be aware, there's evidence that the plane was hit by high-powered rifle ammunition from the ground in Minneapolis. We're following all leads."

"As you should. Has anybody bothered to check on the whereabouts of Wesley Elliot?"

"Our first call. He's still under lock up." The detective paused. "One of the things that's on my list here, a phone call Mac made from his hotel room the night before he left Minnesota. Phone company records indicate that the call was to your home in Jackson, Wyoming. Do you recall talking to Mac that night?"

"Yes."

"Can you share with me the nature of that conversation?"

"Absolutely not." Dane stood up.

"Is there some reason why not?"

Dane grinned to himself, shaking his head. "Well, I guess there is, isn't there? I don't feel it's necessary to tell you about our personal conversation. We were friends, and business partners. We talked about a lot of things. And frankly, Detective Denehy, it's none of your business. You have no authority on this case."

"Ah, but Minneapolis PD has asked for my help. I was the lead detective the last time you were... involved with the MacKendalls. The investigators are interested in what light I can shed on Mac's murder. So, perhaps you could verify for me, then, a report we got that you argued on the phone that night. That MacKendall raised his voice to you in anger."

Dane drew in, and then exhaled, a deep breath, rubbing his forehead with his free hand.

"Is there some particular reason for this line of questioning? It's beginning to sound like I should have my attorney present."

"Maybe you should."

Alex had grown a foot while away at school. Perhaps not a foot, but he was definitely in a different time zone. Since his eleventh birthday in October, he had grown steadily taller, his hair now brushing his father's chin when they embraced at the airport gate.

In the car on the way back, Alex seemed happy and enthusiastic about being in Los Angeles.

"When will be we going to the ranch?" he asked, his fingers twirling the radio dial on the Mustang's dashboard.

"Not sure. Why?"

"Just wondered. How's Donatello?"

"Greg's taking good care of him. You ready to ride?"

"You bet."

"When do you have to be back at school? A week?"

"I'm not going back."

Dane kept his eyes level, on the road ahead. He had expected as much. He'd never liked school much either. "We'll talk about that."

Back in Malibu, Alex tossed his bag into the bedroom Peter had recently vacated, then trotted back downstairs to join his father in the kitchen.

"Do you think you'll like school in Jackson better?" Dane asked, dishing out helpings of cottage cheese on to two plates.

"Doncha got any chips?"

"Nope. You want whole wheat or rye?"

"Neither. I'll just have some macaroni and cheese."

"Not here, you won't. Sandwiches, milk, cottage cheese. Apple or canned pineapple?"

This time Alex only stared as if aliens had abducted his real father.

They ate together at the kitchen table.

"So, what's so bad at Ridgecrest?"

"Aw, the kids there are snobs. All they do is talk about people, all the time."

"Like what people?"

"You know, like kids' dads and stuff."

Dane nodded solemnly. "What kinds of things do they say about kids' dads and stuff?"

"Like, you know, stuff about who they date and stuff."

Now Dane stifled a grin. "So, like, who are we dating now?"

Alex kept his eyes down, pausing to take a sip of milk. Finally, glancing up at Dane, he replied with obvious uncertainty.

"A stripper."

"A stripper," Dane repeated, putting his sandwich down. "And would this be your father who is dating the aforementioned stripper?"

Alex nodded.

"I see." Dane took a long draught of milk. "Seen your mom lately?"

"She was there on Parents' Day."

"Parents' Day? When was that?"

"Couple of months ago. You were at the ranch." Alex poked at the mound of cottage cheese with his fork. "She's split up from Fred."

"That so."

"An' Zoe doesn't want to live with Mom, so she asked Mom if she could live with Fred. Of course Mom said no, 'cuz she dumped Fred already."

"What? What about Mimi?"

"Mimi likes Mom. Oh, and Mom wants you to drop me off at her house for a few days before we go to the ranch."

"She does." Dane had lost his appetite. He folded up the remains of his lunch in a paper towel and tossed it into the trash. This was turning out to be one gem of a day.

Eleven

Hide and Seek

Jessica knelt on the bathroom floor beside the tub and poured a small amount of shampoo into her palm. Humming the theme song from her son's favorite morning cartoon program, she worked the strawberry scented gel into lather and ran it through Devon's wet locks.

"Did you have fun at Aunt Roxie's today?"

"Yeah," Devon replied, holding an empty baby bottle under the water and watching the bubbles escape as it filled.

"How would you like to go on a little vacation?"

"Okay," he said, dumping the water out onto his knee.

"I have a friend who is going to let us stay at his house on a beach."

"Like Uncle Dane's house?"

"Even better than Uncle Dane's. Wait 'til you see it."

Long after tucking Devon into bed, Jessica sat at the kitchen table, making notes to herself on a yellow pad. After reading them over, she laughed a little, for only she could understand the rhyme and reason to her thoughts.

A mixture of "to do" items, people to call, ideas she didn't want to forget. On the reverse side was a list of things of which she would let go; at the top, the first line read *Mr. Romance.*

Flipping back to the important side, she leaned her forehead onto one hand and thought about the dear little baby in Minnesota, the one diagnosed with a heart defect. The emergency surgery to repair a tiny hole in Benjie's heart was scheduled for tomorrow morning, and there was no way she could get there in time. She had her own son to think about.

Irma Carvey had seemed almost gleeful to impart the heartbreaking news. For the life of her, Jessica could not fathom why the woman disliked her so much.

"There's nothing you can do," she had said, sounding much like the evil Miss Gulch on her horrid bicycle. But Jessica felt nothing like Dorothy, and right now she would have given anything to have even a scarecrow for a friend.

Her old schoolmate, Brian, at least, had been genuinely nice on the phone, giving her directions and offering to stock the vacation house with food and linens for her stay. They had not seen each other since college, although his sister Amy had come for a visit just two years ago.

Jessica went to her bedroom and then into the generous walk-in closet she had shared with Mac. In the corner were three pieces of matched luggage, left out from their last, brief vacation to San Francisco. She dragged the largest one out and hoisted it onto the bed with a groan.

Grimly she forced herself to look upon the suitcase as an inanimate object, a utility item she might never have seen before. She could not allow herself to remember that his shirts had lain inside, his jacket and trousers had been folded and carefully packed within its satiny walls.

Steeling herself, Jessica returned to the closet and retrieved the smaller cases. She cast aside the smallest one. There was, of course, a piece missing; the middle-sized rolling case that had gone to Minnesota with Mac.

Quickly she began selecting clothing for her own trip, digging through dresser drawers and rattling garments off their hangers. She'd grab the toiletries in the morning, and pack Devon's bag then also.

Around 1 a.m., she fell into bed, exhausted. She had a long drive tomorrow, and she had to get some rest.

Dane decided that dry popcorn was not all that bad if you dumped enough salt on it. Sprawled on the couch, he glanced over just in time to watch Alexander's eyelids close. He wondered how much his son now weighed; tall and slender, he was a picture of Dane's own childhood years.

He turned the television volume down a notch and sprinted up the stairs to survey Alex's temporary bedroom. Tiny plastic building blocks littered the carpeting. A balsa wood glider sat on the dresser. His duffel bag was stashed in the corner.

Dane turned down the bed and dimmed the ceiling light. Brushing aside the tiny interlocking blocks, he made a path through the room and then returned downstairs to carry his son to bed. He was just returning to the living room when his phone rang.

"You wanted to talk to me? It must be important for you to leave a message." Trina's matter-of-fact demeanor was particularly annoying tonight, especially considering what he'd just learned.

"What're you up to?"

"Not much. Just got home. Why?"

"Thought you might want to come over. I could use some entertainment."

"What kind of entertainment are you looking for?"

"Oh, I don't know. Maybe a little striptease?"

Trina paused a moment, then responded, her voice taking on a wary tone. "Who told you about that?"

"Now that's the interesting part. My son heard about it at school. When were you planning to mention it to me?"

"Well, in your own words, lover boy, it's none of your business." Trina uttered a sigh. "Was there anything else? I've been on my feet all night and I'm whupped."

"I'll bet you are. No, nothing else. Nothing at all."

Dane grinned as he hung up the phone. The last to know. Damn! He'd been so busy following Jessica's every move, he'd lost his focus. He should have had Peter check Trina out.

Later, Dane lay in his bed, his room in total darkness. Yet his eyes remained open. His plans were ever changing. He would not make Alex go back to Ridgecrest; that much was clear. Perhaps Peter would be able to... no. He didn't want to pawn his son off again. It wouldn't hurt to keep Alex out of school for a couple of months while they sorted things out.

He wouldn't be seeing Trina again. She represented just one more complication he did not need. No, he had far greater problems to deal with.

Denehy's implication needled him. That someone thought he could have anything, no matter how remote, to do with Mac's death chilled him to the marrow. He didn't want to think about all the reasons Denehy could dredge up, all the possible implications that could arise.

Lying on his back, Dane felt a weight pressing down on his chest. Indeed, he felt the need to force a deep breath. He decided it didn't matter much what Denehy thought. But the fear that was eating at him, churning in his gut and threatening to reacquaint him with ulcer medication, was that Denehy just might call Jessica.

He had to get to her first.

"Come on, Roxanne. You must know where she is."

"I already told you. She didn't tell me where she was going. She didn't tell Tom, or anybody else for that matter. You'll have to cool your heels, Tarzan."

Dane bit his lip to keep from giving it to Roxanne. He hung up, once again fighting the urge to chuck the telephone, this time into the ocean.

In the garage, he started the '66 Mustang Convertible and headed out of Malibu, pushing the needle with one eye trained on the rear-view mirror.

He already knew there would be no answer at her door, and he trotted over to the garage to peek through the small glass windows. Her car was not inside.

Pacing the front porch, he wracked his brain for an idea. There could be a clue inside.

As he paced, his eyes fell upon the window box, its small geranium plants long dried up. Quickly he felt around the hardened potting soil, his fingers eventually discovering the key pressed deep within. The key Mac had told him about, the night Devon was born in this very house.

Without hesitation, he turned the key in the lock and swung the heavy front door open. He had to hope she had not set the alarm.

He toured the house, fighting off the memories as he walked. It was Mac's house, and Dane could clearly feel his presence. The more he looked, the more knotted his stomach became.

In Jessica's bedroom, he determined that she had packed a suitcase; a smaller one lay discarded beside the bed. Drawers were hastily closed, the closet door still open, clothing obviously missing.

Devon's room reflected the same.

In the kitchen, he found a note to the housekeeper about supplies. Dane sighed in exasperation. He went to the phone but couldn't think of anyone he had not already contacted. Even Jessica's mother had politely claimed ignorance of her daughter's whereabouts.

He started to go, but the tiny blinking indicator light on the answering machine caught his eye. His finger paused only a heartbeat before punching the 'play' button. The first two messages were only himself, casually suggesting she call him back. He grimaced at the sound of his own voice; he detested answering machines. The third message, however, was much more interesting.

"Hey Jessie, it's Brian. I am so glad you're coming up! I can't wait to see you, it's been much too long. Hope you haven't left yet, I just wanted to tell you I'll meet you at the light around 6:00 p.m. with that bottle of champagne we talked about. If I don't talk to you before then, drive safely, if you take Highway 1 be careful around Big Sur, it's twisty and treacherous. See ya."

Dane played the message several times, trying to decipher the message. "Light. 6:00 p.m. Big Sur." Dane rubbed his forehead. "Light? Big Sur, Highway 1, Coast. Light?"

He locked the house and got into his car. Driving back to Malibu, he considered his options, and once home, he dug out a California map and spread it on the kitchen table.

"Six p.m., a light north of Big Sur." Squinting close to the map, he scoured the coastal town names and circled the possibles in red. But there were too many towns large enough to have traffic lights. "Wait a minute..." he said aloud, hurrying into the living room where his notebook computer sat on the small coffee table. He flipped it open and turned it on.

California lighthouses, he typed into the search engine and waited. He was soon rewarded with a clear map of the beacons guarding the Pacific coastline. He focused on those above Monterey.

Grabbing a notepad, he scribbled down the names. "Big Sur. Point Pinos. Santa Cruz. Pigeon Point. Point Montara. Point Surrender. Point Bonita. Point Reyes." Six p.m. She couldn't have made it much farther than the Bay area if she had driven, and he was quite certain she had gone by car.

Dane looked at his watch. It was just after 11 a.m. He had to get moving. After a quick stop at his ex-wife's house, he was on his way.

As he drove, he thought about what he might be walking in to. A lover's tryst? A secret boyfriend? He shook his head, trying not to clench his teeth. Why a lighthouse? If, in fact, the term "light" did mean lighthouse. What was there to do at a lighthouse? She'd taken Devon, another fact of which he was certain.

Touring lighthouses might be fun if he was not so completely freaked out by Jessica's disappearance.

And who was Brian? Brian... Brian Winslow. The night of the masquerade ball, the silent auction donation made by Jessica and someone named Brian Winslow. A weekend... bed and breakfast weekend.

Bells went off in his head. An *L.A. Times Travel* article, a few weeks ago, reviewed a bed and breakfast established within a lighthouse! Excited at this new angle, Dane pulled off the freeway and opened the browser on his phone. Quickly he scanned the information he had previously reviewed at home.

East Brother Lightstation, San Francisco Bay area. That had to be it. But wait; Point Arena was also considered a hotel of sorts, with three full sized homes adjacent to the famous white tower.

"...as seen in the Mel Gibson romance classic, *Forever Young...*" the advertisement stated. He kept reading, finding that even Point Montara was a youth hostel often rented out for weddings and special events.

Dane stared out the windshield, pondering this new dilemma. If he were to drive straight to San Francisco, he could take inland routes and get there faster. But if it turned out that East Brother was the wrong place, he would have missed the other, less likely spots.

He'd stick with the coast.

He stopped for a meal in Monterey. Despite the tension with which he had been living for days, the drive was doing him good. Time to think, to examine his feelings and motivations. Parked in the lot behind a Burger King, he chewed his chicken sandwich slowly and thought about what he would say when he found her.

Because he knew he would find her. He only hoped it wasn't too late.

Twelve

Point Surrender

It was early evening when Dane passed the city limits of Newburg, California. His eyes were straining against the sunset and approaching dusk, and he turned the Mustang into the gravel parking lot outside a diner promising the best ribs on the coast. He wasn't hungry, but he was looking for a good shot of caffeine.

"What can I get you?" The waiter had practically followed Dane to the corner table, pad in hand. He was a big man, with tired but kindly blue eyes.

"Coffee, please."

"Gotcha. Cream?"

"No. Where am I, anyway?" Dane asked with a slight grin.

"This is Riley's, I'm Riley, and you've been on the road awhile."

Dane nodded as the proprietor went for the coffee pot. When he returned, Riley filled Dane's cup and sat down in the booth across from him.

"On up the road there is Newburg. Flea speck of a town, don't blink."

"Is there a bed and breakfast around here?"

"Hastings House, in town. But I think she's all full up this weekend."

"No, I'm sorry, I meant to say, is there a lighthouse around here, like one you can stay in?"

"Well, there's a lighthouse, but it's a private home. I think Brian might rent it out now and then, beings he moved back to the city last year."

"Brian Winslow?"

"You know Brian?"

"Not really. But we have a mutual friend, and I think she's staying at the lighthouse. I wanted to pop in while I was in town."

"Oh. Well, Point Surrender is just across the highway, down a piece on the left. Can't see it from the road and there's no sign, you just gotta know it's there."

Dane wet his lips and nodded slightly. "Thanks. I appreciate the information."

"No problem. Any friend of Brian's – or Brian's friends – well, is good with me."

He found the turnoff with no problem. More gravel, and a newly constructed garage on a bluff. He parked beside the closed garage and walked out to the edge of the cliff, looking out at the ocean below. What he saw nearly took his breath away.

A lighthouse was perched on an outcropping below, its white tower rising from the center of a small one-story house. There were lights burning inside, casting a warm glow on the chilly night. Looking around him, Dane could see a stairway built into the side of the bluff, leading down to the front door of the house.

He hesitated. It was certainly a private looking residence. What if he was wrong?

In the dim light emanating from the front window, he could see the outline of a child's tricycle parked against the house.

He shook his head, looking first back to his car, the locked garage, and then to the house again. Stuffing his hands into the pockets of his leather bomber jacket, he started down the steps, knowing, and yet hoping with all his might, that Jessica was inside.

It wasn't luxury, but it was charming. Brian had seen to everything she could possibly need, even a box of Devon's favorite breakfast cereal. After spending only two nights in the lighthouse, Jessica felt she had been there at least a week. Devon seemed better, but he was still exhibiting regressions she did not expect.

Time. Time was what they both needed, time to settle their problems and get on with life. One day at a time.

The house still smelled of chicken nuggets and French fries, and Jessica smiled as she quietly closed Devon's bedroom door. He'd gone down early tonight after a full day of romping on the beach, chasing seagulls and digging for sand crabs.

She was tired, but less stressed than when she arrived. She put the baking sheet into the sink and half-heartedly rinsed it off, then dried her hands and went to her own bedroom. Even though it was still early, she would not be going out so decided to dress for bed.

Despite recent renovations, the house was still on the drafty side for Jessica. Pulling on her nighttime sweats, she glanced around for her book and remembered seeing it on the small roll-top desk in the alcove off the living room. She went to retrieve it.

Folding her legs beneath her, she curled into the big, padded rocking chair before the fireplace and opened the book. How long had it been since she had indulged in the luxury of reading a good novel? Or any book, for that matter, written for someone older than four years old?

But try as she might, she found herself reading the same passages over and over, like listening to a conversation with only one ear. Finally, she closed the book with a little sigh and stared into the fire instead. She had come to one decision since the great escape from L.A., and that was to sell her house. She had really hoped she could keep it, that she could put the memories aside long enough to move forward. It just wasn't happening. Memories hung on the house, throughout its rooms and hallways, like great cobwebs, catching on her as she moved about.

A call to a real estate broker was now on the agenda.

She would have to find a new house, a house without a history, without ghosts. Fantasizing, she imagined a smaller home decorated in a rustic style, with at least three, no, four bedrooms. She'd need one for Benjie.

Because she was determined to adopt Benjamin MacKendall, to raise him as her own. A little brother for Dev. It would be good for them all.

She replayed in her mind the call to the hospital so far away, made on her cell phone yesterday; Baby MacKendall had done well in surgery and was expected to make a full recovery. And with the memory came an unpleasant thought: what if the baby's heart had failed while in her care? With dizzying regret, she imagined sitting in the director's chair while her tiny nephew suffered in his crib.

She would give up filmmaking. Aside from the fact that there would be no time, she would no longer want to make movies after Benjie came to live with them, right?

Jessica sighed. She had never been so confused in her life, never more unsure of her future. Even back in the early days, when she didn't know where her next rent money would come from, she wasn't so dispirited. All that would change, she was certain, when Benjamin arrived.

Damn Roxanne and her preaching. Benjamin was not, nor would he ever be, the answer to her loneliness. He would not be the substitute for a man in her life, would not fill the emptiness left by her husband's death.

But he would be loved. He would fill a need, and she would be a wonderful mother to him and Devon. Her eyes grew misty at the thought of the two boys playing together, Devon with his golden ochre hair and Benjie with his shining blue-black locks.

Still, there was something missing from the picture. A missing piece to the puzzle her life had become. Jessica took a deep breath, then let it out slowly. She had to admit to herself that there would never be a new man in her life. And she could live with that, if only...

Her reverie was shattered by a brisk knock at the door. Her heart instantly began to pound, so complete was her shock at the sound. She nearly leaped from the rocking chair, running to the door before the caller had the chance to knock again and wake Devon.

Against her better judgment, she pulled open the door without inquiring. The sight of Dane standing on the porch was an even greater shock than the fact that she had any visitor at all.

They stared at each other for several moments.

She was suddenly aware of the chilly, swirling fog creeping into the house, and she motioned for Dane to come inside. Before she could gather her thoughts, he posed the first question.

"Are you alone?"

She stared at him for another moment, then gestured toward the closed door just beyond the fireplace.

"Devon is sleeping."

Dane nodded, some of the apparent tension leaving his face.

"Would you like a drink?" she asked quietly. "I only have champagne."

"That's all you have? I was hoping you had some hot chocolate." He rubbed his hands together, looking around the small living room. "The heater is out in my car."

"Oh my gosh. Come into the kitchen, it's warmer in there."

She put the teakettle on the stove and pulled a canister of instant cocoa from the cabinet. Dane sat down at the kitchen table.

"This your place?"

"No. It belongs to a friend of mine."

"Brian Winslow."

Jessica paused, a mug held in each hand. "You've become quite the sleuth."

Dane would not meet her eyes. Slouching in his chair, hands in his pockets, he looked more like a stubborn adolescent than a grown man.

"I had nothing better to do," he muttered at last.

"I see." Now, Jessica pulled another canister from the shelf, opening it and placing it on the table. "Dev and I baked these yesterday. Help yourself."

Dane plucked a cookie from the can and stuck it into his mouth, giving her a "thumbs-up" gesture.

Waiting for the kettle to heat, Jessica peered toward the kitchen window facing the sea. Instead of the broad expanse of the Pacific, she saw only her own reflection gazing back: stringy hair, drawn cheeks, pallid complexion. And worse, no makeup. The realization of how she must look only added to her misery.

"Dane, if I had known you were coming," she began, a fluster threatening to tangle her words. "Would you watch this kettle? I'll be right back."

In the bedroom, she sat at the small antique vanity and peeked into the mirror with a groan. As irritated as she was at his hunting her down, she couldn't bear for him to suffer her looking this bad. She grabbed her hairbrush and began fighting with her hair, her free hand rummaging through her case for her make-up bag.

Five minutes later she returned to the kitchen. Dane looked up from where he stood pouring hot water into the mugs.

"Sorry. It's been just me and Dev for a few days, I haven't bothered with much."

A half smile turned only one side of his mouth, an amused expression that made her blush. "I forgive you."

She was moving things around inside the refrigerator, hoping to hide her embarrassment until her face recovered. Finally, returning with a can of whipped cream, she turned to him.

"Okay, so tell me why you're here. This better be good." Her serious tone matched her expression. She tilted the whipped cream can over his mug and depressed the nozzle. Whipped cream exploded from the can, over-filling the mug, spattering the table, the wall and Dane's chin.

"Holy shit, woman, I can think of better ways to get even," he said with a grin.

"Oh! Oh, I am so sorry..." Jessica grabbed a paper napkin from the counter and hastily wiped up the mess from the table, and then tossed the napkin into the trash. Looking back at Dane, she saw the small traces of whipped cream on his face. Without thinking, she reached across the table and wiped them away with her finger.

His eyes locked on to hers just as his fingers wrapped around her hand, pulling it slowly back toward his face. Helpless against his power, unable to deny him, Jessica sat mesmerized while Dane pulled her fingertip into his mouth, gently sucking the whipped cream from it before slowly releasing her.

"Yum," he told her, licking his lips and lifting the hot mug. "Now, you were saying? Or would you like me to spray this time?" He took a quick sip of the steaming cocoa, then picked up the whipped cream can. "This could be fun."

Jessica swallowed hard, her chest rising and falling rapidly in response to his actions.

"No, I—I think maybe I'll just have marshmallows." She got up from the table and went back to the cabinet. For the third time in fifteen minutes her face was burning. In fact, she was burning all over. Taking a deep breath, she squared her shoulders and lifted her chin.

Back at the table, she dropped three or four miniature marshmallows into her mug, then looked directly at her unexpected guest.

"You were just about to tell me why you are here. You went to an awful lot of trouble to find me."

"I was in the neighborhood." He propped his elbows on the table, holding his mug close to his lips with both hands. "By the way," he added, before she could protest his dodge. "Do you know just how many lighthouses there are between here and L.A.?"

Jessica could not help a small smile.

"And do you also know, my dear, how comfortable a '66 Mustang convertible with bad struts and no heater is in the dead of winter?"

Jessica covered her eyes with her hand, trying hard not to laugh aloud.

"But I got you this." From the inside pocket of his jacket he pulled a postcard, its edges slightly curled. The picture of Mel Gibson posing before Point Arena bore a pre-printed autograph.

She couldn't help but giggle, pressing the postcard to her chest in glee.

"He's not your type," Dane reminded her sardonically. "Got about fifty kids, too. 'Course, that didn't stop you from coming after me, did it?"

Jessica looked up, her smile replaced by an expression of mock surprise. "I came after you?"

"You know you did. And as for why I'm here, it bugs the hell out of me when people disappear. People I care about." He returned to his slouch, sliding his hips forward and leaning back in the chair. The ball was clearly in her court now.

"I didn't disappear. Rox knew I was leaving."

"You didn't tell anyone, including the great all-knowing Roxanne, where you were going. I call that disappearing."

"Maybe I didn't want anyone knowing."

"Well, that was clear. But unfair."

"It's my life."

Dane pressed his lips tightly together for a moment, then exhaled a deep sigh. "Okay. It's yours."

Jessica shuddered a little as the wind kicked up outside, causing the kitchen window glass to rattle. "Do you mind if we go in near the fire?"

They moved to sit before the fireplace, and Dane added a large log onto the dying flames. Soon, it was blazing. Jessica pushed the heavy rocker away and spread a thick comforter on the floor.

"Dane, I'm sorry if I sounded upset. I can't believe you drove yourself all the way up here looking for me. It was really a sweet thing to do." She avoided his eyes while trying to back-pedal. "I... I was coming unglued down there. I don't expect you to understand.

Nothing, I mean absolutely nothing, was going right for me. The only thing I could think of was just getting away. I knew if I told anybody what I was going through, they'd try to get me into therapy or something. And I don't want that. I'm not off-balance, just confused. And hurting." She stole a quick peek at his reaction, surprised at his sympathetic expression.

"Go on," he encouraged.

Bravely, she continued. "After Mac... after the crash, I was bad, but I hung on. I really thought I was going to be okay. But then, around the time that Charlene... Charlene died, I started screwing up. I didn't even go to her funeral..." she paused, pressing her fingertips to her lips briefly before continuing. "I didn't go, and I felt horrible. Mac would have been so, so disappointed in me! And then that stupid trip to Hawaii, Jesus! What was I thinking? That I could just go on, that I could be normal again, going out with a man I knew nothing about?"

"Jess..."

"Then the fiasco with the film... I thought if I could make that film, could prove myself, that I could make him proud of me somehow... but how can I make him proud, now? He's... he's dead! He's dead."

"Sweetie, stop this."

"My son is hurting so bad, and I can't help him either. How can I fix him when I can't even fix myself? Such a sweet little boy, never did anything bad in his whole short life, and he has to suffer because his father was murdered and his mother is a—a—a psycho." She leaned her face into her hands, the tears leaking between her fingers and running down them.

Only a little hesitant, Dane reached forward and took her into his arms. "Jessie, baby, it's okay. It's going to get better. A whole lot better."

"Oh Dane, you don't understand. My entire life is falling apart. Just when I think it's going to be all right, something else happens."

Gently he rocked her, not unlike the afternoon of Mac's funeral when they had grieved together. "You did the right thing. Being up here, away from all that, you can sort things out. You can be strong again."

She pulled back and looked at him through swollen eyes. "I'm sorry," she whispered. "I didn't mean to lay all that on you. You've been a good friend through all this."

"Not good enough," he responded, stroking her hair away from her face. "Not nearly."

THIRTEEN

All Things Connected

He woke with a stiff neck. The couch was a lot prettier than it was comfortable. Still, he was in the small house on the cliff with Jessica. He would have hung himself on a nail to be with her.

She was still asleep, or at least had not emerged from her bedroom. The creak of an opening door made Dane open his eyes to a small blond boy tiptoeing across the rug toward him.

"Uncle Dane?"

"Hey, sport." With a slight groan, Dane forced himself into a sitting position and held open his arms. Devon climbed easily onto his lap for a hug.

"When did you get here?"

"Last night, after you went to sleep. I surprised Mommy."

"Did you bring her a present?"

"Not that kind of surprise."

"Did you bring me a present?"

"Check this out." Dane reached to the end of the couch where his jacket was draped over the arm. He dug around inside the pocket, finally dragging out a small trinket. It was a tiny viewer dangling from a key chain. Devon immediately held it up to the light.

"It's a lighthouse! Cool, wait 'til Mom sees it! Thanks, Uncle Dane."

"No problem. Hey, should we make breakfast for Mommy?"

"Sure. I can cook good."

In the kitchen, Dane watched with amusement as Devon carefully pulled a carton of eggs out of the refrigerator and slid it onto the counter.

"We like scramblers," he asserted, pulling a wire whisk out of a drawer and handing it to Dane.

"I thought you were the good cook," Dane said, looking at the whisk as though it was a scalpel.

"I can do the toast," Devon said proudly, retrieving the bread from a drawer next to the pantry cabinet. "You do the eggs. And Mom likes pepper."

Suddenly a look of distress crossed the small boy's face, and he turned his back to Dane. Dane narrowed his eyes, wondering what had caused the sudden about-face. Devon's hand was nested between his legs.

"Hey, champ, before we get started, I need to go..." Dane dredged up the words he'd used with Alexander several years before. He lowered his voice conspiratorially, leaning down closer to Devon's ear. "I need to take a whiz. How 'bout you?"

The child spun around, his eyes wide with surprise and interest.

"Yeah," he said, his little fingers obviously clutching his penis.

"Come on." Dane lifted Devon and carried him into the bathroom. "You know, sometimes I have to go so bad, I almost don't make it to the bathroom. I get busy, and I forget to go."

"Yeah. Me too!"

The eggs were only a little rubbery, the toast only a little burned. Jessica was touched at their efforts and smiled while washing down her breakfast with strong coffee.

"You don't scrimp on the grounds, do you?" she asked, peering into the darkness of her cup. Even with a healthy dose of milk, the coffee could have cleaned out the L.A. sewage system.

"I don't make wimpy joe, if that's what you're talking about."

Jessica held the mug to her lips, relishing the hot steam that warmed her face. She watched Dane as he moved about the kitchen, cleaning up the breakfast debris much the way Mac used to do. It intrigued her, for she had never known Dane to be particularly neat. Even his appearance was more carefully attuned. His clean, white knit golf shirt was tucked into his jeans, and she imagined his stomach to be washboard-hard beneath it. The short sleeves, despite the cold weather, showed off his newly muscled forearms.

He caught her looking and she quickly turned her attention to Devon. "Hey you, time to get dressed. We need to take Uncle Dane on a big explore today."

They walked through the small fishing town of Newburg, stopping to peruse the souvenir shops for the usual seaside memorabilia. For lunch, Dane treated them to subs from the Dilly Deli. Devon's improved demeanor encouraged Jessica as she watched his animated, giggly conversations with Dane throughout the day.

The last stop was the local market, where Jessica picked out lobsters and fresh vegetables for dinner.

Back at Point Surrender, Devon retreated to his room for some much-needed down time. It was only moments before Jessica and Dane heard the bleeps and blips of the latest Roblox video game.

"He's only allowed an hour," Jessica said, collapsing on the couch after putting away the groceries. "His dad's rule."

Dane nodded. "I thought of the Mario Brothers as surrogate parents for Alex when he was that age. It was a tough time." He kicked off his shoes and sat opposite her on the couch with his knees up. "Stays awfully chilly in here, doesn't it?"

"For me, yes. Brian's used to it. He lived here for a couple of years."

"Where did you meet him?"

"I went to college with his sister, Amy. Amy and I dated the same guy for a while when Wes and I were on the outs. God. Glad those days are over."

"See? Things are looking better already."

Jessica smiled, suppressing a yawn. They had chatted well into the wee hours of the night before, mostly about trivial, unimportant matters while Dane talked her down from her anxiety attack. He had remained calm, nurturing, caring.

"Tired?" he asked.

"A little." She grabbed the comforter Dane had folded over the back of the couch and threw one end to him, pulling her own legs up. She dragged the comforter up to her chin. "I, um, really enjoyed our talk last night."

Dane covered his legs and adjusted a pillow behind his neck. "Me too. I'm glad you didn't throw me out."

"Of course, I should have," she joked, watching his expression with interest. After a few moments of silence, she ventured some new thoughts.

"I'm thinking about selling the house."

"Oh? And moving where? I assume you have the means to do anything you want, whether you sell or not."

"Oh, yes," she answered, nodding. "We're pretty well set. I'll probably buy something else, another house." Relieved that he had not asked her why, Jessica smiled.

Dane gave her a quizzical look. "I have an idea."

"Okay?"

"Before you do anything, come up to the ranch. You and Dev, come stay with us for a month or two. The weather will be warming up soon... it's incredibly relaxing. Don't make any big decisions for a while."

Jessica tilted her head, her eyes searching Dane's face for his motivation. If there was an ulterior motive, it was well hidden.

"I'll think about it," she offered. "It sounds like a nice idea... only I worry about that Carvey woman."

"What about her?"

"She's keeping a dossier on my every move. She's already compiled a list of all the men I've kept company with since Mac died. I'm a regular trollop in her book."

"What?"

"Oh, it's true. Kyle, Robin – go figure that one! – even you. She is trying to make me look promiscuous."

Dane's eyes twinkled in merriment. "Well, aren't you?"

She kicked him under the blanket.

"Ouch!" Dane grasped both of her ankles and stretched her legs out, pulling her feet into his lap. "That's nothing compared to the dossier I have on you."

"Very funny. I can count on one hand the number of guys I've had sex with in my entire life. Less than one hand. And none of them have been in the last nine months."

Dane's eyebrows lifted slightly. "Well, that's certainly not fair. If you're going to have to suffer that kind of reputation, you might as well be having fun," he said with a grin.

"True," she agreed in jest.

"Getting a little horny, are you?"

Jessica could not stop the rosy heat that spread across her face, or the outraged smile that came to her lips. Had anyone else, anyone but Dane uttered such a comment, she would have slapped them hard.

No, only Dane could get away with talking to her libido, and he knew as much. Even now, he was taking the liberty of massaging her feet through her heavy white socks. It felt too good to be mad.

"Just think about it. We'll find a way to get around that old prude."

Jessica nodded and involuntarily closed her eyes. His experienced hands moved up to her calves, kneading, smoothing, working the muscles into complete relaxation. For the first time in weeks, she drifted off to sleep without her heart aching.

Dane fastened all the snaps on his jacket as he walked along the sand. Another sunset, a completely different day. Yesterday at this time he was anxiety ridden, searching for a missing woman and her little boy. Searching for a part of his soul.

Now, the woman had been found. His soul was still incomplete, but he was feeling better than he had in months. She had confided in him, poured out her fears and her nightmares to him. To him. It was more than he had dared hope for. And she was considering a stay at the ranch.

Denehy's threat seemed far away, now. Maybe I won't open that particular can of worms right now. Surely Jessica would never believe the implied accusation that he was guilty anyway.

The icy wind coming off the sea dragged his hair away from his face. He squinted at the expanse of beach that lay ahead, thinking about how many others had traversed the coast, and about how the waves crashing alongside him were a part of the same ocean that crashed behind his own house in Malibu.

All things connected. He and Jessica were connected, there was no doubt in his mind. And yet, he was afraid of those thoughts, those thoughts of their being together in some form of committed relationship. Even if he could get her to see and acknowledge the connection, what sort of future could they have?

He slowed his pace, pausing to study the sea.

Oh, he glimpsed, now and again, a bright and sunny time, with their boys romping together on the grassy pavilion behind the ranch house, and Jessica reigning over the house like the royalty she surely was. A princess. His princess.

But the vision was cloudy, masked by doubts and old harbingers of doom. It was the same old quandary, the uncertainty about his limits, his ethics.

It was the promise.

Jess was busy in the kitchen when he returned, preparing to cook the lobster. She wrinkled her nose when he came in the kitchen door, dangling a lobster by its tail corner over a large pot.

"I've never done this before," she explained.

"We can learn together."

They didn't talk much while cooking the dinner, and only sparsely during the meal. Devon chattered more than usual, directing most of his conversation to Dane.

"Mommy took a nap today," he was saying.

"I know. She talked herself to sleep."

"I was just up too late," Jessica said, exchanging smiles with Dane. "Feel good now, though."

"I didn't take a nap. I'm too big now for naps," Devon said.

"Me too," Dane agreed. "Girls get tired though. It's all that talking they do. Wears 'em out."

"Yup." Devon nodded, stuffing a forkful of cooked carrots into his mouth.

Devon was asleep by 7:30, and Dane broke open the bottle of Chardonnay he'd purchased in town.

"I'd love a glass," Jessica responded to his offer. "I really don't like champagne, but I didn't have the heart to tell Brian. He was so sweet to drive up from the city and get everything ready for us. Especially with Judy about to have twins."

"Ah. Judy, his wife."

"Of course." Jessica took a sip of the wine and resumed her position on the floor before the fire.

"Well, here we are again," Dane observed, holding up his glass to clink it against hers. "I did some thinking while I walked today."

"That's dangerous."

"I know. I feel bad about what that woman is doing to you. I wish we could blow her off somehow."

"I do too, but unfortunately, she holds all the cards. Without her I don't think I have an iota of a chance to get Benjie."

"And I know how important he is to you."

Jessica looked up. "You really do, don't you?"

"Sure."

"Rox thinks I'm crazy. She thinks it's a bad idea, that I'm only trying to replace the baby Mac and I might have had."

"Are you?"

"Of course not."

"Okay. Then I see we have two options. You wanna hear them?"

Jessica nodded, intrigued. He was ready to champion her efforts! She wanted to hug him.

"One route is to repair your, uh, damaged reputation. Get a little PR campaign going, paint you whiter than lilies at Easter and challenge this bitch to find a hair out of place. We can do it."

"Okay, how?"

"The first thing would be to stop associating with me. We already know she is less than enamored with me, and you might just publicly denounce my, uh, lifestyle somehow."

"Are you crazy?" Jessica put her glass down, concern creasing her features.

"Not at all. Next, you be seen taking up with some respectable people. Get involved in some 'causes'. Visit the President or something."

"Wait a minute. Back up, buddy. Publicly denounce you?"

"Yeah. I'm a bad influence, you know. You need moral role models for your sons."

Incredulous, Jessica began shaking her head. "You listen to me, Dane Pierce. You may not know this, but there is no other man alive I'd rather be an influence on my son, or sons as the case may be. Denounce you? You have been the best friend, the truest person through all of the crap I've had to go through—"

She got to her feet and paced to the front window, staring out at the darkness. Quietly, Dane stood and approached her. Her voice was shaky when she continued.

"I need you in my life, you big jerk. Even if I did try to appear... negative toward you, I'd never be able to pull it off. Never. So think of something else."

He was standing close behind her now, and he grasped her upper arms gently, leaning his chin over her shoulder. "There's always plan two," he said softly, his words sending shivers down her neck.

"Whatever it is, it's got to be better than losing you."

Slowly, carefully, Dane slid his hands down her arms until they reached her wrists, which he took and crossed around her midriff in a gentle embrace. He cleared his throat and Jessica could feel his lips close to her ear.

"We could really blow everybody away and get married."

Jessica whirled around to face him, dislodging his arms from around her and giving him a playful push.

"Now you really are sounding crazy," she told him with a laugh.

Dane's face broke into a cheery grin. "Yeah, crazy," he repeated. "But it would take care of two problems. One, if you marry the offensive scoundrel, you become an honest woman, and two, you have a father for the baby."

"I am already an honest woman. Too honest to get married again. And besides, everyone knows you're a confirmed bachelor."

"Right." Dane nodded his head slowly. "You're right. No one would ever believe it."

"So we need another option, here." Jessica swept past him and crossed to her bedroom door, where she paused and turned to gaze back at him.

"I'll think about it," Dane said at last. "Surely I can come up with something more... practical."

"You do that. See you in the morning." Jessica smiled and blew him a kiss before closing her bedroom door.

Fourteen

Unsettled Unsolved

Dane closed the trunk firmly and turned to the woman waiting beside the car. Down below, he could hear the laughter of a child playing in the yard, and he was glad Devon had not joined them on the cliff.

It was all he could do to not absorb her every fiber into him. Her hair, a mass of sleepy curls, floated about her face in the breeze, inviting his fingers to—

"I hate for you to go," she told him.

Dane pulled her tightly against him, his hands roaming over her back, her shoulders.

"If I don't go, I won't go," he replied. "You need some time to think about things. You stay up here and... think... for a while."

"Okay."

"And don't worry so much. Things will work out the way they are supposed to."

"Okay."

Unable to stop himself, Dane ran his fingers into her hair, pulling it away from her face, and, using every molecule of resistance he could muster, kissed her on the forehead. He was walking the wrong edge of a blade; he couldn't tread lightly enough.

"Call me when you get back. I won't bother you."

"Okay."

He kissed her once more, this time on the cheek, and then abruptly released her. Feeling incredibly awkward, he got into the Mustang and started it up. From the vantage point of his parking spot, he could just see the roundish finial at the top of Point Surrender, and he sighed.

"Dane—" Jessica began, and he swore her fingers were trembling as they grasped the door frame of his car. "Thanks for everything. And thanks for being so good to Dev. He's so much better."

"Sure." Dane nodded, gave her a little wave and headed up the gravel road back to the highway. He couldn't bear to see the tears glistening in her eyes any longer.

He drove straight through without stopping. Six hours of wonder, worry, suffering. Had he done the right things? Said the right things? Had he blown it by joking about marriage?

It was a cheap move to ask her the way he did. Using Benjamin to gain her commitment was wrong. Fortunately, she assumed he was asking in jest. But the way he saw it, it was his only shot. They could go on from there, and she might come to love him eventually.

Damn! He thumped the heel of his hand against the steering wheel. Nine months. It had been almost nine months, and she was still talking about Mac all the time. She was completely ignorant of the tiny needles that jabbed at his heart with every word.

Guilt washed over him time and again. He'd done a good job, made a good show of confidence, friendship, and solidity for her sake. Inside, he was just as anguished as she.

He would never gain the kind of love she had for Mac, but his obsession gave him no choices. He was willing to settle.

But damn, how he'd wanted to taste her lips!

·♥·♥·♥·♥·♥·

She was achy when she crawled out of bed the next morning. Jessica pulled on her sweatpants and groped around for her slippers; it was crispy cold in the house.

In the kitchen, she peered through squinting eyes. Blinding sunlight poured through the kitchen window. Feeling her way across the counter, she managed to put together a cup of instant coffee.

"We could... get married." Dane's words still knocked around in her head; they'd kept her awake half the night. He'd been joking, of course. But still... there was something not quite comical in his suggestion. Something that resembled a testing of the waters.

Joke or not, she had ached at the sight of him driving away; she had longed for a kiss, a real kiss, and the words of endearment she knew he could impart. They had not come, and she'd returned to the house unsettled and empty.

Her eyelids were heavy. Soon, her son would come bounding out of his room. Her smile was melancholy at the thought; Devon had not wet himself once since Dane had arrived.

Jessica rubbed her eyes, and then shook her head slightly. She would force the silly proposal from her mind. It was a non-issue... unless he brought it up again.

Return to routine is what she needed. Mac swore by it.

"Pancakes. Make some pancakes," Mac said, carrying his feverish two-year-old son into the kitchen.

"Pancakes? He needs medicine!" Jessica replied in exasperation.

"Medicine and pancakes. He loves them. We always have pancakes on Sunday morning."

The date on the flour wasn't too old. Jessica scraped together what she could, finding a brand-new griddle in the drawer under the oven. Pancakes it would be. It was Sunday.

·♥·♥·♥·♥·♥·

Sergeant Murdo Denehy pulled a thick file folder from the cabinet and dropped it onto his desk, the emanating wind from which blew several phone messages onto the floor.

From his breast shirt pocket, he plucked a pair of round, gold-rimmed glasses and hooked the wire frames over his ears with a sigh. Methodically he smoothed the sparse hairs back over his very visible scalp with one hand while reaching for a pop-up tissue with the other, wiping the traces of his tuna sandwich lunch from the corners of his mouth.

He opened the file, leaning his head back slightly to get a clearer view through his bi-focal lenses. On top of the various papers and documents filling the folder was a manila envelope. Carefully bending open the tiny brass clasp, Denehy slid out a small collection of various sized photographs. He examined each one closely, laying them side-by-side on the desk beside the file.

"Whatcha got goin'?"

The sergeant looked up as his colleague entered the office. Detective Joe Fusco looked over Denehy's shoulder at the pictures. "I don't remember this case. Recent?"

"No. Almost four years ago. She was an actress."

"Gorgeous. An actress? What was she in?"

"Nothing. Only... trouble."

"Aren't they all," Joe commented, now sitting down at his own desk adjacent to Denehy's. "Unsolved?"

Denehy sighed. "There was nothing to solve. Jackie Spencer killed herself. Shot another guy in the process, an actor."

Joe spun around in his chair. "I remember! That pirate guy. What was his name? Dave something?"

"Dane Pierce."

The younger man quickly resumed his earlier position. "Yeah, that's him. And that's that Dr. Jim guy. The one in the plane crash. Hey, weren't you working on that deal?"

"Mm-hmm. Minnesota wanted to see my file. I'm, uh, working on it on my own time."

"Some connection?"

"Maybe." Denehy continued to turn pages over in the file, eventually coming across a police report concerning the kidnapping of a relatively unknown starlet. He examined a small photograph of a woman, paper-clipped to the report.

"Wow. That's MacKendall's wife. She was kidnapped?"

"Yes. Five years ago. By a crazy ex-husband."

"Where is he now?"

"My first thought, too. But he's still locked up. Not due to walk until next year."

"You're trying to tie this all together, aren't you?"

"I don't know. I just need to re-read all this crap. There's just something..." Denehy ended his statement with a nondescript grumble. Now sorting back to the top of the pile, he fingered a stapled deposition.

Joe retreated to his own desk. "That guy Pierce has got it made. I heard he made about forty million dollars on that desert island flick. Can you imagine? He could have anything he wants. Any car, any property, any woman... anything!"

"Anything." Murdo Denehy closed the file folder and dropped it into his open briefcase. "I'm not so sure."

No, the sergeant was not at all certain that Dane Pierce could have the one thing he wanted more than anything in the world. And he could not help but wonder to what length the star would go to get it.

He took the file home with him. Cracking this case would assure him the election. Even if it weren't a local case, he'd make it one.

It was after sundown when Dane arrived back in Malibu. The house was dark, cold and lonely. Against his better wishes, he had succumbed to pressure from his ex-wife to let Alex stay with her. In retrospect, he was glad Alex had not accompanied him on the impromptu trip.

Dane turned on his bedroom lamp and lay down on the bed. His regret had grown substantially during his six-hour drive home.

What the hell was I thinking? She's better than that. So much better. I just want her too much.

He took a brief shower and then returned downstairs, rooting around in the kitchen for something to eat. The pantry was low on tangibles, so he snagged a bag of small carrots from the refrigerator and went to sit before his computer.

Damn if I haven't blown it—again. She looked perfectly miserable when I left.

I'll back-pedal. I'll remind her that I wasn't serious—that I thought she—ha! As if that would work with her. She knows me too damned well.

Dane stopped typing and stood up, glaring down at the keyboard in chagrin. He glanced toward the kitchen, trying to decide if he should look for a beer. Instead, he sat back down.

She's probably trying to figure out if I've truly lost my mind. I still can't believe I was stupid enough to suggest it.

Perhaps I will just head on back to the ranch. This town always makes me crazy.

She always makes me crazy.

FIFTEEN

Daddy

"While I can't promise anything, I honestly feel you can expect at least two million, probably two million-one for the property."

Jessica stared past the Realtor sitting across from her at the dining room table. "We never used this room, except at Thanksgiving and on rare occasions when Mac would invite over a business associate."

"We can have it listed in the service by Friday. There will be an office exclusive for a week or two, we'll do a nice broker's open house with some hot hors d'oeuvres, champagne, the works." The woman pushed a contract across the table, spinning the document so it would read correctly before Jessica.

"Did you know our son was born in this house?"

"That's nice. Now, what are your plans? It could sell right away."

"I'm not sure," Jessica offered vaguely, one ear tuned on the muted humming emanating from behind Devon's bedroom door.

"We're going to run it as a 'Valentine's Special' in the *Times Real Estate* section. Cover photo."

"No photo. Please."

"Okay, whatever. You said you and your husband had a trust? We can take care of the title issues in escrow. Now if you'll just sign this listing agreement..."

Jessica forced her attention to the multi-page document, quickly reading through the numerous conditions in fine print.

"Lock box?"

"It's a key-safe. So that people can look at the house when you're not home."

"No. No lock box."

"But Mrs. MacKendall, you realize it's the best way—"

"No. Appointments only. I would think that was the norm in this... this price range."

"Well, actually, it is. But I always advise my clients to take every advantage—"

"Not this client," Jessica said, offering a warm, if entirely false, smile. "Mrs. Tuttle, you must remember that I have a very young son. This is going to be hard enough as it is, so I do appreciate your compassion."

"Certainly. Now, getting back to my earlier question, how soon would you be able to move out? You want a thirty-, sixty-, or ninety-day escrow?"

Jessica filled her lungs and looked away. Thirty days? What did it matter, anyway? She exhaled and turned back. "Let's see what an offer brings. I'll be happy to negotiate that."

"Fine. Here's your copy. I'll be here Friday morning to set up the broker's 'open', so what time will you and the little one be leaving?"

"Leaving?"

"Well, it's protocol for the owners to, shall we say, make themselves scarce during the open houses and showings, if possible."

"Scarce. You are expecting us to just go away."

"It is preferable. People feel... conspicuous if the owners are lurking about. You understand."

Jessica paused, then nodded, if hesitantly. "Okay. I'll call you before Friday morning to work that out." She stood then, hoping to indicate that the meeting was over. Mrs. Tuttle snapped up the contract and was on her feet.

"Thank you so much for the opportunity to market your property, Mrs. MacKendall. I'll be in touch."

I'll bet you will, Jessica thought sourly, again pasting an artificial smile on her face as she walked the Realtor to the front door.

Dane eased the silver Carrera out of the driveway and headed south on Pacific Coast Highway. Rita still went by "Pierce," and her newest digs were in the high rent neighborhood of Pacific Palisades. He was impressed at the size of her house as he waited for the electronic driveway gate to swing wide and admit him.

He found Alex skating on the tennis court in the rear. "Where's your mother?" Dane asked, cocking an eyebrow at the back of the imposing mansion.

"Inside. Getting her nails done."

Dane nodded. "You 'bout ready to go?"

"Yup. Hey, Dad, I need some new wheels for my skates."

"Sure. Later. Let's get your stuff." Dane turned and looked for a back door, finding the house had five. "What's the quickest way in and out of this place?" he asked his son, who was unlacing his in-line skates.

"Don't matter. She'll catch us."

"Hmm."

Hearing a door close, Dane looked up to see a young girl standing on the back porch, staring in his direction with curiosity.

"Wow," Dane muttered, wetting his lips and stuffing his hands into the back pockets of his jeans. "That your sister?"

"Of course." Alex squinted up at him as if he had suddenly grown antennae. Dane forced his legs to propel him forward, eventually pausing a few feet from the eight-year-old girl who stared so solemnly.

"Hey, Zoe," he ventured. "What's up?"

She didn't say a word, but her green eyes grew liquid as she focused on her father's face. Overwhelmed with emotion, Dane reached for her just as she chose to raise her arms to him.

Her childish hug was fierce, much fiercer than it should have been for a father she had seen only four times in five years. The muffled "Daddy" that found its way into his ear caused his breath to catch in his throat.

"Hey, hey, what's this all about?" he finally managed, setting her back on her feet and squatting down to maintain his touch. "God, you're beautiful," he murmured.

"Nothing," she said, breaking free to wipe a tear from her cheek. "I'm fine."

Dane nodded. "Good." Clearing his throat, he took the liberty of stroking the girl's brown hair back. "You're really growing up, you know that?"

"Are you taking Alex away?"

"Yes."

"Can you take me away?"

Dane was careful to at least partially mask the surprise he felt at her query. Cupping her warm cheeks in his hands, he kissed her forehead ever so gently.

"Well, not today, sweetheart. But I can talk to Mommy if you want to come for a visit."

Obviously crestfallen, Zoe swallowed hard and turned to go back inside. Dane stood dumbfounded.

In what he might have described as the parlor, Dane found his ex-wife paying the departing manicurist, painstakingly holding her wet nails away from the cash.

"Oh. Hello, Dane. Alex has stacked his crap in the foyer."

"We need to talk, Rita."

"Sure we do." Not a thick, chestnut tress out of place, Rita exemplified the "well-kept-woman." "But not now. I have to get ready for my group."

Her group. He didn't even want to ask. "It's about Zoe."

"She's going through a very difficult time right now. I'd appreciate it if you don't encourage her. She's enough trouble as it is."

"Trouble? That sweet little girl out there? What the hell is going on here?" Dane had kept his temper in check long enough. "What, she wants a little maternal attention?"

Rita spun quickly from where she was delicately tucking her wallet into her purse.

"Watch your step, Mr. Pierce. If you want to talk about parental attention, you'd better take a hard look at your own track record."

"My track record? What about yours? You stole those girls from me. You brought another man into their lives. Now you've ditched him like you did me, and it looks like our kids are caught in the cross-fire."

"That's none of your business. Fred was... a mistake. As were you. And I don't intend to make any more mistakes, so if you'll kindly just butt out..."

Dane's eyes narrowed and he took an aggressive step in Rita's direction. "If you think for a moment I will turn my back on my daughter you are a crazier bitch than I thought. Granted, I can't do anything about it at this moment, but you will see my happy face here again and in short order. I may be almost a stranger, but that little girl out there deserves at least one parent who gives a—"

"Save it." Rita held up her hand defiantly. "Get your lying ass out of my house, and when you get back to that flea trap you call home, you'd better give your attorney a call."

Dane took a deep breath, expanding his chest as he stared hard at the woman he'd taken to the altar at eighteen. Where had that sweet-hearted girl gone?

"Don't worry. It will be my first call."

"You sure told her," Alex said, beaming at his father from the passenger seat as Dane tore through Malibu Canyon.

"She hasn't heard the last of it," Dane muttered, downshifting and slamming the Porsche's accelerator to the floor.

"Uh, Dad? Don't kill us, okay?"

Up shift. Accelerate.

"Zoe's always been whiny. She hates Mom and she hates Mimi."

Downshift. Brake. "What does Mimi think?"

"Mimi's just like Mom. She calls Zoe a brat."

Clutch. Downshift. Gas!

"Uh, I think we just passed a cop."

Clutch. Brake.

"Where did you say that skate store is again?"

Jessica's hand hovered above the telephone, alternately picking it up and replacing it. Finally, she put it to her ear. She shouldn't be afraid to call the woman who had been her best friend since high school.

"Hi, it's me," she said quickly when Roxanne answered. "Got a minute?" Jessica bit her lower lip while waiting for a response. Would it be warm or cold?

"Okay." Wary. Roxanne was wary; that was to be expected.

"How—how've you been?"

"Fine. How's Dev?"

"He's good, thanks." Jessica cleared her throat. "Tom okay?"

"Sure. So, what's up?" A bit of impatience had leaked into Roxanne's voice, and Jessica cursed inwardly.

"I, uh, was wondering if you guys will be around this weekend."

"Nope. We leave for the Bahamas on Friday morning. We'll be gone a couple of weeks. Why?"

Damn. No need to tell her the truth. "Oh, just thought we'd come by ... for a visit or something. No big deal. Kinda ... miss you."

There was a brief silence while Roxanne obviously considered her admission. "Yeah. Me too. Call you when we come back."

"Please do."

Jessica hung up, gently re-cradling the receiver. She had no one with whom to leave Devon, yet she really needed to go back to Minneapolis.

Benjamin was doing well, but the news was mixed: the foster parents were hesitant about adopting the baby, a baby with a defective heart. Still, Irma Carvey was anything but encouraging when Jessica broached the subject of re-activating her application.

"She has no right," Jessica said aloud, thumbing through her dog-eared address book. "She's just plain mean." Page after page, no names would work. "There's got to be someone who can watch him," she muttered. While she wasn't against taking him along, she knew that another airplane ride might dislodge the fragile web of healing that had begun at the lighthouse.

Her mother. She could fly her mom to L.A. for a visit. But before she could lift the receiver to call, the doorbell rang.

Better not be another darned broker, she thought. "Dev? Still in your room?" she called as she walked to the front door. Satisfied with his acknowledgment, she looked out the stained-glass panel bordering the front door and was surprised to see the outline of a deliveryman behind a lush floral arrangement. Quickly she swung the door open wide.

"Wow. These are beautiful," she breathed, taking the two-dozen red roses and placing them on the counter. "I wonder who sent them?"

"Should be a card," the deliveryman said, but after carefully digging around the arrangement, Jessica could find none.

"Hmm. Interesting," she muttered, closing the door. She went back to the flowers and took a deep whiff. "Nice." She smiled to herself. They had to be from Dane.

She went immediately back to the phone and instead of calling Seattle, she dialed Dane's now familiar number.

"I just called to thank you," she said simply, walking around the cut-crystal vase as she talked. "They're beautiful."

"Beautiful?"

Jessica giggled, and then turned as the doorbell rang again. "Hold on."

At the door, a sheepish grin accompanied the small gift card the deliveryman held out. "Sorry. It was on the floor of the truck."

Jessica wasted no time in tearing open the envelope.

"Sorry I missed Valentine's Day. Hope we're still friends. Love, Kyle."

The smile ran from her face like melting ice. She picked up the phone, now unsure of what to say. "I'm back," she said finally.

"You were saying?"

"Oh, nothing. What's going on at your house?"

"You don't want to know, believe me. Rita's on the warpath about Zoe, her lawyer's talking to my lawyer... I'm about ready to pack it in. Thinking about going back to the ranch. You?"

Jessica sighed into the phone. "I want to go back to Minnie and re-open my adoption case."

"Is there anything I can do?" Dane's voice carried a note of sincerity that touched her.

"Not unless you want to watch Dev for me," she said with a mirthless laugh. "I've run out of babysitters. I'm thinking about calling my mom, so you know I'm desperate." Jessica wedged the phone between her ear and shoulder as she carried the roses to the dining room table.

"I'd be happy to."

The words caused her to lose her grip on the phone and it tumbled to the floor, sliding across the dark Oriental rug beneath the table. Quickly she scrambled to retrieve it.

"You what?" she finally panted, getting to her feet.

"He can stay with me and Alex. Just a few days, right? It would do him good to pal around with some dudes for a change. Bring him on."

Jessica felt inexplicably warm all over her body. Dane's words were more than welcome, more touching than any bouquet of flowers.

"I'll—I'll ask him if he'd like to. That would be really nice," she said, her voice cracking with emotion.

Bless you, Dane.

Damn you, Kyle.

Sixteen

Unexpected Ally

Jessica rolled her suitcase from one moving walkway to the next, weaving her way around Minneapolis-St. Paul International Airport like a seasoned pro. Anyone looking twice at her might suspect her celebrity, for the sunglasses were not exactly necessary on this typically gray, mid-March afternoon. Still, for what it was worth, she never went into public without them.

The limousine was another giveaway, but she ignored the few gawkers at the curb and waited while the driver dropped her case into the trunk. Forty minutes later she had checked in at the Gifford Hotel and was back in the hired car on her way to the hospital.

The floor nurses were all friendly, and the nursery attendant happily wheeled Benjamin's bassinet closer to the window for her benefit. He was sleeping peacefully, nearly recovered from the heart surgery he'd undergone a month before. And despite the informal "gag order" that had prevailed during her last visit, the staff seemed anxious to help her cause this time.

"Mrs. MacKendall? If you'll step into this closet they call my office..." the head nurse was saying. Jessica tore her gaze away from the child and followed the woman who beckoned.

The woman closed the door and sat down. "What I am about to tell you is entirely off the record, and I would be forced to deny this conversation if confronted."

Her eyes wide, Jessica nodded emphatically. "Of course."

"The week Benjamin had his heart repaired, I guess the local papers had nothing better to talk about, so they did a story about the little guy. They even got the hospital administrator to complain about the cost of the surgery, and about the child's orphan status."

Jessica nodded, anxious to hear where the woman was leading.

"We started getting calls and donations like crazy. One of the docents set up a bank account to collect the money, and it was a wonderful thing. And then something very strange happened." The nurse looked Jessica plainly in the face. "A man demanding to remain anonymous funded the entire surgery and after-care. It was a sizable sum of money if you know what I mean. And if that wasn't strange enough, he wanted to know if we needed blood for the boy."

Jessica's mind was racing. "So you think..."

"He's the boy's father, is what I think. His call was directed to me. Not one to let an opportunity go by, I suggested that yes, we could use blood donations, just in case anything went wrong."

"Did you find out who he is?"

"No. His own physician took care of the procedure. It was done under what they call a 'veil of anonymity'. However, his blood type matched Benjamin's. AB positive."

"Not that common," Jessica murmured.

"No, it's not. The reason I am telling you all of this is that the woman from Social Services stuck her nose into it, and now she also suspects the baby's father is identifiable. She will use this information against you. Irma and I go way back, and I have my own reasons for wanting to see her go down. I will help you any way I can, but no one can know."

Jessica nodded slowly, letting the information sink in. "What do you suggest I do?"

"If you can find this guy and get to him before she does, you might convince him to relinquish his rights before she twists everything into a square knot."

"Is there anything else you can tell me about the man? Is he in this city? Did he mention my sister-in-law at all?"

"He didn't say anything except that he was a concerned citizen. But unbelievably, I got the phone number he called from." She opened her desk drawer and brought out a small note pad. "Here it is. I haven't had the nerve to call it. Perhaps you will."

"Really?" Jessica stared at the slip of paper in her hand before finally folding and putting it into her purse. "It could be just an anonymous number..."

"I hope not. Irma is scrambling right now to find a new adoptive family. Believe me, Mrs. MacKendall, I don't know what her motives are, but she is bound and determined that you not be allowed to adopt your nephew."

"I don't know how to thank you, Mrs.—Mrs....."

"It's Nadine Carvey. Miss Nadine Carvey. Irma Carvey is my step-sister. Now, would you like to go hold that little bugger a bit?"

As Jessica stretched out between the cool, crisp sheets in her hotel bed, she marveled at the day's activities. She had expected none of what had transpired. The inside information about the mysterious donor, and the opportunity to finally hold the baby in her arms was unforgettable.

She had called Dane just before retiring. Devon sounded happily tired and completely comfortable with going to sleep on the trundle bed in Alexander's room. Dane had put all her fears to rest.

"He's taking good care of us. Don't worry," Dane had assured her. "Just don't forget about us."

"Impossible," she had responded with a smile. How true. While absurd to suggest that she could forget her own son, it was as unlikely that she could ever forget Dane Pierce.

Even now, in the dark hotel room, his green eyes teased her from the far corner of her heart's memory. She no longer cared to remember the bad times, the times he had disappeared, the times he had wreaked havoc on her relationship with Mac. What she did call to mind was his oft-concealed goodness. The subtle, cherishing way he had cared over the years.

And as in most nights' past, her thoughts turned to Mac and her last words with him. While her husband was not angry when he left for Minnesota on that last May morning, neither was everything exactly right between them. They had... was squabbled the right word? Mac had been uncomfortable about their discussion concerning Dane. She had refused to believe it at the time, tried hard to ignore the fact that he seemed to be angry with Dane all over again.

There was no basis for it. It had been three years, at the time, since Mac had walked into their house and witnessed a good-bye kiss he was never meant to see. Innocent, at least on Jessica's part, and nothing more than a brief show of affection for a departing friend.

Dane was leaving for Cambodia, though it hardly mattered to Mac; he saw only a faithless wife and her ex-lover locked in a passionate embrace.

Discomfited by the vision, Jessica tossed in the bed. Mac had left her for months. Pregnant, alone, devastated. Unaware of the depth of Mac's anger, Dane had left the country as well.

It had been the worst period of her life. Worse than miscarrying her first child at twenty years old. Worse than being abducted and beaten by her ex-husband.

Why am I dredging this up now? It's all behind me.

Again, she turned in the bed. Why, indeed. Dane came back into her mind, and this time the memory was of the two of them on the beach in Amande. Filming had wrapped on Lost Season, and she had called Mac at home to tell him the news. A woman's voice on the phone had rocked her world.

Dane was there to set it straight.

"I've heard making love on the beach is not all it's cracked up to be. Gets a bit gritty," she had teased, dropping the Hawaiian print wrap dress around her ankles.

"Not if you're careful," Dane had responded, his keen eyes taking in her surprising immodesty. "But then, who wants to be careful?"

He always said the sexiest things. She blushed in the darkness, remembering with startling detail the events of the night in question. They had made love until, exhausted, they fell asleep just before sunrise, when a jet would take her back to Los Angeles and the man who loved her.

And while it niggled at her for a time, she had eventually managed to disallow the notion that she was also leaving behind the man who loved her.

The adoption board accepted her new application. Jessica managed to avoid a confrontation with Irma Carvey, and armed with her new information, happily boarded the plane for home.

She had pictures, too. Pictures of nine-month-old Benjamin MacKendall sitting up in his bassinet.

Dane would help her find the father. Things were looking better and better.

She grabbed a taxi at the airport and headed for home. She wanted to change and unpack before retrieving her son. A mountain of business cards lay haphazard on her counter, all from agents previewing or showing her home to prospective buyers. She had agreed to leave a key with the real estate office in her absence and made a mental note to pick it up as soon as she could. She waived aside the melancholy that accompanied the thought of moving.

After slipping into more comfortable clothing, she sorted through the mail. A large, costly and ornate envelope that certainly must contain an invitation of sorts immediately intrigued her. The sending entity's address included a logo: a small, embossed gold design replicating an Oscar statuette. The Academy of Motion Picture Arts and Sciences was requesting her presence to accept an award; a posthumous Oscar for Cory MacKendall.

"Oh my God," she whispered, her eyes immediately filling with tears. The letter fluttered in her trembling hand. She was to call the coordinator as soon as possible with her response and the number of people who would accompany her to the awards. "Oh, Mac..." She fairly whimpered his name, dropping into the nearest chair to recover.

Ten minutes later, she had decided what to do. Bringing the letter with her, she got into her car and headed for the beach.

The last thing Dane expected was a call from another film director. Crawling out from beneath a blanket-and-clothespin "fort" loosely constructed on the deck, he reached for the phone, hoping to hear Jessica's voice.

John Lauder seemed as surprised as Dane when the two began to talk.

"Didn't think you'd answer, Pierce. You at home?"

"I'm helping out a friend this weekend. What's up?"

"I want to talk about this piece of crap deal Jessica has dropped in my lap."

Dane's hackles went up at the negative implication in Lauder's voice. "She had no control over what happened with that Quill asshole."

"She should have known he wasn't up to it. A good director—"

"A good director would have been on the set when he was supposed to be there, from the start."

"She knew I had other commitments."

"You never should have agreed to do it if you weren't available. Come on, John. Don't try to pin this on Jess. Her heart was in exactly the right place."

"I should have known you would jump to her defense. Anyway, I didn't call to trash Jess. I like her. She's tough. Very green, but tough enough. So, you guys gonna go after the little fag?"

"I beg your pardon?" Dane's eyes shifted from the giggling masses behind the blanket tent to a scene inside his head. "Quill's sexual preferences are not an issue here, and I think you'd better drop the homophobic monikers from here on in. And no, we're not going to press the issue. Yeah, he breached. We'll probably shelve the project. You wanna sue us? Go ahead."

"Dane, Dane, no reason to get pissed off. I wasn't saying—"

"You weren't saying what? So, what was the purpose of your call? You already know it all." Dane pressed the "off" key on the phone, knowing that he was being reactionary. Knowing that he had been inordinately abrupt with John Lauder. But just let anyone, anyone at all suggest that Jessica was anything less than perfect...

"Ah, hell." Dane shook off the feeling and rejoined the boys in the tent. And anyway, he hated telephones. It was only a minute before he heard the front screen slam.

"Anybody home?"

Dane poked his head out from beneath the hanging blanket, his face coloring in a hot blush at the sound of her voice as she trotted happily into the living room. Getting to his feet as quickly as he could, he met her halfway.

"Sure, just walk right on into my private sanctuary," he scolded, watching with interest as she marched up to him and, lifting herself as tall as her feet could stretch, pursed her lips demonstratively.

Incredulous that she was inviting him, he pursed his own lips and offered a warm, if chaste, kiss.

"How are all my favorite boys?" she asked, now brushing past and leaving Dane in a decided fluster. "Devon! Mommy's home," she called.

They ordered pizza.

Dane could not keep his gaze off her. She was positively glowing.

"I have a big surprise," she announced, once most of the pizza was gone. Reaching into her purse, she withdrew a folded letter. "Boy, do I have a surprise. A couple, actually."

Dane watched her animated expressions as she read the letter from AMPAS. "And guess what?" she announced at the end. "You are all going with me."

"Aw, Jess, I don't think—"

"And I don't think you'd better say a word. If you don't go, I'll cry. I'll cry and cry. Won't I, Devon?"

"Yeah. Mommy will cry."

"So, you will all be my dates. I'm not taking any 'no's' here. And anyway, they made a special arrangement to let me bring three guests."

Dane sighed. He hated the Oscars, unless, of course, he was nominated. And worse, AMPAS hated him. Unless, of course, he was winning. He did not have the heart to disappoint her, however.

He just wished it weren't for Mac.

I am incredibly selfish. I should be stoked that she wants me to go.

I can do this for her. I have to do this for her. But I can't help thinking about how different things would be between us if all the crap that's happened just didn't. My feelings about Mac are so twisted up. If only he hadn't read the journal. If only he'd never found out about my feelings for Jess.

Dane paused, his unseeing eyes searching the air around him for the vision that would allow him to finish his entry. He looked back down at the keyboard, his fingers only barely resting there.

Looking back, it was stupid of me to write all that stuff down. My shrink would say I was trying to get caught. I can't imagine how Mac must have felt reading it, finding out that I wished he were out of our lives.

I need to go back and find the journal and destroy it. Maybe it's turned to dust by now, there on the closet shelf. One of these days I will be able to do that.

For now, it is all I can do to go day to day, barely holding on to my self-respect, trying to keep my promise.

I feel like he is watching me.

Seventeen

Oscar Night Proposal

Jessica had Devon and Alexander fitted for matching tuxedoes. Her own attire presented a real problem, however, for even if she had truly reconciled with Roxanne, Rox was soaking up the sun in the Bahamas and would not return in time to put anything together. Her last-minute invitation had not been publicized; not one designer had called to offer a gown, and she was loath to initiate a call herself.

She could recycle one of her old dresses. In her bedroom, she hastily slammed hanger after hanger aside, pulling out two "possibles" and draping them across the bed.

The first was the white, bead-spangled sensation she had worn to the Bellerive premiere. It was a spectacular dress, Roxanne's first formal gown.

Jessica fingered the iridescent bugle beads so carefully sewn into the white lace. It had been a calculated risk, wearing white. But she was an unknown starlet, newly signed to the much buzzed-about epic, *Lost Season*. All heads turned her way when she timidly joined the after-show party on the arm of Cory MacKendall.

Mac had helped her out of the dress later that New Year's Eve, carefully draping it onto the hanger on which it still hung. She had not worn it since. With a heavy sigh, she returned the untouchable gown to the closet.

The other dress would need considerable reconstruction. A black velvet and taffeta creation, Roxanne had designed this one for a very pregnant actress now attending the *Lost Season* premiere.

The right tailor could make it over into something that would work. She hoped.

By the next afternoon, Jessica happily acknowledged her hunch was correct. The dressmaker recommended by her management agency removed a couple of yards of velvet and with a little creative stitching, maintained the simple beauty of Roxanne's original design. Jessica chose a single teardrop diamond pendant and matching earrings, elegant vintage black evening gloves and the sexiest little sling pumps in her closet.

Fortunately, her hairdresser was a retired stylist, able to come to her house on the day of the awards show. Jessica endeavored to sit still while Devon ran screeching through the house chasing a radio-controlled electronic dog.

"Is he always this spirited?" the beautician asked, gently re-adjusting the position of Jessica's head.

"No. Sometimes he's worse," Jessica replied. "And I still have to get him ready. The limo will be here in an hour."

"That soon?"

"The arrival of the guests is almost as big a deal as the show itself. They start early."

By 3:30 p.m., Jessica judged them both attractive enough to meet even the Queen. The limousine appeared in the driveway at 3:35; Dane emerged looking like the Hollywood deity he once was and could very well be again. Jessica watched from the window, mesmerized, as he leaned back into the car briefly, then trotted briskly up to the front porch. His tuxedo was flawless... merely an extension of the man beneath it.

She smoothed down her dress. *My God, I'm panting!*

She opened the door.

They stared at one another for several moments, each taking in the other's appearance. Jessica sought Dane's eyes, his approval—and received it. He seemed tongue-tied for the first time she could remember.

"Hey Uncle Dane! We match!" Devon exclaimed, wriggling past his mother and onto the porch.

Dane broke into a grin, and Jessica grasped his hand. "We'd better go. I am so nervous!"

"Right this way." He took a few moments to secure Devon into the limousine beside Alexander, and then returned to intercept

Jessica on the porch. "You look... absolutely, unequivocally, stunningly beautiful," he told her.

"Thank you," she said, after taking a moment to absorb the compliment. "You clean up pretty well yourself."

The Oscar ceremony was being held at the Kodak Theatre in Hollywood. In keeping with past years' traditions, portable bleachers were erected to hold the die-hard fans that had been arriving since early morning. The entire entry had been carpeted in a red plush, and ten-foot-tall Oscar replicas flanked the doors. The atmosphere was electrified as limousines lined up down Hollywood and Highland Boulevards waiting to deliver their famous passengers.

Jessica sat back in her seat, her eyes only occasionally leaving Dane's. Unlike the early years when she was as much a fan as she was a celebrity, Jessica was less impressed with the throngs of media that crowded the event. There were more important issues at hand.

Dane, however, did glance out the side windows. "The barracudas are circling," he said of the many reporters and TV cameras hovering.

"A wise man once told me we don't have to talk to them," Jessica told him.

"Whew. Glad to hear that."

"Is it big inside?" Alex wanted to know, leaning close the window, his eyes wide.

"Very big," his father told him.

"Wow. Have you been here before? Is this where you won your Oscar?"

"We were on Amande when I won. But it was just as exciting," Dane assured, winking at Jessica. "Okay, gang. Looks like we're next."

Once the door was pulled open, the evening began in earnest.

Dane stepped out first, and then offered his hand to Jessica. The boys tumbled out together, and Dane immediately lifted Devon into his arms. Despite the late afternoon hour, strobe lights flashed from every direction, and the crowd roared in approval. Jessica took Alexander's hand and the foursome moved down the red carpet together.

Everyone wanted an interview. The fashion divas ogled Jessica's dress. The hosting television network dispatched their entertainment editor with a microphone, as did the cable news and movie magazines represented. A particularly cloying man with an earring pressed Dane for a statement.

"So, what will you and Hollywood's most eligible widow be doing after the show? Heading out to any of the big Oscar bashes?"

Dane cleared his throat and momentarily set Devon on his feet; the interviewer purposely pulled the microphone closer to Jessica, so that Dane was forced to bend to respond.

"We promised our kids ice cream and games. A little private party of our own," Dane offered with a dazzling smile, caught by the questioner's own photographer.

"And the kids get to stay up all night, right?"

Dane shook his head, reaching down to tousle Devon's hair. "It's off to bed after that."

The event was heavily organized, and security was tight. Unlike regular award winners who would be announced by category and approach the stage from the audience, Jessica would be brought backstage in advance and introduced on stage.

It was hard to concentrate on the program. She had seen none of the nominated films, but she did watch the overhead monitors and noticed her face as well as Dane's displayed more than once. When it was time to go backstage, he reached across the two boys sitting between them and squeezed her hand.

She was given specific instructions, and her jitters escalated until she thought she would faint when they announced the award. Surprisingly, she began to calm as she approached the lectern, hearing mostly the swishing of her taffeta ruffles instead of the thunderous applause the audience provided in memory of her late husband.

"This is such an honor," she began, looking from left to right across the veritable sea of faces, some anxious, some bored, some familiar, many unrecognized. "When he made *The Horseman*, Mac was really terrified of making the leap onto the big screen. He worried that if he were terrible, his new friends would hate him, and if he were wonderful, his old friends would abandon him. It turned out he was wrong on both counts." She paused, gathering her ad-libbed thoughts, her impromptu speech. "Of course he would want me to thank you all. He would want to thank his late mother, for her undying faith in him, his children for their devotion, and his many,

many fans for believing in him. His managers, his peers, those before him who inspired him so..." Jessica went on to list the names of the few people who had made a difference in Mac's life. She had almost finished her brief speech without a single tear. She paused, looking back toward the seat she had recently vacated.

"More than acting, Mac enjoyed being a director. Nothing excited him so much as driving the bus, creating a film out of words on a page. He credited his friend Dane Pierce with strapping him into the director's chair, and for showing him the professional ropes."

Her statement re-ignited the applause as the cameras closed in on Dane's face as he leaned down to hear his son's whisper.

"Thank you again, everyone."

Tears of joy, remembrance and relief now spilled over Jessica's lower lids as she was ushered gracefully offstage. During what was, to the outside world, a commercial break, she rejoined Dane and their sons. He stood and leaned across the boys to kiss her cheek.

"Would it be terrible for us to leave now?" she whispered before he could return to his seat.

"Terrible or not, let's go."

They sat on the deck. She was cold and wrapped in a blanket. He was warm enough just sitting beside her.

"You didn't have to say that, about me," he told her, his eyes watching the breaking surf. Above them, the midnight moon danced among the passing clouds.

"It was the truth."

"He would have done it without me."

"It doesn't matter."

"You're right."

"Thanks for going with me, anyway," she said. "I don't think I would have gone by myself."

"It was arduous."

She glanced over at him then, and he could see the warmth in her eyes. He weighed the moment, and then reached for her hand, barely visible where it clutched the blanket's edge.

"How's the real estate circus going?

"It's a circus all right. The phone never stops ringing, there's an endless parade of people—mostly just wanting to see where Dr. Jim lived. It's disheartening."

"Sounds like you're ready to come up to Jackson?"

A smile washed her sour expression away. "Maybe I am. Tell me again how much I'll love it."

Dane paused, taking a moment to massage her hand, her fingers, her wrist. "The phone doesn't ring unless I allow it to. There's no Playstation, no strobe lights, no dead plants in pots. There's a Japanese soaking tub, a real wine cellar, a hay loft and five horses in a nine-thousand square foot heated barn."

"Is the house heated, too?"

"By more than one source." He pressed her hand between his own. "There's a little spring that runs alongside the property, there's trout, twenty-five acres of quietness... there's a library, too."

"How about a kitchen?"

"A kitchen and a cook. By the way, has Devon ever been fishing?"

"I don't think so."

"Riding?"

Jessica giggled. "Does the carousel at the mall count?"

"How about wading in a stream? Catching pollywogs and bullfrogs and—"

"Okay! I'm sold."

"Yeah?"

"Yeah. I've got to get away from the house, Dane. It's making me crazy. If you're sure..."

"I've got your rooms all ready. I'll be going up in a few days with Alex. You and the little tough guy can come up any time you want. Whenever you're ready." He pulled her hand to his lips and kissed the back of it. She gently tugged it away and started to stand up.

"We'd better go inside. I should get home."

"Home? Dev's already in bed upstairs."

"I've got to get some sleep."

"I have some here."

Jessica gave him a level stare, and he made sure he did not flinch.

"What are you proposing?" she asked at last.

"Only that you let someone else take care of the details for a while. You go upstairs, take a shower, the sheets on my bed were just changed yesterday..." Dane started to chuckle but continued anyway. "I'll bunk down here and make you some rubber eggs in the morning."

Jessica shrugged. "Well, when you put it that way..."

"I do. I'll put it any way you want it. Just... stay."

He put his arm around her shoulders, and they walked upstairs together, stopping to peek in at their respective sons, already long asleep.

In his bedroom, Dane tossed her a clean t-shirt, and then pulled a turquoise silk kimono out of the closet.

"Got this on my infamous trip to Cambodia." He left her then, and she took his advice and showered in the master bathroom, then pulled the t-shirt down over her damp curls. She climbed into bed with a sigh, leaving the small bedside lamp on.

Visions of the evening re-played in her mind. She remembered someone saying that the Oscar program drew around a billion viewers worldwide.

"He deserved it," she whispered, thinking about Mac and his too-short professional career. "He was so good."

"Why, thank you," Dane said, approaching the bed and sitting on its edge. Jessica gave him a playful punch. "Just wanted to say goodnight," he said, stretching his arms wide and yawning. "It's been a big day. You have a good time?"

"It was wonderful. Right down to the ice cream. You?"

"Tolerable."

Jessica was quiet for a moment. "I only wish Mac could have—"

She was cut off by Dane's finger, pressed gently to her lips. "Shh. Time for sleep." He caressed her cheek, sliding his fingers into the hair above her ear and around to cup the back of her head. With his other hand he deftly switched off the table lamp.

Without another word, he leaned closer until his lips surprised hers with an unexpected kiss. A kiss that began so innocent, a harmless symbol of an affectionate wish for a good night; a kiss that evolved into a powerful demand for reciprocal love.

Without question, Jessica parted her lips, grasping him around the neck and returning his gesture with equal passion. Her hunger too long un-sated, she was unable to react any other way.

And there was history here. She knew his lips, his tongue, his mouth. The years of being kissed only by Mac were suddenly washed to the side, and the memories of days and nights spent in perpetual obsession came flashing back. The raw sexuality was still there, and Dane Pierce still wanted her.

He released her now, his chest rising and falling in rhythm with hers as they each recovered from their dizzying encounter.

"What are we doing?" she whispered at last, running a hand across her own forehead.

"Surrendering." Even in the darkness, Jessica could see the uncertainty on Dane's face. He reached out and grasped her chin, giving it a gentle shake. "Goodnight, sweetie."

Jessica blew all the air from her lungs through pursed lips after he had closed the bedroom door. The kiss had put a whole new spin on her trip to Wyoming. On her life.

There goes another damned night of sleep.

Eighteen

Bail Out

Woodson Rawlins leaned forward and fired up his e-cigarette then settled back against the couch in Dane's living room. Dane blinked his eyes several times. "You know those things are bad for you. So, are we about done?"

"What's your hurry? Got a plane to catch?"

"As a matter of fact, I have to pack. Going back to the ranch tomorrow." Dane stood up and gave his waistband a little tug; he really needed to buy some smaller khakis.

"You really hate this town, don't you?" his manager said with a chuckle.

"No. I'm allergic to it. Breaking out in hives."

Rawlins took a drag. "Okay. We're moving *Mr. Romance* from the back burner to the closet. You ought to put it in turnaround. You have any interest in that Miramax deal?"

"Nope."

"Disney's not your style, eh? How about—"

"I hate baseball movies."

"Right. Hey, I did get a hold of a property last week you might want to look at. Air traffic controller with big problems meets a female pilot with big problems."

Dane sat back down. "Who's doing it?"

"Castle Rock. There might be a backend deal."

"Anybody attached to it?"

"Oh, there's a bunch of names they're spewing, but I don't think anything's signed."

"Call Rettner and see if he wants to talk."

"Gotcha." Rawlins snuffed out his smoke, then stood up himself. Barely 5'2", he wore lifts in his shoes, thinking no one knew about them. Dane tried not to look.

The phone interrupted his musing, and Dane reached for it while glancing at his watch. It was after midnight.

The woman's voice was shaking with thinly concealed anguish. Trina Vidal was in trouble.

"Where are you?"

"Rampart Division. Downtown. I know I shouldn't have called you, but... there's nobody else. It's a bum rap, too. I—I just need you to post bail for me. I'll pay back every cent, I promise..."

Dane's hand went to his forehead. Every thought that came to mind was one he could not voice. Still bruised from her deception, his first inclination was to let her sit in jail. Still, he had developed an unexpected soft spot for the girl. And besides, she knew some of his secrets.

"Dane? Are you there?"

"I'm on my way." He put the phone down and drew in a deep breath. "I've gotta go," he said, hoping his manager would leave without asking for an explanation. It was, however, not to be.

"Who was that at this hour? Some broad?"

"Yeah. Some broad. No, a friend. I have to go bail her out."

"Literally? Are you nuts?"

"Been accused of worse," Dane replied, searching the kitchen counter for his wallet. "I'll talk to you tomorrow. Let me know what Rettner says."

"Dane, man, you can't show your face down there. It will be all over the papers, the net, E-Weekly..."

"You want to go for me? Think your wife would understand you bailing an exotic dancer out of jail?"

The man closed his eyes and sighed. "I'll go with you. Hopefully, we can get in and out without much trouble."

If Trina had not been so battered, Dane would have sworn it was a trap. He was not quick enough to turn his head before the flashes went off as he and Trina exited the station and hurried down the steps. Reporters? At 1 a.m.? Were they like zombies, roaming the streets at night? Woodson Rawlins seemed beside himself.

"Well, this will look good," he said in the car, turning around from the driver's seat to peer at Dane and his "friend."

"Woody, shut the fuck up." Dane took Trina's chin and turned her face from side to side, examining the cut on her lip and the bruises around her eye. "Who did this to you?"

"It doesn't matter. He thought I was offering more than a peek."

"And you weren't," Rawlins said with a sarcastic slant to his lips.

Dane issued a glare. "You should have given the cops his name. How can you let someone get away with this? They thought you were turning tricks."

"It's not the first time."

Dane just shook his head. Trina was one messed-up chick. "Where can we drop you?"

"Anywhere."

"Give me an address or I'll take you back to Rampart."

Trina muttered an address in Hollywood, and Dane eventually let her out of the car. She declined a walk to the door.

"I'm sorry about this. Really. It won't happen again. And—thank you," she said, keeping her eyes averted.

"Oh, don't mention it," Dane said lightly, his own eyes roaming over the night sky. "My sterling reputation can stand a little tarnishing now and then."

"Yeah, right. See ya."

Probably not. Dane got into the front seat and Rawlins drove him back home. Not a word was spoken the entire way.

·♥·♥·♥·♥·♥·

"This is incredibly hard," Jessica murmured, carrying the yellow tablet with her as she went from room to room, making notes. Each piece of furniture was to be tagged with a destination. Some would be sold, some donated, some stored. She did not know how long she would be in Wyoming, but she had to assume that the house would sell and close escrow within the next few weeks. Mrs. Tuttle had indicated that two offers were being written.

In short, she might not get another opportunity to organize her move. She ignored the fact that she had no new home picked out. She had not even looked.

The good news was that Lydia had returned to work and was even now answering the phone as it rang.

"It's Mr. Pierce," she sang out from the kitchen.

Jessica put down her tablet and picked up the phone in her office. "You getting ready to leave?"

"Yeah," Dane responded. "I just wanted to touch base with you. When do you expect you'll be up?"

"We reserved our tickets this morning. We're leaving a week from today. April sixteenth, I think."

"Great."

"Dev's really excited. I couldn't back out now if I wanted to. Which I don't."

Dane chuckled but said nothing more. Jessica felt something amiss. "Everything okay?"

"Sure. I had a tough night last night."

"Oh really? What happened?"

Again the silence.

"Dane?"

"Oh, it was nothing, really. Woody was here, we were up late, we had to go help a friend out with something... nothing important. So... be sure to bring your heavy coats, it's still nippy up there. Had a snow just two weeks ago."

"Devon will love that. He's in packing his toys right now."

"Make sure you give me your flight number. I'll have the jet waiting in Salt Lake to bring you on up."

"I can't wait." Jessica caught her own reflection in the mirror. The smile on her face surprised her. "Have a great flight, and I'll talk to you soon."

"I'll call you tonight."

Jessica found herself waiting for that call. "Lydia? Where did we leave the portable?"

"I think you were sitting on the couch last."

Idly, Jessica thumbed through the home flyers Mrs. Tuttle had left her. Nothing looked remotely appealing. The homes were nice enough, certainly costly enough, and were in all the "right" neighborhoods. She looked up from time to time, glancing around the living room at the walls she would be replacing. It did not feel right to stay in this house, nor did it feel right to be looking for a new one.

She stacked the flyers up and put them on the counter. Her lack of enthusiasm depressed her, and she longed to get moving.

"Lyd?"

"What now, Missus?" Just back from Argentina, the girl Jessica had re-hired as her personal assistant was baking a cherry pie. Her comical response brought a smile to Jessica's lips.

"You think we could move our flight up?"

Lydia appeared in the doorway, and Jessica gave her a beseeching look. Lydia propped her hands on her more-than-amble hips. "No, I don't. We won't be ready any sooner!"

"You're right. You're always right."

"That's why you hired me. Now, you want some pie, or what?"

Jessica patted her stomach. "I've really got to start watching..."

"Yeah, right. You are a twig beside me. And in Dane's eyes you are walking perfection. Have some pie."

In Dane's eyes. Jessica paused a moment to stare at Lydia's bright smile. Even though Lydia was a good ten years younger, she often saw things through the eyes of a mature woman. I'm so lucky to have her, Jessica thought, spooning a scoop of vanilla ice cream onto the top of her pie.

Lydia went about tidying up the kitchen. Her coffee-bean brown hair was pulled into a tight ponytail and hung to her waist in a thick broom. She wore no bangs, little make-up, and her equally dark brown eyes nearly always twinkled with contented joy.

Jessica remembered approaching Lydia at the preschool Devon attended, just days after the plane crash. The job was to be temporary, a generous "loan" from the preschool, and Lydia went back to the school after a couple of months. But she had missed Devon and Jessica, and she had eventually offered to return permanently. Jessica thanked God every day.

"Devon MacKendall, if you want some pie, you'd better get your handsome self in here right now," Lydia was calling down the hallway.

"Why did you say that? About Dane, I mean?" Jessica asked.

"Do you think I'm brain-dead? A person would have to be in a coma not to see how he is around you. I should be so lucky to have a man like him around me someday."

Jessica sat very still, her tongue savoring the over-sweet cherry pie filling in her mouth. Suddenly her mind switched gears. "Has

Roxanne called lately? Have I missed any calls?"

"Not that I know of. Except for that Wagner guy that you said not to give to you."

"Kyle? When did he call?"

"Mmm, three or four days ago."

"Really."

She was almost asleep when the phone finally rang on her nightstand. Still, she grabbed it on the first ring.

"Hi. Sorry it's so late." Dane sounded more than weary.

"It's okay. I was still up. Everything okay?"

"Colder than a witch's—uh, well, let's just say it isn't sunny California."

"That's a good thing." Jessica closed her eyes, imagining Dane's mouth as he formed the words. It didn't really matter what he was talking about. She wondered what the house looked like, where he was sitting, standing, lying down...

"Jess?"

"I'm sorry, what did you say?"

"I asked if Lydia was coming with you."

"If it's okay."

"It's a good idea. We can use the help. My girl just quit."

It was a brief phone call, and despite her earlier sleepiness, Jessica tossed in her bed. She considered the sleeping pills her doctor had prescribed just after Mac's death but decided against them. There had to be a better way to start sleeping at night.

Too much was happening and not happening at the same time. Her attorney had recommended that she again hire a personal manager, but she was reluctant; she and Mac had handled all their own affairs for the past few years. She wasn't even working; she should be able to deal with her life. Unbidden, her mental "list" came to mind.

The murder investigation had stalled.

The sale of the house would be one less thing to worry about, except that she had to find a new one. She had not made the time, yet, to follow up on the lead on Benjamin's father. And why was that? What was she afraid of? The prospect of a successful adoption had improved, now that the other couple was supposedly opting out; yet her "reputation" was not getting any better. Irma Carvey probably already knew she was moving in with Dane.

Moving in with Dane? Was she? Jessica's eyes opened wide in the darkness.

Oh, Mac. I'm sorry... I really want to do this. It will be so good for Devon... he needs a man in his life... Dane is wonderful for him... and anyway, it's not like I'm sleeping with him.

"How long before this is over, Jessica? When can I stop wondering?"

"I don't know what you mean." She had taken a tiny step backward, distracted and unaware of her own movements.

"Of course, you do. Let's see, how did it go tonight? He doesn't want you to marry me, right? We're not right for each other... or maybe, the marriage doesn't even matter. Maybe it would be more interesting for him to be 'the other man' this time."

Stop it. Go away! It's over... I can't stay married to a dead man, Mac!

But the memories would not stop until the entire scene had played out. It was so long ago, and yet... so vivid it might have been yesterday...

"Fight with me, Jess, c'mon. I'm ready. I'm as mad as hell. Don't walk away leaving me to believe you still want Pierce..."

"No!"

> *"He snaps his fingers and you jump in your car, no, into my God-damned car, and run off to be with him. He wants you now, doesn't he? More than ever..."*

This is crazy!

Jessica threw back the covers and went to the bathroom. In the medicine cabinet was the almost-full prescription bottle with the child-safe cap. Blinking against the too-bright bathroom light, she twisted off the cap and looked into the small bottle of capsules, tears filling her eyes until she could no longer focus.

And before she could change her mind, she dumped the entire bottle into the toilet and flushed them away.

Back in bed, she lay flat on her back and stifled her own sobbing.

I can do this. Things will get better.

Holding her eyes tightly closed, she sniffed, and swallowed hard.

I won't sleep with him. I promise.

Nineteen

Jackson

Roxanne was still mad at her. Why, Jessica wasn't sure. She hung up the phone feeling empty and confused. It seemed to have started just after the Halloween party, but was really evident during the weeks Roxanne had watched Devon while Jessica worked. They had barely spoken since.

Regardless of what had touched her off, Roxanne was tight-lipped and made no effort to warm up when Jessica called to tell her good-bye. She seemed unimpressed either way that her best friend would be gone an indefinite length of time and would be living with a man she disliked.

Jessica tried to push the sadness aside and instead focused on moving from point A to B, B being Wyoming and perhaps, some sense of salvation.

Her "to do" list looked better. As a result of Roxanne's cold reception, Jessica decided to have her mail forwarded to the ranch. She would leave a voice-mail number with a select few, including Sgt. Denehy and Mrs. Tuttle. Gretchen, her ex-housekeeper, would be happy to house-sit for her, and Jessica decided to give the woman Mac's antique roll-top desk as a gift. Gretchen was tearfully grateful.

On a whim, Jessica called the adoption services office where her case was being handled, to be certain they had the direct phone number of Dane's home in Wyoming. She did not want to risk missing a call.

"Mrs. MacKendall? My name is Russ Morrison. Irma Carvey is on vacation. Is there something I can help you with?"

"I have an application in process, and I wanted to make sure you have the phone number where I will be staying over the next several weeks."

"I see. The problem is, I don't seem to have a file on you. But go ahead and give me the number. Perhaps it's just misplaced somewhere on Irma's desk."

Jessica gave the man the number, along with her personal voice mail number and e-mail address. "I'd really appreciate any news as it becomes available, Mr. Morrison. My little nephew is my priority right now. .

"MacKendall... oh, that's right, the little heart patient. He's your nephew?"

"That's right. And I understand," Jessica began, swallowing hard, "that the Bandorfs, the couple that was trying to adopt him, may have changed their minds. I hope that I will be seriously considered at this point."

The man paused, and Jessica could hear the shuffling of papers. "I have Benjamin's file right here. I see quite a list of prospective parents, but your name is not on it."

Jessica's heart began to flutter. At a loss for words, she could only gasp for a moment. "Mr. Morrison, I was the first person to apply. I have a copy of my signed and dated application right here. I would be happy to... to fax you a copy..."

Now Morrison seemed as flustered as she. "Well, yes, if you can snap a picture of it, I would like to see that application. In fact, we are beginning interviews next week. I'm sure there's just some mix up here, Mrs. MacKendall. I'll have Irma call you just as soon as she returns."

"I'd really prefer you call me, Mr. Morrison."

"I'll do what I can."

Thoughtful, Jessica re-filed her application and stuck the folder into her suitcase. Before leaving, she had one last call to make.

The phone rang three times before the sergeant picked it up. "This is Denehy."

"Sgt. Denehy, this is Jessica MacKendall."

The policeman picked up his pen and straightened his back. "Mrs. MacKendall. What can I do for you?"

"Well, I was wondering if there was any news."

"I'm sorry to say, no. Whatever leads there are, they aren't particularly valid ones. But we will continue to work on this, you have my word." Denehy removed his glasses and rubbed his eyes, then leaned back in his chair. "Mac was a friend of mine. I won't let this rest, Mrs. MacKendall."

The silence on the line made him wish he had not spoken so freely; the young widow was undoubtedly anguished over her husband's death. Yet it was only a moment or two before she responded.

"Thank you. And if you don't mind, I have a favor to ask."

"Shoot."

"I was wondering if you could advise me on how to go about finding a private detective to help me find someone."

"Who and where? L.A.?"

"I need to track down my orphaned nephew's biological father. Possibly in Minnesota."

Denehy scribbled some words on his notepad. "I'm not sure that would be very useful information. Might be best to just let that go."

"It would be very useful information, to me. Never mind. I'll find someone in Minneapolis to help me."

As promised, upon their arrival in Salt Lake City, Dane's Lear Jet scooped them up. It was a short flight into Jackson, and Greg Singleton was at the airstrip with an over-sized all-wheel drive truck, a brand-new child's car seat installed in back.

It was a brief ride to the ranch. There was, indeed, snow on the ground, and the three travelers from Los Angeles stared in wide-eyed excitement.

"Can we make a snowman, Mom?" Devon wanted to know.

"Sure..." Jessica murmured, glad that practical Lydia had bought gloves and snow boots for them all.

Peter met them at the door. Jessica was in awe of the size of the main house, covering nearly five thousand square feet. Only the back half had second story rooms; the front living room and entry had high, open beamed ceilings.

"Dane will be back shortly. He had to make a run in to town," Peter told her. "I'll show you the rooms."

There were seven bedrooms in the house, two modest ones on the main level and five more upstairs. The room Dane had designated for Jessica was spacious and decorated with contemporary, western treatments. A small fireplace was built in one corner: a generous, full bathroom in another. A four-poster bed was central, with a writing desk against one wall. The last wall opened to a balcony through French doors, providing a westerly view of the ranch and its adjacent creek.

Jessica stretched out on the bed. The room was perfect, except for the steer horns over the mantel. Those would have to go.

She wondered for a moment why Dane had chosen to put Devon in with Alexander. Surely there were more than enough rooms to give each boy his own.

She was contemplating her still unpacked bags when there was a subtle knock on the door. Too comfortable to get off the bed, she called out her permission to enter.

He didn't say anything at first. Dane seemed content to just gaze upon her, crossing his arms across his chest as he leaned casually against the doorjamb.

"You like?" he said at last.

"I like." She forced herself to sit up, despite her weariness.

"Can I get you anything?"

She stared at him, awash with conflicting emotions. In her mind's eye she rushed him with a heart-smothering hug. Instead, she just ogled.

The jeans were worn and seductively snug, leaving nothing to the imagination; his snap-buttoned western shirt was carefully tucked in, and he was wearing leather boots.

"You never told me you were a cowboy."

"Let's keep it our secret. How was the flight?"

"Boring." She crawled off the bed now and retrieved the first of her three suitcases.

"Here, let me get that," Dane said, easily hoisting the heavy case onto the bed. "Jesus, woman, what the hell you got in here?"

"Just clothes."

"Planning to stay awhile, are you?" he asked with a grin.

"Maybe." Jessica turned to the dresser and pulled open the top drawer. "You did clear out all those other women's clothes?"

"All cleared." He stood behind her, and she was suddenly affected by his proximity. His outline in the mirror, taller and slightly to the side, melded with hers seamlessly, looking as natural as if... as if it had always been that way.

Impulsively she whirled about and hugged him, then tore away to begin her unpacking. From the corner of her eye, she watched as he left her, a bemused smile on his lips and shaking his head.

Dinner was a cheerful affair, with everyone around a six-foot diameter, solid ash table. While it wasn't immediate, Jessica began to relax as the night wore on, and she was more than ready for a restful night's sleep at 10:30 p.m.

It would be the first night Jessica would remember sleeping the entire night since Dane's visit to the lighthouse.

TWENTY

Cappen Catchup Pops the Question

Wyoming was good.

Without being intrusive, Dane saw to their every need, coming in and out of the frames that made up Jessica's days and evenings. He made good his promise to teach Devon, on a small scale, the ways of the great outdoors, and with Alexander on his other side the three became a team of wilderness explorers not to be reckoned with by the females of the house.

There was a happy camaraderie at the ranch. Peter and Lydia faced-off daily in a comic show of one-upmanship when it came to arranging meals, shopping and even deciding what occasional video the children would watch in the thirty-seat screening room at the rear of the house.

Dane seemed delighted enough just having them there; he made no overtures, and Jessica decided her life had taken a turn for the better at last. Comfort was the by-word of the day, the week, the month.

By May Day, the snow was melting; only patches of the mostly dirty cold stuff remained along the sides of the narrow road leading to the ranch. A blindingly white sun splashed warmth on Jessica as she took a now daily walk to the stream just before lunch.

In the pocket of her patchwork quilted jacket was the wrinkled scratch paper Nadine Carvey had given her. Finally mustering her courage, she had dialed the number early this morning and was now puzzling over the answer she had received.

Expecting a business, a private residence or most likely, a blind voicemail service, Jessica was completely tongue-tied when an automated voice offered to direct her call to the proper office at the Minnesota State House of Representatives. She hung up quickly, her mind tangled in confusion.

"Bizarre," she whispered, jotting down the name carefully on the back of the paper and tucking it into her pocket.

Now, as she walked along the creek side, she pondered the implication. Was it possible that Charlene was dating a politician?

Dinner was to be pizza and root beer, Dane had decided, when Jessica returned to the house that afternoon. Peter had gallantly offered to escort Lydia to a movie in town, and Greg normally ate alone in his small caretaker's quarters beyond the barn.

The boys were entirely willing, as it was, to eat pizza until they could hold no more, and after the last slice had been consumed Alexander brought out a selection of board games.

Reluctant at first, Jessica finally took the fourth seat at the game table and rolled the dice. Soon she was happily caught up in the game, delighted by her son's shining eyes and her benefactor's contented smile.

She could not remember ever seeing Dane so at ease.

"I think it was Captain Ketchup, he did it with the eggbeater, in the... in the attic!" Dane announced.

"Daa-ad..." Alexander complained, rolling his eyes. "There's no Captain Ketchup."

"Yeah, Uncle Dane, there's no Cappen Catchup..." Devon mimicked Alexander's exasperated expression and Jessica giggled.

"Aw, you guys just don't know how to play this game," Dane admonished with a smile. "You gotta be creative."

"How could you kill somebody with an eggbeater?" Alexander demanded.

"Well, it would be a lot more interesting than with a stupid 'lead pipe'."

"The candlestick is my personal favorite," Jessica said, folding her hands demurely.

Dane winked at her. "A true romantic."

Soon it was yawns all around and Jessica ushered the boys upstairs for a bedtime story. Devon did not make it past page three, and Alexander was fading by the end of the book.

In her bedroom, Jessica washed up and changed into a satin nightshirt and matching shorts. Then, realizing she had left her magazine downstairs, she went to the living room to retrieve it. As she was returning to her bedroom, she noticed a light coming from the office down the hall. Hoping to find Dane, she decided to investigate.

The light was from the small, green-glass banker's lamp on the massive oak desk. Dane sat with his back to the door.

"Hey, Cappen Catchup," Jessica began, pausing in the doorway.

Dane spun about in the broad, leather executive chair, a look of surprised delight crossing his face. "Come on in," he said, then turned back to the object of his attention.

It was a wooden box; Jessica could see as she drew closer to the desk. It was about the size of a shoebox with a hinged lid, ornately carved with letters across the front spelling "Mother." Inside the box were photographs.

"Whatcha doin'?" Jessica asked, hopping up to sit on the empty corner of the desk.

"The old memory-lane thing. I was looking for a picture I told Alex about, a horse I used to ride when I was a kid—and I got hooked..." He swept up a handful of photos from the desk and handed them to her.

Jessica could not keep the smile from her lips. "This is you? What an ornery little devil."

"As you can see, I haven't changed."

"This is your mother..." Jessica leaned closer to the light to get a better look. "... and your dad. Wow. You look like him."

"So they said." Dane began digging in the box again. "Here. This is my favorite." He withdrew a photo, its color faded and the corners worn.

"They look so happy," Jessica said softly, her eyes looking from one face to the other and misting over in the process. "Were they?"

Dane turned his own eyes briefly on to hers. "Blissfully. This was taken right before the accident."

Jessica nodded. "You had a happy childhood?"

"Yeah. I did, in fact. It was so good, I used to worry that something would happen. At night, I would lay awake hoping that a bomb wouldn't land on our house, or a hurricane knock it down or something."

"A hurricane. In Southern California."

"I was neurotic, what can I say?"

Jessica giggled at the rosy blush that colored Dane's cheeks, then looked back at the photograph. "They really loved each other; you can tell even from the picture."

"Yup. In a way, as bad as it hurts, it was at least good that they went together. Even though I would have given my own life for her to have survived, I know she would have been miserable forever without Dad. She always used to talk about how they would grow old together."

"That is so sad," Jessica said.

"I was going with Rita at the time. I once asked Mom about whether or not I should marry Rita, and she asked me if I could see myself growing old with her."

"And? Could you?"

Dane shook his head slowly. "All I could think about was, years and years of guaranteed sex."

Comically outraged, Jessica gave his shoulder a punch. "That's typical."

"I was twenty years old. Almost half my life ago." He paused, as if weighing his next words. "What about you? Did you think about that growing-old shit?"

"I can't tell you what I was thinking when I married Wes. It just seemed like the right thing to do. Of course, my folks tried to talk me out of it, but I just wanted to be out. But the night before the wedding, I had second thoughts."

Dane nodded, and Jessica knew where he was heading. It was the same place she was. "I never expected that I wouldn't grow old with Mac. I didn't think too much about the future, really. Except that... oh, never mind."

"Except what?"

"It's stupid."

"Can't be."

Jessica looked down at her bare knees, avoiding Dane's prying eyes. She wanted to confide, wanted badly to tell him about her fears. The power he had over her was almost palpable; she felt him drawing her in. "I had a worry, too. I was afraid, somewhere really deep inside, that he would leave me someday." Her own voice sounded childlike, and she swallowed. "If he ever got mad about something, I worried that it was my fault."

"Did he get mad very often?" Dane's words were guardedly concerned, gentle.

"No. Not really." Jessica straightened and squared her shoulders. Boldly she looked into his eyes. "I don't know why I even brought it up. Anyway—" she continued, handing him back the photo, "that's a love to be cherished."

Dane nodded slowly, then sighed. "You know I'm going to be thirty-nine soon?"

Relieved that he allowed a change in subject, Jessica laughed nervously. "Old man," she chided.

"Indeed." Lightly he ran his fingertips across the glossy finish on the photo. "And I want that. I want that for myself."

"That?"

"I want what they had."

"You'd better get busy and find somebody then," Jessica warned. "You're not getting any younger."

"Oh, I've already found somebody. There's just one problem."

The smile on Jessica's face remained frozen there, but a very definite knot was twisting her stomach into a bow. "Problem?" her lips repeated, when inside her mind raced around the words "I've... found somebody."

Dane gathered up the snapshots and carefully put them back into the box. "I made this in wood shop for my mom. Back in high school. Maybe it was junior high."

"It's beautiful. You were talking about a problem?"

"Hmmm? Oh, yeah. This girl, uh, woman, she's already told me she doesn't ever want to get married again. I can't say as I blame her, she's had a really tough time."

Jessica could feel every ounce of blood drain from her face, and a static hiss was growing in her ears. Dane looked at her now, concerned, watching her expression intently.

"You okay?"

"Sure. Of course."

"Oh. Good. Anyway..." He paused, carefully peeling her white-knuckled fingers from the edge of the desk and smoothing her palm against his own. "If this lady were to reconsider that rather rash decision, I would promise her my very best behavior. I'd promise her a lifetime of devotion."

As enlightenment filled her head, so did the blood rushing back into her face. Jessica's lips parted slightly, her eyebrows lifting so that she knew she must look just like Lucille Ball.

"'Course, if she doesn't reconsider, I'll have to understand. I'm not much of a prize, after all." Despite the normally comic, self-depreciating comment, Dane's voice was soft and completely sober. "It's a big decision. There are kids involved..."

Jessica struggled to find a voice. Her hand, now pressed gently between his, craved his warmth.

"You're really serious this time, aren't you?" she finally managed.

"I was serious last time. I've... always... been serious."

"I see."

Dane brought her hand to his lips, kissing the knuckles and the bare space on her ring finger. "So, what say ye? Is the galley maid willing to take a chance on the dread pirate?" Then, more gently, "You wanna be my girl, Jess?"

She brought her free hand up to her face, pressing three trembling fingers against her lips.

"I'm just so—so stunned. I don't know what to say, just yet..."

"Think it over." Carefully he released her hand, then pushed back in his chair and stood up. He stared at her for a few moments, tucking his hands into the back pockets of his jeans. "At the risk of sounding trite, we could have a real family." He paused to wet his lips. "You, me and the boys—it could be... really, really nice."

Jessica felt rooted to the desk. But when Dane again approached her, she was able to drop her feet to the floor and stand before him.

Dane placed a hand on each of her shoulders, looking down at her solemnly. "Look, am I on Mars or something? If I am, just tell me, Jess. I won't get mad, I won't hold you responsible, I won't ever bother you about—"

"Shut up," she said, placing her hand over his mouth. "I'm the one who's been on Mars. Let's—let's talk about this tomorrow, okay?"

He smiled then, and they both felt the relief. Jessica hugged him, pressing her cheek hard against his chest and closing her eyes. As she started to draw away, he caught her forearm and gently pulled her back to him.

"Oh yeah," he said, sliding his fingers firmly around the small of her back and pressing her lower half against his. "The proposal comes with this."

The naked emotion in his eyes startled an already shaken Jessica, but she was ready for the kiss, willingly exchanging a little of her power for an equal portion of his. One long, sumptuous kiss, filling her with a passion she almost wished she didn't feel. Almost.

When at last he drew his lips away, Jessica dared one last look into Dane's eyes before running from the room.

Jessica listened as the small mantel clock in her bedroom counted off three bells. The storm had sneaked in during the night, and a steady rain fell upon the roof above. Back in her sweats, she tiptoed downstairs and curled herself into the rocker, the fireplace now only a glowing memory of an earlier blaze.

She knew she would never sleep again. The few restful weeks she'd had with Dane in this house were now just a blur, a bit of unimportant history considering the new challenge before her.

Dane had re-entered her life in a big way. Not only had he effected untold benefits on her son, but he had also rocked her very core. And now, his talk of a future together had presented an enigma she was ill prepared to solve.

"I want what they had." The words still rang in her ears, in her heart. A part of her was reeling with immeasurable joy; a part of her was filled with unbelievable remorse.

She twisted in the chair, hoping to find a more comfortable position. In her hand she clutched a postcard. She pulled it out now, turning it over to read the words in the dim ember-light.

"Wish you were here," he had written. "Love, Dane."

Well, it didn't really say "Dane." Rather, a large "D" followed by a squiggly line. But it clearly read "Love."

And therein lay the problem, she finally realized. When someone asked you to marry them, shouldn't they say, "I love you" first?

She didn't doubt that he loved her. His caring was obvious. But did he love her the right way, enough to sustain that lifetime of devotion he'd offered?

Perhaps he was truly only seeking someone with whom to settle. A "growing old" partner. His mother's legacy.

No, Jessica labored under the possibly old-fashioned belief that to marry, you must be in love, and she wasn't sure Dane was in love with her. No matter that she wasn't quite sure she was in love with him.

And even if she were... would it be right, considering all that had happened? Would she ever be able to forget, or at least set aside the pain of the past?

"You know, I almost like you Pierce, but you're bad news—and I don't ever want to see your face here again, you got that?"

"Go ahead, MacKendall, finish the job. Finish what you started in Amande." Dane had baited. "Come on, if it'll make you feel better."

But nothing had ever made Mac feel better about Jessica and Dane's friendship. Up until the very day he left for Minneapolis, the cloud had lingered above them, tainting their marriage to the smallest degree.

Love or no love, could she even consider marrying the man responsible?

Twenty-One

A Matter of Commitment

The woman pushed her shopping cart forward aggressively, impatiently dodging other carts as she gathered her week's groceries.

Packaged, single-serving frozen dinners. Soup for One. A quart of milk. Cup O'Lunch.

It was the same every week. Except that this week, her cart held one additional item: a chocolate cupcake in a small pink bakery box. It was, after all, her thirtieth birthday.

No one knew of course, except her sister. Her older, decidedly mean sister.

At the cash register, she tapped her foot while waiting for a chatty couple to finish their business with the checker. Her gaze darted swiftly across the covers of the magazines displayed beside her basket. Tempted to buy one, her hand reached out, but she pulled it away. It was a waste of money. It was different than the days when she bought the magazine in hopes of gaining a new snapshot of him.

Now, there would be no new photos. Not ever.

Pushing her basket forward just enough to slightly bump the one ahead, she paused when a cover on the lower rack caught her eye. The tabloid section. She usually ignored them; this one she could not.

Whipping the splashy periodical off the rack, she tossed it into her cart. She couldn't wait to get home to read the front-page story.

Irma Carvey lived on the third-floor apartment across the street from her office. Edgy, she carried the bag of groceries up three flights rather than wait for the sluggish elevator.

Hurriedly putting away the milk and margarine, she grabbed the newsprint and trotted briskly to her bedroom, where she sat down at her small corner desk and carefully spread the periodical open. A taut smile spread across her naked lips, and she paused to look up at the photos taped to her bedroom wall. Clippings, snapshots and traditional 8 by 10 glossies, all pictures of the same face; the same pair of loving brown eyes, golden ochre hair, dimpled smile. All likenesses of a man who would have loved her, had they ever met. Had he not died.

Unconsciously, she reached up to press a peeling strip of tape to the wall. Pins and nails were against the rules.

Suddenly, everything was extremely clear, and she knew why Jessica MacKendall could not be allowed to adopt baby Benjamin. Why she must be prevented, at all costs, to gain custody of Cory MacKendall's nephew. There was no question in her mind, now.

She looked back at the pages covering her desktop. This article would help eliminate one of the obstacles, clearing the way for her to make her move.

Benjamin Cory MacKendall belonged to her, and she would stop at nothing to bring the child home.

·♥·♥·♥·♥·♥·

"Let me get this straight; you called the number, and it was the Minnesota Senate Office?" Dane looked over his shoulder at Jessica, who, perched on a bale of hay, watched as he curried Whiskey.

"House of Representatives. The nurse believes the man must be Benjamin's father. Charlene was probably having an affair with the guy."

"Is there more than one kind of affair?" Dane hid a smile. Charlene dating a politician was so left field, and yet bizarrely cliché. "So, what do you want to do about it?"

"I'm not sure." Jessica got to her feet and went to stand beside Dane as he ran a brush down the big horse's back.

Her proximity gave him pause. It was a feeling he would be hard-pressed to describe; anticipatory, excited, mildly aroused. He knew it was partly because she had not yet given him an answer, and partly because he always felt a little inside out when Jessica was around.

Whiskey swung his huge head around and snorted in complaint about Dane's divided attention. Jessica took several steps backward.

"You're not afraid of him, are you?" Dane asked, watching her expression closely.

"I don't get along too well with horses," Jessica confessed, warily eyeing Whiskey's flaring nostrils.

"He's harmless."

"To you, perhaps. You probably weren't thrown, bitten or kicked as a child."

"I was, but not by a horse," Dane quipped, but chose to save further discussion about Jessica's phobia for another time. It was a miniscule problem considering the other challenges he now faced, one of which he had, admittedly, created for himself.

"Did I tell you I heard from my attorney about Zoe?" he asked suddenly, and Jessica turned her attention from Whiskey's face to Dane's.

"No, how's that going?"

"Not great. I'm hoping we won't have to go to court. Rita's become a bitch on wheels. I've gotta do something, and quick."

Jessica sat back down on the hay bale. "What about Melissa?"

"She's already a lost cause, I'm afraid." He moved to the other side of the horse, working steadily with the brush, admiring Whiskey's shining auburn coat. "That isn't to say she's happy, but she's her mother's daughter, if you know what I mean."

"Can you bring Zoe up here for a while?"

Dane paused momentarily; he had hoped Jessica would be amenable to the idea. "I'd like to."

Grooming completed to his satisfaction, Dane stashed his tools, secured the stallion in his stall, and then washed up in the mudroom at the rear of the barn. Taking Jessica's hand, he led her outside and then into the adjacent hay barn, where they climbed a rough wooden ladder into the loft.

"Wow. I feel like I'm in a Jimmy Stewart movie," Jessica commented, carefully stepping onto the hay-strewn floor. Dane unlatched and pushed open a wide door at the front of the loft, exposing a westerly view that always took his breath away.

"Take a look," he told Jessica, who grasped his arm for support as she wobbled onto the mound of straw.

From a distance came the voices of children. Dane pointed to the uppermost view of the creek, where Alexander and Devon frolicked on the banks.

"Is it safe?" Jessica asked suddenly, her face awash with concern.

"The creek's about eight inches deep and I doubt if we have any of those killer tadpoles yet," Dane told her.

Apparently satisfied, Jessica made herself comfortable sitting in the hay, and Dane sat opposite her.

"So, what's on your mind?" she asked, wrapping her arms around her bent knees, her eyes still trained on the boys.

"Guess I wanted to ask you the same thing," Dane began. Try as he might, he could not read Jessica's mood; she could go either way. "Any thoughts about last night?"

Jessica did not answer at first, instead focusing her attention on rearranging the straw into a mound against which she could recline. Dane smiled as he watched her, still anxious but delighting in her every movement.

"I have lots of thoughts," she said at last, sighing and venturing a look into his eyes. "And I'm—I'm scared. I don't know how else to put it. I just... don't know what I want to do."

Dane drew in a deep breath and felt his eyes narrow involuntarily. He was loath to show his disappointment; still, she wasn't saying 'no.'

"I think we just need a little more time," she was saying, again avoiding eye contact. "There's so much at stake. Do you think... do you think we could just go on like we are for a while? I'm just so—"

"Done. Whatever you want. Just be honest, tell me if you think it's a bad idea. I can live with that."

Now she looked up, and Dane saw real hope in her expression. "Thanks. I just don't want either of us to make another mistake. I want you to know that I've been so much better, being here, with you and the boys. It's been wonderful."

"I'm glad."

"Devon loves it here, too."

Conversation was again put on hold as Jessica lay back and closed her eyes. The respite was brief, however, and eyes wide with terror, she tore away from the hay mound, tumbling awkwardly against Dane.

"Something's moving in there!"

Dane maneuvered her into his embrace, now chuckling. "You probably collapsed their living room."

"Whose living room?"

"Oh, the rats, mice, whatever."

Grimacing, Jessica pressed her face against his shirt, wiggling closer to sit on his lap. It was almost more than he could bear.

"Jess."

"I hate rats!" she proclaimed, her voice muffled as still she hid her face.

"Jess, look at me."

Jessica slowly turned her head toward his face, and Dane decided it was more than he could bear. His lips found hers in a heartbeat and heeded his obsessive demand for a kiss. The tightening of her arms around his neck fueled his need for more, and together they rolled into a passionate mass of reckless desire.

How long had they been in the loft? Jessica struggled to sit up, pulling her t-shirt down and picking off pieces of clinging straw. Beside her, Dane laid back, his eyes fixed on the ceiling of the barn, his face flushed with dissipating passion.

Quickly she glanced out the gaping loft door, vainly hoping to see her son still playing by the stream.

"Dane. The boys. They're gone."

"So?"

"Here we are, necking like a couple of high school juniors, and our sons are missing!"

"I doubt they're missing." He reached up and pulled her back down against him. "Necking? Is that what you call it?" A bemused smile played upon his mouth.

Jessica's heart was still fluttering, and she fixed her gaze on his lips. Sensuous was the only word that would come to mind. His eyes were boldly consuming her, and she could not help but liken him to a mouse that had just stolen the cheese from the trap without getting his tail caught.

"Making out?" she asked, tracing a finger around his still smiling lips.

"It could be more," he said, slowly running his hand smoothly down her back and over the swell of her bottom, his hand finally coming to rest on the back of her thigh. "You say the word."

Jessica felt her face grow flushed once again. She had not felt so aroused in a long, long time. Kyle's aborted attempt at seduction had been juvenile beside Dane's encompassing control. And it had always been this way.

There was no denying that she could easily become Dane's bed partner. Sexual compatibility was not an issue. The sparks had flown from the first touch.

No, it was a matter of commitment. Commitment to love.

·♥·♥·♥·♥·♥·

"I need to go back to L.A.," Dane announced at breakfast a few days later. They had taken to eating the morning meal together, Jessica feeling a sense of routine would be good for the boys.

"Whatever for?" she asked now, cocking her head in question.

"He's gonna kidnap Zoe."

Dane turned sharply toward his son, his expression serious. "Not exactly. You be careful about saying things like that. Don't wanna land your dad in jail, do you?"

"Are you, Dane?"

"Of course not. But I am hoping to bring her back with me."

"She's a cry-baby," Alexander asserted.

"She's your sister. Be glad of that. And I'm her dad, too. She probably wouldn't be a cry-baby if she were in a happier house, right?"

Alexander peered solemnly at his father before nodding his head in agreement. "Mom's a bitch."

Jessica felt the color fade from her own face at the word issued by Alexander's lips. She looked from Devon to Dane and then back to Alexander in shock.

"I'm sorry?" Dane asked, putting his fork down and leaning slightly closer to his son. "What did you just say?"

"Nothing."

"I heard something, and I didn't like what I heard. I want you to apologize for your language and promise not to ever talk like that again. You hear me?"

"You talk like that. You talk worse."

Dane closed his eyes briefly and exhaled a sigh. "Let's just cut to the apology, okay? I happen to agree with that description of your mother. But it's not okay to call her names. Especially at the breakfast table."

Alexander held his head high, but his eyes diverted down. “Sorry.”

“Well. You were saying about going to Los Angeles?” Jessica said quickly, before more attention could be paid to Alexander’s impropriety.

“I may have to meet with my attorney. I’m hoping she’ll just let me have Zoe without going to court. The kid’s miserable. I talked to her on the phone last night.”

“That is just so sad.”

Dane nodded, pushing his plate aside. “You don’t mind my going for a while?”

“Of course not. We’ll all be fine.”

Dane left the following morning, and Jessica felt oddly disconnected.

TWENTY-TWO

Dane's Girls

"Honestly. What were you and Mom thinking? It's no wonder she's messed up. If I were her, I'd get a lawyer and sue you both." Melissa took the straw between her lips and executed a calculated sip.

"Sue us? Why? For being irresponsible enough to have another daughter when the first one was already so rude?" Dane grinned at his eldest child across the table, and then looked for the third time at the closed ladies' restroom door.

The twelve going-on-eighteen-year-old ignored her father's comment. "For giving her such awful names. How can she go through life being a ZIP?"

Dane grimaced. Rita had insisted upon giving the baby girl her mother's name. It hadn't occurred to either of them that Zoe Irene's initials might create a problem for her in later years.

"And lately, she's eating everything in sight. It's embarrassing for me and Mom. She's such a little pig."

"That's enough. She's coming back. Just eat your lunch."

"You expect me to eat this... this crap?"

"That happens to be very good crap."

Zoe slid into the booth beside her older sister and picked up a fork.

"Tell me what you two have been up to lately. We need to catch up."

"Like what?" Melissa snorted.

"Like, how's school, what lessons does your mom have you suffering through, stuff like that."

"School's, like, the worst ever."

Dane cocked his head and turned his attention to Zoe, who looked up, her face a blank.

"School's okay."

"I'm cheerleading," Melissa said suddenly.

Dane nodded. "What about you, Zo? Doing anything besides school?"

"She dropped out of dance," Melissa blurted. "After she quit gymnastics. She flunked out of Tindale's, too."

"I think your sister can speak for herself, thank you. What's Tindale's?" Dane asked, directing the question to Zoe.

"They teach you manners and dancing and stuff. It was boring."

Dane sat back in the booth and sighed. "I see. Well, I was wondering if you guys would like to come up to the ranch for a while. I think you'd have a great time."

"You're kidding, right?" Melissa asked, picking at her salad.

"Are there animals?"

"You bet. You like animals?" Dane asked, encouraged by Zoe's interest.

"Some, yeah."

"Oh, gross. Horses and pigs?" Melissa wrinkled her nose.

"No pigs."

"Alex is there, isn't he?"

"You've got quite a mouth on you, girl." Dane shook his head. Melissa was becoming more like Rita every minute.

Melissa pushed her plate aside. "As if Mom would let us go, anyway."

"Tell me more about this Tindale lady."

"She has this club," Melissa began, rolling her eyes as her sister snagged a cherry tomato from her salad. "Mom has to get in or she'll die."

"Die? Really?"

"But it's like, you know, really-really hard to get in. You have to be really like Miss Perfect or they won't let you join. Mom's totally losin' it."

Dane nodded slowly, filing the information away.

"Are we gonna get dessert?" Zoe asked.

"How about a bowl of strawberries?"

Melissa sneered. “She won’t eat them unless they’re floating in whipped cream. Anyway, Mom’s gotta get all these other women to, like, say she’s cool and all. She needs one more.”

“Can I have a sundae?”

Dane turned his attention back to the younger girl. Her wide set green eyes pleaded for the ice cream. He patted his own stomach and smiled. “I don’t know about you, but I’ve been trying to eat a little better lately.”

“I heard Mom tell Aunt Lena that you haven’t looked so good since you met each other,” Melissa admitted. “Don’t tell her I said that.”

“Please?” Zoe begged again.

Dane’s heart went out to her; she was so needy he could feel the pain. “How about we split one three ways?”

“Not me,” Melissa said, again rolling her pre-adolescent eyes. “I’m not gonna grow up fat and homely.”

Dane could feel his face harden involuntarily. “Suit yourself. More for us, right Zoe?”

Thrilled by her father’s decision, Zoe batted her eyelashes playfully. “My name is Ashley. Ashley Marie Pierce.”

“Like you could really, honestly change your name. How stupid can you get?”

“Well, Miss Ashley, should we have whipped cream and nuts?” Dane asked, ignoring Melissa’s latest barb.

“No nuts. We need a cherry, though.”

“Mom’ll kill you.”

“Mimi, I’m not worried about Mom. I am, however, worried about you,” Dane said, signaling the waitress.

“And why should you start worrying now? You never worried before.”

“I—” Dane was quick to begin a defense but was interrupted by the waitress taking their dessert order.

“And if you’d been around even half the time, you’d know that nobody calls me Mimi anymore,” the girl continued.

“I do,” Zoe mumbled, her eyes trained on the retreating waitress.

“You don’t count.”

“And anyway, Dad’s being nice to us now and I hate you to be mean to him so shut up.”

Dane felt like he was watching a tennis match. He cleared his throat. "I stand corrected, Miss Pierce," he murmured. "I think we all need to work on being a little nicer to each other."

Melissa uttered a bored sigh, prompting Dane to mimic her with one of his own. The three sat in silence until the dessert arrived, and Dane forced himself to dip into it with a spoon. The look of sheer delight on Zoe's face warmed him, however, and his smile returned.

"Come on, it's good," he said, picking up a clean spoon and holding it toward Melissa. "We don't have to tell Mom."

Melissa looked from the spoon to the sundae, then to her father's eyes, clearly torn. Dane was surprised at his own realization that his daughter was not choosing between thin or chubby, or even between her obsessive mother and suspiciously available father. Instead, Melissa was straddling the line between the comfort of childhood and the angst of adolescence.

"Just a taste."

Dane was careful not to smile too broadly.

In the driveway at Rita's estate, Dane stayed Melissa's hand before she could throw open the Mustang's passenger side door.

"I need a favor, 'Lissa."

Wary, the girl narrowed her eyes.

"I'm gonna have to do some serious combat in there. I need you to go upstairs and help Zo pack some things."

"You're really gonna take her, then?"

"I think it's best."

Melissa looked uncertain.

"You're welcome to come, too." Dane squeezed her hand.

Her expression now unreadable, Melissa got out of the car and stood by, waiting for her sister to climb out of the backseat.

Rita Pierce was lounging beside the pool. "Tired of them already?" she asked, her eyes well hidden behind designer sunglasses.

"On the contrary, we're just getting started," Dane replied, sitting on the stone planter wall.

"And what's that supposed to mean?"

"Zoe's gonna take a little vacation and visit the ranch."

"Like hell, she is," Rita muttered, turning her head to the side and away from Dane.

"We're leaving this afternoon. She's packing right now."

"Over my dead body."

"I was hoping we wouldn't have to resort to that."

"You're so droll, Dane. Really. I hope that piece of crap car of yours isn't leaking oil on my driveway."

"I'll have her call you every few days to tell you how happy she is," Dane said, standing and turning to go.

Rita sat up and whipped the glasses from her face. "You can't be serious. You think for a minute I'd allow you to take my daughter away from me?"

"Why not? You took her away from me, before she was old enough to have a say in the matter. Now she's old enough, she wants to go, so we're going."

"I'll call the police."

"Please do. And while you're at it, call that Tindale broad, too. Perhaps she'd like to know about our latest scandal."

Rita seemed to choke on her own tongue. Sputtering in rage, she fairly leaped from the lounge and gave chase as Dane sauntered toward the back of the mansion.

"You won't get away with this!"

"With what? Taking my little girl home for a visit? Getting her out into the fresh air of Wyoming, teaching her to ride a horse that isn't shellacked?" Dane stopped and spun around to face his ex-wife. "I'll tell you something else. She asked me to take her. She begged to go. To get away from you. And if you don't think I'd take you back to court to get custody of her, and Melissa too, for that matter, you're sorely mistaken. And I'd win, too, you can count on that. So, let's make this easy on ourselves, and more importantly, easy on them. Just lay off."

Rita's gaping mouth slowly closed, and Dane reached out to her, drawing two fingers gently down her cheek. "What happened to you, anyway?" he asked, then turned away while shaking his head.

•♥•♥•♥•♥•♥•

Jessica hung up the telephone in the kitchen and shuddered.

"Who was that?" Lydia asked, peeking into the hot oven at the tray of cookies baking inside.

"Russ Morrison. He's with the adoption agency in Minnesota. I can't believe it! He's setting up an interview for me!"

"Oh, Jessie, that's wonderful! I'm so happy for you. But you look worried."

"I'm nervous about the whole thing. I wish Dane were here."

"Be home tomorrow, right?"

"Supposedly. This thing is taking so darned long. I'm afraid to get my hopes up again. Every time I do, something goes wrong."

"Things like that always take time. You've heard what they say about a thing being worth waiting for, something like that?"

"As usual, you are right," Jessica agreed, absently popping a cookie into her mouth. "And Benjie is definitely worth waiting for."

Dane's call from Salt Lake City later in the evening surprised her.

"You'll be here tonight?"

"I couldn't stand another night away. It'll be late—they're just fueling the plane now. Could you make sure her bed is ready?"

"The bed is already turned down."

"Thanks, sweetie. See you soon."

Jessica toured the house before settling onto the couch to wait for Dane's arrival. The boys were asleep, everything was quiet. It was half-past eleven when she heard his truck pull into the garage.

She followed him as he carried his sleeping daughter up the stairs and into the room she and Lydia had readied for Zoe. Tenderly Dane covered her sleeping form and bent to kiss her peaceful brow.

"She got a little airsick," he whispered, stroking his daughter's hair away from her face. "I think she's okay now."

Back downstairs, Dane reached for Jessica and took her into his arms. "I missed you," he said into her ear, causing shivers to ripple throughout her body.

"Missed you, too."

He kissed her then, a single, deeply satisfying kiss that reconnected them after his brief absence. Jessica shivered again in his arms.

"You okay?"

"I'm fine. I'm just... glad you're back. You must be tired."

"Burnt, yeah. Duking it out with Rita wasn't exactly easy. We'll talk tomorrow."

They didn't talk about much the next day. Dane delighted in showing his "baby girl" around the ranch, and Jessica watched a side of Dane she had rarely seen. Peter commented as they stood together outside the corral where Dane walked Whiskey in a circle, Zoe planted firmly before him in the saddle.

"She's definitely likin' bein' a daddy's girl."

"She should," Jessica mused, briefly thinking about her own late father and the times they had shared. "But I think Dane's enjoying it even more than she is."

"He's lucky, eh? I'd hoped to have some wee ones of me own, but lady luck has always looked the other way."

"You sound like you've given up! Don't be foolish, Peter."

"Ah, Jess, you're an angel to say it. But I ask you, what woman in her right mind, or otherwise for that matter, would want to start up with a crusty ol' Brit like me? A roly-poly, balding, near-sighted Limey who's most comfortable in the kitchen?"

It was an inopportune moment for the comment as Lydia stepped from just behind him and climbed up to stand on the split rail fence surrounding the corral.

"What's on the menu tonight, Limey?" she teased with a little giggle. Coloring, Peter turned and huffed back toward the main house, leaving Jessica to stifle a laugh.

"Dane says we're going to a summer festival deal tonight. There's a "mountain man" competition, dancing, face painting, booths, all that stuff."

"Great. At least I won't have to argue with him about dinner!" Lydia asserted, then turned to follow Peter back into the house. Jessica watched her go, a broad smile on her face. Something was brewing.

It wasn't long before Jessica found herself adoring Dane's daughter as much as he did. The exposure to outdoor activities had put a rosy bloom on Zoe's cheeks, and she played big sister to Devon much better than little sister to the pouty Alexander.

Every day brought another level of contentment to Jessica. Likewise, her problems took more definite, more manageable shapes, and she felt better focused than she had in months. Months?

She stared at the calendar on the kitchen wall. Tomorrow would be May 19th. Tomorrow was the anniversary of Mac's death.

Where had the year gone? A series of pictures rushed by in her mind, but not nearly enough scenes to make up an entire year.

Preoccupied, she lifted her jacket off the pegged rack bedside the door and met Dane as he came in from outside.

"Going somewhere?" he asked, shedding his own windbreaker and helping her on with hers. "Nippy outside."

"Just need to take a walk."

"You don't look like you want company."

She only smiled and gave him a quick kiss on the cheek. "Be back soon. The boys are—I mean the kids are upstairs."

"Don't get lost," he called as she trotted down the porch steps.

Don't worry. I'll find my way back. Somehow.

She walked until the chilly air had her winded, and she found herself on the top of a small hill. The sun hung low in the western sky. Her hands well nested inside her pockets, Jessica stared at the farthest horizon and then sat down on the grassy hilltop.

"I can't believe you've been gone a whole year," she said quietly, her eyes roaming over the treetops, a bird in flight, the distant clouds. "Where are you, Mac? Where are you, really?"

She listened to the wind in the trees, the bird's wings. Were these the sounds given her by her late husband? The man to whom she had sworn a lifetime of love, truth and fidelity?

"I haven't been back to visit the... the grave, you know it just didn't seem... right, for you to be there..." she murmured, now looking down at the individual blades of grass before her. "It's not like you're really there." Her voice caught in her throat. "It's not like you're really anywhere. I mean, where you are, it's where you'll always be, in my heart, okay? Oh snap."

The lump in her throat had grown almost too large for her to speak aloud. She swallowed hard. "He's different, Mac. He's better than before. He's good to me, and good to our son. Devon needs Dane in his life... and so do I. Would it be so awful...?"

Jessica squeezed her eyes tightly closed, waiting for the memories to begin washing over her. Waiting for the fear and humiliation to set in. Instead, the cry of the hawk overhead startled her, causing her to look skyward as the bird circled above.

The old pain did not return. Instead, the vision that filled her was of Mac's shining adoration. The little salute he was fond of giving her when they were dating. The sympathetic and loving eyes that were saying, *It's okay. I will always love you.*

Suddenly, she was gasping for air, her heart thumping in her chest as though she had run a great distance. Jessica got rapidly to her feet, taking in big gulps of air, her arms spread wide in gratitude. Had she purposely conjured an approval? Or were the visions sent from beyond, somehow, to tell her not to worry? She did not want to wait for an explanation, did not want to allow the old doubts to creep in. When her breathing had calmed sufficiently, she began descending the hill, slowly at first and then picking up speed until she was jogging back toward the house. Dane was out in front, playing tug-of-war with one of his favorite Labradors.

"Hey, woman, you got a bear after you?" he called as Jessica trotted briskly up to him and threw herself into his waiting arms.

"I am a bear!" she proclaimed, wrapping her legs around him, reveling in his embrace. And when he again placed her on her feet, the light in his eyes was such that Jessica stood transfixed, unable to move at all.

"Take me to where you've been," he murmured, his fingers moving slowly against the tresses of hair that hung down her back.

"I'm still there," she told him, now laying her cheek against his chest. "And I want to stay."

He didn't seem at all surprised when she came into his bedroom after midnight. Wearing the silk turquoise robe he'd given her, Jessica sat down on the edge of his bed and sighed.

"I need to talk," she began, fiddling with her finger as if twisting a non-existent ring.

Dane hoisted himself into a sitting position and turned on the bedside lamp to its dimmest setting.

"I've been thinking about us. I have some questions, I guess."

"I'm listening," he said quietly.

"About getting married. I need to know... why."

Dane tilted his head. "Why? Well. I thought this was going to be hard," he said with a smile. "Like whom would keep the checkbook, where we would go for our honeymoon, you know, hard stuff."

Jessica lowered her chin in a mock pout.

"Okay. Why. Well, I think we're good together, Jess. For the first time since we met, I feel like... like we're finally in sync. Crazy as it sounds, it's like everything that went before led up to this, right here and now." He paused, looking briefly away and then placing his hand on her knee. "I don't mean what happened to Mac. I never wanted that to happen, believe me. But the fact remains that you and I, we're here now, finally together."

Jessica drew in a deep breath. There had to be more, and she waited quietly.

"Not buying it, huh?"

"Keep talking."

Dane was quiet for a time, then threw back the covers and got out of bed. In another time and place, his immodesty would have stunned her. Yet the sight of this completely nude man crossing the room in the dim light didn't faze Jessica. If anything, it delighted her; still she remained stone-faced.

He was digging in his top dresser drawer. "You have a right to ask," he said, now returning to the bed. "Okay." He sat beside her and took her hand. "You want to know why I want to spend what's left of my life with you? It's a simple answer, really." He slipped a small band onto the nervous ring finger of her left hand. Jessica uttered a tiny gasp, staring in wonder at the ornate, diamond and platinum filigree ring.

"Oh, my..."

"It was my mother's. She was the last to wear it. She would have wanted you to have it."

"Why me? We never even met."

"Because you are the woman I love. The woman of my heart."

Jessica felt her pulse quicken. "Could you just say that first part again?"

Cupping her right cheek, he moved his lips close to her left ear, speaking softly yet plainly. "Losing your hearing, are you?" Jessica shivered as he kissed the spot on her neck just below her earlobe. "You are the woman I love, and damn it if I haven't loved you from the very beginning." Slowly easing her back on the bed, Dane trailed his lips down her neck and around to the other ear. "Forgive me," he whispered, his words hot and moist, tantalizing her senses. "I've hidden it so long, it's still hard for me to say it."

"Hidden?" she managed, her own hands traveling across his naked flesh, down his back, absorbing the tautness of his muscles as she reacquainted herself with his form.

"It doesn't matter now." Dane stopped kissing her and looked into her face. "I do love you, want you... let the heavens witness that I promise you my love forever, Jessica. Forever. If you want it."

"I do. Oh, I do. I didn't think you knew. I didn't think you would ever really love me, this way. We really do have a chance, don't we?"

"More than a chance, if you love me even half as much—"

"You know I love you. I've never stopped loving you."

He paused then, searching her eyes for the truth she was doing her best to convey. "So it's yes?"

"Yes. Let's do it."

His sigh signaled a combination of relief and barely restrained desire; Jessica surprised herself by wriggling out of the silk robe beside him, pressing her nakedness against him.

"Ah, you came prepared," he murmured, pulling her closer and launching a full assault on her eager sensuality, triggering reactions she had all but forgotten were possible. She proved his match, however, alternately giving and taking whatever she felt would give them both pleasure.

And when the play was over and a sweet rhythm developed between them, Jessica closed her eyes and succumbed to Dane's never-ending power over her. The term "lover" had never carried any significant meaning before. He was her friend, her champion, her benefactor to some degree. Now, once again her lover; her fiancé, soon-to-be her third and final husband.

Lover. The word rolled passively through her head as he worked the magic, shared the fever, and woke the passion within her.

From the first day she'd laid eyes on Dane Pierce, she'd wondered what it would be like to share his bed. It had not taken long to find out. The excitement was unfathomable... and yet lacking. Because sex without commitment would never be good enough. And now, surrounding her finger was a circle of commitment that fulfilled the act, fueled and validated the inferno of their physical love.

Yes. Dane had always loved her. But only now was he ready to trade his disclaimers for a future. The realization drove Jessica to a new, exquisite reality, allowing her to forget, for a time, that anything or anyone else even existed. So complete was their unity, there was no question in her mind that he felt the same.

Twenty-Three

Faith

"I asked for Russ Morrison."

"He isn't here. Is there something I can do for you, Mrs. MacKendall?"

Yes. Quit your job and move to Siberia.

"I want to update my application."

"In what way?"

"Please, change the records to show that I am getting married soon, and the Wyoming address will become permanent."

"And the prospective groom?"

"Dane Thomas Pierce." Not that it's any of your business.

"Ah. I might have known."

"And just what is that supposed to mean?" Jessica asked, feeling her hackles rise.

"Well, after that... shall we say... telling article in Hush... I clipped it out. Thought it would make a nice addition to your file."

"I wouldn't put much stock in any tabloid story, Miss Carvey. Surely you realize—"

"Surely you realize just how slim your chances are of adopting a special-needs child when you are associated with... a philanderer, a man who's already abandoned two of his own children..."

"I beg your pardon?!" Jessica's temper flared at the implication made. "Your information is incorrect, at best. And none of your business anyway, I might add."

"Oh, but it is my primary business to see that little Benjamin is placed with upstanding parents, responsible parents of good moral character. I'm sorry but I think you're wasting your time."

Newly enraged, Jessica slammed the phone back onto its cradle.

Wide-eyed, Lydia watched from the doorway. "Need anything from town?"

"Yes." Jessica was thoughtful, pushing her sparse bangs away from her forehead. She lowered her voice. "See if you can find a copy of Hush Magazine."

"Sure."

"And if there's anything, you know, too obvious on the cover, don't let anyone we know see it."

"Gotcha. Anything else?"

"Not right now, unless you want to strangle Irma Carvey for me."

·♥·♥·♥·♥·♥·

"Okay. What've you got?" Murdo Denehy sat down at the long precinct conference table while his partner closed the office door.

"The Internet is crammed full of stuff about this guy. Articles, bios, fan clubs, the works." Joe Fusco sat opposite Denehy and opened his steno notebook.

"Go ahead."

"Thirty-eight years old, born November 29th in Glendale. Went to school locally, journalism major. Father was a philosophy teacher, mother taught art and voice lessons and was an ex-Miss San Fernando Valley."

"Was?"

"They were both killed in a train wreck a few years back. New York State. Pierce married his high school sweetheart, Rita Herrington, when they were just kids. They have three children. Around the time he started winning Oscars and shit, she left him."

"Hmmm. Poor guy."

"Right. Word was, he was already banging other chicks. That's when he met Ms. MacKendall. 'Course, she wasn't MacKendall at the time."

"They did a movie together."

"Yeah, and had a brief tumble, after which he dumped her, and she married MacKendall."

"Anything about the Spencer woman?"

Fusco flipped a few pages ahead. "As a matter of fact, I spent about two hours going over the archived chat logs of the fan club. It's divided, about whether it was an accident or suicide. A couple of people even believe he killed her. But just about all of them think that Jessica MacKendall was the motivating factor."

Denehy chewed his lip for a moment. "Did you see anything about Mac and Pierce ever squaring off?"

"A woman interviewed for Pierce's unauthorized biography worked on the *Lost Season* movie as Jessica's stand-in. She claims Pierce was a tyrant on the set and nobody would stand up to him. He once called out another actor who invited Jessica to dance. And," Fusco paused to again thumb through his notes, "I quote, 'Cory MacKendall was the only man who didn't lie down before Dane's arrogance.' She goes on to say that Mac and Pierce had apparently tussled over Jessica, and Pierce came away the worse for it."

"You got her name?"

"I can get it. You find anything?"

"Oh, hell. I've poured over this damned case off and on for weeks. There are some holes in it, but nothing I can nail down.

"During the months just prior to Jackie Spencer's death, we were investigating several acts of 'harassment and vandalism' reported by the MacKendalls. We even had Mac's sister in the lock-up at one point. He had her released the day of the shooting. After that, Mac asked me to drop the case. At the time I kind of figured the dead girl was behind the whole thing. Now, I'm not so sure."

"You gonna pick up Pierce?"

"Can't. It's not our case. But I'm keeping my eyes on him."

"You've seen this, right?" Fusco said, slapping a copy of Hush Magazine down on the table before the sergeant.

Jessica closed the front door and leaned against it. She felt antsy, unsettled, and needy. Trotting briskly up the stairs, she sought out Dane. She found him in his office, fingers tapping lightly on the keyboard of his notebook computer.

He jumped and nearly left his skin behind.

"Sorry, I didn't mean to startle you," she said as he spun around in the over-sized executive chair. "Whatcha doin'?"

"Nothing important." He beckoned with his fingers, and she climbed onto his lap, her knees straddling his legs. "Where is everybody?"

"Lyddy took the brood to town. Peter's... somewhere, I don't know." Jessica squirmed uncomfortably; her simple cotton dress was hiking up around her hips.

"What's on your mind?" he asked, unbuttoning the top button on her dress and kissing her throat.

"We need to talk about... some things." *If he does that again I won't be able to talk about anything.*

"Like?"

"Like going back to Minnesota. I have that interview set up, and I want you to go with me."

"You sure?"

"Absolutely. As my husband."

Dane took a breather from his preoccupation with her chest and looked into her eyes. "And this appointment is when?"

"June 20th."

"Then we'd better get to planning a wedding." Sliding forward on the chair, Dane got to his feet and lifted Jessica with him. Without further discussion, he carried her down the hallway and into her bedroom, where he laid her carefully on the bed, then joined her.

Jessica giggled. "I still can't believe we're going to do this," she said.

"We have no choice." The gleam in Dane's eyes was filled with affection and humor, and Jessica felt a sudden rush of emotion throughout. Quickly she pressed her lips against his, drawing in a kiss that she hoped would convey how much she loved him at that moment.

"Mmm... I'm liking this," he murmured, pulling back just enough to get a hold of the next button on her dress, then the next, until her delicate cleavage was exposed to his eyes. Jessica held her breath as he slipped his fingers into the cup of her bra, lowering his lips to perfect some adoration upon her flesh.

"Ah... we were talking about the wedding..."

"We were? Oh, yeah." Dane lifted his head and pulled her back against him, returning his attention to her neck. "So, when?"

"Uh... June... June... oh, dammit Dane!" Jessica gave him a playful, yet firm, push and tried to rearrange her bra.

"June 14th. Flag Day. That way I'll always remember it. Now, come here, wench."

His hand was on her thigh, sliding upward until he encountered her panties. Jessica felt her face begin to heat up, her foot lifting involuntarily to wrap seductively around his leg. And before she knew what was happening, the panties were on the floor, and she was clawing at Dane's belt buckle.

It was over quickly. Jessica lay panting on Dane's chest, listening to the rapid beating of his heart beneath her ear. It had been this way for days; since the first night they had made love in Dane's bed, they had taken every opportunity to be intimate. Passion was the order of the day.

"Not much time to plan a wedding," he said, idly stroking her hair.

"Plenty of time. We don't want any big affair."

"Certainly not."

"Just a few friends. We'll get married right here on the ranch."

Dane turned his head toward her face. "Wonderful. Do you want to call Roxanna, or should I?"

Jessica's smile faded at the sound of Dane's pet name for Roxanne. She had put off thinking about contacting her friend. "I will. Surely, they'll come, won't they?"

"Who knows? I haven't seen either of them since the night of the auction." Dane pulled himself free and stood from the bed, reassembling his pants and belt. "Let's call them right now."

Jessica sighed and sat up. "I'll be down in a few minutes."

She took her time freshening up from their afternoon frolic. She frowned, then giggled at the sight of a new, faint pink mark on her neck. Dane Pierce was nothing if not a passionate lover.

He was in the kitchen, waiting beside the telephone. Wordlessly, she took the phone he handed her and dialed the familiar number, trying to remember to breathe between rings. Tom Jarrick's friendly greeting allowed her to exhale.

"Well, hello, stranger! We were just talking about you. Still living in Jellystone Park?"

Jessica laughed. "Close to it. I have some exciting news to share with you guys. Is Rox home?"

An eternity passed while Tom went in search of his wife. When Roxanne came on the line, Jessica was again holding her breath. Behind her, Dane ran his knuckles delicately down her spine.

"How's everything?" Jessica asked, trying to keep the quiver from her voice.

"No complaints. How do you like it up there?" The words were friendly, but the tone was lackluster. Jessica forced herself to smile.

"It's absolutely breathtaking. How soon can you come up?"

Roxanne was quiet, as if she couldn't find an answer to Jessica's simple question. Jessica noticed her own hand trembled as she held the phone. Roxanne finally spoke.

"I don't know. We're in the middle of a big remodel right now, and I've got three gowns to deliver by July 1st. You know how it is..."

Jessica wet her lips and glanced at Dane.

"Tell her," he mouthed.

"What if there was a wedding to come to? A wedding for someone who... who would really cry a lot if you weren't here?"

"Not you and Dane?"

Jessica swallowed hard and reached out her hand. Dane took it and squeezed. "Yeah. We're getting married on June 14th, and I really... I really need you to come."

The silence on the phone line was palpable. Jessica released Dane's hand and waved him away, reluctant to have him see her grovel. "Rox? Come on, at least say something. If you think it's a stupid idea, it's okay to tell me, but don't give me this silent treatment. Please?"

"Of course it's not stupid. I'm—I'm happy for you, Jess. I wouldn't want you to be alone. I'll—I'll talk to Tommy about coming up." There was a pause, and Jessica tried to think of something else to say. But Roxanne continued. "I guess I'm just a little surprised, that's all. I don't know why. God knows Dane never got over—" Roxanne cut herself off, then changed her tone. "Look. I've gotta go. I've got a client waiting. But we'll be in touch, I'll let you know, okay?"

"Sure." Jessica made no effort to hide the disappointment in her voice. From the corner of her eye, she could see Dane standing in the doorway. She hung up the phone and sighed.

"Well?"

"She had to hang up. She'll call back and say when they'll be up."

Dane gave her a skeptical look, crossing his arms across his chest. Jessica ignored him.

"Now, I have to call Chrissie."

Her sister was overjoyed. "We'll be there!" she proclaimed. "Unless I go into labor first."

"Don't even say that," Jessica said with a giggle. "You aren't due until—"

"July first. It's cutting it close."

"Luckily, you're not that far away. Oh, I am so glad you're coming!"

"I'm happy for you, sissy. Can I talk to Dane?"

Surprised, Jessica handed the phone over and stood by, her palms pressed together before his chest. Dane grinned and waved her away as she had done him earlier.

Jessica reluctantly wandered into the living room, her emotions a jumbled mess. Roxanne's reaction bothered her; at least she had not been cold or unaffected.

Opening the front door, Jessica went out to the porch and sat on the steps. The afternoon sun was already high, and she wondered when Lydia and the children would return.

Soon, Dane was beside her, his arm slipping around her shoulders, a smile on his lips.

"What did Roxanne really say, sweetie?"

A single tear slid down Jessica's cheek and she hastily brushed it away. "Nothing, really."

"She'll come around. Don't worry."

Memorial Day weekend was a huge affair in Jackson Hole. While Dane tried to remain unobserved among the throngs of tourists crowding the small resort town, he nonetheless carted his children around to various holiday events. They also celebrated Jessica's birthday in high style by throwing a barbecue at the ranch for the few neighbors Dane had come to know.

Her gift, however, got mixed reviews.

Named after Jessica's character in *Lost Season*, "Mariah" was a gentle mare, smallish and exquisitely formed. Jessica eyed her with caution.

"She... she's beautiful," Jessica stammered, holding tightly to Dane's arm as he led her around the horse. "I suppose I'll have to learn to ride now."

"Sweetie. Do you really think any wife of mine could stay afraid of horses for long?"

"I didn't realize that was part of the proposal," she chided, allowing him to direct her hand to the horse's mane, dragging her fingers through its silky tresses.

Dane threw back his head and laughed. "Don't look so panicked. You'll like it." He leaned down and whispered into her ear. "It's almost as good as sex."

Jessica blushed. "I'll remember that."

They walked back toward the front porch hand in hand. They'd nearly reached it when a Federal Express truck roared up the private driveway and stopped to deliver a large, flat box addressed to Jessica.

She hurried inside with the package, sitting on the couch to open it. "It's from Rox," she said excitedly. "What could it be?"

Carefully she slit open one end of the box with the knife Dane handed her. Inside, another box slid out onto her lap. Jessica wasted no time in whipping off the lid.

"Oh, my..." she gasped, lifting out a captivating wedding gown of handmade ecru lace. Holding it up by the wide, crocheted straps, Jessica stood and allowed the long dress to fall against her body. Layer upon layer of intricate lace panels draped over one another, cinching at the waist without a seam. Simple, feminine, so typical of Roxanne.

Jessica spun toward Dane, shaking her head slowly.

"There's a card in the box," he told her, retrieving the envelope and handing it to her.

"You read it," she whimpered, temporarily overcome with emotion.

Dane cleared his throat. "Haven't seen you in a while but this should be close... will make adjustments when I get there... remodel on hold... blah blah blah..."

"What blah blah blah? Read it all!"

"You are one lucky woman to snag Dane. He's such a sexual dynamo..."

Jessica snatched the letter from his fingers and carefully draped the wedding dress over the back of the couch.

Dane chuckled. "And you thought she wasn't coming."

Jessica resumed reading the letter. "'We'll be there on the twelfth. Sorry this is late, you didn't give me much notice, hope you had a wonderful birthday... Love, Rox.' Can you believe it?"

"Actually, I can."

"I can't wait to try it on."

The next few days flew by for Jessica. Putting thoughts about the adoption aside, she focused on the wedding plans and preparing the children for the event.

Devon seemed excited at the prospect of gaining a second father, and Zoe had warmed to Jessica immediately. Jessica was reminded of Mac's daughter Megan and regretted that she had not made better efforts to stay connected. Megan had turned eleven in April, and they had shared a brief telephone conversation. Megan seemed distant, and perhaps Jessica was a painful connection to her father, as was Megan to Jessica. I need to resolve that, Jessica vowed to herself.

Uncharacteristically tired in the middle of the day, Jessica went to her bedroom for a brief nap, taking Devon with her. As she pulled off her son's shoes, she noticed a flat paper bag on her dresser.

"Comfy?" she asked as Devon wiggled his bare toes.

"Uh huh. Are you gonna take a nap too, Mommy?"

"Yes," she confirmed, but instead dumped the contents of the bag onto the dresser. The June issue of Hush Magazine lay before her, with a note from Lydia saying she'd finally located a copy.

Jessica was ill prepared for the back-to-back photos of Dane Pierce on the cover. She sat down on the edge of the bed, frowning at the pictures. The one on the left was of Dane and herself as they arrived at the Academy Awards the month before. Shining and gorgeous, they did indeed epitomize Hollywood's A-list. The other photo was not so complimentary.

An unshaven Dane had his arm around another woman; a nighttime photo, and they appeared to be in front of... yes; the caption clearly said Rampart Division, L.A.P.D.

Jessica tilted her head. What was this about? Blinking several times, she swallowed and folded the magazine so that she could attempt to read the article. But her eyes would not stray from the photo. The woman in the picture looked familiar.

"Mommy?"

"In a minute, Dev." Quickly Jessica forced herself to skim through the paragraphs. The words "exotic dancer" leaped out at her. The author was speculating that Dane Pierce had bailed the woman, one Katrina Vidal, out of jail, the night after the Oscar ceremony.

Jessica wracked her brain to recall the night. He had called late; he was leaving for Wyoming the next day. There was something about helping someone out.

She looked back at the headline with despair. *Dane Does Double Duty.* Below the photo of herself was a quote.

"A little private party of our own," snickered Hollywood's most eligible bachelor, when asked what he and the recently widowed MacKendall would be doing after the show. "It's off to bed after that."

Taking a deep breath, she closed the magazine and slipped it into her dresser drawer beneath her underwear, then stretched out beside her sleeping son. Unconsciously stroking his blonde hair, Jessica could not begin to sleep now. And it came to her then, who the woman in the photo was. The petite redhead from the costume ball. Miss Red Corvette.

An exotic dancer. *How could he?*

She awoke with a start. Devon was sitting up, looking at her.

"You sleeped a long time," he said, patting her cheek with his small hand.

"Guess I did," Jessica said, her mind hazy as she forced herself to sit up. Remembering the magazine article, her mood rapidly deteriorated. "Let's go downstairs. Lyddy's probably got a snack for you."

After depositing her son with Lydia in the kitchen, Jessica wandered out to the barn. She wasn't ready to confront Dane; she needed to think through what, if anything, there was to say. She remembered with chagrin her words to Irma Carvey. Tabloid stories were never to be believed. Her own publicist had warned her many times in the early days, when she would see her name associated with all kinds of lies and sordid sensation.

Inside the barn, she stood before Mariah's stall and watched the horse. She did, indeed, seem like a calm animal. Jessica issued a little huff; Dane would force the issue, wouldn't he?

I can do it, she thought haughtily. I can learn to not be afraid. They're just big dumb animals, right?

Carefully she unlatched the stall door and crept inside, then closed the door behind her. Mariah lifted her head and issued a snort.

"Nice horse," Jessica said softly, steeling herself to move closer, to stroke the mare's mane the way Dane had shown her. "Good girl..." This is easy. She's not really so big, not nearly as big as Whiskey or Barleycorn. Mariah turned her head to look Jessica squarely in the eyes, pushing her muzzle at Jessica's hand. Startled, Jessica backed away, and the horse turned to follow.

"Oh, snap. This isn't what I wanted to do." Backed into the corner of the stall, Jessica flattened herself against the wall. "Good girl," she panted, as Mariah took another step toward her.

What am I going to do now? This horse is going to step on me, or bite me, or God knows what! She took a deep breath and attempted to calm herself. "This is ridiculous. It's just a horse. Just a horse. A gentle horse, Dane said you were gentle, you'd better be, or I'll kill him... oh Dane, where are you?"

This is almost more than I can handle. Truly more than I deserve. Somehow, I always believed it could be this way, but I figured I'd missed my chance. To be given another one is...

Dane stopped typing and frowned at the words on his screen. The wedding was three days away, and it was like he was waiting for something to happen. To go wrong.

Closing the computer, he stood up and stretched. What else did he have to do today? Jessica had taken care of most of the arrangements. Tom and Roxanne would arrive tomorrow, Christine and Nick the following day. They had invited some high-profile friends from L.A., and the immediate neighbors.

Down in the kitchen, Dane sat at the breakfast bar beside Devon and stole a strawberry from his plate.

"Hey!" Devon complained, then laughed at Dane's comic attempt to hide the evidence.

"Where's your mom, slugger?"

"Don't know. She went outside. We took a big ol' nap today. Well, she did. I was awake the whole time."

"Sure, you were. Lyd, you know where Alex and Zoe are?"

"Peter took them to the Perons'. They have a couple of baby goats just born today."

Dane nodded and decided to look for Jessica. He almost didn't check the barn; it was the last place he would have expected her to go. Still, the barn door was not closed as tightly as he or Greg would have left it.

"Jess?" he called, once inside.

"Yes! I'm over here."

"Wow. You're really determined, aren't you?" he said with a laugh, leaning against the outside of the stall door.

"Could you, please, just get me out of here?"

"What? Are you glued to the wall?"

"No. Just—just move her aside so I can get out."

"Move her? Are you kidding?" Dane chuckled. "She's a stubborn little gal. Kinda like you. Beautiful, but tough."

"You said she was gentle."

"Did she kick you or something?"

"No, but..."

Dane couldn't help but enjoy Jessica's dilemma. He shook his head slowly. "How did you get back there, darlin'?"

"I walked in, fool. I came in here to think. I know you always come in here when you need to think."

"And just what important things do you have on your mind?"

Jessica tossed her hair behind her shoulder. "Katrina Vidal, for one!"

Dane felt his eyebrows lift in surprise. He rubbed his chin thoughtfully, watching the defiance on Jessica's face grow. "She was my trainer. What about her?" he finally asked.

Jessica set her jaw but lowered her eyes. "Are you still seeing her?"

Dane eyed Jessica, wondering just how much she knew and how much she needed to know. "Come on out and we'll talk about it."

"Make the horse move."

"Come around her. She won't hurt you."

"Please, Dane, just... she's blocking my way."

"Let's show a little faith here, Jess." Giving her a hard stare, he lowered his voice. "In me. Jesus, we're getting married in a couple of days."

Jessica remained frozen in her spot, looking from the horse's big head to Dane's eyes.

"Do you really think I'd be sleeping with a stripper and proposing to you at the same time?"

Their eyes locked on one another, an eternity passing before Jessica began to slowly approach the horse, edging her way around the mare and closer to the stall door. Dane opened the door and she hurried out.

Stunned, Dane watched as she stormed past him and toward the house. And when his wits returned, he broke into a jog to catch up with her.

"Hold on there," he called, grasping her arm and trying to impede her flight. "We need to settle this right now."

Jessica turned, her face filled with confusion. "Okay. Let's. Why were you bailing her out of jail, and why didn't you tell me? You were sleeping with her, weren't you?"

"Hell, yes. I did. A few times... months ago. Last winter. It was a nothing sort of deal. But we stopped seeing each other, and then she got picked up on a bum rap. She had no one else to call that night. I probably shouldn't have done it, but I did. And out of respect for her, I didn't tell anyone. Not even you. I guess I should have, and I'm sorry."

Jessica stared at him for a long moment, her thoughts unreadable.

She's trying to believe me. And how can I blame her if she doesn't? My track record stinks.

"Before you go trying and convicting me, you might want to remember a time when you were doing the explaining, to someone else who preferred to believe the worst. I'm not any guiltier than you were then."

At his reference to the incident, so long ago, that had caused Mac to leave her in devastation, Jessica's eyes grew soft and saddened. Wordlessly and with some obvious hesitation, she wrapped her arms around Dane's waist and hugged him tightly, then pulled quickly away and strode purposefully toward the house.

God, help me keep this woman. I will do anything.

Twenty-Four

Third and Final Husband

The champagne flowed freely on the afternoon of June 14th. Dane wore a light linen suit and a perpetual grin, most often turned upon his glowing bride, and Jessica felt her world just might be coming together at last.

The heavy, crocheted gown needed no alterations. Roxanne and Jessica took a short walk to the rear, grassy backyard and sat down together at the patio table. Inside, the reception was in full swing.

"Dane looks like the cat that swallowed the canary," Roxanne observed, and Jessica gave her a smiling shrug. She was too happy to consider analyzing anything about anybody else today.

"He always looks that way."

"I heard he bought you a horse."

Jessica nodded her head slowly. "That, he did. He can't stand it that I don't ride."

"He's a man used to getting his own way."

Jessica started to question her newly re-acquainted friend but remembered her credo for the day: nothing was important enough to cast a shadow on her wedding day. Besides, Roxanne was still acting aloof and detached. It wouldn't do to rock the boat. Not today.

Silently, they watched the children playing on the lawn. Devon was delighted to see Christine's daughter again, and together the preschoolers ran rampant. Zoe shadowed her father most of the time, quietly observing the goings-on. Peter had enlisted Alexander's help in making sure the guests' glasses stayed filled.

"When's Chrissie's baby due?" Roxanne asked.

"Oh, about any minute now."

"The ceremony was nice."

"Dane wrote some of that."

"How's Devon taking all this?"

Jessica looked squarely at Roxanne. "He's completely devoted to Dane. He's already calling him 'Pop'."

"Will he go by Pierce?"

"Dane wants to adopt him, but not change his name. If we get Benjamin, he will be Benjamin MacKendall Pierce. Looks like we might get legal custody of Zoe, too."

Roxanne's eyes drifted back to the children on the lawn. "I hope it all works out for you."

Jessica lifted her chin. Roxanne's statement, while appropriate, was decidedly flat. Still, she chose to ignore her friend's melancholy mood. "I always thought I'd have more children. Of my own, I mean."

"Has Dane considered trying to reverse his vasectomy?"

Startled, Jessica turned back. "Why, I have no idea. We've never discussed it. It's been a long time... does that really work?"

"Sometimes. Some people think it's worth a try. But I would imagine it might be a little risky adding even more kids to Dane's plate."

"Risky?" Jessica asked, finally allowing her patience to be tried. She was ready to shake Roxanne.

"I just don't see him as much of a patriarch, if you grasp my meaning." Roxanne stood. "I'm expecting a message from an important client. My cell has no service out here. May I use your computer to check my email?"

Jessica stood also, looking away and wetting her lips. Drawing in a deep breath, she didn't look back at Roxanne. "Of course. It's upstairs in Dane's office. I need to see to our guests anyway."

·♥·♥·♥·♥·♥·

Peter Welles was filling the coffee pot when Jessica wandered into the kitchen the next morning. An ice pack tied onto the top of his perpetually worn baseball cap, Peter was practically staggering as he struggled to walk erect.

"Coffee, dear?" he asked, a grimace on his normally cheerful face.

"Sure. Where's Lyd?"

"Sleepin'."

Jessica lifted an eyebrow but held her tongue. Neon lights could not have made the word "hangover" more apparent.

Peter squinted at her from across the kitchen. "I see you're none the worse this morning."

Jessica crossed her arms and grinned. "As wedding nights go, it was tolerable." She shook her head. "But Mr. Pierce is nursing a bit of a headache this morning, so don't feel bad."

"Oh, I do. I feel terribly bad, for both of us." Peter clasped his hands in prayer before the coffee brewer. "C'mon, you wicked machine!"

"You know what they say about a watched pot," Jessica advised. Peter only grumbled in response.

As soon as the coffee was done, Jessica poured a cup and trotted back upstairs to the bedroom she now shared with Dane.

"My angel," he murmured, sitting up and taking a sip of the coffee. "Happy honeymoon."

"Thanks. Happy honeymoon to you, too."

"What do you say we ditch all these people and take off for Cancun or something?"

"Sure. Then Paris, Naples, and let's not forget Rio."

"Rio has possibilities," Dane allowed. "Or we could go back to Amande."

"Amande?" Jessica paused, her hand on the drapery cord.

"Sure. We have friends there, remember?"

"I remember eating bullfrogs. And bugs. And you and Mac fighting."

"We had the best reason in the world to be fighting." Dane's eyes were warm and thoughtful. "Do you also remember the balmy nights, the white sands, and the steel drum band?"

"I remember fainting a couple of times." Jessica sat down on the edge of the bed, her vision leaving Dane and traveling back to the days spent filming *Lost Season*. "I remember dancing with you in the cantina."

"I remember mad, passionate, unprotected sex on the beach."

"You would."

"And you do."

"How could I forget? I could barely walk afterward." Jessica went to the dresser and began brushing her hair, a rosy blush tinting her cheeks. The sight of the new rings on her finger gave her pause. "We can go back if you'd like. It might be fun."

"Ah, the mention of lovemaking and you're in, eh?"

"That's not what I meant. And anyway, what would we do with the kids?"

"Leave them here. We'll only be gone a few days. Pete and Lydia can handle the little squabs while we're gone, then we'll go out to Minnie and visit our new son."

Jessica whirled about, hairbrush poised. "Oh Dane, do you really think we'll get him someday?"

Dane crawled out of bed and took her into his arms. "Of course, we will. I know I haven't been much help to you on this. I needed to get things squared away for Zoe, but it's looking better all the time. We'll get Phillip Stern in on it. There's no reason in the world we can't make this work."

"I hope you're right."

"Oh, by the way, there's a little wedding gift for you in the closet," Dane said, reaching for a pair of swim trunks he'd draped over a chair.

Jessica shoved open the sliding door and turned around, puzzled.

"That cardboard tube there. Hand it to me." Dane took the tube and slipped his fingers into one end, withdrawing a rolled stack of blueprints and spreading them out on the unmade bed. "What do you think?"

Jessica peered at the plans and her heart quickened. "This is a house," she murmured, turning the large sheets on the bed like a massive book. "For us?"

"Yeah. I found this nice lot on a hilltop in Malibu, and figured we'd need a winter home that was a little more suitable than the beach house. Like it?"

"God, it's beautiful! I can't believe it! Big enough for all our various children, too."

Dane once again pulled her close. "Of course, we should keep the beach house, too, for when all our various children become too taxing..."

She accepted a kiss, then smacked him on the behind. "You'd better shower and get dressed if we're going to Amande."

When she returned to the kitchen, Tom Jarrick was sitting at the table perusing the newspaper. Dark eyebrows knitted in concern, he frowned as he turned the pages, yet brightened when Jessica sat down across from him.

"Mrs. Pierce! What's that saying? Always a bride, never a... damn. Slips my mind."

"Very funny. Roxanne still in bed?"

"She's getting dressed. We are going to venture a little horseback ride this morning."

"Good luck. Lord knows there's an assortment of horses to choose from out there."

"She's hesitant. Always worrying that she might fall or something. She's afraid to risk another miscarriage. Of course, she always assumes she might be pregnant."

Jessica lowered herself slowly into the chair across from Tom. "What miscarriage?" she asked.

Tom again creased his handsome forehead. "You didn't know?"

Jessica shook her head. "When did this happen?"

"I'm sorry. I didn't realize she hadn't told you." Tom's face reflected his astonishment. "It was in January. While you were working on that picture. She was already still so distraught about Mac. There was no physical reason the doctors could determine. She was only three months along."

Jessica drew in a deep breath. She couldn't fathom why Roxanne would not tell her something so important. Unless... unless she hadn't been listening.

"I am so sorry, Tom. She didn't tell me. I'm... I'm just speechless. I wish I had known."

"She's been getting some counseling. It's been really rough." Now Tom sighed. "It might be better not to say anything right away. Put a little space around it. You two can slowly get back in touch, and she'll tell you about it herself. We're still trying, but I don't think her frame of mind is conducive to, well, conception."

Jessica nodded slowly. So many loose ends could be tied by Tom's story. Her heart ached for her friend, who'd had to suffer so many losses in such a short time.

"She really dislikes Dane," she murmured, more to herself than to Tom.

"No, she just really loved Mac. We all did." He placed a fatherly hand over hers. "For the record, I can't think of anyone I'd rather see you with than Dane. He's a good guy, and nobody can challenge the fact that he would lay down his life for you. You've both been through enough. You should be able to shape a marriage that works."

"Thanks, Tom. That means so much to me. Please, would you let me know if anything else happens, in case Rox doesn't tell me?"

Tom was quick to assure her that he would keep her informed.

With a heavy sigh, Jessica turned her thoughts to her new husband and children, and the hastily planned honeymoon.

•♥•♥•♥•♥•♥•

"Married! Damn it! That figures."

Denehy hung up the phone and thumped his fisted hand on the desk. "That figures," he repeated. This was a challenging setback.

"Married. Big deal. Anyone could find some big creep with an inflated ego to marry," Irma Carvey mumbled, scrunching up the phone message and tossing it into the wastebasket. "Sad, really."

Thumbing through the papers in her file, Irma pulled one out and put it on top. Mr. and Mrs. DeWitt would be Benjamin MacKendall's proud new parents. Not wealthy, certainly not socialites, but they met the criteria with flying colors. Hell, they even had a swing set in their backyard, and three other children, all with good teeth and clean socks. They'd welcome another boy into their family, they claimed.

In fact, she was betting her entire life savings on their greed.

For on paper, Chuck DeWitt ran a profitable mail-order business from his home. His tax returns were neatly in order, and he had fifty thousand dollars in the bank. Had the funds been verified? Of course. Irma had seen to it herself. The source of the recently deposited funds? Carefully she penned the letters, "I-N-H-E-R-I-T-A-N-C-E." Verified by? "I.C."

The governess job she had been offered in upstate Michigan provided for her to bring her young son. A perfect arrangement. Perfect for her, for Benjamin, and for the formerly bankrupt DeWitts, who cared a lot more about their sudden windfall than they did about gaining another child.

Now, all she had to do was get that MacKendall woman out of the picture. For good.

•♥•♥•♥•♥•♥•

Amande.

It was not at all as she remembered it. They had been told about a renovation, but neither Jessica nor Dane expected the changes to the Marquis they discovered when exiting the limousine at the hotel's new grand entrance. The broad expanse of window glass behind the registration desk revealed an endless beach of crystalline white sands, beautifully maintained and dotted with relaxing, presumably wealthy, vacationers.

"Where are the bungalows?" Jessica asked the registrar, who was busily punching numbers into a state-of-the-art computer system.

"Bungalows?"

"The little cabins you used to have on the beach," Dane said, gesturing past the long, three story hotel buildings to each side of them.

"Oh, those were torn down before I came here. The place became so popular they had to expand."

"Popular? Nobody came here before."

"Before. Yeah, before that movie it was dead, I hear."

"Movie?" Jessica asked, coyly pulling her sunglasses away from her face. "What movie would that be?"

The young clerk looked up from his keyboard. "It was called Lost Season, Mrs.... Mrs.... oh, shit. I mean, oh gosh, I'm sorry. You're..."

"Mr. and Mrs. Roger Boyer. Could we have our keys now? You can send the bellman with our bags," Dane said impatiently.

Jessica offered a broad smile at the flustered clerk, allowing Dane to usher her away toward the elevator.

"It's on the top floor," the young man sputtered after them.

"Penthouse usually is..." Dane muttered, and Jessica giggled.

"Not exactly a twelve-hundred-dollar mattress," Dane complained, stretching out on the bed with his arms folded behind his neck. "It'll do, though."

Jessica pushed aside the draperies and opened the French doors leading to a large, private patio deck. The view was unrivaled. "Oh Dane, you must see this. It's... stunning."

"Not the same, though."

"Nothing is the same, really. Everything is always changing."

"Except for one thing." Dane beckoned for her to join him on the bed, where he encircled her with his arms. Holding her close, cuddling her against him, he pressed his lips to her forehead. "This... will never change."

Jessica didn't answer, having no appropriate response in mind. She was still in awe of his affection, still getting used to his tender love.

They lay quiet for a while. Jessica thought Dane might have fallen asleep; it had been a long, tedious trip. But soon he issued a deep sigh.

"How are things with Roxanne? She seemed okay at the wedding, right?"

Jessica mirrored his sigh. "Not really." She didn't want to disturb the gentle ambiance that surrounded them, but knew she had to tell him what had transpired. "She was still very aloof. I talked to Tom about her the next morning. He told me she had a miscarriage in January, and that she hasn't been the same since."

Dane uttered a groan.

"After that false pregnancy she had a few years back, this was a terrible blow. And she never told me about it. She's going through therapy and everything."

"Man. That's rough."

"Did you know that Tom had a vasectomy reversal?" Jessica said, her voice sounding more conspiratorial than she had planned. She sensed Dane was grinning, although her eyes were still closed as she lay against his chest.

"It's not the kind of chit-chat in which we usually indulge, darlin'."

"And now, she worries all the time that she'll be pregnant and lose another baby. It must be hell." Jessica nestled closer. "Anyway, that was really cool of him to do that. His son was already grown when he met Rox. She wanted—still wants—a baby with him and I don't blame her. It's the ultimate connection."

"Mmm."

"I still can't understand why she didn't tell me, or why she's so uptight. We've been like sisters... for years. It's like she blames me for something."

"I gave up trying to understand her a long time ago. Don't lose too many brain cells over this, okay? It might not be worth it. We've got a lot of issues to deal with already."

"I know. I just... just hate it."

"Mmm."

They dined by candlelight in the hotel dining room. They had "dressed" for dinner, and Dane looked as handsome as she'd ever seen him. The flickering flames gave a glint to the jade in his eyes, eyes that focused on hers with both desire and devotion. Emotions at a high, Jessica felt an on-going rush that would not subside. She could barely eat.

It did not feel like they were married. It was more like a date, despite their long history of entanglement. There was no idle chitchat, no talk of the children or the ranch or the next film. She forgot, for the time, that this was the man who had once broken her naïve heart, who had nearly trashed her marriage but had gone on to help deliver her son, who had risked his life more than once for her. Instead, this was the man she wanted to keep under lock and key. A man whose love and attention she craved and would forever cherish.

Their love, she knew, was impossibly complicated. But tonight would be different. Tonight would be a simple man, a simple woman, an exquisitely uncomplicated affair between two people addicted to love and addicted to each other.

They walked on the beach, neither aware nor caring about the hour. He led her to the place they both sought, a small alcove of boulders cropping out of the sand.

"Care for a quick tumble?" he asked, his eyes crinkling in merriment as he pretended to loosen his bowtie.

Jessica laughed. "No, thank you. I'm not into quick, and I'm too grown up now to think that sex on the beach is all that glamorous."

"Ha! You'd rather be tied to that too-soft mattress upstairs, would you?"

"I'd rather be tied to you." She reached up and gave the bowtie a little tug.

"Ah, but you are. For life, woman."

Her smile faded at the implication. Life, she'd learned, was a tenuous thing. Yet despite the comic expression, she knew Dane's words were from the heart, and she felt her blush spreading all over again. She made a solemn, silent vow to make the most of their life together.

It was dawn before they both slept. And while Dane did not actually tie her to the bed, he did see that her every desire was met.

And Jessica was far from worrying about satisfying Dane; their lovemaking had never been so complete. In her fairy tale state of mind, she wished it could last forever.

TWENTY-FIVE

Disappointment and Deceit

"What? I can't believe this! We had an appointment! This is absolutely... irresponsible and really, down right mean." Jessica was on her feet, arms akimbo, her voice rising beyond propriety in the small office. Irma Carvey leaned back in her chair, fingers laced in her lap.

"Mrs. Pierce. I warned you that approval of your petition was not likely. I'm sorry you made this trip for nothing. Mr. Morrison was unaware that Mr. and Mrs. De—uh, another couple, had already been awarded custody."

Jessica walked to the only window in the room and looked out. A few older children were tossing a basketball around in the play yard below.

"And you couldn't even make a phone call to let us know?"

"I regret that we couldn't reach you in... wherever you were entertaining yourselves..."

Ignoring the obvious barb, Jessica responded coldly. "You could have called our home. We are constantly in touch."

"Oh, yes, that place where you left your existing children to stay alone with an unmarried, undocumented couple. That home."

Dane stood up. "Jess, let's get out of here."

Jessica whirled about and again approached the desk. "This is utterly preposterous. If my husband were here, he would never stand for this. You wouldn't have given him all this grief!"

Irma Carvey smirked and closed the file on her desk. "I thought your husband was here, Mrs. Pierce."

Jessica colored. "I meant... my *late* husband."

"Despite the fact that it is, unfortunately, a moot point, Mr. MacKendall was a blood relative. You are not. Good afternoon."

Seething, Jessica stormed from the office with Dane close behind.

He didn't know how to approach her. He'd rarely seen such rage in the woman he now called his wife. They went to lunch, and he ordered her a drink.

"What's this for?"

"To calm you down."

"I don't need calming down. I need an attorney. Or a gun."

"This isn't over yet," Dane said, handing her the Bloody Mary the waiter had delivered.

"You bet it's not over. God, I hate that woman!"

"She's a peach, all right. I've already put in a call to Phillip."

"Somehow, I don't think there's anything he can do," Jessica bemoaned, then drank half of the spicy cocktail in one draught. "She's a witch."

"That may be, but we can't give up yet."

Her agitation wore Jessica out. By bedtime she was lethargic and withdrawn, and declined Dane's half-hearted advances.

·♥·♥·♥·♥·♥·

The following morning, she was alert and matter-of-fact, and anxious to get home to Devon. Dane, however, had more business to attend He bid her an affectionate goodbye at the airport and then drove his rental car to the Marian Pierce House.

"Gosh, if we'd known you were coming, we would have cleaned up a little," Paula said as Dane came around the front counter and into the back office.

"No problem. I just need to look through some of the financials, correspondence, that kind of stuff."

"Sure. You can use Char's desk. We, uh, left it the way it was."

"Great."

Dane spent the better part of the day digging through ledgers, files and notebooks. Anything that seemed even remotely interesting was painstakingly copied and stuffed into his briefcase. Last, he tackled Charlene's own desk.

"I suppose the police or the Feds have already been through this?"

"No, not really," Paula answered with a shrug.

Dane lifted his eyebrows but did not comment.

He'd almost finished, coming up with nothing more than an invitation to Jessica and Mac's wedding and a half empty prescription bottle for Valium. In the lowermost drawer was a small clutch purse. Dane started to leave it there, but decided he'd make a thorough search or none at all. Unzipping the top, he winced at the sight of two wrapped tampons stuffed into one side section of the purse.

"Damn," he muttered, gingerly pushing them aside. Beneath them was a small cluster of cards rubber-banded together. A credit card, bearing a woman's name he did not recognize, was on top. A well-worn letter, folded ridiculously small and dated thirty years before, was from Chuck MacKendall and begged his only daughter to come home. Last, two photographs.

One, faded with age, was of two tow-headed children with huge brown eyes, possibly three and five years of age. The boy bore a remarkable likeness to Devon.

Dane sighed heavily and slipped the photo into the breast pocket of his shirt. The second photo was recent; Dane's heart began to pound with anticipation. Charlene looked good; her waist long hair, back to its natural, gleaming blond, hung in waves around her. A happy, contented grin adorned her face. Dane smiled despite his grim determination. Next, his eyes examined the young man in the picture with Charlene. Dark, unshaven and sleepy looking, the man had his arm around Charlene.

"Paula? Do you recognize this guy?"

"Uh... that would be Frankie. She dated him for a while. He was no big deal. Stayed here a couple of nights to dry out."

"Has he been around at all since?"

"Nope. Didn't show for the funeral, either."

"Got a last name?"

"No. We don't require it. That's all I know. Except that he drove a nice car. But some of them do. Dealers."

"You think he was? A drug dealer?"

"Could be. No way to know, now."

"Hmmm." Dane pocketed this photo as well and packed up to go.

Back in his hotel room, he laid out the individual pieces of potential "evidence," carefully examining each one. Beside them he placed the photograph of Charlene's erstwhile boyfriend.

He sighed. "Frankie" did not, in any way, resemble a politician. For one thing, he was too young. Probably even younger than Charlene. And anyway, he was likely only one of many male companions Charlene had entertained during the past few years.

Far more interesting was a sizable donation funding most of the newly completed wing. The donor was a local man, one Steven F. Conway.

Dane had only skimmed the information while sitting at Charlene's desk. Now, upon closer inspection, the words seemed to leap out at him.

"Bingo." Dane took his yellow highlighter and dragged the point across the words beneath Conway's name. Minnesota House of Representatives.

There it was. A connection. But why? While it was certainly not unusual for politicians to make charitable contributions of this sort, it struck Dane as odd. A visit to the representative was in order.

•♥•♥•♥•♥•♥•

"Mr. Pierce! What a pleasure to finally meet you. My girls will never believe this. Here, have a seat." The congressman released Dane's hand and gestured to a large leather chair opposite the desk behind which he was now sitting. "To what do I owe this pleasant surprise?"

"I appreciate your seeing me on such short notice. I was just in town, cleaning up things a bit at the House. My late partner was a fastidious bookkeeper, and I fear I've let things go somewhat since she passed away."

"I know what you mean. I'm terrible at record-keeping."

"Yeah, well, I hear they don't give awards in heaven for keeping every gas receipt. I did notice, though, your generous help in building the addition. I wanted to thank you for that."

Steven Conway grinned, looking down at his fingers, which were fiddling with a gold letter opener. "It was a very worthy cause." He was older than Dane had imagined. In his fifties, with a shining scalp and a small, ski-slope nose. A friendly face, nonetheless.

Dane nodded, his eyes traveling over the other items on the congressman's desk. They lit on a pewter-framed photograph of the man, a woman and two middle-school aged girls. "Lovely family."

"Oh! Yes. Aren't they beautiful? They make my life worth living. You have kids, Mr. Pierce?"

Dane started to suggest that he preferred 'Dane,' but decided he liked the formality and the implied respect. "Yes. I have two daughters also, and two sons. Handfuls, all of them."

"I hear you. I have a son too, but the rascal wasn't around the day we took that. Baseball game he couldn't get out of. I'm sure you get that."

"Indeed, I do. So, I understand you've just announced a run for the governor's seat?"

Conway blushed. "Why, yes. News travels fast, doesn't it? But yes, I think I can fix a few things for Minnesota. It's not an easy job, that's for sure. Rogers has had a time of it."

"I wouldn't know, to tell you the truth. I'm strictly a California boy. But I wish you the best of luck. I know Charlene thought a lot of you."

"Charlene?"

"MacKendall. My late partner."

"Oh, yes! I'm sorry. I didn't think of her by her first name. A tragedy, that. I only met her once or twice, toured the facility, met the staff, but she was a very nice girl. Worked hard for that place. Lord knows it's been a help to the community."

Only met her once.

"You think so?"

"Oh, absolutely. A lot of young people have been rescued from terrible situations. At least that's what I've heard."

"Well, good. That's what she wanted. That, and a child of her own. Did you know she was pregnant at the time of the crash?"

"Yes, I remember something about that from the news. An awful shame."

"My wife and I are trying to adopt the child."

"Oh?" Conway looked up, and then his gaze drifted to his telephone as if he expected it to ring. "Well, that's... that's very noble."

"Well, technically, he is my wife's nephew. It's a family thing. But I guess there's some hang up with the biological father." Dane watched closely for Conway's reaction, however, the politician only stood and picked up his Daytimer from the desk. Clearly, the interview was ending. Dane wasn't sure what to think.

"It's been a real pleasure, Mr. Pierce. I'd like to talk with you some more, but I'm late for a meeting. I thank you for your support, and for taking the time to stop by."

"I'll be in touch, Mr. Conway. You can count on it."

·♥·♥·♥·♥·♥·

"When are you coming home?" Jessica asked, her voice tinged with what sounded to Dane like a touch of self-pity.

"In a few days. I have some business in L.A."

"What kind of business?"

"My physical, for one thing. I'll stop in on Phillip Stern, and Woody wants me to meet with Rettner about that pilot flick. Can you spare me for a bit?"

"If I have to."

Now, she did have a decided pout in her tone. Dane took a deep breath. "I'm sorry, sweetie."

"Did you hear anything more from those jerks at the adoption office?"

"We won't hear anything more from them, Jess. We need to create a little stir of some kind. I'll see what Phillip says, okay?"

"Okay. I miss you."

"Miss you too. Take care."

Irma Carvey dropped her office keys into the white letter envelope and sealed it, then placed the envelope squarely in the center of her bare desk. No one had been surprised or moved in any way by her sudden resignation. Now, only the short drive to the Bandorfs' house stood between her and her new "son," Bailey. She'd never liked the name Benjamin.

Mrs. Bandorf had been crying. "We bought him this new little Vikings shirt for a going-away gift," she said, dabbing at the corner of her eye.

"It's cute. Now, if you'll just help me get his bags into my car, I can get on my way to his new parents. They are so anxious."

"They should be. He's just a... a joy," Mr. Bandorf said, taking a suitcase in each hand and brushing past Irma, who was bouncing young Benjamin in her arms.

"Now, now, don't let him see you upset. You knew, as foster parents, this would eventually happen. Don't spoil things for him. Children are very receptive."

"It's just that... that we did apply, you know... I still don't know why we were turned down. We've had him since he was born. He's like a part of us now," Mrs. Bandorf lamented. "I'm sorry. You're right. I'll be fine."

"It's too bad, Mrs. Bandorf. I'm sure you're quite qualified. For whatever reason, the new parents were more qualified. I'm sorry. Truly. Now, I'll be on my way. I wish you the best of luck."

Irma could see the Bandorfs embracing in their driveway as she drove away. "A shame, really. Oh well."

With her kidnapped orphan just beginning to whimper in the backseat, Irma Carvey got on the Interstate and headed north.

Jessica hung up the phone. Dane hadn't answered at the house in Malibu, and his cell phone was never turned on. The weather was warm, the children were romping outside; she had long stopped worrying about their every move, lulled into complacency by the tranquil peace of the ranch and surrounding wilderness. She roamed the house, bored, discontent and with growing anxiety. She really did miss Dane and felt slighted by his going to Los Angeles instead of coming home.

It was with this thought in mind that she leaped for the phone when it rang. Roxanne's voice on the line was more than just surprising.

"Have you got a minute?"

"More than a minute. What's up?"

"I'm calling to say I'm sorry."

Jessica felt her cheeks grow warm. She could barely believe her ears and was preparing to exonerate her friend when Roxanne continued.

"I can't keep it inside any longer. He's no good for you, he never has been, he's never done anything but hurt you. I'm sorry, Jess, but I need to tell what I know, and I hate that it will upset you but it's for the best."

"What are you talking about? Who's hurt me?" Alarms began going off in Jessica's head. She already knew what Roxanne would say.

"Dane Pierce. He's not a good person. You can't see that, but you don't know what I know. You obviously haven't read what I've read.

Mac was a good man, and he deserves justice. So, I'm sorry. It... has to be done." Roxanne's voice diminished with her last few words, and the line dropped. She'd ended the call.

Slowly Jessica lowered the phone, her thoughts stricken with fear and confusion. Then, she picked it back up and hastily dialed Roxanne's number. She did not leave a message when the call went to voicemail.

The blow was a heavy one. Wandering to the couch, Jessica sat down and tried to make sense of Roxanne's words. Her friend's voice had sounded vague and disassociated, as though she was talking to herself and not Jessica.

I should call Tom. Rox has gone off the deep end.

But before she could determine how to reach Roxanne's husband, the front door swung open wide and her own walked into the room.

Twenty-Six

Suspect!

"Come in, Mrs. Jarrick. Have a seat. I'll be right with you." Murdo Denehy pulled out a chair for his guest and crossed the room to refill his coffee, holding his mug up in offer. Roxanne declined with a shake of her head. Denehy returned, picked up his pencil and took a deep breath. "Well. Shall we begin? You had a statement you wanted to make?"

"Yes. I have knowledge of Dane Pierce's guilt."

"Guilt in what way?"

"I believe he killed Mac MacKendall."

"I see. Now, you say you have knowledge. Would you also have some sort of... physical evidence pertinent to this crime?"

"Not in my possession, no. But I know about it, and where it is."

Denehy tapped his pencil eraser on the table. "You know where it is. In what form, may I ask, is this purported evidence?"

"It's a computer. He, Dane, that is, wrote in his computer about killing Mac."

"And you read this... accounting? In the computer?"

"Yes, I did. It was at his house. I already suspected as much, but when I was there for the wedding, I found it. I would have copied it to a disk, too, but Tom stopped me."

"Tom?"

"My husband. There's also a journal somewhere. Dane said something about it being too bad that Mac had read the journal, and that now he'd have to destroy it."

"Do you know where this journal might be?"

"I have an idea."

"I see. All right. Let's get this all down. I'm going to videotape you, is that okay with you?"

"Of course. Whatever it takes to bring justice."

"Fine. Let's begin. Tell me everything you remember reading, and the exact location of this... computer the last time you saw it."

·♥·♥·♥·♥·♥·

The hot water felt good. He thought about inviting Jessica to join him in the hot tub but decided he really didn't want any company while he mulled over the events of the last 72 hours.

Like a jigsaw puzzle, the bits of information he had gathered had yet to be put together. One thing was for sure; Steven Conway was a piece that didn't seem to belong. He didn't fit the role Dane had conjured, that of the philandering congressman courting the young ex-hooker and getting her pregnant. Something about his integrity, his pride, and the expressions on the faces of his family members. More, it was Dane's own instinct that caused him to shake his head. Yet there was something. Some connection, and an acknowledgment, if fleeting, that Conway knew more than he was willing to let on.

Dane filled his lungs and exhaled slowly, leaning his head back and closing his eyes. There had to be something he could do. If Conway wasn't the answer, perhaps there was another angle, one he'd missed. The doctor, for example, who had handled the blood transfusion. Maybe he should talk to the nurse at the hospital.

Charlene was, or had been, he reminded himself, a very private person.

With a silent smile, he remembered the day he'd talked with Jessica on the telephone, and she'd mentioned Charlene's pregnancy. He had been flippant, reminding her that he could not take responsibility for the baby; Jessica was aware of his inability to father children since his vasectomy eight or nine years ago. No matter that he'd not been intimate with Charlene for close to four years.

Dane sighed. Eventually he would have to face the fact that the adoption would not occur. The cards seemed stacked against them, and he was doubtful that even proof of the father's paternity would have much bearing on the case.

"Damn," he muttered. *Too bad I'm* not *the father. That would solve everything.*

No. There would have to be another way to get Jessica the baby she so wanted.

Dane reached for a hand towel and ran it across his face. There was one way. If he was brave enough to try it.

She was on the phone when he passed through their bedroom on his way to the shower.

"I know, honey. I miss him too. Every single day," she was saying, her voice low and fraught with melancholy. "No, of course no one could ever replace him."

Dane pretended to ignore her but left the bathroom door ajar.

"Megan, listen to me. I loved your daddy. He was the best. I would give anything if he could come back, but he can't, and there's nothing we can do except go on and make the best of things."

Setting his jaw, Dane reached into the shower and turned the knob on full force.

·♥·♥·♥·♥·♥·

"Sure. I was there. MacKendall punched Pierce in the face."

"What were the specifics of the fight, Mr. Wagner?" Denehy switched the phone to his other ear and grabbed up his pencil. "They were arguing about something?"

"Well, it was over Jessica. They hated each other. Word was, Mac couldn't stand the way he treated her. They were both jealous as hell. That asshole Pierce thought he had her under his thumb, then the white knight showed up on his steed. Of course, we all know how that played out. She dropped the scum ball when Mac finally found the cojones to take her."

Denehy tried to ignore the fact that Kyle Wagner had an obvious dislike for Dane Pierce.

"But this fight. What did Pierce do to provoke it?"

"Well, I wasn't actually there, mind you. But he was always baiting people, like he hoped they'd take him on. No one would. He was the boss, right? Cross him and you were off the film. Period."

"So, you didn't see MacKendall hit him?"

"Well, no, not actually. But I did see them square off in the hospital waiting room. Then they went to the cafeteria to get coffee.

It happened in there. They were alone. Pierce came out with a black eye."

"I see. Listen, Mr. Wagner, thanks for the information. I may be calling on you again."

"She's a nice girl, Detective. She likes Pierce, but he's gotta be bad for her."

Murdo Denehy hung up the phone. Jessica MacKendall Pierce was a nice girl, and he hoped he could prove his case before something terrible happened.

He added the notes from his phone call with Kyle Wagner to the file, bradding them in just above the deposition of the hotel maid who'd recounted the eavesdropped phone call between Mac and Dane. MacKendall had asked for extra pillows and had been on the phone when she'd brought them. He'd hurried about the room, she explained, in search of his wallet to tip her, the phone wedged between his ear and shoulder. She'd taken the time to check his bath towels and toiletries while he searched.

"Well, I've changed my mind. It's not a good idea... No, in fact, I don't trust you. It was stupid of me to think that you could ever... that's not true and you know it... You can just forget it. What? Listen pal, you made a promise to me..."

She'd been a little sketchy yet was certain of the gist of the conversation. But the most striking recollection was that of Mac's final words to Dane.

"Are you threatening me, Pierce? Because if you are, I say, bring it on, boy. Because guess what? I keep my promises. I said I will never leave her, and I won't. You'd have to kill me first."

Denehy shook his head. He would make this case stick. Because if there was anything of which he could be certain, it was that Dane Pierce would stop at nothing to possess Jessica. Not even murder.

Jessica watched Greg's truck until it disappeared down the unmarked road that led to the main highway. Dane had insisted upon driving to the airport, Greg beside him in quiet compliance.

The tension had been high during his brief stay. She had not related Roxanne's phone call to Dane and had regretted it since. The talk with Mac's daughter had further unnerved her, and Dane himself had seemed self-absorbed and withdrawn. They had not made love in the two nights he'd stayed.

Oh well. She felt her period coming on anyway. Jessica made a mental note to write out a message to herself as Dr. Anderson wanted her to keep a record. Her hormone levels were all over the map and he had suggested that she should consider a supplement of some kind, an idea she always pooh-poohed. She was reticent to take even an aspirin.

She turned back from the window and found Zoe at her side.

"What's up, sweetpea?"

"I miss Daddy already."

"Me too. He'll be back soon, though. He's just got a few matters to tend to in L.A." Jessica bent and gave the girl a warm hug. "You talk to your mom on the phone today?"

"Yeah. She says I gotta go back to school soon."

"Well, she's right. As much as I love having you here, you can't miss school. How do you feel about going back home?"

Zoe looked down. "I hate it. But Daddy says I can come back at Christmas."

"You know what? You're going to be fine. You've changed since you came here. Have you looked in the mirror lately?" Jessica took Zoe by the hand and led her to the guest bathroom. Indeed, Zoe had lost the baby fat look, had more color and less worry in her face. "Check this out." Jessica pulled the girl's mop of mouse brown hair back from her face and lifted her chin a bit, then dragged most of her thick bangs back as well. "What do you say we go into town and get your hair all fixed up? Then we'll shop for some new school clothes."

"I think Mom already bought me some," Zoe said, her expression dour.

"And they probably won't fit," Jessica added with a giggle.

Zoe's face brightened. "Yeah, right. Okay."

The shopping trip went well, Jessica delighting in the results of Zoe's "makeover" day. Breathless, they carried in their packages and shared the contents with Lydia, who clapped her hands with joy. Zoe was mugging for Jessica's camera when the phone rang.

"You have news?" Jessica asked upon hearing Sergeant Denehy's voice on the line.

"Yes, Mrs. MacKendall. I have some information you might want to know about."

"It's Mrs. Pierce, Detective."

"Right. Sorry. Look, I'll get right to the point. I've taken three depositions that may shed some light on your husband's... your late husband's murder. I'm sorry to tell you that Dane Pierce has been implicated."

Jessica's breath caught in her throat. It was only a moment before she was recovered enough to speak. "I don't know what you mean. Dane had nothing, nothing whatsoever to do with Mac's... death. There's obviously been some mistake."

"No, no mistake. Two individuals have come forward and are willing to testify that... that Dane was motivated and desirous to get Mac out of the picture."

Jessica forced a chuckle. "So, you're talking about opinions and hearsay. Sergeant Denehy, surely you realize that there are people in this world who may not be fond of my husband. And I'll be the first to say that Mac and Dane had their differences. But they were friends. They were like brothers, at times. You're barking up the wrong tree, so to speak."

"I wish I were, Mrs. Pierce. But this isn't looking good for him. And one of the witnesses says she knows of written evidence."

'She' knows. It could only be Rox.

"I don't think I want to be a part of this conversation any longer."

"Wait. Can you honestly say that you don't think your husband, your current husband, ever wished ill upon Mac MacKendall? Isn't it true that for a time, you and Mac were estranged—nearly broke up—all due to Dane Pierce's continual pursuit of you, a married woman?"

"That's really none of your business."

"Okay." There was a pause, and Jessica noticed that she was beginning to shake.

"Is there anything more?" she asked.

"Just this. If you should think of anything, anything at all that could alter the course of this investigation, please call me. Even if it further implicates Mr. Pierce. You owe it to yourself, and Mac, that justice is served, Jessica."

Jessica bristled at his use of her first name. "If you mean, will I turn on my own husband, you're crazy, Detective. I love my husband, not that it's any concern of yours. And besides, should any charges ever be filed, what I know or do not know about his relationship with Mac will never become public knowledge. I know that as his wife, I cannot be compelled to testify against him."

"And did you ever consider, Mrs. Pierce, that perhaps he knew that fact also when he got you to marry him?"

As a cold chill engulfed her body, Jessica hung up the phone without saying goodbye.

The talk with Rettner went well. Dane felt better than he had upon his return to L.A. For now, all he wanted to do was put the adoption, the unknown father and the murder investigation out of his mind. And what better way than to start a new film?

With some regret, he boxed up his "investigative" materials and shoved them into his file cabinet. Surely Phillip Stern would produce something and this would all be for naught. For now, there would be pre-production meetings, costume fittings, rehearsals. Location selections and product-placement deals. As a co-producer, Dane would have a hand in every aspect of *Unstable Airspace.*

Including the casting of the leading female role.

Jess would be perfect for this, he thought with a heavy sigh. But his new wife had made her wishes clear; she wanted a year off. At least a year, she had asserted. And he would give her that. He would, in fact, give her anything she wanted.

Even a baby?

The thought reminded him of one of his excuses for coming back to Southern California. Dr. Segal and his annual physical. It was nearing the fourth of July, and it would be better to try to get in before the long holiday weekend.

"You're sure you want to do this?"

"Quit asking me before I change my mind. Yes."

"It might not work."

"Fine. Just... do it."

"Okay. Monday afternoon. I want to see your labs first. Stomach okay these days?"

"Doc, my stomach is cast iron. I'm still working out, I'm married to a wonderful woman, I've got my daughter back, and life is grand.

Now, is it time for me to turn my head and cough? I've got work to do."

Dr. Segal smiled and shook his head. "Same old Dane."

·♥·♥·♥·♥·♥·

Sal Cicerelli would direct. Together, Dane and Sal watched the screen tests of the actresses that were vying for the lead role. Dane rubbed his eyes. "I don't know. You choose."

"Not easy, is it? Okay. I pick... Suzanna King."

"Nope. Not her."

"Fiona Collins?"

"Forget her. Her lips are too big."

Sal chuckled. "And you wanted me to choose."

"Lisa Lee."

"Okay. She was really my first choice." Sal patted Dane on the head and stood up to stretch. "We've got an early day tomorrow. Get some rest, will you?"

"Sure."

Back at the beach house, Dane poured over the script, striking out lines and adding them, scratching notes in the margin. He lamented that his copy was already dog-eared, and production wouldn't even start for weeks. A new copy would be forthcoming, however, as soon as his changes were effected.

At 1 a.m., he took a shower and lay atop his bed, turning on the TV. With a heavy heart, he realized he hadn't called Jessica in two days. He imagined her at home, rattling around in the big house with the children, lazily living out the end of the summer. The phone on the bedside table interrupted his thoughts.

"I can't sleep," Jessica said simply, and Dane smiled.

"Me either. How are you, sweetie?"

"I'm... nervous."

"About what?"

"Everything. It's just... I don't know."

Dane pulled himself to a sitting position. "Cough it up, darlin'. What's bothering you?"

"Denehy called me."

Dane groaned. "And what did that idiot want now? Do they have any new leads?" He waited for his wife to respond; her silence put him on edge. "Well?"

"I don't know how to tell you this. Some people think... that you're involved." Jessica paused, then hurried on. "I told him he was crazy! You couldn't possibly have wished Mac any harm. I don't know who would say such awful things."

"Any number of people, Jess. Don't let it bother you. It's just talk, idle talk."

"Right. Of course."

"You do know that, right? You don't think—"

"He said there is someone who has some written evidence. Something you wrote about Mac. Is that true?"

Damnation. God damn it!

"Jessica. You just said that you knew I'd never... what the hell is going on? It's... lies. All lies. This is... crap! That's what it is. That asshole Denehy is running for District Attorney. He just wants the press. It isn't even his case! He has no authority."

There was silence on the line. Dane took a deep breath; his heart was pounding in his chest and his palms were damp. *Calm down. You're just making this worse.*

"I'm sorry," he said, his voice strained. "I'm just so... offended by all this. I already knew that Denehy was making accusations. I had hoped he'd have the good sense to leave you out of this, Jess. He has no leads, so he's trying to create a scenario that just doesn't exist. That's all it is, sweetie. Let's not get kerfuffled. Because then he wins."

"Okay. Whatever you say," she said, but Dane was unconvinced of her sincerity. He hung up the phone knowing that neither of them would be able to sleep.

Labor Day found Jessica saying goodbye to her new, upgraded stepdaughter in Salt Lake City. She'd taken the short hop flight to Salt Lake with the girl, Devon and Alexander in tow, and couldn't have been prouder of Zoe's new look and demeanor. A chubby, despondent child had become a healthy, happy, pre-adolescent with a sunny smile and a new, flattering wardrobe. Secretly, Jessica wished she could be a fly on the wall when Rita laid eyes on her daughter. She only hoped Rita wouldn't find a way to punish Zoe for the change.

At least Dane, she knew, would be watching.

"You call me any time, you hear?" Jessica said, tousling Zoe's new, chic haircut. "At least once a week. I'll be missing you so much!"

Zoe hugged her hard and then took the flight attendant's hand. Blinking away her tears, Jessica took the boys by the hand and turned back toward the airport lobby to look for her brother-in-law, Nick Reeves.

It was Alexander's first trip to the lodge. In the back seat of "Uncle Nick's" van, Devon bounced up and down with excitement. "Did Aunt Christine make cookies?"

"You bet. And Angel can't wait to see you."

Jessica smiled. She had not seen her twin sister since the wedding and was anxious to meet her new little niece, Bridgett. The baby had, thankfully, waited until after the wedding to be born, coming about the time Jessica and Dane arrived on Amande.

"She is just so precious," Jessica said, cradling the baby as she paced the warm kitchen in the lodge. "Bridgett. What a wonderful name. How lucky to have two girls."

"I know. Nick still wants a son, of course..." Christine said, folding her arms and leaning back against the sink counter. "I'm not of a mind to have any more right now. Vaginal delivery isn't all it's cracked up to be, by the way."

Jessica laughed. "I do remember something about discomfort," she said. "Though I imagine having the electricity on does help?"

"That's right, you had Devon during a power outage. I'd forgotten!" her sister said with a grin. "That must have been a treat."

"Dane was running around like a madman lighting a Coleman lantern, and getting clean towels, and I nearly broke his hand in the process..."

"Dane? I thought Mac delivered the baby."

Jessica's smile faded. "Why, yes, of course he did. It's just that Dane... Dane was there the whole time. He had to break into the house that night... Mac wasn't home... until later."

Dane. Odd that she had only remembered Dane being there, at first. And even odder, it was a comforting feeling.

"Right. Seems to me Dane has always been there." Christine responded. "Well, do you remember how to change a diaper?" she asked brightly, and Jessica let the feeling pass. As she laid the baby on the changing table, a new feeling took its place. A fullness, tinged with a bittersweet warmth. The scent of baby powder and the sight of two tiny feet jabbing at her belly overwhelmed her maternal instinct and she closed her eyes briefly.

Dash the thought, Jess. It ain't gonna happen.

She had trouble falling asleep. Alone in a king-sized bed, Jessica tossed half the night. Dane had been in Los Angeles for over two months, and filming of Unstable Airspace was just beginning. He'd promised to come home next week. And while he called nearly every night, their conversations had become trite and perfunctory. Dane seemed distanced by more than the miles, and Jessica worried about the reason. Ever since the late-night phone conversation where she had related the accusations, Dane had grown cooler and more aloof.

It's the film, of course. He always gets this way.

She recalled the day they'd met, on the set of Bellerive. He'd taken a few moments away from his preoccupation to talk to her but had gone back into his manic-film mode soon after. Always driven by perfectionism, Dane was hard to live with while working. She should be glad he wasn't home.

Yet she wasn't. Glad, that is. She missed him, wanted him by her side. But until he came home, she could not begin to repair the damage she may have done by her inopportune moment of doubt.

She had heard nothing more from Roxanne and had tried to set the whole incident aside. It was too painful to think about. Phillip Stern had filed an appeal to the adoption outcome, but Jessica knew in her heart it was a mere formality, and that after several months of waiting they would hear that the case had been thrown out. By now, little Benjamin had celebrated his first birthday and Jessica could only hope that he was happy with his new family.

It had been okay, really, until she'd lost her new daughter to school and met her new infant niece for the first time. Now, the longing for a baby had returned full force, landing her back into an emotional maelstrom.

She turned once more in the bed. He'd be home soon, and everything would be fine again.

Twenty-Seven

Mom Two

The drive from Jackson Hole's small airport to the ranch was the longest part of the journey for Dane. Chagrined to find himself nibbling at his own thumbnail, he cursed. *It shouldn't be this way. I should be happy to be coming home to the woman I love. She should be happy I am coming home. But is she?*

She'd been less than cheerful on the phone. Chilly, perhaps. Maybe it was just himself. His craziness over the film. His worry that the adoption appeal was going nowhere.

She did embrace him, long and hard, at the front door. But eye contact was brief before their sons came bounding up to him, each wanting an affectionate turn at their returning father.

"We got the adoption papers on Devon," she said at the dinner table.

"'Doption? What's that?" Devon wanted to know.

"It means—" Jessica and Dane both started at once. Jessica looked to Dane, who continued. "It means I'm your legal father now."

"But not your real father," Alexander shot back.

Jessica looked alarmed and Dane sighed. After a warning look at Alexander, he turned to Devon. "I'm as real as they come, sport. When you're older, you'll understand the difference between a legal father and a biological father. But for now, it's not real important. Let's just say I'm your second father, and I love you just as much. Forever. Okay?"

"Forever unless you die," Devon said matter-of-factly, and Dane didn't know whether to laugh or cry. Jessica cleared her throat.

"No, Devon, your first daddy still loves you, too. You know that. Even from heaven, people can still love and watch over you. Right, Dad?"

"Sure," Dane murmured and put down his fork.

"Not hungry?" Jessica asked.

"I guess not. It's the—"

"Film, I know. You never eat. By the looks of you, you haven't eaten well in a while. We'll have to fatten him up while he's home, right boys?"

"Ice cream," Devon said. "We always used to eat it. Mommy doesn't buy it anymore. She says it makes her sad about my first—"

"I'll buy some! Now, finish your dinner. It's bath night," Jessica said quickly.

"Sad?" Dane asked.

Jessica just shook her head and looked back toward Devon.

"I don't want to take a bath. I'm big enough to take showers," Alexander stated flatly.

"Fine." Jessica said, the strain in her voice barely disguised by her light tone.

Dane cleared the table while Jessica took the boys upstairs. Peter had taken Lydia to a show, suggesting that Dane may like an evening alone with his family. Now, loading the dishwasher, Dane felt out of sorts.

A sensation was returning to his stomach. Not a pain exactly, just an odd discomfort that gnawed at him. When had it started? He paused, plate in hand, wondering why the feeling had surfaced so strongly tonight.

No, he wasn't the "real" father. The real father was dead. Worse, she wasn't buying ice cream because it reminded her of Mac? *Give me a break!*

The discussion at the dinner table had been difficult, and it had added to the already growing monster inside him. His last visit home, back in June... Jessica was talking to Megan about Mac. She'd said something about still loving Mac and having to just "go on and make the best of things." Was that what their marriage was about, just an attempt to make the best of things?

And before that. In the adoption office with that Carvey woman, Jessica had referred to Mac as her husband. Dane had tried to ignore the comment at the time; it was an easy mistake to make. Still...

She was telling Devon that Mac was still here, still watching. Dane dropped the plate into the dishwasher rack and slammed the door.

Well, maybe he was still here. Still watching.

·♥·♥·♥·♥·♥·

"You've been drinking," Jessica murmured, her lips trailing from Dane's earlobe to his cheek. On his first night home, he'd complained of fatigue and had gone to bed early. Tonight, he knew, she would not let him off so easily.

"Just a shot of Jack. I'm still tense from L.A."

"I think the airlines should pass out anti-depressants upon arrival at LAX," she quipped, sliding her fingers through his hair. "Except for the wedding, I haven't seen you take a drink in ages."

"No big deal," he said hoarsely. "L.A. isn't so bad. I've just got a lot on my mind."

"The film's going well?"

"Yeah. Great."

"Any news from Phillip?"

"Nope." Dane sighed and turned to face her. She looked like an angel to him, the moonlight from their bedroom window casting a halo effect around her face. "Sweetie..." He took a moment to draw a finger down her cheek, wishing with all his might that the badness inside him would go away. "It's probably not going to happen. I wish I could do something, but every direction I turn is blocked."

She looked into his eyes then, and he tried to see what was there. Disappointment? Despair? He was unsure.

"I know. I've already figured that out for myself," she said. "Can we just forget about all that, just for tonight?"

Not sure if the Jack Daniels was helping or hurting his cause, Dane whispered his agreement and took her into his arms. He would, for tonight, try to forget, and focus his every fiber upon pleasing her. There would be plenty of time to worry in the days to come.

·♥·♥·♥·♥·♥·

Her father was laughing. His eyes shone clearly in the dim room, and he shook his head slowly as if some sour, melancholy joke had come to his mind. He was younger than she could remember him ever being. Jessica could not see her mother's face but knew it was wrinkled with age, could hear the wrinkles in her voice as her words condemned the handsome man reclining in the easy chair.

Jessica stayed hidden in the shadows. She trembled at her mother's ire, wishing she would stop yelling at her beloved father. "Stop," she murmured, taking a step forward. "Stop it. He didn't do anything wrong."

Her parents continued to argue. Torn in confusion, Jessica rounded the front of the living room couch, making herself known to her mother. "You want everything perfect," she ventured, surprised at the childlike sound of her own voice. "Leave us alone."

"He will spoil you," her mother said, turning to face Jessica in the darkness. "He will get bored and leave you. He will never take care of you the way I did." Before her eyes, her mother's face faded away and another one took its place. His fist was raised.

"Don't hurt him." Jessica's body jerked abruptly, and she rolled over in bed. The warmth of Dane's torso against her back was comforting, and she nested against him as he slipped an arm around her waist.

"Okay?" he whispered groggily.

"I was dreaming about Mac."

·♥·♥·♥·♥·♥·

"Okay. That's a wrap for today."

"Are you sure? I didn't like the way that last line came out. Let's do it again," Dane called from across the set.

"Dane, c'mere," Sal Cicerelli called, looking down at his shuffling feet. When Dane stood before him, Sal looked up at him and shoved his hands into his pockets. "Look, man. I have the greatest respect for you, for your work. I mean, you're the man in this business. But here, now, today, I'm the director. I call the shots. That take wasn't even a hair's breadth away from perfect." He held up his thumb and first finger to demonstrate. "Now go home and get some rest. You're starting to look haunted."

Dane took a deep breath. "Right. You're right, of course. I'm sorry, Sal. I'm outta here." He turned and started to walk away when the director called after him.

"You wanna get a drink later?"

Dane turned and gave Sal an appraising eye. "Sure. That would be great."

He went home to clean up before going back out. He was about to leave the house to meet Sal when the phone rang.

"Hello Mr. Pierce. Murdo Denehy here. Have you got a minute?"

"Actually, no."

"I've heard you're quite an eloquent writer. We have this inner-city mentoring program we're test driving this fall, and we're recruiting local celebrities to take part and assist these disadvantaged teens. I thought you might be interested in giving a little talk on the benefits of journaling."

"What the hell are you talking about?" Dane asked, trying to shrug into his jacket while jockeying the telephone. His stomach was beginning to churn.

"Just a thought. Sorry to have bothered you."

Journaling? Seething, Dane stared at the phone in his hand. The line was dead.

He's baiting me. Nothing more. He couldn't know about the journal.

The Club wasn't crowded, and he spotted Sal at a corner table. They chatted about the film, Sal's grandkids and the latest tax on the film industry. Sal ordered a second round.

"I remember sitting in a bar in New Zealand with Mac," he said suddenly. "He was just a picture of misery."

Beyond caring about what he said, Dane shrugged. "So what was the almighty Cory MacKendall upset about?"

"The same thing you're upset about. His wife."

Dane turned slowly to look at Sal. "I'm not upset about anything. Hell, life's a bowl of fuckin' cherries, ain't it?"

Sal smiled. "Yes, my friend, it is. Of course, you have to watch out for the pits, as they say. I have some advice for you."

"Sal, forgive me in advance. I've never been known for my impeccable manners while drunk. Not that I am drunk, mind you, but I'm hoping to be soon. So, anyway, please save your advice for someone who needs it. Mac probably needed it. I don't."

"Sure. You don't. But humor me, I'm a lot smarter than you are." The older man smiled and took another swig of bourbon. "The word of advice is mellow. M-E-L-L-O."

"W."

"What?"

"You forgot the W, asshole."

"If you don't, you'll lose her for sure. She's a fine woman, Dane."

"Damned straight, she is."

"He almost lost her."

"He never lost her." Dane signaled the waiter. "He still hasn't."

"Mac's dead, man. He's gone, she's yours. Don't make a stupid mistake."

"What do you know about mistakes? You're the director, remember? Not me."

Sal shook his head.

"And anyway, what makes you think I'm upset about my wife?"

"He wasn't as perfect as you think."

"No?" Dane pulled his wallet from his pocket and tossed down some bills. "Another for me and my guru, here." He swallowed the last of his drink. "I used to call him a Boy Scout. And he was. Through and through. Not a misshapen bone in his body. Not an unkind thought. He probably even orchestrated their timing in the sack so that—"

"Is that what worries you? You think he was a better lover? Hail, Mary!!"

Dane only glared.

"I'll tell you this. And I tell you this with the disclaimer that he was my friend and I liked him. He was every bit as insecure as you are right now. He worried night and day. Do you want to know what he worried about? You, my friend. You. And her."

"Well bless my soul," Dane muttered sourly. "He's getting back at me now for all that worryin', isn't he?"

Sal blew his breath out in a muted, frustrated whistle. "He's dead, man. You're alive. Make the most of it before it's too late."

"Actually, that's 'make the best' of it. I've heard that one before." *Easy for him to say. He's not being accused of murdering his wife's ex.*

October 30th was Alexander Pierce's twelfth birthday. Standing at the front window in the great room, he stared out at the pouring rain, unaware that his stepmother was watching from the hall. Jessica could feel his depression.

"Want to play a game?" she ventured, knowing well he did not.

"Has Dad called?"

"Not yet. He will, honey. You remember how he is when—"

"He's working on a picture. I'm sick of hearing about the picture! I'm sick of being stuck here! I want to go home."

"This is your home, Alex," Jessica said, the lameness of her words wrinkling her nose. "Come on. I'm bored too. Want to go into town?"

"Why not." Alexander's tone was lackluster, but he wandered to the peg on the wall that held his coat. "And I hate raincoats."

Jessica informed Lydia that she was taking Alexander into town, then grabbed her own coat off the wall. Soon, she was maneuvering the SUV down the muddy road leading away from the ranch.

"He's not coming home for my birthday, is he?"

"It doesn't look that way. It doesn't mean anything, Alex. I remember when he was in Cambodia, really, really sick, and all he could talk about was getting home for your birthday. It motivated him to get well faster."

"Hrmph."

In Jackson Hole, the streets were mostly deserted. They wandered in and out of the tourist shops, Jessica offering to buy anything that even remotely piqued Alexander's interest.

"Did you speak with Mom One today?"

"Yeah. She said my present was returned in the mail. The delivery company couldn't deliver it. She said it's Dad's fault for not having the address posted at the end of our road."

"Dad has very good reasons for keeping the road anonymous looking."

"I know. So people won't bug us."

"Is she sending the gift again?"

"No. She said she'll give it to Dad when she sees him. He goes there to see my sisters."

"Well, that's good, isn't it?"

"If he ever comes home."

"He'll come home, sweetheart."

They stopped in front of a magazine rack. Jessica focused on the decorating periodicals, wary of the variety of "movie" magazines and gossip rags. Alexander browsed those offering computer game reviews.

"Hey, Mom Two! Look, it's Dad!"

Jessica bit her lip but reached for the magazine. *Movies Now!* was on the set of *Unstable Airspace* with some exclusive photos of the cast!

"Hmm. Wonderful." Jessica thumbed through the high color, glossy pages. Yup, there was her husband, looking thin, looking tough, looking... at the starlet from the film. Lisa Lee Falconi. The girl, a twenty-something starlet from Reseda, California, was looking thin, looking sexy, looking... at Dane. Was it off-camera, or a still from the picture?

"Stars Dane Pierce and Lisa Lee chum around during a break in the action..."

Jessica's teeth began to grind. She remembered, all too well, a day when that photo was of her and Dane. A day when Dane was still married to Rita. Alexander's "Mom One."

Quickly she deposited the magazine back onto the rack. "Come on. Let's get some ice cream."

The counter in the ice cream shop was empty, so they sat on stools and devoured the largest sundaes they could handle. Jessica scraped the last of the hot fudge from the bottom of the bowl and popped the spoon into her mouth with a satisfied "Mmm."

Alexander couldn't quite finish his. "Wow. I didn't think you could do it, Mom Two."

"I adore ice cream," she said simply, sliding off the stool and patting her stomach. "And these pants were already too tight. I can barely walk!" Jessica giggled and Alexander laughed.

"Aw, you're not fat," he said with a little blush.

"I am, too! And I know why," Jessica said, brushing her hair away from her face. "I've done nothing but sit around since I moved up here! Sit and eat. It's no wonder I'm becoming such a cow. I couldn't get a role now if I tried."

"You won't, will you?" her young companion asked, a wary expression on his face.

"Nope. I'm off the market right now, kiddo."

With Alexander contentedly lugging a 3,000-piece Lego building set to the truck, Jessica counted their trip to town a successful birthday activity. Despite the loathsome picture of Dane and the new leading lady in his life. Er, film.

Twenty-Eight

Mrs. Pierce Goes to Town

"Looks like our winter is finally here," Jessica said while dressing Devon in his warmest pants and sweatshirt. "November is warm at home, compared to here."

"I love snow, Mommy."

"Good for you," Jessica said. "I'm glad." Snow falling gently outside while you were cuddled up inside with the one you loved, before a roaring fire... she loved that kind of snow. Snow that blew in and turned your carpeting into permafrost every time you opened the door, froze your windshield wipers to the glass and disguised the road leading back home was a nightmare.

And yes, the road was the one leading back home. As much as she loved the ranch, Los Angeles was and would always be her home. It was where she'd grown up, gone to school and worked all her life. And right now, it was where her husband was living.

Her connection, of course, was the telephone. Every time it rang, she leaped on it like a cougar after a famine. This call, however, was not good news.

"Don't go far," she called after Devon who was going out the front door as she reached for the phone.

"Hello Jessica-my-love."

"Teddy! What a surprise! Gosh, it's great to hear your voice. Tell me Spielberg wants me for something. Anything!"

Theodore Langley chuckled, then clucked his tongue. "Now sugarplum, you told Uncle Theo that you were unavailable. You want a deal, just say so. But listen, I've got some bad news. Kyle Wagner was killed last night."

Jessica sank into her rocking chair. "Oh, no... What happened?"

"Car accident. Word on the boulevard is, he was lately into speedballs. He probably shot up before getting behind the wheel."

"Speedballs? Isn't that cocaine and... and..."

"Heroin, darling. A real suicide cocktail if you ask me. Anyway, I knew you two were friends, so I thought I'd let you know. They're talking funeral on Friday. Dane's still in town, isn't he?"

Last I heard, she thought with chagrin. Surely, he'd heard about Kyle but had chosen not to call her. Probably spending all his time "chumming" around with that Lisa Lee woman. "Yeah. He is." Jessica pushed her bangs back and blew out a heavy sigh. "I'll... I'll be there. Somehow. Would you call me back when you find out where and what time?"

"Sure, Jessie. Sorry for the bad news, love."

•♥•♥•♥•♥•♥•

She had the limo driver take her straight to the cemetery. The crowd of celebrities was impressive, and many made subtle efforts to welcome her home.

The funeral was graveside. Jessica melted into a group of people with whom she was comfortable and only half listened to the minister's eulogy while keeping an eye out for her husband. Yet Dane didn't show. She wasn't really surprised; when she'd called him about Kyle, he'd remained cool and unemotional. He would try to make it, he'd said, but wasn't sure. He was working.

Holding her chin high, Jessica purposely disengaged herself from the surroundings. It was so like the sunny hillside where Mac had been laid to rest, and she couldn't afford a breakdown now. She dabbed at her cheeks during the appropriate moments and finally spotted Teddy just as the final "amen" was spoken. But before he could join her, another familiar face came into her line of vision.

"Mrs. Pierce? Have you got a moment?"

"I find this a most inappropriate time, Sergeant Denehy." Jessica kept her pace as she crossed the grassy cemetery toward the waiting caravan of limousines.

"Terrible about Mr. Wagner. It was drugs. And what a strange coincidence."

"And what coincidence is that?" Jessica asked, still walking and hating herself for taking the bait.

"That he died, of course, just after offering to depose information that would be pivotal to our case."

"Our case?"

"Mr. Wagner was to be a prime witness in the investigation of your husband's involvement with the murder of your... husband." Denehy cleared his throat awkwardly after realizing the redundancy of his statement. Jessica ignored it.

"Witness?" Jessica stopped and turned to face the man. Several yards to her right, cameras were snapping, clicking and buzzing. "To have a witness you must first have a crime. To have knowledge of a crime you must have evidence. Real, tangible evidence, of which you have none. Not that you are even legally involved in this investigation." With as much arrogant confidence as she could gather, Jessica resumed her march to the car. "Meanwhile, Mac's real killer remains unfound while you insist upon hounding an innocent man. Good day, Detective."

Soon, Teddy was beside her. "Sorry I didn't see you, darling. Want to get some coffee?"

Jessica spent the midday hours with Teddy, reminiscing and trying to avoid the inevitable sadness.

"Seriously, Jess, if you want me to put you back out there, people have been begging for you. I've got a stack of scripts chest high for you to read. Oscar could still be yours, my love."

"Nope. I'm not ready. I'll know when it's time."

"Okay. You just say when it is."

She bid her agent goodbye in Beverly Hills, where she spent the next two hours at her favorite salon. A body wrap would take care of those pesky extra pounds. A deep pore facial, a new haircut with highlights and the sexiest little black dress she could find were also on the agenda.

"Pretty smart, if I say so myself." Jessica turned before the dressing room mirror, murmuring to herself. The "fashion consultant" stood by, a wistful smile on her face.

"It's the right choice. Black is always the right choice. He'll eat you alive in that."

"I'd settle for one of those long, slow, deep, soft kisses that last three days."

"Right now, I'd settle for a leer," the woman countered comically. "You're a lucky girl, Mrs. Pierce."

"I know," Jessica muttered. *I will be even luckier if I can get my husband back.* She could only hope her simple plan would work.

She took the limo to the studio where Dane was supposed to be working. She wasn't all that surprised when the receptionist haltingly advised her that Mr. Pierce was on dinner break.

"Where did he go?"

"I'm not sure..."

"Isn't that his Mercedes in the lot outside? Why, I'll just bet he's across the street at Francois'. Do you think?" she asked coyly, watching the agitated woman's reaction to her suggestion.

"Oh, I doubt that. No, he probably got a ride with someone else to dinner."

"Well, it's worth a shot, isn't it? Thank you."

Was Dane's secretary really biting her nails?

Jessica shook her head and got back inside the limousine. She wasn't about to cross the busy boulevard in her stiletto heels.

The maître 'd looked pleased, then nervous, recognizing her immediately before agreeing to check for Dane's presence in the dining room. Her assumptions had been correct; Dane was not alone.

"Right this way, Mrs. Mac—Pierce."

Jessica looked past the maître 'd's shoulder and offered a false smile. "I can see myself to the table, thank you."

Squaring her shoulders, Jessica paced herself, moving directly but unhurriedly toward the corner booth occupied by her husband and the starlet creating the latest, and best, Hollywood buzz. Acquaintances nodded and smiled, some of them giving her a side-eyed, pitying look.

She paused at the table's edge, looking only at Dane, who turned his face to hers without the slightest trace of surprise.

"Good evening, Mrs. Pierce," he said.

"Hello, darling. I hope I'm not interrupting anything... important."

"Not at all. Lisa, my wife Jessica; Jess, this is Lisa Lee."

Jessica put out her hand. "Lisa. Lisa... Vulturi, isn't it?"

"Falconi. And I was just leaving."

"Oh please. Don't go on my account." Jessica's words gave no hint of sincerity.

The actress stood. "Thanks, Dane. I'll give you my answer tomorrow." The stewing starlet sashayed from the room, and Jessica hesitated only a moment before slipping into the booth beside her husband. He spoke first.

"To what do I owe the pleasure of this visit? Kids okay?"

"Of course, they are. You knew I'd come for the funeral."

"The funeral of a heroin addict. Did you know his trial was coming up next week? He was out on bail for major drug trafficking. I find it a bit odd; I didn't think you and Wagner were all that close. Or were you?"

"Closeness has nothing to do with it. It's a matter of respect."

"And you didn't respect Charlene?"

Jessica drew in her breath. *That was unfair.* "That was different." Before she could lose her resolve, Jessica wet her lips and laced her fingers. "I missed you."

If Dane flinched at all, Jessica did not detect it. His eyes focused across the room, and he picked up his drink for a sip. Boldly, she assessed him. So much like the day they'd met, it was unnerving. He was lean; preoccupied; self-important. But she'd learned, since then, that how he appeared could be entirely opposite... completely irrelevant to the way he felt.

His expression was shuttered.

"You hungry?" he asked at last, his tone clearly indicating that she should not be.

"We need to talk," Jessica answered, hating the sound of the words as they tumbled off her tongue.

From his wallet, Dane plucked a couple of bills and tossed them down, then stood from the booth. He offered his hand. Jessica got smoothly to her feet, ignoring the almost discreet glances from the infamous patrons around them. *They are wondering if we'll be tabloid fodder tomorrow.*

Outside, he signaled the valet. "It's across the street," he directed, gesturing toward the studio parking lot. He turned to Jessica. "You have a car?"

"No." Jessica fidgeted with her purse.

It was only moments before the red-jacketed attendant drove up in a brand new, black Mercedes-Benz.

Jessica sat stiffly in the passenger seat as Dane put the car through five gears and headed west on the freeway. It nearly made her ill, the discomfort she felt riding beside the uncommunicative man whom she'd thought she knew so well. *Say something, dammit!*

But Dane did not speak. Now, winding through Malibu Canyon, Jessica hoped the whiskey did not compromise his judgment. She also hoped he was not aware of just how tightly she was clutching the door handle.

This is crazy. Where is he taking me?

Before she could summon the courage to ask, Dane made a left turn onto a road marked "private drive."

"The gates aren't in yet," he murmured, bringing the car to a stop before a beautiful contemporary house centered on a large estate-sized lot. Once again, he offered Jessica his hand as she struggled to exit the low vehicle in her high, backless pumps.

He preceded her up the few steps of the wide front porch and unlocked the front door, swinging it open and stepping aside to allow her entry.

Jessica walked inside, the clicking of her heels on the stone entryway echoing throughout the vacant house. She turned a full circle, taking in the details of the not-quite-finished home, then looked at Dane.

"This is it, isn't it? Our house?"

"Yup."

"It's... it's beautiful. It's almost done. Why didn't you tell me?"

Dane offered a slight shrug and sauntered past her. She followed him into the kitchen.

"I love it," she said quietly, running her hand along the smooth, cold, granite countertops, and the custom cherry wood cabinets. She opened the enormous sub-zero refrigerator and was surprised to see bottles of white wine and three or four cans of beer, alongside a case of bottled water.

Dane reached in and snapped up one of the wine bottles. "Care for a glass?"

"Uh, sure."

From an otherwise empty cabinet, Dane took down two Styrofoam cups and sloshed some Chardonnay into both, then handed one to Jessica. "To... to what? You pick."

Jessica caught his gaze and did her best to hold it. "To us, of course."

"Right. To us." Quickly swallowing most of his wine while Jessica quietly sipped at hers, Dane dumped another ounce or two into his cup and walked from the room. Jessica followed as he went wordlessly from room to room, switching the lights on and then off for her appraisal. They ended back in the living room.

Jessica kicked off her shoes and went to stand before the floor to ceiling windows. "You can see the pier," she murmured, holding the cup close to her cheek.

"So, what do we need to talk about?"

It was difficult keeping the hurt expression from her face. Jessica fought to stay in control, for she believed it to be the only way she could communicate effectively with Dane. Tears would only drive him away.

"Well," she began, trying to clear her voice without sounding insecure, "let's start with this house. When will it be ready to move in?"

"When I tell them to finish it up."

"I guess the question is, then, do you want us to move in."

"I guess the question really is, do you want to move in?"

Jessica frowned and took a step toward her husband, who was leaning against the massive fireplace mantel. "Why in the world wouldn't we want to?"

Dane shrugged and polished off his wine. "You like the ranch. It's better for the kids."

"Right now, it's not. What's good for the kids is being near their father." *Not to mention what's good for me.*

Dane ignored her statement and headed back to the kitchen. Propelled by his lack of response, Jessica followed quickly behind him. "What's happening? What is really going on here? Are you tired of us already?"

Dane was reaching into the refrigerator. "Tired of you? No." He again refilled the cup in his hand. "Tired, yes. Tired of trying. Tired of trying to be something I'm not."

"I don't know what you mean. You... you're talking in circles. If you're mad about something, just say it. If you don't find me... if I'm not what you want anymore, just tell me."

"You don't have a clue, do you?"

"There you go again. Don't be cryptic with me, Dane. At least do me the courtesy of being honest. Mac may have had an unreasonable temper sometimes, but at least he always said what was on his mind. None of this silent, distant crap you're giving me!" Her words surprised them both. Dane suddenly became a lit fuse.

"Ah. There we go! It's just the three of us now. To us, you wanted to toast? Us? You, me and Mac. He's never left your side, not once, has he? He dogs us like a bloodhound. He's there, when we're eating, walking, talking—" Dane's anger bubbled quickly to the top and outward, and Jessica took an involuntary step back.

"I don't know what you're talking about."

"Christ! He's even in the sack with us, isn't he? Isn't he?"

"No! Of course not! He's dead. He's gone, and I—"

"And you miss him every damned day. Is he there, telling you what to say and do? How to be? Is he there to remind you of how a real hero acts?"

Dane slammed the refrigerator door and breezed past her on his way back to the living room, the neck of the half empty wine bottle in his fist. Jessica stared after him in outraged awe. Finally finding her feet, she stormed after him.

"So that's what this is about. You think I'm comparing you to him. Well, I guess your shoulders are just so damned broad I never noticed that big chip before." Jessica shook her head slowly. "And to think that I foolishly thought this was about you and me."

Dane sat down and leaned against the wall, staring at her, his expression sullen. "It's true and you know it. It was asinine of me to think I could ever possibly be anything to you, after him. Mr. Stand Up Guy, Mr. Family Values, Pancakes-on-Sunday and Dinner-on-the-table-by-six Mac MacKendall."

"Please, don't."

"It's not your fault, sweetie. I misled you. I misled myself. It was wrong for me to suggest that I could make you happy. And it was even more wrong for me to break my promise."

"What promise?" Jessica asked, lowering herself to sit on the carpet in front of him. "Tell me, Dane. What promise?"

Dane's sour expression slowly changed to one of mock enlightenment. "That's why he won't leave us alone. It's so simple. It's the fucking promise. How stupid... how blind could I be?"

"Dane, listen to me." Jessica took the cup from his hand and put it on the hearth. "We need to talk this out because you are wrong.

You're wrong! You couldn't be more wrong." She attempted to take his hands in hers, but he pulled his away.

"No, I screwed up, big time. I gambled and lost. So what else is new?"

"How can you say that? We have so much!"

He refused to make eye contact, and Jessica felt her own anger growing. "So that's it, huh? Just say it's because of Mac and walk away. Just make it easy on yourself." She got to her feet and placed her hands on her hips. "Do you know why I came down here? Why I humiliated myself in front of that... that little trollop you were seducing back there?"

Now Dane did swing his vision upward to meet her eyes. "Probably to lambaste me for not getting Charlene's baby for you. I blew that, too, didn't I? Ah, but your other husband would have had no problem."

Jessica shook her head in frustration and began to pace the empty living room, struggling to voice her tangled and painful thoughts. "I'm sure you don't know it, but I haven't been able to sleep since you left for L.A. Even before you left, I knew something was wrong, but I chalked it up to some kind of adjustment period. Yeah, I was rationalizing. I know it now. But a few days ago, I got out of bed, alone, alone again, and realized that I was losing my husband. Again. Only this time, I had a chance to do something about it. And I'll be damned if I'll let you just cruise out of my life like some... some ransacking pirate sailing off to sea."

Jessica paused to draw in a deep breath, and then narrowed her eyes as she peered down at Dane. "But go ahead. Feed your jealousy, your jealousy of a dead man. And for the record, Mac was anything but perfect. And I loved him. But you know what, Mr. Smart-Ass Know-it-All? I loved you first. And yes, you were a complete jerk to me. You broke my heart, and I forgave you. You wanna talk about gambling? I put my whole marriage on the line just to keep you in my life. Have you forgotten that when I was married to that other man, I flew halfway around the world, seven months pregnant, because I was terrified that you might die?"

The memory of her trip to Cambodia brought a stinging to her eyes. She had been afraid to even breathe until the doctors had finally said that Dane would live.

She placed her palms out between them. "If you'd rather sit there and get shit-faced drunk, and feel sorry for yourself, just do it. But know this, Dane Thomas Pierce, I am your wife, and you are my last chance for happiness. I will not go through this again for anything or anyone in the world. It just isn't worth the pain." Jessica's voice grew softer and more broken as she spoke. Deflated, she lifted Dane's keys from the fireplace mantel and slipped into her shoes. "Have a good night with your ghosts. I need to go."

And she was in the car, trying her best to force herself to put the car into gear; he was knocking on the driver's door window. She locked him in her gaze and lowered the window.

"There's so much you don't know," he began, the cockiness gone from his voice.

"Then tell me."

"I can't."

"Goodbye, Dane."

Twenty-Nine

A Killer in the House?

Doc says that my tests came back good. Gotta watch the booze, though. As if I didn't know that.

God, I miss Jess. Too bad it's not me she is missing. Despite what she said, I know she would rather be with him. She will never be free. Come to think of it, neither will I.

I'm sure she's even madder now that our appeal was denied. I can't believe Denehy would sink low enough to leak his suspicions to the adoption board. Slimeball.

Surely something must change soon. It's ruining me.

Dane looked up from his computer and toward the television, where the news was broadcasting. A congressman from Minnesota was in town, attending a nuclear arms discussion being held at Camp Pendleton, California.

"So what?" Dane muttered and started to look back at his keyboard when Steven Conway's name was mentioned. An advocate against nuclear arms, Conway was briefly interviewed outside his West L.A. hotel.

His interest re-ignited, Dane pulled out the file of information he'd all but forgotten over the last several weeks. Again, reading through the notes, he pondered his earlier thoughts. He had to have missed something. Boldly, he picked up the phone and dialed.

"Nice to see you again, Mr. Pierce. Glad you caught me. I was going to visit my son before flying home."

"He live around here?"

"Yes, but I just found out he's out of town. I just missed him."

"Funny, I thought he was a child. Like your daughters."

The two men took their seats in the downtown restaurant Dane had picked.

"No. He's older... from a previous ..."

"Ah. Well. I thought this might be an opportune time to talk about fattening your campaign coffers."

"My constituents have been very generous. It's people like you and Miss MacKendall who have helped keep the right folks in office."

Dane nodded thoughtfully. "You sure you didn't know Charlene?"

"No. As I mentioned before, I only met her while touring the facility."

"Really. I thought for sure you two knew each other better. She spoke of you on several occasions."

"I'm flattered, I guess," Conway said, shaking his head slowly. "She wasn't exactly the kind of woman that fits into the political scene, if you catch my drift."

"No, what is your drift, Congressman?"

"First of all, I'm a married man, Mr. Pierce."

"So am I. Forgive me, but—so?"

"Good point." Conway looked weary. "Surely you don't imagine... a man like me, a younger woman... with tattoos, no less..." he chuckled. "No offense to Miss MacKendall. She was a nice person."

"Yes. She was."

"Shame about that adoption. I was sorry to hear about that."

"Mm hmm."

"What a run of bad luck. But you came here to talk about the campaign."

Dane smiled. "I wasn't around much the last time you were running. Charlene was really impressed with your platform. She was your true supporter."

The congressman seemed to wince. Dane continued. "I'm really a California boy. Minnesota politics only matter when they affect the business."

"Well, I can assure you, my position has only strengthened over the past four years."

"Good." Dane leaned forward, offering a sly smile. "You sure you and Char weren't more... intimately acquainted?"

"I beg your pardon, Mr. Pierce. That's preposterous."

"Then perhaps you spent some time lurking about her bedroom windows?"

Conway stood abruptly. "Whatever are you getting at?"

Dane leaned lazily back in his seat. "Just trying to figure out how you knew about those tattoos. As brash as she was, Char was modest about her body. Hell, I'd been sleeping with her for three months before I caught a glimpse of them. And here you, by your own admission, a total stranger..."

The representative from Minnesota took his seat. "Can I buy you a drink, Mr. Pierce?"

"Not tonight."

"Funny, I took you for a drinking man."

Dane chuckled, unwrapped a stick of gum and slid it into his mouth.

"What is it you want?"

Chewing his gum thoughtfully, Dane looked around the restaurant at the other, unsuspecting diners. "You surprise me, Congressman." He reached into the breast pocket of his sports coat and withdrew two envelopes. He placed them side-by-side on the table. "You asked about my kids." Opening the first envelope, Dane pulled out some photos. "This is my oldest son, Alexander, my wife, and our son Devon. I'm not his birth father, of course. His real dad is gone now." He turned the photos toward the politician. "This little guy is Benjamin. He's Charlene's son. We named him Benjamin, hoping to adopt him one day. I'm not his biological father either." Dane pushed the second picture closer to the perspiring man across the table from him. "But I'd do anything for these boys."

Conway averted his eyes. Dane patted the second envelope.

"These are the results of a blood test performed on Benjamin, and on the mysterious blood donor who came forward during his open-heart surgery. Guess what." Dane rearranged the photos. "Cute little kid, isn't he? Too bad his mother had to die before she could tell us who the father is."

"Perhaps you could be the father, Mr. Pierce. A little influence imposed in the right direction, and those could be your blood records in that envelope."

"I've considered that option. However, it's not a very well concealed fact that I underwent the knife about eight years ago to see to it that little accidents like this one didn't happen to me." Dane pressed his fingertips together. "I love my wife, Mr. Conway. Her late husband, and his sister, were friends of mine. The least I can do is see that the child is placed in the right family, and with the help of the biological father, I just might be able to do something. Now, shall we talk about the tattoos, what's in this envelope, or your campaign? Your choice."

"I never saw the tattoos, myself," Conway remarked at last, still not meeting Dane's eyes. His voice was soft and woeful when he continued. "Those blood tests may, in fact, be mine, but I am not that little boy's father."

"You sound mighty sure of yourself."

"I am quite sure." He turned to face Dane. "A few minutes ago, you said you would do anything for your sons. Well, Mr. Pierce, so would I. Hopefully, your sons will grow up strong and healthy, make you proud. But if they don't, if they go astray somehow... how will you handle that? Hmm? And what about their children, the innocent by-products of careless indiscretions... if they needed care, you would step forward, wouldn't you?"

Dane narrowed his eyes, his mind racing through the scenario the congressman was painting.

"So where does it end, Conway?"

"As a father, it never ends."

"And as a public figure? As a law making, and hopefully law abiding, citizen?"

Conway issued a deep sigh. Dane gathered the envelopes and tucked them back into his pocket. "Where did he go?"

"Who?"

"Your son. You said he left town."

Steven Conway looked forlorn for a moment. "He meant well. He was worried about the election. She wanted to get married."

"Char? Married? That's a joke."

"It was the baby. She wanted respect. I told Frankie he had to do right by her, something I wished I'd done many years ago. Frank's mother... well I guess that's irrelevant, now. But he's so headstrong. He'd really cleaned up – didn't want to associate with that scene down there. So, they argued. He thought she was threatening him. He wanted to scare her, so she'd leave us alone."

"Wait a minute. Frankie is your son? The drug dealer?"

Conway said nothing. Dane frowned. The puzzle pieces were knitting themselves together. Frankie Conway was more than just the baby's father. "Scare her?" Incredulous, Dane leaned close to the politician's face. "*Scare* her?" Dane's voice reflected the horror of his realization. "He killed her! The mother of his child! And her brother!"

Now, people in the surrounding tables began to stare. The maître 'd signaled the waiter, who approached the table.

"Can I get you gentlemen anything else?"

"No. Thank you." Dane fell back against his chair; his guest sat stock still in his. The unexpected turn of events had put a new spin on Dane's plans to get Conway to confess. "You know I can't sit on this," he finally said.

After a long moment, Conway broke the silence. "I'll bring him in."

Dane swallowed hard and tried to slow his breathing. "Look. I'm... I'm sorry it had to be this way. I'm sorry I suggested what I did about you and Char. It was not meant to degrade you."

"I know that, Mr. Pierce. I guess I knew all along that someone, somewhere, would find out. However, I doubt very much that Frankie's conviction will help in your attempt to adopt the child. It will, most likely, only complicate matters. I wish you luck, however. And I'm truly..." his voice began to roughen, and he cleared his throat. "Truly sorry about the MacKendalls."

Dane took a moment to rub his eyes. When he opened them, it was to see the Minnesota State Representative retreating slowly from the room, head held high. A moral, well-liked politician who loved his family and his country. A man whose career was now over.

His legs shaking with adrenaline, Dane made a dignified effort to retrieve his car from the valet. He could barely discern the road ahead as he began the drive home; his sinuses were swelling, and his eyes burned. Finally, after exiting the freeway onto a darkened stretch of Canon Road, Dane Pierce pulled over and parked his car. Lowering his forehead against the steering wheel, he began to weep.

He didn't go to work the next day. He didn't answer the phone or go out. He did sit on the beach, despite the overcast sky and chilly air.

"What do you want for your birthday, darling?" his mother asked, her fingers subtly toying with the single strand of pearls around her neck. "What would make you happy, Dane?"

He was nine or ten. She'd baked him a round layer cake, and he was putting on the candles before his father came home from work.

"Didn't you already buy my presents?" he'd asked in surprise.

"Of course, I did. But you never tell me what you want so I choose things I think you'll like. Isn't there anything you have your heart set on?"

Only Jessica.

His birthday was two weeks away, just after Thanksgiving. He'd be going home next week. He'd make it a quick trip. No sense in prolonging the agony. She wouldn't want him around much anyway. Still, he labored over her last words to him.

I loved you first.

If she was telling the truth, then he'd made a big mistake. A monumental mistake. Again.

He went back to the house with a heart as heavy as the sand upon which he walked. There were messages on his answering machine, the only one of any interest being from the detective bureau at L.A.P.D. A Lieutenant Fusco was calling to offer an apology on behalf of the department. Frankie Conway had surrendered to authorities that morning and was undergoing psychiatric evaluation prior to being charged. Sergeant Murdo Denehy had withdrawn his hat from the race for the D.A.'s seat and would be taking a voluntary leave of absence.

Dane snorted at the implication. “Should be a permanent vacation,” he muttered.

In the afternoon he slept some, then drove his Mustang around Los Angeles with no destination in mind. Near the airport, he stopped in at a topless bar.

With some semblance of decorum left, he kept in the shadows and ordered a drink he didn't touch. At one end of the bar centered in the room, a short, abundantly endowed redhead was swinging around a heavily chromed pole. Wearing not much more than a G-string and a cheap rhinestone tiara, her bump-and-grind was impeccable. Dane stopped the waitress and gave her a hundred-dollar bill to give to the dancer when the set was over.

Breathless and wearing a sheer silk peignoir over the skimpiest bikini possible, Trina Vidal slid into the booth across from him, delicately folding the note and slipping it between her breasts.

“I can see you're not doing your routine,” she said accusingly, but her eyes were sympathetic. She hailed the waitress and ordered two Perriers.

“I don't know why I came here,” he said miserably.

“Let me guess. Your wife locked you out of the house?”

Dane only frowned and withdrew into more of the shadow in which he was sitting.

“Uh... okay, your movie deal got canceled. No? Christ, man, what happened? Your dick fall off?”

At this comment Dane sat up, ready to be mad at her. Instead, he burst into laughter and Trina joined him. Reaching forward, she stroked his cheek affectionately. “Is there anything I can do, big boy?”

“Naw. Not really. I thought maybe... but it wouldn't work.”

“Ha! It did fall off.”

Again, they both shared a good laugh, Dane shaking his head at her comic expression.

“Well, that's gotta be it, otherwise my heart will be broken. Can't have that, can we?”

“No, I guess not.” Dane's smile faded. Her comment about the broken heart reminded him again of Jessica. “I shouldn't be here.”

"No, you shouldn't. But you are, and I've only got ten minutes before I get to pump up all those redneck slobs again. If there's something I can do for you, better ask now."

Dane's smile, melancholy, returned and he took Trina's hand. "You're a good friend, Katrina Vidal. Just listening to your inane prattle does me good. You be careful out there, you here?"

"Not me I'm worried about, Romeo. It's you. You're the one wearing your insides on the outside these days. You better patch things up with the missus quick. No sense in all three of us bein' miserable over this. I gotta go change. Thanks for the c-note. Love ya." She gave him a quick kiss on the mouth and disappeared through a curtain of hanging beads.

Dane sipped on the Perrier and left halfway during her second act.

THIRTY

Redemption and Revelation

Jessica had never known Peter Welles to be a nervous man. Yet, as she watched him scurry about the kitchen one morning, it occurred to her that he had been agitated of late. And she was willing to bet it had nothing to do with her own troubles with Dane.

"What's the matter?" she finally asked.

"Matter?"

"You're hoppin' around here like a rabbit with a hound after you. Is something bothering you, Peter?"

Peter stopped and stared directly at Jessica. "As a matter of fact, yes."

"Well, let's talk about it. Perhaps I can help."

"It's complicated and not very pretty," he answered, his tone slipping decidedly back into the Cockney slang he'd spoken since his childhood.

"Shoot."

"In a word, it's Lydia."

Jessica smiled. "Go on."

"I want to marry her."

"I doubt you'll get much resistance from her, dear. So, what's the problem?"

"Oh Jess, it's... it's... oh buggers. I'm already married."

Jessica couldn't keep the shocked expression from her face. "What?"

"It's true. I married me a London whore while on 'oliday. She up n' stole all the money Dane gave me and gambled it all away. I 'ad to borrow to get back 'ere. But it's a legally binding marriage. I can't marry another until I'm free of 'er."

"Wow," Jessica whispered. "That's terrible. What can you do? Won't she divorce you?"

"I imagine she would, were I there, but I'm not. I've no address or phone number for her. And anyway, I just can't ask Dane for any more money. I feel bad enough as it is."

"Nonsense. Make your reservation. We don't have to tell Dane why you're going if you don't want to. I'll bet you could find her."

Peter's face brightened for a moment, then fell. "Lyddy doesn't know about her either. My... wife."

"Well... that's another story. The last thing you want to do is start out a marriage with a secret. Tell her, she'll understand."

"You think so?"

"I know so. Would you like me to make your travel plans?"

"I'm very capable of some things, Mrs. Pierce. I can do my own calling."

"Put it on my credit card. You have the number."

"Yes, Ma'am. Thank you, Jess. You're a love."

"Just one thing. When are you going to propose?"

"Before I go. And I will tell her the whole story, I promise."

Jessica beamed. The happiness on Peter's face helped to momentarily set aside her worries. "I'm so happy! Lydia can be a December bride!"

"December sounds good to me. If she consents. What will we tell Dane?"

"If we must tell him at all, I'll think of something. Some business matter you left behind that needed attending to. Something like that."

By the following afternoon, Peter was gone, and Lydia was wearing a delighted glow. Jessica began making plans for a December 15th wedding, and Lydia was content to let her. As Dane's phone calls became fewer and farther between, Jessica decided to delay calling him with the good news. Peter would be back before she had to lie for him. Dane wouldn't come home until Thanksgiving.

And what would happen when he did come home? Their last meeting was terrible. Worse, it was heart breaking. She'd left him in the house he'd had built for them, alone, unwilling to spend another moment trying to change his mind.

No, she'd given it her best shot. If anything were to change now, it would have to be his doing.

She was wearing down physically as well. It was the cold weather, the lack of exercise, and she wasn't eating right. It was all these things, and none of these things. She had thought that the relief, when Mac's true killer was found, would be enormous. And while she was resting easier now that the murderer was no longer at large, she was more relieved that Dane truly did have nothing to do with Mac's death. Still, it shamed her to think that she could entertain any other thought on the matter. And she had yet to apologize.

Oh, she had been so convinced that his love was pure, that his heart was completely devoted to her! They would be together forever.

"Like that will ever happen for me," she said sullenly, crossing her ankles on the coffee table before the television. "There's no such thing as forever. I might as well pack it in and forget about men and love. I have my child." *He's all I need. Devon will always love me.*

Bored beyond tears, she flipped the stations with the remote. "I hate television," she said aloud, tossing the remote onto the couch cushions beside her. The news was on, and she only half listened to the broadcast while wallowing in her depression.

A reporter was interviewing someone from the Minnesota Adoption Board. Jessica sat forward and picked up the remote, turning the sound louder.

"Channel Thirteen has been following this story from the beginning, when little Benjamin MacKendall was delivered by Caesarian section of the comatose sister of the late Cory 'Mac' MacKendall, TV's popular Dr. Jim. What effect, if any, will this news have on the outcome of the adoption? Does the identity of the child's biological father have a bearing on the case?"

Russ Morrison was looking uncomfortable, straightening his tie. "It may. It's a complicated situation since the adoption would have been final in three days. We are definitely taking a close look at the code to see where a case like this falls, whether or not a precedent has been set, and of course, what are the best interests of the child."

Jessica's fingers flew to her throat. What did it mean? Would the case be reopened? *Not that we have a chance. Especially not now.* She sat back against the couch and sighed. Dane had gone to so much trouble to find out who the father was, never realizing how close he was to discovering the killer. She owed him that. But even if they were to review the Pierces' application, it was common knowledge that Dane and Jessica Pierce were practically estranged. All of Hollywood knew, so it would do no good to try to hide it from the authorities in Minnesota.

The news program broadcast a photo of little Benjamin. Jessica closed her eyes, trying not to cry.

Lydia drove her to town. They ordered a turkey and all the trimmings for a grand Thanksgiving dinner. On a whim, Jessica decided to add to her wardrobe, and dragged Lydia with her into the only dress shop in town that carried the designs she liked.

"Man! These can't be eights. They won't even zip!" she cried from behind the louvered dressing room door. "Lyd? Can you find me a pair of tens?"

Lydia complied and Jessica turned for her.

"They're cute! Wish my butt was as small as yours," Lydia said.

Jessica shook her head. "This is ridiculous. I'd better lay off the ice cream! I haven't been this heavy since... since Devon was a baby." She looked back into the mirror with dismay. "Even my bra is tight. Guess I'd better find the lingerie section."

"Jess, you don't look fat at all. Honest. And anyway, Dane will be so glad to see you—he wouldn't notice if you were twenty pounds overweight!"

"Why do you always think I'm dressing just for Dane?"

"Well you are, aren't you?"

"No. Absolutely not. And yes, he would notice if I were that big, which, thankfully, I am not. Yet. But at the rate I'm going..." She frowned. "And he won't be glad to see me."

Lydia shook her head. "You're blind, you know that, girl?"

"You're starry-eyed, yourself, *girl*."

Lydia laughed. "Maybe I am."

Back at home, Greg was more than ready to be free of the boys. "I thought you guys were never coming back! Dane called. Wants you to call him back."

The smiled she'd been wearing upon her return fell from Jessica's face. "Oh. Did he say where I should call him?"

"He's on location. Cell phone."

Jessica went upstairs to Dane's office to call. Heartbeat thumping in her ears, she paused before pressing the last two numerals. "Calm down, dammit."

When she felt she could breathe normally, she completed the call.

Dane answered on the first ring. "I had some news I thought you should know. It's about Benjamin."

"I saw the report on TV. It's good news, I hope?"

"No, it's not. They, uh, can't seem to locate him."

"What do you mean, locate him? Isn't he with his adoptive family?"

"No. This couple claims Irma Carvey bilked them and took off with the baby. The police are perplexed. No one knows where she is."

Jessica uttered a quick gasp. "How... how did you find all this out?"

"That nurse at the hospital, Irma's sister? She called here looking for you. She got the scoop from a friend. Morrison thinks the couple is actually in on the scam."

"Oh, Dane..."

"I'm sorry, Jess. I'm doing everything I can to find out more. They've put out an APB on that Carvey woman."

"That black-hearted bitch! She wanted Benjamin for herself! God, kidnapping is a felony! She must be crazy."

"We knew that a long time ago." Dane paused. "I'll be home next week," he added.

"Yes. We're all looking forward to it. Lyddy and I already bought the turkey," she said quickly. And despite what she had said earlier, she found that she was looking forward to seeing Dane.

"Great. It will be fun. Hey, I'll let you know if I hear anything new, okay?"

"Please do. And Dane..." Jessica pressed two fingers against her lips, then planted the tiny kiss against the mouthpiece of the phone. "I never said thank you for... for finding out who killed Mac. I still can't believe you were able to do that. And thanks for letting me know about Benjie. I really appreciate it."

"Sure. Bye."

"Help me! Somebody, God damn it! Oww... Damn it that hurts!"

Sal Cicerelli dropped his megaphone and ran with the others onto the runway where Lisa Lee Falconi laid screaming and cursing. "Get the EMT's out here! Hurry!" he hollered over his shoulder, then squatted next to his leading lady with concern. "Where does it hurt, Leese?"

"Here, and here. Ow!"

"Looks broken to me," one the grips stated flatly.

Dane watched from his director's chair, his legs stretched out before him and crossed at the ankles. It figures, he thought. If you step off the top of a moving stairway, you're going to fall. If you fall twenty feet, you're going to break something. He sighed.

He was still musing when Sal returned.

"Well, we're screwed. At least until January. We might as well break for the holidays."

"No pun intended."

"No. Surely not." Sal grinned. "Go home to Jessica. Surprise her with a lavish gift."

"My last lavish gift didn't go over very well," Dane recalled aloud. "She's afraid of horses."

"I always buy my wife jewelry when she's mad at me."

"Jessica... is not mad at me."

"Okay. Buy her jewelry anyway."

"It's not what she wants."

"And that is—?"

She wants a baby.

Dane forced a laugh. "She may want a new husband, by now."

"I doubt that. Back in June, I'd never seen a happier bride. And that was only, what? Five months ago? You couldn't have wrecked your marriage yet, could you?"

"I could have," Dane said with a smile. "I certainly could have."

"Jewelry."

"Yeah, yeah. All right. Diamonds. Rubies. Emeralds—" Dane was interrupted by his cell phone. "Yeah?"

"Daddy?" It was a girl's voice, but not Zoe's. She was frightened and trying not to cry.

"Mimi? What's wrong?" Dane demanded into the phone, getting to his feet.

"It's Mom. She won't wake up. I'm scared she's dying!"

"Okay, baby, tell me where she is. Is she in bed? On the floor? Where?"

"She's... she's on the couch."

"Did you shake her? Real hard?"

"Yes! She just flops around! Daddy, can you come?"

"Melissa, did she take something? Pills or something?" Dane felt his blood pressure rise. "Mimi? Are you there?"

"She's... she's drunk, Daddy. She's just drunk, again. But usually she's awake by now."

"Is she breathing? Did you try slapping her? Go ahead and smack her across the face, honey. I'll wait."

Now Melissa was openly crying. "Okay," she whimpered. Dane could hear his daughter's efforts to rouse her mother. "Mama! Mama, please!"

Dane began to pace, then turned and walked in the direction of the lot where his car was parked.

"Dane! Where're you going?" Sal called after him.

"Got an emergency," he called back. "Call ya later!"

Dane kept Melissa on the phone as he took to the freeway. Afternoon traffic was brutal, and he skirted the trouble spots as best he could, resorting to surface streets around the major intersections. Melissa had opened the gates as he'd requested, and he sped up the driveway and parked.

Melissa held the door open for him. "She told me never to call the doctor when this happens," she said, standing to one side as Dane strode briskly into the house.

"Living room?" he asked as they walked.

"Yeah."

Dane rushed to the couch where his ex-wife lay sprawled. "Rita! Come on. Come on, Rita." Grasping her chin, he turned her head from side to side. He pulled open one eyelid and tried to see her pupil. Looking around, he found an empty bottle of gin on the floor. "Rita!" he repeated. "Mimi, get me a glass of cold water."

His daughter complied and Dane dumped it onto Rita's face. The woman sputtered and groaned, then returned to her comatose-like condition.

"Crap. We need to get her to a doctor. I don't want to second-guess this."

"Don't call an ambulance. She'll kill us. The neighbors might see."

"Do you know where the nearest hospital is?"

"Yeah, we pass it all the time on the way to school. It's just down the hill."

"Where is your sister?"

"Upstairs, in her room. She won't come down. I think she's too scared."

"Go get her."

"She won't come for me. You go."

With a deep sigh, Dane turned and took the stairs two at a time, opening doors and calling Zoe's name. He found his youngest sitting in the corner of her bedroom, a box of chocolates on her lap. Her eyes were round with fear and confusion.

"Come on, Zo. We're gonna take Mom to the doctor."

"She's dead."

"No, she's not. She's just very, very sick. Now come on." Zoe got to her feet and Dane was dismayed to see the chocolate stains on her shirt. The weight she'd lost during her summer in Wyoming was creeping back on. "Come on, sweetheart. After we take care of Mom, I'll take you up to see Jessie. Would you like that?"

Zoe's face grew hopeful.

"Now grab your jacket and come with me."

Downstairs, Melissa was ashen. "Daddy," she ventured. "Mommy's... bleeding."

"Bleeding? Where?"

Melissa pointed to a spot-on Rita's head, above her ear. Gingerly she lifted a strand of Rita's chestnut hair, exposing an ugly red gash on her scalp.

"Where's the phone?" Dane asked. "Neighbors or no neighbors, we need an ambulance."

"Will she be okay?" Melissa asked as she lost sight of the gurney carrying her mother down the emergency room corridor.

Dane looked at Melissa, feeling it was the first time he'd really seen her today. Pale, drawn and much too worried for a thirteen-year-old, Melissa was obviously frightened. Zoe, sitting in the administrator's chair, seemed oblivious to her surroundings. Dane went to Melissa and gently, if hesitantly, embraced her. His daughter looked up at him briefly before dissolving into a torrent of tears.

"She didn't mean to do it. It's only because that horrid woman turned her down," Melissa sobbed. "Now, she's so sad she drinks all the time. I can't take care of her anymore! I can't! I can't..."

"Shh. It's okay, darlin'. We'll get Mom all fixed up good as new, Okay? Don't worry. You don't have to worry any more. I'll take over from here. I promise. It'll all be fine." Dane struggled to comfort the girl who was caught between the childhood she craved and the adulthood that was coming all too soon. With remorse, he realized that he had not held this daughter in his arms since she was a toddler.

After what seemed like an eternity of waiting, a doctor appeared and beckoned to Dane.

"Well, we're going to keep her a couple of days. She has a concussion, caused by the conk on the head. Looks like she hit a sharp corner or something. She has a dangerous amount of alcohol in her blood, and unfortunately, some traces of barbiturates. Probably Vicodin. She's basically a mess and I'll be recommending..." the doctor paused to glance at Dane's children, sitting together now on the waiting room couch. "A good facility where Mrs. Pierce can get some... rest."

Dane nodded and filled his lungs. "Thanks, doc. Can I see her?"

"Not right now. If you want to come back later this evening, she might be able to talk to you then."

Dane put the girls into his car and took them back to Rita's house. He was glad it was Saturday, and they would not have school in the morning. Thanksgiving was just days away. After throwing a snack together for the three of them, Dane picked up the phone.

"Tom? It's Dane. I have a favor to ask."

He was unprepared for anything but a hearty welcome for his daughters while he tended their mother. What he heard, instead, was that Roxanne was sick and recuperating from a severe anxiety attack.

"She'd be glad to do it, you know that, if she could. It's been a tough time. It seemed to happen just after that guy confessed to killing Mac. She just came unglued that morning. Doctor says she'll be better after a few days' rest."

"I am so sorry, Tom. What a terrible... Is there anything I can do?"

"Sounds like your plate is pretty full already. But thanks."

"You keep us posted, will you?"

"Sure will. Dane, I'd watch them myself but I'm spending all my time with Rox. I'm worthless without her."

"No excuses are necessary, friend."

"I'm sorry about Rita."

"Brought it on herself, I'm afraid. The girls are taking it hard, though. I'll be in touch."

Dane ended the call but held the phone in his hand. "How's your Gramma doing these days?" he asked Melissa, who was getting milk for her sister.

"She's okay. Mom doesn't always talk to her when she calls, though."

"I'm going to call her."

"Mom will be—"

"Mad, yeah, I'm sure. Mom is out of choices right now."

Rita's mother was quietly aghast at Dane's revelations about her daughter.

"She's going to need you, Irene. I'm taking the girls up to the ranch for Thanksgiving. The doctors are going to send her down to..." Dane paused and walked into the adjoining dining room, "the Monroe Institute. It's a drying out farm for A-list drunks and drug addicts."

After extracting a promise from his ex-mother-in-law, Dane had one more call to make. Luckily, Trina was still at home.

"I don't do kids, Dane."

"You owe me."

"I do owe you, but—"

"No 'buts,' darlin'. I know this is a big one, so I'll owe you back some. Deal?"

He could hear Trina sigh over the phone. "Just one night?"

"I'll pay you whatever you would have made tonight."

"It's not the money. I'm just not... oh, hell. Give me directions."

The nurses and technicians came and went. Some of them may have recognized him, but if they did, they hid it well or it did not matter to them. It was a private room, the lights dimmed for the night and quiet except for the not-too-distant beeps and rings and clanks of the instruments on the ward. Dane shifted in the "guest" chair, leaning forward, his elbows propped on his knees as he braced his chin against his clasped hands. Watching Rita sleep.

She didn't look so bad. How long had the drinking been going on? Melissa had lied for her mother, he knew. It might have been a gradual increase, over the years. Perhaps when she parted ways with Fred. Or even back before then, when she'd found out about Dane and... whoever it was. Whatever girl she'd heard he'd been seen with.

He closed his eyes. It wasn't a pleasant memory, certainly one he'd like to forget.

A glance at the wall clock above Rita's bed indicated it was almost time for them to bother her again. A blood draw, perhaps. A 1 a.m. injection of some kind. A change in the I.V. drip. A movement from the bed caught his eye. Rita was waking up.

"What the hell are *you* doing here?" she said hoarsely, looking around. "And where is here, anyway?" She attempted to sit up, but Dane was quick on his feet and held her back.

"Don't. You're all wired up. It's Mercy General, you... fell and bashed yourself on the head."

Alarm crept onto Rita's face. Alarm and the obvious worry about the obvious problem; someone, possibly many someones, knew about her drinking.

"Where are the girls?"

"They are asleep, at home, with a sitter. Don't worry. It's under control."

"And I suppose I have you to thank for that. Well, no thanks."

Dane shook his head. "You really hate me, don't you?"

Rita turned her head away, grimacing. "Christ that hurts."

"It should. You put a good-sized dent in your noggin."

"Like you really care."

"I do care."

Rita turned back to look at him, still frowning. He couldn't tell if it was from the pain in her head or because it was his face to which she'd awakened.

"Is that all that happened?" she asked guardedly.

"If you mean does anyone know you were stinking drunk, yes, they do. Everybody knows, so you can quit worrying about them finding out. Your daughters will forgive you."

Rita's eyes filled with tears, and she looked down at her hands. "How do you know?"

"Because they forgave me, and what I did was a lot worse. That's how I know."

His ex-wife sniffed and tried to brush away a tear. "They never stopped loving you. Melissa defended you forever. We finally called a truce and agreed not to talk about you at all."

Now it was Dane's turn to battle a lump in his throat. He'd had no idea of his oldest daughter's devotion.

"I hear you've stepped in it again with the new one. What's up with that? She asking too much? Like wanting you to stay around some?"

Dane didn't answer.

"You might as well pack it in. You'll never be good at that relationship crap. You can't commit."

"What did you say?"

"I said you can't fully commit to anyone. Don't sneer at me. I know. Not to be trite, but I've been there."

"I didn't give up my whole day and night to be pissed on, Margarita. I do have better things to do."

"Like what? What's left to do? One of these days, you're going to have to stop blaming every woman you meet for your mother's death." Rita groaned and lay back, closing her eyes.

"Leave her out of this. My mother has nothing to do with our splitting up, or my problems with any other woman, for that matter. I don't know where you're coming from."

"It doesn't matter," she murmured. "Could you please call a nurse or something? My head is killing me."

He was tempted to leave while the nurses huddled over Rita, poking, prodding and making notes. Something made him stay. The first rays of light were just beginning to color the draperies when she spoke to him again.

"It wasn't all your fault," she said softly. "It was mine, too."

Dane pushed his hair back away from his forehead. "How do you figure?"

"I sat by and let it happen. I didn't fight for you. I was bitter, I was younger, I wanted you to just come back and apologize. Instead, I substituted someone else to make me feel important."

"Rita—"

"No, Dane, it's true. I should have come back to L.A. and hauled you out of bed and made you at least talk it out. I know, now, that you can't take the heat. You not only get out of the kitchen, you get out of town. And right now, you're even out of state, aren't you?"

Dane squirmed in his chair. Damn this woman for being right. "It's not that simple."

"It never is simple, is it? That's what scares you. You're so afraid she'll leave you, like Mom did, so you make sure you leave first. Am I right?"

"Mom didn't leave me, God damn it! She died! It wasn't her choosing."

"Be that as it may, she wasn't there anymore, and it hurt."

Dane gave his ex-wife a level stare, and she turned away. After a time, he was able to speak again. "What ever happened with Fred, anyway?"

"Oh, Fred, the-tennis-pro-Fred? Hmm," she responded with a little smile. "Let's just say he was encouraged to swing his racket elsewhere."

"And... Was this before, or after, you lost the baby?"

"There was no baby."

"But you told me—"

"I lied."

Dane wet his lips. This conversation was more than he could handle at one time.

"I wanted to hurt you, like you were hurting me."

"We weren't very good to each other, were we?"

"Could have been better," Rita acknowledged. "You still have a chance with... what's her name? Jessica? Unless she's already given up the fight."

Dane recalled the night Jessica had shown up at the restaurant, and their subsequent argument at the new house in Malibu. Jessica had done exactly what Rita regretted not doing—she'd shown up, prepared for battle, hoping to take her husband home with her. Instead, he'd forced her to leave him there, drunk and unwilling to abandon his unjustified self-pity.

"I'm sorry," he finally said, and Rita lifted her eyes to peer into Dane's face.

"For what? For how you treated me, or how you're treating her now?"

"For everything. Such a fool..."

"Are you sleeping with someone else yet?"

"No, I'm not."

"Then don't blow it."

The morning nurse brought medication and interrupted their talk. "How are we doing this morning? Ready to get out of bed?"

"*We* are feeling shaky," Rita grumbled. "Can I have some coffee?"

"I'll have some decaf brought in with your breakfast."

"Decaf? Worthless."

Dane smiled in spite of himself. "Look. I'd better get back to the house and check on the girls. I'll be back this afternoon to drive you up to Monroe."

"Monroe? Oh, no, you don't. I'm not going there. You can just forget that idea, Mr. Pierce. I'm going home, today, to my own house and—"

"And to what? A new bottle of gin?"

The startled nurse faded away and Rita gave Dane a steely look.

Dane sighed. "I made a deal with your doctor. You check in at Monroe, he keeps this whole little incident under wraps."

"And if I don't?"

"No telling who might find out."

"Crap. What about the girls?"

"They're going up to the ranch with me for Thanksgiving. I'll keep them until you're out of treatment." Rita's startled expression spurred him on. "Melissa needs a break from the responsibility of taking care of you. You need to go back to being her mother, and she can go back to being a kid. Got it?"

Dane nearly laughed out loud at the sight awaiting him in Rita's kitchen. Trina was digging browned scrambled eggs out of a skillet, grumbling something about cold cereal, and the girls were both giggling from their seats at the breakfast bar. Dressed in well-worn jeans, ragged at the bottoms and adorned with rhinestones, the babysitter also sported a short, midriff-baring top and high-heeled cork sandals. Her magenta hair popped out above a green bandana wrapped around her forehead.

"Daddy! Trina is soooo cool!" Zoe exclaimed, hopping down from the stool and running to meet her father.

"Yeah, she's cool, all right," Dane agreed, lifting Zoe into his arms. "Glad to see we've all acclimated," he added, grinning at Trina.

"We're having a bang-up time, Dad," Trina agreed. "Hope you warned these ladies that I can't cook worth a darn..."

Thirty-One

A Walk in the Snow

"Ten weeks. Minimum. And that's if they let him re-enter the U.S. with that expired visa on his record."

Lydia's face was a picture of despair, and Jessica's heart ached for her. "That's not so bad, Lyd. Could be worse. At least his, uh, wife is willing to cooperate. It will pass before you know it."

"Things are so hard now. Immigration is just awful. I was so hoping we could get married sooner, like we planned, before Christmas."

Jessica sighed. "Well, it doesn't look like that will happen." She put her arm around her personal assistant and friend. "Look. If Pete can't come home, then we'll just have to package you up and mail you to England."

Lydia looked stunned. "Me? To England? Are you serious?"

"Of course, I'm serious. You need to be with Peter, and that's that. Call the airline, then get yourself packing. You can be there by Thanksgiving."

"They don't exactly celebrate it over there, Jess."

"So what?" Jessica giggled. "You won't have any trouble finding a turkey then."

Jessica hoped she would not regret sending Lydia to Great Britain. Although Dane had mentioned coming home, she forced herself not to count on it. He could bail out at the last minute, and she'd have a very cozy holiday with Devon and Alexander. And a large turkey, to boot.

Fortunately, Lydia's passport was in order. The recent trip to her mother's home in Argentina had proved beneficial. In a flurry of anticipation and excitement, Jessica bid her goodbye and Lydia was off to meet her betrothed in London.

•♥•♥•♥•♥•♥•

The midday sun took the chill off the brisk November air. The drive to the Monroe Institute had been sobering, riding along with the woman Dane thought he'd known so well. Rita had resigned herself to the future and was mostly quiet along the way. Her only request was that he take good care of the girls and tell them she loved them; that she'd be home and back with them soon. They did not talk about the admonitions she'd flung his way from her hospital bed, nor the duration of her drinking habit. He gave her a brief hug when it was time to go.

Now, hours later, Dane steered the Mustang between the iron gates of the memorial park, slowly maneuvering along the narrow roads that passed between the different burial "regions." Near the end of the last road, he pulled over and sat in the car for several minutes before forcing himself to get out.

It was another fifty or sixty yards to his first destination. His mother's crypt, set on a small knoll, was no different than it had been the day she'd been laid to rest there. Yet he was different. Placing a small nosegay in the permanent bud vase on the front of the crypt, Dane sat on the adjacent bench and smiled. Rita's words were coming back to him in a big way. He'd been completely devoted to Marian Pierce, and she had left him.

"Ah, Mom," he whispered. "What should I do?"

He didn't really expect an answer. Getting off the bench, he placed his hand against the small brass placard bearing her name. "I'll do the right thing. Right? I will." *I hope.*

Farther up the hill was the gravesite of his best friend. Nothing fancy, not showy, Mac MacKendall's final resting place looked just the same as most of the plots in the park. Dane shoved his hands into his pockets and stood at the foot of the grave.

"Damn you, MacKendall." Dane shook his head slowly, a bittersweet smile curling his lips. "This is all your fault."

Right. Like he ever did anything but try to protect what was rightfully his.

"I'm, uh, sorry for what I said that night. You didn't deserve it." Dane looked over his shoulder, hoping there was no one within earshot of his confession. "I just... I just love her so much, dammit. I'm not telling you anything new." He leaned his head back, peering at the sky above, wondering if Mac was watching from somewhere on high. "I can't change what happened. I've wished a hundred times, a thousand times that I could. If I'd said something different, or done something different... maybe if I hadn't made that stupid promise..."

The surrounding silence unnerved him, and Dane was getting no answers. What had he hoped to find? To hear? After another glance down at Mac's headstone, he turned and made a quick trek back to his car. There was one more stop to make.

The house in Benedict Canyon was, for the most part, exactly as he'd left it five years before. The bloodstained carpet had been replaced; there was no physical evidence of the grisly morning Jackie Spencer had shot herself, and him, on the living room floor. A crew routinely removed the cobwebs and cleaned up the yard. It was colder than he could stand, however, and he flipped on the forced air heat before touring the big house.

It's probably time to ditch this place, he thought, realizing he hadn't missed the house and he could transfer the assets into the new home.

Driven by some unseen force, Dane went into his old bedroom and directly to the closet. In the back corner, on a high shelf next to the spot where he used to keep his Stetson was a locked cashbox. He took it down and unceremoniously blew the dust from the top. From the keys in his pocket, he selected one and slid it into the lock; the key turned easily and with a tug on the handle, the box was open.

Inside laid the journal.

March 16:

If I had any doubts about MacKendall they have been dashed, and I have the sore jaw to prove it. Too bad he is such a fool he can't see what he is doing to her, and to himself...

I drove him to the airstrip this morning, playing the role, being his "friend" when in truth I am hoping he takes a wrong turn and ends up in the Bermuda Triangle... or worse. And now she is sad. I can only hope that his abrupt departure will turn her off and buy me some time with her...

Dane groaned at his own words of years before. Flipping a few pages, he read more.

Try as I might, I cannot seem to put her in the background. It upsets me to think that I could become so completely enticed by one woman. She is like a tattoo upon my soul. This is insane.

"This is insane. Why am I doing this?" Dane snapped the journal closed and carried it downstairs to the large, rustic den. He sat down on the brown leather couch and held the book against his chest. Rubbing his eyes, he tried to focus on the cold, empty fireplace before him.

Mac was leaning against the mantel, his eyes blazing. His voice was thick with anger, and he began to pace as he spoke.

"...yes, I read it. Read every damned page."

"You had no right—"

"I know that, and I'm sorry. Nevertheless, I read it."

"You're sorry. And did you do that to punish me, or yourself?"

Mac stopped pacing briefly and stared at him.

"You're pissed off," Dane recalled saying.

"Christ, Dane, you're in love with my wife! How do you expect me to feel?" Mac began pacing again, his agitation building. "I thought—I thought that was all over. I thought we were friends!"

We were friends, Mac. You were the best friend. Like my brother.

Dane again rubbed his eyes. Mac wasn't really here. Mac was dead. But when he looked again, the apparition was still seething. Dane's own words came back, as if the confrontation had been only yesterday.

> *"You are the last jerk on earth I wanted to get close to. You beat me hands down at my own game. And you don't play dirty. You make me sick with your morality, your reason, and you're a lousy drinker. You're forever making me look bad. But the night your son was born, it occurred to me that I didn't have to compete with you, and, I won't. You have my word, Mac."*

My word.

> *"...just one word of caution," Dane had added. "If you ever, ever take off on her again, I'm only giving you twenty-four hours to get back. After that, she's fair game."*

> *"You won't ever have to worry about that."*

> *"I won't. It's you who should worry, pal."*

Twenty-four hours to get back. How stupid. As if he could come back at all.

> *"I won't worry."*

But Mac did worry. *And that's why he called me that night from his hotel room.*

Dane sighed and got to his feet, pacing before the couch himself. He was still holding the journal, and he was angry with himself for writing it. For still having it. For reading it again. He threw the book onto the couch. It was time to pick up his daughters and go home. If Wyoming was still to be his home.

·♥·♥·♥·♥·♥·

More antsy than ever, Jessica roamed the big house, frequently tuning in the all-news television stations for any updates about Benjamin and the wicked Irma Carvey. She was rewarded, at last, on the day before Thanksgiving.

Neighbors had turned her in. The cameras zoomed in on Irma's staunch, pale face as authorities in Minneapolis handcuffed the former adoption agency clerk. A stoic Russ Morrison stood by.

"Who's that, Mommy?" Devon wanted to know, climbing into his mother's lap.

"A bad woman," Jessica murmured, her eyes focused intensely, hoping to get a glimpse of her young nephew. Unfortunately, the media was not yet privy to the boy's whereabouts at the time of the arrest. "A very bad woman."

Her mind racing, Jessica stood and placed her son on his feet. "Devon, go find Greg, will you? Mommy needs to talk to him. I think he's in the barn. And put your coat on!"

Devon scampered from the room and Jessica picked up the telephone. "Northwind Airlines, reservations please," she said to the information operator. After the airline answered, she was put on hold. Still, she watched the television screen. After a minute or two, Greg tramped into the great room, stomping snow from his boots at the door.

"You needed something?"

"Yeah, could you please pick up Alexander for me today? I don't want to miss this... this program." Her excuse sounded so hollow, but she believed Greg would understand what was going on. "Please?"

"No problem, Mrs. Boss. I'll leave in about five minutes. I need to stop at the tack store anyway."

"Thanks."

"I wanna go!" Devon shouted, bouncing in front of his mother to gain her attention.

"No, not this time, Dev. Be still."

"But tomorrow's no school an' I can't go."

"Tomorrow's Thanksgiving," Jessica said. "I wonder if we'll be alone."

"Pop's coming home," Devon said importantly, marching back and forth before the fireplace.

"Maybe."

"No, really. He said."

"When did he say?"

"Today. On the ant sheen," Devon said, pointing to the answering machine on the bar. "He said he'll be home soon."

"How soon?" Jessica asked, alarmed as she crossed to the machine and stared at its display window. "Devon, it doesn't say anyone called. Are you sure?"

"Pop called. He's coming. I raced the message."

"You what? You erased it?" Still on hold, Jessica hung up the phone in frustration. "Devon MacKendall, how many times have I told you not to play with this machine! Now I can't hear Daddy's message!" She stared with disdain at the archaic device. Her exasperation escalated.

"I want to go with Greg!" Devon shouted back at her, kicking his foot demonstratively and knocking over the fireplace tools. The clatter was deafening.

"Okay. That's it. Go upstairs to your room, right now!" Jessica demanded, pointing toward the staircase in anger. "Go!"

A change in the news program caught her ear and she turned.

"We're outside the police station where young Benjamin MacKendall has been reunited with his foster parents. There's no hiding the joy on the faces of this young family as they greet the little boy who lived with them almost from birth. This is the same couple, we understand, who tried to adopt MacKendall, even after the open-heart surgery that would have turned many prospective adoptive parents away. A heartwarming scene, coming to you live from downtown Minneapolis."

Jessica slowly lowered herself to sit on the couch. The woman holding Benjie was crying, smiling through her tears and kissing the tot repeatedly. There was no mistaking the enormous love and relief on the faces of both the parents. Hollowness began to spread throughout Jessica's chest. She would not need to call the airlines back.

So, Irma had hoodwinked them all. The couple Jessica thought had withdrawn their application had not. The baby clearly loved the couple. There was no room in the equation for Jessica.

Clicking off the remote, Jessica sat in silence for several minutes, her heart so heavy she felt it difficult to breathe. The quiet of the house enhanced the feeling. In fact, the house was too quiet.

"Dev?" she called, looking toward the stairway leading to the second floor. "Dev? You can come down now. Mommy's sorry."

No sound returned from Devon's bedroom door.

"Devon?" Jessica took to the stairs and hurried up to the first bedroom on the left. The door was open, the room empty. "That little scamp." The other rooms were vacant as well.

Back downstairs, Jessica hurried into her down parka and stepped outside, eyes perusing the courtyard and the driveway. All was quiet.

"Devon! Where are you? Come on out, Mommy's sorry!"

While she knew Devon was hardly strong enough to open the heavy barn door, she looked inside anyway. Whiskey, king of the stable, looked around as if indignant at her intrusion. "Don't say it, Whisk. I know. I shouldn't have yelled at him." Whiskey blew her a raspberry and Jessica retreated from the barn.

Jessica spent a good fifteen minutes searching the immediate grounds for her son. A rising panic threatened her already shaky frame of mind. Where could he be?

Forcing herself to calm down, Jessica tried to focus her thoughts. Looking around, she was surprised to see footprints in the snow. Small ones that she'd missed before. They seemed to lead past the barn but disappeared into the snowbank Greg had created when clearing the driveway that morning. It was possible Devon had wandered off in the direction of the small, forested hills beyond the frozen streambed. How could she cover so much ground alone? With some trepidation, she looked back toward the barn and set her jaw.

·♥·♥·♥·♥·♥·

"Mimi, look! Snow! It's real snow!" Zoe jabbed at the window with her finger. Her sister, mesmerized at the sight of the white-blanketed runway, nodded slowly.

"Get your jackets back on. It's chilly out there," Dane told them, unbuckling his seatbelt and getting to his feet. "I've got a car waiting to take us to the ranch."

After securing his daughters in the backseat of the four-wheel drive Suburban, Dane slid behind the wheel and began the short drive to the ranch.

"Can we make a snowman, Daddy?" Zoe asked, now drawing happy faces in the fog on the door window.

"After we get you some gloves and snow boots."

"Does... Jessica... know we're coming?" Melissa asked, her arms crossed against her chest.

"Sure, she does. I'm sure she and Lydia have cooked up something nice and hot for your dinner. And don't look so nervous. You'll like Jess."

"Jess is cool," Zoe agreed, and Dane grinned at her in the rearview mirror.

The house was empty when they arrived, but a pot of coffee had just been brewed in the kitchen.

"She's probably at the school picking up your brother. Why don't you show your sister your bedroom? I'll bring your bags up in a bit," Dane told Zoe, and the girls happily clattered up the stairs. He poured himself a cup of the steaming brew and sat down to a stack of mail he found in a rack on the kitchen wall. All of it was unopened and addressed to him.

He'd been waiting a half hour or more when Greg and Alexander burst through the door, laughing and tramping in snow.

"Dad!" the boy shrieked and rushed to embrace his father, much to Dane's delight.

"So, you did call. Devon was right," Greg commented, reaching out to shake Dane's hand. "Where's the missus? I need to talk to her about some things before I take off."

"And where are you off to?"

"Portland. Goin' home to see my mama for the holiday."

"That's great. Uh, Jess didn't go with you?"

"Nope. She asked me to pick up Alex. She was watchin' some news show. I think it was about Benjamin."

Dane's eyes swept the room and rested on the television, which was off, then back toward the front windows of the house. "Well unless she bought another car while I was gone..."

"No, I was in the truck. There's no other vehicle on the premises besides your rental."

They took a few minutes to search the house. Jessica and Devon were nowhere to be found.

"They were fighting when I left. Devon was being a little shit about having to stay home."

Dane put on his coat and gloves, and turned to his children, all three of which were at various levels on the staircase. "You kids stay put. I'm gonna take a little walk. Greg, if you need to leave before I get back, just make sure the kids are locked in. And have a nice visit with your mom, you hear?"

"Sure, Boss. Thanks. Tell the missus and the little squirt bye for me."

Dane looked around the courtyard. He was about to enter the barn when a movement in the distance caught his eye. A lone horse with no rider was approaching; an unmistakably large, auburn steed with a proud, arrogant attitude was slowly making his way toward the barn. With a nervous sigh, Dane met Whiskey halfway.

"All right, you old nag, what did you do with my woman?" The big roan horse snorted and turned his head away. Dane reached beneath Whiskey's belly and tested the buckle on the surcingle. "Not bad, Jess," he muttered. Hoisting himself onto the horse's back, he steered the horse close to the house where Greg was watching from the porch. "You cinch this saddle?"

"Nope. She musta done it herself. She's been practicing."

Dane nodded and tugged the reins to the right, heading up the hill and away from the house. He shuddered a little, the frigid air turning his breath into small white clouds around his face. A gnawing began in his stomach, a small worry that he tried to ignore.

Why can't horses be like dogs, he wondered in irritation. "Come on, Whisk, where'd you leave her?" He thought he might be following some tracks, but the snow was old, and the trail was unclear. It was twenty minutes before he thought he heard voices. He pulled Whiskey to a stop.

"If you hadn't run off like that, this wouldn't be happening." Jessica's voice was brittle with irritation and fear, sounding close to tears.

"I'm sorry, Mommy." Devon sounded even worse. Then, "Look! It's Pop!"

Dane slid from the saddle and bent to receive the child who thrust his small body into his stepfather's arms. "Hey, Champ, you been out for a walk in the snow?"

Jessica paused in her tracks. Jamming her gloveless hands into the pockets of her jeans, she glared at Dane.

Dane stared back at her, an uncontrolled smile forming on his lips. She looked so incredibly beautiful, her cheeks blooming with a blush he'd missed so much. Her face seemed fuller, softer, and the icy breeze caused the long curls to dance around her neck.

"How about a lift?" he asked, swinging Devon up onto the saddle just behind the horn, then turning to offer Jessica his hand.

"Uh uh. Not on your life. I wouldn't get back on that... that hack... if you paid me."

"Suit yourself. It's a long walk back."

Jessica merely crossed her arms and started forward, stumbling a little but with her chin held high. Dane shook his head and climbed on to Whiskey's back behind Devon.

"Mommy forgot to tie Whiskey up to the tree, when we was fighting, and Whiskey went away! He was probably hungry or somethin'," Devon explained. Jessica glowered.

"You hold on to the horn. We'll talk about it when we get home," Dane advised, trying to sound firm and fatherly despite his amusement. He kept Whiskey at a slow, ambling walk so as not to leave Jessica too far behind.

The evening was strained at best. Greg had gone, and Dane and Jessica were alone with their blended family. Only Zoe seemed joyful, delighted to be back in the home she loved and where she felt content. A suitcase full of Barbie dolls was spread open before the fireplace. Melissa sat with a book; Alexander and Devon remained in their bedroom building with snap-together blocks. Jessica busied herself getting ready for the following day's dinner while Dane caught up on his mail.

"What in the world made you take Whisk for a ride? Your own horse not good enough?"

"Greg told me Mariah is pregnant. I didn't think I should saddle her. And I couldn't get near Barleycorn."

Dane scoffed and picked up another stack of mail. "So, Lydia went too?" he asked, not looking up as he tossed most of the envelopes, unopened, into the recycle bin.

"I felt it was the right thing to do."

"Hmm."

"You have a problem with that?"

"Nope." A pause. "Just thought you might have mentioned it sooner."

"Like when? Was I supposed to call you off the set to ask permission?"

Dane looked up, the strain in Jessica's voice resounding off the walls. "The film's been shut down."

Jessica, her back to him as she stood at the kitchen sink, paused momentarily to think about Dane's words. When he didn't continue, she ventured her curiosity. "Permanently?"

"No. But at least until after New Year's. Lisa fractured her ankle."

Jessica sucked in her upper lip but did not turn around. She was relieved, despite her growing disenchantment with Dane, that he would not be seeing the starlet for a time.

"What a shame," she murmured, wringing out the dishcloth in her hands. "Bet you're disappointed."

"Not in the least. I wasn't really there. It wasn't going too well to begin with. Maybe after the holidays..."

"Yeah, maybe." Jessica crossed to the refrigerator and opened it, peering in for some item she'd already forgotten she was looking for. "Zoe's gained weight," she said, wanting to change the subject.

"Rita hasn't been the most... attentive mother."

"She should just stay with us."

"From one dysfunctional family to another."

Jessica whirled around at the subtle sarcasm in Dane's voice. "And what's that supposed to mean?"

Dane grinned at her, a detached, melancholic musing that unnerved her.

"It means absolutely nothing," he said, getting up from the chair on which he'd been sitting. Dane retreated from the room, his murmured postscript wafting back to Jessica's ear. "Not a thing."

THIRTY-TWO

The Chase is On

It was, undoubtedly, the most dismal Thanksgiving Jessica had ever experienced. She had thought the prior year's unhappy event at her brother's home would be the worst she would ever have to suffer through. By noon on this gray November day, Jessica already knew that last year had been a walk in the park.

"Do you know where your father went?" Jessica asked the sisters, who were playing a board game on the great room floor.

"Nope. Just said he'd be back later." Melissa, lying on her stomach, got to her feet and straightened her sweater. "Need some help?"

"Well, yeah, actually I could use you both in the kitchen."

Eagerly, both girls followed Jessica and donned the whimsically patterned aprons Jessica had bought for them. Together they scrubbed and peeled, chopped and seasoned, kneaded and baked. At 4 p.m., the dinner was nearly finished.

"Not too shabby, if I say so myself," Jessica murmured, carefully lifting a lattice-crusted cherry pie from the oven. "This is so clever, Mimi. How is it that you have learned to cook so well? Does your mom cook a lot?"

Melissa's face became shuttered. Exactly like Dane, Jessica thought with surprise.

"She used to," Melissa said, then brightened. "The cranberries! We forgot to cook them!"

"We have the canned stuff," Jessica said quickly.

"No. These only take a minute. Takes lots of sugar, though."

"Great," Jessica lamented, smoothing her own apron across her stomach. "That's just what I need. Zoe, go tell the boys to wash up and come downstairs. I want them to finish setting the table."

Dinner was exactly as Jessica had hoped it would not be. Dane, melancholy and withdrawn, sat at the head of their table and, after carving the turkey, ate his meal in near silence. Melissa, Jessica supposed, was thinking about her mother, and Zoe was unusually reserved. Only the boys chattered during the meal.

"Aren't we gonna have to say what we're thankful for?" Alexander wondered aloud, looking first at Jessica and then with obvious reluctance, his father.

"I think it would suffice to say we're all delighted to be here," Dane said flatly, and Jessica's stomach tightened. Grudgingly she forced another bite and offered the closest thing to a smile she could muster. She caught Dane's eyes briefly, but her husband returned his attention to his plate.

I'm glad someone has an appetite, Jessica thought sourly.

"Frank Conway was arraigned," Dane muttered.

"Of course. I know. I didn't want to be there."

"They'll nail his ass, don't worry."

"I'm not." Jessica refused to meet Dane's eyes, if he was even looking her way. She presumed he wasn't but didn't want to risk it.

Afterward, it was with some relief that she found herself cleaning up alone. Lost in thought, she slowly rinsed each china dinner plate and loaded them into the dishwasher.

I have to get out of here.

Dane had said nothing meaningful since his arrival. The fact that he'd slept in Peter's bedroom sealed the verdict: their marriage had failed. Jessica couldn't bring herself to examine the reasons. She'd thought about it so much already, and there were no new angles. The fact remained that Dane was powerless against the demons holding his heart captive, and he didn't love her enough to fight them.

Now, her biggest regret was allowing Devon to become so attached to Dane. It would be difficult for the little boy to lose another father. But she had little choice. Staying in a painful, loveless marriage would be worse, and Devon would surely suffer for it.

Pretending not to notice Dane and Alexander as they sat before the television in the great room, Jessica trotted briskly up the stairs, tuning out the annoying cacophony of the football game in progress. She would pack tonight and get a flight out tomorrow. And with any luck, she could slip away without confrontation.

"Did you even tell him goodbye?" Jan Taylor asked, pouring a cup of hot tea for her daughter.

"I left him a letter."

"A letter? A 'Dear John'? Oh, Jessica."

"I know, it was cowardly. But I knew we'd argue, and I would end up bawling and upsetting the kids. They were upset enough as it was. They were up when we left."

"Did you tell him where you'd gone?"

"Just that I was going to visit you. I seriously doubt he has any clue about where in Washington State you live." Jessica rubbed her eyes and then glanced up as her mother's kitchen clock chimed eleven. "You don't think he'll follow me, do you?"

"Honey, I barely know the man."

"He won't. Anyway, he's got the kids to worry about."

Jan nodded, sipping her tea. "Devon sure is fond of him."

"Dev idolizes Dane. He asked about fifty times when we'll see 'Pop' again. I feel so guilty about this whole mess."

"Maybe it isn't such a mess. Could be you just need some time apart. To think things over."

"Time apart is not the solution, Mom. We've had plenty of that. I've done everything I can think of to make things work. Dane just seems to have given up on us. He can't get rid of that stupid notion."

"What notion?"

"For some reason he keeps thinking I'm still in love with Mac. He keeps comparing our marriage to mine before. I can't make him see how wrong he is. And there're things he's not telling me. I begged him to come back to me!"

Jessica's mother was quiet for a moment, resting her hand over her daughter's. "Mac was a hard act to follow," she said gently. "Dane has every right to worry. It doesn't help that he was Mac's friend, or that he's a substitute father to Mac's son."

"You sound like you're defending him."

Her mother did not respond to Jessica's accusation. Instead, she looked up brightly. "What's up with Roxanne these days?"

"We're not speaking."

"And why not? You've always been so close."

"She told the police that Dane killed Mac."

If her mother was surprised at Jessica's bold statement, she did not show it. Jessica continued.

"We haven't been friends for a while, Mom. She had a miscarriage last winter and didn't even tell me. I still don't know what I did wrong."

"It might have nothing to do with you," her mother said at last. Jan rose from her chair and put her cup in the sink. "I've got to get up early, dear. I promised my grandson he could go with me to feed the horses in the morning."

"Good. That might cheer him up. On top of everything else, he argued with Alex as we were leaving."

"He'll be fine. You'll all be fine."

Doubtful, Jessica rose also and followed her mother's lead. Bed sounded good.

Before retiring, Jessica tiptoed into the attic room with the sloping ceiling where Devon lay sleeping, innocent of all. She was already worried about how the events of the last eighteen months would affect his adulthood, how he would relate to the women and men who would pass in and out of his life. Closing her eyes tightly, she could only pray that he would turn out okay.

Later, lying in her own bed, her thoughts turned back to Dane and what he might have felt while reading her brief note, relief or pain. She wondered if he would stay in Wyoming over the holidays or beeline it back to L.A. She labored over whether she had made the right decision or not.

Devon's excited shouts brought Jessica around the next morning.

"You should see! They've got a new baby horse! Mom, get up!"

"Okay, okay, give Mommy a minute, will you?" Jessica begged, struggling to sit up from the unfamiliar mattress. Devon stepped back and gave her a winsome smile, and for just a moment, Jessica was certain she was looking into the face of a five-year-old Cory

MacKendall. The image shook her. "I'll be just a minute, sweetheart. You go on back downstairs and I'll be there soon."

In the kitchen, her mother was putting out a plate of muffins and scones.

"There's coffee, honey. My neighbor brought over the pastries. Help yourself."

Desirous of nothing more than a sugar-and-caffeine rush, Jessica did help herself as she watched Devon romping in the pasture behind her mother's house. "Looks like he's having fun," she said, gulping a healthy dose of coffee while peering out the kitchen window. "He loves horses. Dane's got him riding well now."

"Feel any better?" Jan asked, her face a picture of pity and yet a certain determination that bothered Jessica.

"No. Not as tired, but I'm still... still... upset." It wasn't the right word, but her mother's expression unnerved her.

"Oh, before I forget, I've got some mail here for you. Seems the post office was unable to deliver it to your address in Wyoming, something about there being no address on the road? Anyway, it looks important. Only how they found me I have no idea."

Jessica took and then slit open the certified mail envelope, quickly skimming the letter inside. "It's about Wesley."

"What about him? He's not out, is he?"

Jessica glanced up at her mother's wall calendar. "Yes, he was paroled a week ago. It's policy to let the victim know. And they couldn't find me. That's just great. As if I don't have enough to worry about."

"Well, he doesn't know where I am. I moved up here the year after they locked him up." Jan picked up a piece of paper from the kitchen counter, and after a moment of obvious uncertainty, she cleared her throat. "Jessica. I've been thinking, and I feel you're being too hasty about Dane. You haven't even given this marriage six months and you've already packed it in. Men are... not all that... astute about their feelings. Sometimes you have to drive the bus yourself."

"I tried driving the damned bus, Mom. I used all my power. And for what?"

"I'm only saying, don't rush into a major decision. Here, I want you to take a few days off, just by yourself. I've made reservations at a wonderful little bed and breakfast up in Port Townsend for you.

You can take Daddy's car and be there in an hour. Kick back, think things through, maybe give Dane a call." She forced the paper she'd been holding into Jessica's hand.

"I can't do that. What about Dev?"

"Devon will be fine here with me. I raised three pretty decent kids myself, you know. And I need to get to know my grandson a little better."

"But... but..."

"But what? I dare you to think of a reason why you shouldn't go. And you'll love this little inn. It has a ring of familiarity to it. Very relaxing there. The town is just as laid back and easy going as can be."

Jessica stared at the paper, then back at her mother's determined expression. "Well... if you think it would be okay... I could use a break."

"Settled." Jan went to the back porch screened door and hollered. "Devon! Come inside and see your mama."

Just outside the town limits of the small burg in which her mother lived, Jessica began to cry. Her father's shiny red Cadillac fairly glided down the blacktop, the well-maintained engine purring and unhurried. Hastily she brushed the tears aside.

"Oh, Daddy, why can't any of them be like you?" she whimpered, blinking quickly to clear her vision. "I'm such a wreck. I can't seem to do this marriage thing at all." *Even my marriage to Mac was flawed and messy.* "Ha! And Dane thinks it was so perfect."

After a time, she calmed down and her mind cleared a little. She started looking forward to relaxing alone for a few days. Devon had been no less than thrilled to stay with his grandmother and the horses she boarded.

The inn was, as her mother assured her, a beautiful relic of elegant days gone by. Jessica parked the Caddy in front on the curbless street and pulled her travel bag from the back seat. Taking a deep breath, she turned the small knob on the manually-activated bell.

After a few moments, the wide front door swung open and a young woman stood smiling at her. Jessica dropped her bag in surprise. "Amy! Oh my gosh! Is it really you?"

"It's me! I couldn't believe it when your mom called me. She kept the card I sent her when we bought this place last year. Come on in!"

Jessica picked up her bag. "Brian told me you were living up here. But I was such a mess at the time... like when am I not a mess! I totally forgot about it." Stepping inside, Jessica again flung her bag down and embraced her old roommate.

"Well let's get you into a room so you can freshen up and gather your wits. Then we'll talk. Gosh, it's great to see you."

Jessica loved the suite Amy had reserved for her. Pink floral prints were everywhere. A huge private bath adjoined the room, complete with a claw foot tub and pedestal sink. A view from the bay window looked over Puget Sound. "This is just perfect," Jessica murmured while unpacking her bag. "I can't believe this. Thanks, Mom."

Soon, Jessica was sipping wine in the living room while Amy arranged cheese and crackers on a large platter.

"We set up wine and cheese nearly every night for the guests," she explained.

"Where is Casey?"

"Down at the wine shop buying some Pinot Grigio. A special request from the couple in the honeymoon suite across the hall from yours."

"Ah. Well, I can't wait to meet him. When are you two getting married?"

"Umm, don't know. We're not sure we want to be married. It's like, we don't know anyone who's all that happily married."

"I hear you," Jessica muttered, taking another sip of wine. "You might just be right."

"Well, really, I hope I'm not. I do want to have kids someday, and I think I'd like to be married when I do."

"That could be a good idea." Jessica sighed, looking around the lovely room filled with antiques and charm. She would not, could not, add the thought of not having more children to her growing list of woes. "What's to do around here? Where should I have dinner?"

"With us, of course. Don't be silly. But tomorrow you might want to wander downtown, there are lots of shops and restaurants, boutiques and touristy type stuff. I might be able to slip away and go with you for a while. Hey, we even have a movie theater!"

"No lie?"

Jessica found Case McKenna to be a warm, if quiet, gentleman. As Amy's significant other, he was a matching bookend for her friend. Educated, witty, and yet down to earth.

"MacKendall, McKenna. Yes, I thought of that right away," Jessica acknowledged over dinner.

"Weirder still, McKenna isn't my birth name. My folks were named Jenner. I moved in with my aunt when my, uh, dad passed away. Uncle Steve thought it would be easier if I went by McKenna; it was a small town." Case shrugged.

"I see." Jessica nodded, thinking about her own phone book length collection of names. Perhaps Dane had been wise not to have Devon take the Pierce name during the adoption.

The adoption. Another messy situation. Jessica dabbed at her lips with her napkin. "So. I'm going to play tourist tomorrow and spend all my money," she said with a chuckle.

"That could take a while," Amy said with a smile, "if you brought your credit cards."

After the dinner dishes were cleared away, Jessica retired to the living room with Amy. The girls chatted before a comforting fire, and Jessica was only remotely aware of Case's voice as he checked in a late arriving guest. The creaking of the staircase faded, and Amy grinned at Jessica.

"It was his turn," she explained.

"Do you usually get guests this late?"

"Sometimes. We were expecting this one, though."

Jessica nodded. "You have such a different life than I do. Seems like so much fun."

"I'd love to be in a movie," Amy said, rocking on the floor, her arms wrapped around her bent knees.

"Okay. We'll trade." Jessica giggled. "Not sure when I'll ever do another picture, though. Haven't felt much like it."

At Amy's prompting, Jessica described the mechanics of filmmaking and how long it took to put together a complete production.

"Amazing," Amy murmured, the firelight reflected in the dream-like expression in her eyes.

Jessica agreed but offered a caveat. "You really do give up a lot," she reflected. "It's really, really hard to have a normal life. I never thought—" The words stuck in her throat as a woman walked haltingly through the doorway.

Amy got quickly to her feet. "You made it! I was getting worried." Without a shred of hesitation, Amy embraced Roxanne heartily.

Over Amy's shoulder, Roxanne looked expectantly at Jessica.

"I got a little lost," Roxanne said quietly. "But I'm here now."

Jessica knew she should stand and greet her former best friend. Instead, she was rooted to the spot, a stone pillar unable to express any emotion.

Roxanne soon pulled away and Amy grabbed a clean wineglass from the nearby sideboard.

"Join us for a bit of the grape, girlfriend?"

"Don't mind if I do," Roxanne finally answered, accepting the glass with a half-hearted salute before sitting at the opposite end of the settee from Jessica.

The conversation became stilted, Jessica only speaking when necessary to maintain decorum.

"Catch me up, Aim. Tell me about that lighthouse," Roxanne ventured, not looking at Jessica.

"Point Surrender." Amy shuddered visibly and took a gulp of her wine. "Let's just say it's a whole helluva lot better now than when I stayed there."

"Why is that? It was lovely when I was there," Jessica countered.

Amy's face took on a serious, cloaked expression. "Did you go up into the tower?"

"No. It was locked. Your brother told me it was because I had Devon with me."

"Did you?" Roxanne asked Amy, her eyes round with curiosity.

"It was before Case and I were... together. We'd only just met—it's a bit of a long story, but—we were up there, it was a stormy night, lots of wind, waves, like a hurricane. We needed to get the light working. There were boats," Amy said, her eyes looking beyond her friends on the couch and into the past. "We argued, I fell down those spiraling stairs... I lost my baby later that night." Amy swallowed hard and attempted a vague sort of smile. "She would have been about a year old now."

"Oh, no..." Jessica heard herself whisper. "I'm so sorry."

"It was horrible. The good news is, Case and I got together, and he took me away from that... place. Brian and Judy fixed it up then moved to San Francisco."

"That's awful," Roxanne said. "I had no idea."

Jessica turned toward Roxanne with an accusing look. "Sometimes people don't share their heartaches with those who would want to help them." Turning back to Amy, Jessica gave her a sympathetic smile. "My daughter would have been around six by now."

Amy covered her mouth briefly. "I'd forgotten you lost a baby. It's so sad. Both of us."

Once again Jessica turned her eyes upon Roxanne, who was staring into her lap.

"My son would be six months old right now."

A gasp escaped Amy's lips. "You, too, Rox?"

"Last winter. I'm—I'm sorry I didn't tell you guys. I just couldn't." Roxanne looked like she was about to flood tears, and Jessica took a deep breath.

"I can't imagine why," she said finally.

The silence that followed lasted longer than was comfortable for anyone. Amy stood and placed her glass on the fireplace mantel. "I'm sorry, girls, but I've got to hit the sack. Coffee's on at seven-thirty, breakfast at eight-thirty. Sleep well."

The silence continued after Amy's footfalls had long died away. It was Roxanne who finally spoke.

"It's more than just the baby."

Jessica raised an eyebrow in Roxanne's direction. "I'm listening."

"Tom didn't think we'd really get pregnant. But it turns out that micro-surgery really works. He was beside himself."

"Why? Didn't he want a baby?"

"It was more complicated than that. I wanted the baby to be legit."

"I don't understand."

Roxanne looked up from where she'd been twisting the corner of a small throw pillow in her lap. "Tom and I... we never really got married. We lied."

Jessica nearly choked. Quickly she put her wineglass on the coffee table. "What?"

"When I told you Tom was divorced, I didn't know he'd lied to me. He has a wife, and she's institutionalized. It's a very well-kept secret."

Jessica shook her head. The thought of straight-arrow, easy-going Tom Jarrick living a lie was an impossibility. "What's wrong with her?"

"She's legally insane."

"Oh, God."

"He said he couldn't divorce her. I was pressuring him. I wanted him to find a way. We argued for days, and one night Robbie came in on it. He sided with his dad, of course. Devon was there, too, playing in the back room. I didn't want him to hear us. I was mad at you for being late. I didn't know you were late because Robbie had walked out on you."

"Huh?" Jessica's confusion grew with each revelation. "Robbie walked out on me? What do you mean? Robbie?"

"Robin. Tom's son. He goes by Quill. It's his mother's maiden name."

"Robin Quill is your stepson? How did I not know that?"

"He obviously didn't mention it after he realized you didn't recognize him. He came to a party at your house a few years ago. I thought I should say something, but..." Roxanne shook her head.

"He did mention a connection, but I never put it together. He's clearly a troubled young man."

"To say the least. And I should have spoken up. But I was already mad at you because you... you had everything I didn't. You had a wonderful marriage, a beautiful son. When Mac died, I was devastated, but you seemed to pick up your life and just go on. I couldn't imagine doing that."

"Rox, I wish you'd said something..."

"I was always saying something. Just not the right things."

"You thought Dane killed Mac."

"I don't know what I was thinking. I was taking meds for depression. I was out of my head. Tom started thinking I was going the route of his first wife. He almost went out of his mind trying to straighten me out. Dane was just... convenient, I think. It made sense to me. He's always loved you, obsessed over you. I became consumed by the idea that he did it. I wanted him to have done it."

Jessica looked toward the fire, which was beginning to die out. Roxanne's confession was tearing at her gut. "Dane cared about Mac."

"From where I stood, he couldn't have been more hateful." Roxanne sighed, and raked her fingers through her dark bangs, pulling them away from her forehead. "I sneaked around, Jess. After the wedding, I was using his computer to see if my orders were in, and it was too tempting. I know my way around that stuff now, and there was this document he'd been writing, a diary—"

"Stop. I don't want to hear about it."

"It was personal. I shouldn't have read it. I know, now, what an awful thing I did."

"It might have helped send him to prison, or worse."

Roxanne's fingers fidgeted in her lap. The only sound in the room was the crackle of the log in the fire. Roxanne's story was heartbreaking, overall, and Jessica's empathetic side began to surface.

"I wish you'd confided in me. I'm so sorry about Tom and his... wife, the baby... even Robin. I didn't have a clue about any of that. I need you to know," Jessica said, forcing her hand to reach for Roxanne's and grasp it, "I'm still your friend. And for the record, yes, I did pick up my life and go on. But it wasn't without heartache. Losing Mac devastated me, too. It was like losing myself. I was so empty. I had nothing inside anymore. Until Dane came back into my life. He was the one, the only one, who truly came to my rescue. Without judgment or demands. He was the one." Jessica stopped, noticing that her chest was heaving in evidence of the strong emotions within her. "I love him, Rox. He's as flawed as they come, and I still love him."

"Then why are you here without him? Your mom said you were having trouble."

Jessica suddenly felt very tired, and she withdrew her hand. "Yeah. We are. Dane has issues about Mac... Mac and me. We're working on it."

"I hope you can forgive me."

Jessica looked Roxanne in the eyes. "I do forgive you. Please promise me we can be close like we used to be. That you'll tell me when things happen. There've been so many times I wanted someone to talk to..."

With elephant tears streaming down her cheeks, Roxanne dissolved into Jessica's arms.

Roxanne said her goodbyes just after breakfast, and Jessica had to tear herself away from her best friend. The call from Janet Taylor had prompted Roxanne to squeeze in a brief, thirty-six-hour visit between fashion events in Los Angeles, but Jessica was glad, nonetheless. It was good to see Roxanne going back to work as well.

The last remnants of fog were just lifting as Jessica made her way down Main Street, her woolen jacket buttoned up to her chin. The town was every bit as charming as her mother said it would be. Only an occasional passerby smiled in recognition, but no one approached her. Midafternoon she stopped and gorged herself at the local pizza pub, then continued her shopping down the opposite site of the street. Shopkeepers kindly offered to deliver her purchases to the Winslow McKenna Inn, and she gladly accepted, succumbing to a need to feel unfettered and free. Yet keeping her arms free of packages proved a lot easier than keeping her mind free of the thoughts she'd hoped to avoid.

"Dane," she whispered, stuffing her hands into her jacket pockets. "If only you weren't such a... such a kook." She smiled inwardly at her own choice of words. Her mother wasn't all that far out in left field. There had to be a way to shake some sense into Dane, to make him remember that they were truly right for each other.

Jessica recalled with bittersweet irony their hasty honeymoon in Amande, and Dane's vow that they would always be together. Yet that very promise-keeping ethic was now keeping them apart. And what was that promise, anyway? He'd mentioned it more than once.

It had something to do with Mac, and she'd been unable to get Dane to reveal it to her. She should have tried harder. Maybe she still could.

Dane hugged both girls together and individually before leaving them in their maternal grandmother's care. His own concern surprised him as he watched for signs from his daughters, signs that they also felt a loss at his departure.

"I hope things work out for you," Melissa said.

Dane forced a tight smile. "It will be okay."

Zoe clung to Dane's side. "When will you come back, Daddy?"

"Soon, sweetie. Soon." Dane gently extracted himself and sought out his son, who was sitting on the back porch of Rita's mansion. "Hey, sport. I gotta go now. You help your gramma with those bratty sisters, okay?"

"Sure."

"Why the long face? I'll be back soon."

"Sure."

Dane issued a deep sigh and sat down beside Alexander.

"Are you going after them?" the boy asked, looking not at his father but at some nonspecific spot on the back lawn.

"Them, who?"

"Mom Two and Dev."

"Don't know. I don't think she wants me to."

"Dev said you would."

"Dev said what?"

"He said you'd come and bring him and his mom back to the ranch."

Dane shook his head slowly. "Wonder what made him say that?"

Alexander shrugged. "He kept saying, 'Daddy told me he would always take care of me and Mommy.'"

"I might have said something like that at one time or another. I don't remember."

"No. He wasn't talking about you. He was talking about his other dad. Uncle Mac. He said his other dad said that you," Alexander emphasized with a finger pointed at Dane's chest, "you would always take care of him if he ever needed it. Kinda weird, huh? Why would Uncle Mac ever say that?"

Dane frowned and got slowly to his feet. "I'm not sure, but I think I'd better find out."

Alexander stood also, and after a moment of hesitation, embraced his father. "I told him he was dumb. I didn't want them to go. Will you tell him I'm sorry?"

Dane felt as if the air had been sucked right out of his lungs. The feeling began when Alexander revealed Devon's words to him and continued right up until he boarded the flight to Seattle the next day.

"Can I get you something, Mr. Pierce?" the flight attendant asked, leaning down slightly. "We have mimosas made up this morning, or perhaps a Bloody Mary?"

"Coffee, please." Dane pushed his seat back a notch and looked out the window. First class was mostly empty on the 5:50 a.m. flight out of LAX. He was edgy; too much was happening, too many details to think about. His future seemed to be teetering on the brink of a precipice, and everything was riding on his ability to put the past behind him.

As part of his attempt to do just that, he'd made another stop at his former estate home the night before, intending to retrieve and destroy the hateful journal. It was no longer useful, and its very existence was threatening to him. Now, gratefully accepting the mug of steaming coffee, he recalled his shock at arriving at the Benedict Canyon house to find the small, rear bathroom window smashed. A quick glance around created a new knot in his stomach: the journal was gone. He'd had every opportunity to keep it safe, hell, destroy it, and now it was missing.

Dane shook his head to clear it. Reaching into the breast pocket of his shirt, he withdrew Jessica's letter for the third time since boarding.

"I'm not certain what to do next, only that we can't go on the way we are. But I'm also not ready to talk about divorce. It would be terrible for Devon. So, please, if we could just leave things alone for a while..."

Dane sighed and refolded the letter. *Leave things alone. What does that mean?*

"Cream?"

"Uh, no. Black is fine."

Okay. We can leave things alone, just as soon as I talk to Devon about what his father really said. Because if Mac did say I'd be there for his son... for his wife...

A light wave of dizziness washed over Dane, and he reached for the coffee on his tray. He hated the fact that his hand was trembling. The coffee was too hot, searing his throat and gullet but the pain did serve to clear his head, if only momentarily.

It had been no small feat getting Janet Taylor's address out of Teddy Langley, Jessica's agent. It was a miracle that Dane had even thought of calling Langley at all. Now, if he was able to find Jan's house, he might just find the answers he so desperately sought.

THIRTY-THREE

From the Mouths of Babes

"This is the best you can do?" Dane asked, staring at the keys to the four-cylinder economy car the clerk handed him.

"I'm sorry, sir. If you'd reserved... there is that big summit meeting in Seattle this week. We're tapped out of the big cars. I can give you an SUV if you'd like."

"Crap." Dane swallowed and looked around. People were beginning to stare. "Okay, hell, give me a damned SUV."

Another clerk, on the telephone with his back turned, called over his shoulder. "We're out of SUV's, too."

The young man working with Dane sighed. "Well..."

"Nothing else but that... that roller skate out there?" Dane asked impatiently.

"Give him the Hummer," the other clerk called.

"A Hummer. That's just great." Dane shook his head and took in a deep breath. "Just give me the damned keys, will you? And I need directions."

He was on the Bainbridge Island Ferry before he calmed down. Leaning against the rail, the cold wind in his face, he watched the retreating Seattle shoreline. His insides were burning. He'd had enough Seattle's Best java on the airplane to drown a fish, and certainly enough to re-ignite his dormant ulcer.

The directions to Jan Taylor's farmhouse seemed simple enough, if he could thread the mile-wide Humvee through the network of narrow two-lane roads on the small island. What would he say when he got there? What if Jessica refused to see him?

She'd have every right. I really, really screwed up this time.

But whether she'd see him or not, he had to talk to Devon. And Devon would be happy to see him, he was certain.

The exit traffic at the Bainbridge Island terminal distracted him for a time as he tried to move the vehicle between the smaller cars all opting for the same lane. Yet it took almost no time to find himself traveling down the country road toward his mother-in-law's home. She answered the door immediately.

"Why, Dane. What a surprise. Please come in."

Whatever he was expecting, it wasn't this welcoming woman with the sympathetic smile on her face. "Thanks. I don't suppose..."

"Jessie's not home. But sit down. Would you like some coffee?"

"Uh, no. Thanks. Had enough already. Is... Dev here?"

"He is, yes. He's out back watching the mares. Why don't you rest a bit before you see him? You've probably been on the road awhile?"

"Yeah, I have. Left L.A. early this morning. Where'd Jess go?"

"She's... taking a little vacation. Up the Sound. How 'bout I make you some eggs?"

Dane could not hold back a smile. "That sounds good, actually." He followed her into the kitchen and sat down, watching with amusement as the woman bustled about, pulling together the ingredients. "It's been a long time."

"What, since we've seen one another or since you've eaten a decent meal?"

"Since we've seen each other. My ex-mother-in-law fed me yesterday."

"Would seem you've had good luck with mothers-in-law, at least."

"She's pretty fair. Her daughter's not so bad, either, now that I think about it."

"I heard she's been ill."

Dane stretched his legs out and sighed. "Is that what Jessie called it? Ill?" He chuckled to himself. "She's doing okay. She'll get out in a month or so."

"The girls are with their grandmother, then?"

"Yup."

"You know Dane, the reason I wasn't at the wedding was that my daughter—your wife—did not invite me."

Dane lifted his eyebrows but did not voice his response. Jessica had never elaborated on why Janet had not shown up. Finally, he concocted a suggestion. "Maybe she felt two weddings were enough to invite you to?"

Janet stopped stirring the scrambled eggs and turned to look at Dane, her expression quizzical. Dane cocked his head to the side in question, and the two burst out laughing in sync.

"Could be," Janet agreed, nodding. "Could be."

She joined him for the meal. "Devon's already eaten," she explained. "He just can't wait to get out there with the horses. I'm not much of a horse person myself, but he sure has taken to them."

"That doesn't surprise me." Dane felt a welling of pride. "He's a great rider, already. I was planning to give him Mariah's foal this spring, but..."

"But what?" Janet asked sharply, as if she'd just been waiting for the comment.

"Well, it doesn't look too good for us still being together as a family. I suppose I should still give him the horse, but I don't know when or where he'd be able to ride it."

"Nonsense."

"Huh?"

"I said, why don't you go talk to him now?"

Dane frowned and got slowly to his feet. "Right."

Devon made a mad dash for Dane when the latter waved to him from the back porch.

"Pop! You're here!" Throwing his small body into Dane's arms, Devon snuggled his face against Dane's neck. "I knew you would come."

"You did, huh? Why is that?" Dane asked casually, carrying the boy back toward the horses and finally perching him atop the split rail fencing the corral.

"Because you always take care of us."

"Well, I try to. Is there another reason why you knew I would come?"

"No, just my daddy, my other daddy who got kilt in a crashed plane? He told me if he ever crashed, that you, but he said you were called Uncle Dane then, he said you would take care of me, and Mommy too, because you loved us almost like he did."

It was several moments before the lump in Dane's throat shrank enough to allow him a voice. "He said that, did he? When was this?"

"One time when I was scared, he was crashing his plane. He said he wouldn't. But he did. But it wasn't his fault."

"No, son, it surely wasn't his fault." Dane wrapped his arms as tightly around Devon as he could without crushing the little boy. "He was right about the other thing, though. I will always, always take care of you and Mommy."

"Yup. 'Cuz you're my pop."

Dane blinked away the moisture filling his eyes. "Hey. Did you know that Mommy's horse is going to have a baby? What do you think about that?"

"Sure you can't stay for dinner?" Janet Taylor asked, her hand absently stroking her grandson's hair as he stood by her side at the front door.

"I've lost too much time already," Dane said. "You say it's about an hour's drive?"

"Give or take. Depends on traffic at the bridge."

Dane nodded. Unable to stop himself, he stepped forward and gave Janet a hug. "Wish me luck."

"I don't think luck has much to do with it. But I don't think you're going to need it anyway. Jessie might surprise you. You be careful."

"In that? Are you kidding?" Dane responded, gesturing toward the oversized vehicle parked near the porch. "Thanks for everything."

The drive to Port Townsend was uneventful. The scenery was tranquil, and a pleasant sort of anticipation began to spread over Dane.

So. Mac had effectively made him Devon's unofficial godfather. It made sense. Hadn't Dane himself, after taking a bullet from Jackie Spencer's gun, charged Mac with Alexander's future? It was only natural that Mac would expect the same when it came to his own son.

But his wife, too?

It was open to interpretation.

Pensive, Dane drove on. Interpretation of the words of a not-quite-five-year-old boy, a boy who needed a father, and more, a happy mother. Yet this same boy was incapable of creating a lie.

Or was he? The tiniest sliver of doubt crept into Dane's mind. It was a fact that, even at five, Devon had become a pint-sized manipulator when it came to getting what he wanted. Was it possible that his memory of his father's assurances had been slightly skewed? That Devon's overwhelming desire for family caused him to tweak Mac's words? To insure his mother's happiness?

Interpretation. I can choose to interpret this any way I want. Who would challenge me? Certainly not Devon.

Gripping the steering wheel and taking a deep breath, Dane sped past the Port Townsend city limits, determined to win back Jessica's heart.

For good this time.

"I didn't think I'd be able to get away at all," Amy was saying, reaching for a packet of sweetener. "My Wednesday girl didn't show up today, so Case and I had to do everything. That's the downside of this business."

"Still, it looks like a lot of fun."

"It is. But I don't want to do it forever. So, did you spend all your money yet?"

Jessica grinned. "Not quite. Did get a few things for Devon. And a beautiful, hand-glazed crock for Mom. I want to go back to that store; they were closing when I was there yesterday."

"Sure. Let's go there when we're finished here."

The girls chatted amicably, reminiscing about their college days and carefully side-stepping their individual heartaches. From her discussions with Brian, Jessica knew Amy had been through her own turmoil in recent years. Yet things looked quite rosy for her now.

"I've been thinking about what you said, about not knowing too many happily married couples," Jessica ventured, her eyes momentarily focused on her plate. "Some people do have good luck with it."

Amy smiled. "Sure. I know that. I mean, Rox is happy, right?"

Jessica's own brief smile faded. "Yeah. She's happy. Hey, your brother Brian and Judy are happy. Chrissie and Nick are blissful!"

"And you and Mac were happy."

Now Jessica looked up, feeling her face grow hot. "Of course."

"Oh, Jess, I'm sorry. I didn't realize it was still so..."

"No, really... I'm fine. It's just that I... I really thought that Dane and I ..." Jessica smiled brightly. "But I don't want to spoil our time together. Let's get out of here and do some serious shopping, okay?"

"You're on. You've still got, oh, at least a million to spend, right?"

They were digging through a bin filled with silk scarves when Amy's cell phone purred to life. "What's up?" she asked, her face taking on an animated, concerned expression. "But they said they were staying another night! Great. Okay, I'm on my way. No, it's okay. It won't take long anyway." Shoving the phone back into her purse, Amy turned to Jessica with an apologetic smile. "I've got to get back to the Inn. The Heimlich's are maneuvering out the door and Case is having trouble with the credit card line. It's all choked up."

"Well, you sure wouldn't want him to get blue. I'll just see you later," Jessica quipped, waving her friend off.

She spent the rest of the afternoon wandering through the shops and boutiques, her mind still unable to focus on anything but her dilemma. Passing a video store, she paused, then returned. Where but in this quirky town would she find a vintage shop still renting DVDs? A good movie would help. While the Inn did not have televisions in the guest rooms, Amy and Case had given her carte blanche usage of their cozy living room on the third floor.

Casually glancing over the titles, Jessica paused in the 'romance' aisle, only to be stopped cold by the cover of *Lost Season*. I'm haunted, she thought with disdain. *I will never get away from this.*

As she put the movie case back on the shelf, a man appeared beside her and touched her gently on the elbow. Jessica nearly leaped from her skin.

"I'm sorry, but would you mind autographing that for me? I'd be so honored." The shopkeeper was a kind enough looking man, but Jessica was still shaking from the surprise.

"Of course. No problem." Hastily she scribbled her name on the cover of the box and exited the store.

The sun was setting on the water, and the temperature had dropped considerably since her mid-afternoon lunch with Amy. It was time to head back to the inn, which was more than a mile up town. She turned and headed in the general direction of the hilly neighborhood where Amy and Case lived, moving slowly and without purpose. She'd only walked a block from the store when she acquired the odd sensation of being followed. Not sure why, she turned, only to see the thinning crowd of tourists behaving normally, peering into store fronts and walking tiredly toward their rental cars parked at the curb.

As she gained another short block, she again turned around, but saw nothing out of the ordinary. A very young mother hustled across the street, clutching an infant; a teenaged boy took a drag from a cigarette, squinting his heavily made-up eyes toward the sunset; a man in an overcoat stared into a shop window. Had she seen him earlier?

"You are losing it, girl," she murmured, yet she wished she had driven her father's car instead of walking. "You've lived in L.A. too long."

The feeling grew. Finally, she crossed the street and entered a small gift shop. Glancing over her shoulder, she saw the man in the coat crossing also.

"I'm sorry, Ma'am, but we're closing," the woman behind the counter said.

"Oh. I didn't realize. Things close early here, don't they?"

"I guess that depends upon where you're comparing 'here' to."

"I'm from L.A.," Jessica said, hoping to engage the woman in conversation for just a few more moments.

"Ah. Yes, we do roll up the sidewalks earlier here. Was there something specific you were looking for? We open at nine a.m. tomorrow."

"No, just killing time. I'm staying at the Winslow McKenna Inn."

The woman just smiled, her keys in her hand.

"Well. I'll, uh, just be going then. I'll come back... tomorrow." Jessica gritted her teeth and turned toward the front door.

Taking a deep breath, she stepped outside and once again began walking up the sidewalk, cautiously looking from side to side. The man was nowhere to be seen.

Relaxing a little, her gaze wandered to the small boat dock at the end of the street. Normally bustling with activity during the summer months, it was now deserted but still charming. On a whim, she decided to walk the length of it, her thoughts returning to her husband and her ultimate dilemma. She looked over her shoulder once to be sure she was alone.

Jessica made it a slow stroll. The waters were dark now, the sun having just dipped below the horizon. Overhead, seagulls screamed and soared, diving in their last dip of the day. Across the water, she could see wooded Marrowstone Island and she wondered what it would be like to live surrounded by water. So beautiful.

If only Dane was here to enjoy this with me.

She was near the end of the dock when a voice came from behind her. She did not understand the words, but she spun quickly around. The man with the overcoat. A man whose face she knew.

Jessica was unable to withhold a gasp. "I don't believe this," she murmured, her hand flying to her neck. "What are you doing here? You nearly scared me to death!"

"Hello, Jessica. I was hoping you'd have a moment to talk."

"Not to you. How did you find me?" Jessica tried to calm her breathing and then set her jaw. "Not that it matters. I have nothing to talk to you about."

"But I have something to talk to you about. You'll be sorry if you run from this."

"Are you threatening me, Sgt. Denehy? Because if you are, there are legitimate law enforcers in this town who would be happy to escort your... you out of here."

The detective smiled. "Why all the hostility? Come on. I think you'll find what I have to say very interesting."

"I'm on my way to dinner. Please, just crawl back under whatever rock you slithered from." Jessica tried to skirt the man, but he stood squarely in her path.

"It's about your husband," Denehy began, slipping his hand inside his overcoat. "Did you know he had you followed?"

Jessica stopped and took two steps backward, facing the detective, her mouth slightly open in surprise. "Whatever do you mean?"

"All the way to Hawaii and back." Denehy withdrew a black book and held it up for Jessica to see. "That's only the tip of the iceberg. There are all kinds of surprises in here."

"What's that?" Jessica demanded, reaching for the book, but Denehy quickly lifted it out of her reach.

"Ah, ah, ah! Now we're interested, are we? Want to get some coffee and discuss it?"

"No. Just tell me whatever is so damned important so that I can go. I'm losing my patience." Jessica made every effort to sound assertive and confident, but her words failed her. "If you're still trying to place blame for Mac's death on Dane, you're beating a long-dead horse, Sergeant. Now unless that... that book contains a written confession in Dane's hand, you are wasting your time and mine."

Denehy smiled, an almost sympathetic smile, Jessica thought.

"Perhaps it does. I guess you could say... it's up for review. Analysis."

"The killer confessed. Wasn't that enough for you?"

"Sometimes it takes more than one to kill someone, Jessica."

"I'd prefer you didn't call me that." Once again starting forward, Jessica tried to maneuver past the man. "I'm leaving now."

"What about his lies? It doesn't matter to you that he lied about his relationship with Mac? Mrs. MacKendall?" Denehy opened the book to a bookmarked page. "And I quote: 'If only there was a way I could get rid of him, get him out of her life for good.' He's talking about Mac. That he wanted your husband dead is clear. There's more, too. It's enough to reopen the case, in my opinion."

"Well, Sergeant, your opinion doesn't count much anymore. And while I hate to be cliché, you aren't half the man Dane Pierce is. You aren't even fit to wipe his boots!" Jessica filled her lungs with air, feeling her power returning. Returning in a big way. "Yes, I know Dane and Mac weren't the best of friends Yes, they were jealous of each other. But that doesn't equate to murder. I've told you before, I love my husband and will stand behind him until the end. The end of everything." In anger, Jessica whipped the black book from Denehy's hands and stepped away from him, her chest rising and falling in anxious gasps. It was then that she noticed the man who'd silently joined them on the dock.

Swallowing hard, Jessica looked past the detective to Dane's face, and then to the journal in her hands. Dane's journal. She'd seen it once before, years ago, when she'd discovered it on the floor of his car while on a date. He'd taken it from her that night, hastily tossing it into the back seat. Now, the journal was back in her hands. Three or four torn slips of paper, acting as bookmarks, extended from the top of the closed book.

"Go ahead. Open it." Denehy suggested, staring hard at Jessica.

Jessica ran her hand over the cover, feeling the suppleness of the soft, black leather. The gold embossed name in the lower front corner had nearly worn away. Inside were the words, the answers to the questions she could not ask. The key to the mysterious "promise" and Dane's obsession with keeping it. This was her chance to finally find out. Hugging the journal to her chest, Jessica returned Denehy's stare. Her anger at the man threatened to bubble over, overshadowing her need to delve into Dane's personal diary.

"There is nothing between these covers that could change the way I feel about my husband," she said with a forced calm reserve. "This... this doesn't belong to me. And it certainly doesn't belong to you." This time Jessica succeeded in getting past the stunned policeman, walking the three or four yards farther to stop before Dane, who stood watching with his hands shoved into the pockets of his jacket.

Denehy turned around, his face pinched in concern. "Uh, Mrs. MacKendall, that's state's evidence. You can't—you can't—"

"I can't what, Sgt. Denehy?" Jessica called over her shoulder, then turned and held the journal out for Dane, whose expression was one of interest and surprise. "Is this yours, darling?"

Slowly Dane withdrew his hand from his pocket. "As a matter of fact, it is. It was stolen from my house a few days ago." Taking the journal, Dane stared at its cover as if he'd never seen it before. "You, uh... you're welcome to read it."

Jessica peered into Dane's eyes. If called upon to describe the feeling inside, she would have been forced to decline. A rush, a massive, spreading warmth overtook her, but her eyes never left his. "It's not necessary," she said slowly. Vaguely aware of Denehy's complaints at her back, Jessica didn't move.

Dane opened the journal and fanned its pages briefly. A slight smile turned up the corners of his mouth. "Not necessary," he murmured, now closing the book and grasping it in his right hand. He looked past Jessica to Denehy. "When you get back to L.A., you'll find a copy of the police report on the break in. Insurance will pay for the damage, of course. This was the only thing stolen. But since it really has no value..."

Jessica watched in silent surprise as Dane curled his arm back and then flung the journal into the ocean as though it was a Frisbee.

Denehy shook his head slowly, and, after looking from Dane to Jessica and then back to Dane, walked off the dock, leaving the Pierces alone.

It was several moments before either ventured any kind of movement. Cloaked in the declining dusk, Dane Pierce took a deep breath, wrapped both arms around Jessica and buried his face in her hair.

•♥•♥•♥•♥•♥•

At the Winslow McKenna Inn, the private bathroom in the suite Jessica had rented was filled with burning candles. Candles of every shape and size surrounded the huge claw foot tub, and Jessica was already mostly hidden by thick, frothy bubbles as Dane unbuttoned his shirt.

"Is it hot?" he asked, tossing the shirt aside and unbuckling his belt.

"It is. And delicious."

Next went the jeans and briefs, and Dane stepped into the tub, sitting opposite his wife. The water rose dangerously high. "No sudden movements," he warned with a smile.

"You know I like it slow," Jessica said, her voice low and sultry, and then she giggled. "I'm rotten at the coy stuff, aren't I?"

"You are as coy as a vamp in a silent picture, sweetie." Dane reached for his wineglass on the tub side table. "Don't ever change." He took a sip and stared over the top of the foam at his wife's face, which was moist from the heat of the water. Her hair was piled onto the top of her head and held by a silver clasp. Her eyes held warmth and a hint of mischief that was hard to miss. "Forgive me?" he asked impulsively.

Jessica cocked her head, and a dreamy, trancelike expression replaced the smile on her face. What was she thinking? Was she remembering the times he'd treated her badly, the times he'd trounced on her heart? Was she wondering if his involvement in Mac's murder was real, or just the inane ramblings of a guilt-ridden detective? Was she still weighing the good against bad, sizing up the outcome of her decision to marry the man who'd made such a stupid promise? A promise she knew nothing about...

"Yes," she said suddenly, and the bubbles that had gathered against the hair on Dane's chest parted as Jessica's toes emerged from the water. Dane watched with heated interest as her big toe, its nail painted in bright, lipstick red, pressed against his skin and slid down his chest, disappearing back below the foam. "Yes, I forgive you," she repeated. "And I'm so glad... so glad you are not perfect."

Dane sighed. *Am I supposed to wonder what the hell that means?* "We'll I'm glad that you're glad, because perfect is something I'll never be." Dane reached into the water and grasped Jessica's foot, pulling it back out of the water and to his lips.

"Mmm. There are some things, however, that you do perfectly," Jessica teased, the smile returning to her face. "Don't ever change."

"I'm not sure I could change. I'm pretty rooted to my asinine ways."

The dreamlike mask of Jessica's face remained. Reaching out, she took Dane's glass and stole a sip of his wine. "I want to thank you," she said at last, curling her fingers around the glass and holding it against her cheek.

"For what?"

"For not giving up on me."

Dane took a deep breath and held it momentarily, expelling it with a low whistle. "Jessie, I really never even had a choice. And I'm so sorry for all the times I... made it hard for you. So many times I —"

"Stop." Jessica sat upright and returned the wineglass to the table, then leaned forward and pressed two fingers to Dane's lips. Dane closed his eyes, allowing the immense delight created by her touch to flow throughout his being. Jessica's soft voice continued. "I understand enough now to know you were right when you said we were meant to be together. It was your belief that brought you back to me."

It was the eve of his thirty-ninth birthday. And it looked like he was finally getting the gift he really wanted.

•♥•♥•♥•♥•♥•

In the pasture behind Janet Taylor's farmhouse, Jessica curried the new filly while Dane watched.

"You almost look like you're enjoying that," Dane said.

"I am enjoying it. I figure I should start out small. Some fears are harder to overcome than others."

Dane smiled. "You've got that right."

It was quiet for a time, each of them lost in thought until Dane again spoke. "I still can't believe that asshole followed you up here."

"He said he saw me at Sea-Tac International. He followed me to Mom's, then to Port Townsend. Gives me the creeps. Reminds me of Wesley."

"Who's out of prison, right?"

"Yeah. They sent me a letter to the ranch, but someone took down our address numbers..."

"Someone who meant well."

After a time, he took the brush from her hand and gently grasped her by the waist. "So have you decided what you want to do?"

"Yes. Have you?"

"Yes."

"Well?"

"No, you go first." Dane lifted his hands and stroked the hair away from her face. "Tell me."

"I want to have Christmas at the ranch. I want the kids with us. I want to forget about all the crap we've been through and just go ahead."

Dane blinked and looked toward Jan Taylor's back door. Grinning, he shook his head. "That, and the cake your mother is baking in there, are the best birthday presents I could have hoped for."

"Yeah, like I could use more sweets," Jessica said with a smile, unsuccessfully trying to 'suck in' her slightly rounded tummy.

"You look absolutely ravishing to me."

Jessica rolled her eyes and looked away. She had thought she would never hear words of endearment again. Now, back in Dane's protective grasp, she couldn't be happier. No matter that the adoption had failed. No matter that her husband was making a picture with another woman. No matter that she would have to be happy with the children she already had in her life. Nothing mattered more than the love of this one man. And this time, she vowed, she would not let misconceptions and preconceived notions get in the way of their happiness.

Thirty-Four

A Hero's Promise

The first lavender hues of the dawn were barely visible. Jessica, her body warm and cocooned against Dane's, was torn between staying nested and getting up to begin their first Christmas morning together.

Compromising with herself, she dallied another fifteen minutes, snuggling and kissing Dane's face as he lay in half slumber. Finally, she crept from the bed and donned her turquoise silk robe.

In the kitchen, the coffee maker was already brewing, and Jessica turned on the oven to bake the breakfast strudel and Serbian eggs she and Melissa had prepared the night before. On the great room hearth, the Santa plate, with its half-eaten cookie and empty milk mug, sat waiting for the children, along with the over-stuffed stockings that hung from the mantel. She noticed with amusement that her own stocking was also filled. From the hall closet, she brought out a small bag of gifts she'd purchased for filling Dane's.

Finally sitting down with her coffee, she watched the pink layers of sky become golden ones, relishing the few moments alone before the chaos of Christmas came tumbling down the stairs.

And tumble they did. Two boys, two girls and one slightly groggy father soon dashed away the silence and filled the great room with excitement and joy. The strudel was baked, the cocoa was melting mini marshmallows and the children's stockings were unceremoniously dumped onto the carpeting. It was all Jessica could do to slow them down long enough to snap a few photos. Before long, the room was knee deep in discarded wrapping paper and bows, toy packaging and tissue.

"Time for breakfast," Jessica finally announced, and Melissa was quick to help serve the eggs and turkey sausage.

"Wow, Mom Two, this is awesome," Alexander said, reaching for a slice of Dane's toasted beer bread.

"Yummy!" shouted Devon, and Dane fondly tweaked the youngster's nose.

"Fill your stomachs; we've got a big day ahead of us," Dane suggested.

The "big day" included a massive snowball fight in the yard; a snowman building competition, boys against girls; and a sleigh ride into Jackson for the afternoon church service.

By late afternoon, two boys and two girls were tired and content to play quietly with their toys while Jessica and Dane cleared away some of the spoils of the morning. When the phone rang, Jessica grabbed for it, thinking it was perhaps her sister or brother calling.

"Jess?" A woman's voice. Jessica frowned and Dane paused, his hands still filled with crumpled gift wrap.

"Yes? Who is this, please?"

"Okay, it hasn't been that long!"

"Rox? Oh! Hello!"

"Just wanted to say, Merry Christmas..."

"Merry Christmas to you, too! How are you?"

"I'm... good. I'm better. Just wanted to make sure you aren't still mad at me."

Jessica put up her hand as if Roxanne could see her halting gesture. "Rox, don't even go there. You... you weren't well. We know that now. Please don't give it another thought."

"It's important to me that Dane knows how sorry I am. Truly."

"He forgives you." Jessica looked hard at Dane, mouthing the words, "You do, don't you?"

Dane looked uncertain and then smiled and shook his head "no."

"Rox, why don't you and Tom come up for a visit? We'll be up here another month. Please?"

"We'll talk about it. Is it cold there?"

"Is it cold? Is it cold? Ha!"

The children were tucked into bed, eight goodnight kisses having been bestowed. Dane descended the stairs and joined his wife before the fire, where Jessica sat looking through the stack of Christmas cards they had received.

"This is my brother and his wife," she said, handing Dane a photo card.

"I see the resemblance."

"To me?"

"To Bill Gates."

"Ah. Yes." Jessica giggled. "Here's the one from Chrissie and Nick."

Dane took the snapshot of Angel and Bridgett and smiled, slowly shaking his head. "Reminds me of when Mimi and Zoe were little like that." Quietly getting to his feet, Dane retrieved an unopened card from the mantel. "This came yesterday. I thought you might want to open it."

"Minnesota? Who do we know there?" Once opened, a photo and a letter fell from the otherwise unremarkable card. Dane leaned closer to see. The picture was of a little boy with shiny black hair and big, brown eyes, possibly eighteen months old. Quickly, Jessica flipped the photo over. "Oh, my. Look. 'Benjamin MacKendall Bandorf, age one and a half.'"

Jessica read the letter from the Bandorfs aloud, then clutched it to her chest and smiled. "This makes me so happy. It was the right thing, what happened. These people are wonderful for him."

"I'm glad you feel that way. I've wanted to talk to you about that. I still feel bad that it didn't work out the way we planned."

"It worked out fine."

"But I promised you."

"Dane," Jessica said softly, reaching for his hand, "there are just some promises that cannot be kept."

Dane nodded slowly. "I know. Some promises should never be made in the first place." He took the picture of Benjamin and stared at it. "Cute little guy. Do you think we did the right thing by not challenging the adoption?"

"Of course, we did. His life had already begun with them. And look. They are keeping in touch with us... what more could we want?" Her eyes misted over, then brightened. "Hey, we never opened our own stockings!" Jessica scrambled to her feet and unhooked the two remaining stockings from the mantel. "Here you go, stud. Enjoy!" she said, tossing Dane's into his lap.

After laughing over a variety of dime store items, Dane dug out a small package from the bottom of the stocking and removed the wrapping paper. Inside was a box, and inside that, a gold pocket watch. Quickly he looked up at Jessica.

"Go on, open it, silly!"

Dane pressed the tiny button on the side, and the watch cover flipped open. Opposite the watch face was a small photo of the four children.

"It's a composite. I could never get them all four in one place so the guy in town put it all together for me."

"It's... it's wonderful, Jess. Wow. Thanks." He gazed at the picture and smiled. "It would be hard to get more than four in there." He turned the watch in his hands, carefully closing the front and finding the inscription on the back.

To my real hero: Love forever, Jessica

"I..." At a loss for words, Dane cupped the back of her head in his hands and pulled her lips against his for the deepest, most meaningful kiss he could create. There was nothing he would not do for this woman, nothing he would not give her, especially with the new confidence that she was rightfully his. At last, they parted, and he was reminded of something. Something equally important. "Now you. Go ahead." Dane gestured toward the untouched Christmas stocking on Jessica's lap.

"Oh! Okay. Here goes." Like a child, Jessica pulled two small, wrapped gifts from the stocking. "Which one first?"

"Uh... that one."

"Okay." Quickly she pulled the shining gold paper from the smaller package. Inside, a velvet jewelry box. Clearly holding her breath, Jessica tilted the lid backward to expose the diamond tennis bracelet that lay inside. "Oh, how pretty! Oh, Dane, I love it!" Snatching it from its velveteen bed, Jessica was quick to open the latch and wrap it around her ankle. Stopping just short of hooking it, she gave Dane a coy smile. "Would you mind?"

"I'd be delighted, Ma'am." With great ceremony, Dane latched the delicate hook and gave her ankle a lustful stroke for good measure. They replayed their previous kiss with just as much feeling and passion as before, and Dane felt hard pressed not to lift his bride to the sofa right then and there. But there was that other gift. "Don't forget the other one."

"Oh, right! I don't know how anything could top this," Jessica said, admiring the bracelet one more time as the diamonds caught and magnified the dancing firelight. She took up the second small package and shook it, then pressed it to her nose. "Not perfume..."

"Nope. But something I hope you'll be able to use, soon."

"Hmm. What could it be..." Jessica took her time peeling small strips of paper from the box. Soon, it was evident that it was a commercial product with large black letters on the front of the packaging. "What the..." Removing the remaining wrapping paper, Jessica held up the box. "Is this some kind of joke? What would I do with an in-home pregnancy test?"

Dane took the box from her, turned it around and shoved it back into her hand. "The same thing any other woman does with it. Read the directions!"

Jessica went silent, and Dane suddenly feared she was going to cry. "What does this mean, Dane?" she asked carefully. "The only way I could be pregnant is if you... if you..."

"Glad to hear that," Dane quipped. "Look. First you go into the bathroom; you open the box, take the little stick thing out and pee on it. The guy at the drugstore said..."

Suddenly Jessica threw the kit to the side, got to her knees and grasped Dane by the shoulders, pushing him flat out on the floor. "Did you do it? Did you really? Oh, God, Dane, when did you do it?"

"In July. Right after we got married. And it seems to me... I'm no expert, but..." Dane slid his hand across Jessica's tummy affectionately. "So, are you gonna go use it, or what?"

Her eyes blazing with joy, Jessica whipped the kit from the floor and skipped off to the bathroom, giggling hysterically.

Dane lay back on the carpeting and stared at the ceiling, the myriad of shapes created by the firelight entertaining his eyes. He chuckled to himself. Maybe this promise business wasn't so difficult after all.

THIRTY-FIVE

Epilogue: Full House

"I must be suffering from heatstroke. How much did you say?" Jessica asked, squirming uncomfortably in the posh chair before Teddy's desk.

"You heard me right. He's the man, baby. The biggest director in Hollywood, and he'll hear of no one but you for the part. Ever since I let it leak that you were back in town, your price keeps going up!"

You're not the only one leaking, my friend. Jessica stole a glance downward at her blouse. Why hadn't she put nursing pads in her bra? "Teddy, I'll have to let you know after I talk to Dane. It's important to me that he's in on any decision. I want to read over the script again, too. And I'm throwing this huge party tomorrow. You are coming, aren't you?"

"Of course, sweetpea. March fifteenth, right here on my desk calendar. I wouldn't miss it for all the men in West L.A."

"Good. Now, I've got to run. I'm... I need to get home."

She wasted no time jamming the new Jaguar into gear and finding the freeway on-ramp. She looked at the clock every few minutes, racing against it to get home in time. Her new silk blouse was already stained, but it was not the condition of the blouse that concerned her. Teddy had kept her longer than she had planned.

Finally, she cruised into the triple-wide garage at her Malibu home and bounded from the car, rushing inside in search of Dane.

"I'm home!" she called, hurrying through the kitchen into the living room where Dane sat in the large rocking chair, a finger pressed to his lips.

Jessica stopped short. The drapes had been drawn against the noonday sun, and the television was on at low volume. The small bundle held against Dane's chest stirred.

"How's she been?"

"She's been great. Asleep for an hour and a half."

Jessica exhaled the breath she felt she'd been holding since leaving Hollywood. "I'm sorry I'm late. You know how Teddy can be." Peeling off her pink suit jacket, Jessica peered down at her blouse and grimaced. "I'd better change. I'll be right back."

In her bedroom, Jessica practically ripped the clothes from her body, changing into a fresh white cotton nursing blouse and a pair of shorts. At the dressing room sink, she splashed cool water on her face before realizing her make up would be ruined.

"Darn it," she muttered, wetting a washcloth and trying to repair her face. Leaning close to the mirror, she carefully wiped beneath each eye. Something moved in the mirror behind her, and she froze, watching for it to appear again. A tiny face, held by her father's capable hands, peeked around the edge of the door frame. A small fist rubbed at her eye.

"I'm awake, now, Mommy," Dane's high falsetto advised from beyond her view. "And I'm hungry!"

Jessica giggled and dropped the washcloth, eagerly taking her daughter from Dane's arms. "How's my little girl?" she cooed, cradling the baby and walking back to the living room and rocker.

"What do I need to do for tomorrow?" Dane stood beside the chair, looking down at his wife as she prepared to nurse the baby.

"Everything's about done. Just call your daughter and make sure she's all set."

"Don't know why I have to do all the work..."

Zoe Irene Pierce had made up her own guest list. A tenth birthday party was very special, Jessica had assured her step-daughter. The beginning of two-digit ages. Several friends from school, her assorted brothers and sisters, and her mother finished off the list. Jessica had stressed about 'the mother,' at first, but Dane had assured her that Rita would die before making a scene. That left only one name to worry about: Trina Vidal. When Jessica had asked Dane for his thoughts on this last party guest, he'd merely chuckled and walked from the room.

"It's okay, isn't it? I love Trina!" Zoe demanded, her young face screwed into a scowl.

"It's okay," Jessica eventually decided. After all, there were enough adults attending to dilute the mix. Roxanne and Tom, Teddy and his partner, and Peter and Lydia, just home from Great Britain. Woodson Rawlins would probably show up, as would Sal Cicerelli and his wife.

Jessica busied herself dressing the baby in her cutest little pink dress and bonnet, while Dane led the caterers to the backyard, overlooking the Pacific, where the party was being set up.

Soon, the festivities would begin.

My name is Zoe Irene Pierce, and this is my very first diary. My mom bout it for me today for my 10 birthday. It even has a lock and a little key. She said I can right down my thots here. and no one can read them but me. She is helping me.

I had a big nice party today. everyone came even Tosha from school. All my famly was here too. Alex is my brother, he's 13 and thinks he is so smart. Mimi is 14 and she was so bord but too bad. Devon is my step-brother, hes kinda a brat but I like him o.k.

I have a new baby sister, her name is

J I L L I A N L E I G H

but I had to ask my mom how to spell it. She is so cute and little. My dad almost fanted when she was born.

My dad is a famis movie star and everyone likes him. My stepmom (J E S S I C A) is a famis movie star too. She is

B E A U T I F U L and nice. I want to be a famis movie star too. Trina says I can be if I want to. Trina is my grown up friend. She bout me real lipstick for my birthday. Yea!

Megan came to the party. She is my cousin I think, she is Devon's other sister. I think she likes my brother Alex, she sits by him all the time.

Uncle Peter brot me a big big big big! stuft panda bear. He said he wants a little girl like me when Ant Liddie gets her baby. Liddie said I can babysit.

Uncle Teddy came too. He gave me COLER PICTCHERS OF COLIN STARR!! even ottografed. Yea!!

Ant Rox brot me a dress she made herself. it's dark blue with lots of sparkles! it fits grate. Uncle Tom gave me the biggest hug ever. He's so cute!

JeSsica got me lots of new close. She is always so nice when I come. Sometimes dad and Jessica get mad but they always kiss and make up. Jessica might get a MO VIE DE AL.

Well, that's all for now. Dad says I haff to be careful about what I write in here, like don't say anything bad about someone. But I told him, its got a lock!

Oh, also, dad thinks I can be a movie star too. he says movies are in our blood.

Zoe looked back to the top of the page and began reading over her entry. After reading it through twice, she sighed, and then tore the page from the book. She picked up her pen and began again.

My name is ASHLEY MARIE PIERCE and this is my very first diary.

Dear Reader...

Thank you for reading A HERO'S PROMISE, Book 2 of the StarCrossed Romance saga!

If you enjoyed this book, now would be a great time to post a review. Many thanks!

Now, turn the page for an excerpt from THE GYPSY IN ME, Book 3, which takes up twelve years later...

Next Up ...

The Gypsy in Me

It's been twelve years since Jessica and Dane solidified their marriage and added baby Jillian to their "yours, mine and ours" brood. Six kids, growing up in the shadows of their superstar parents and trying to come into successes of their own. A blended family with its own special brand of neuroses. Melissa, Alexander and Zoe Pierce, each with an entirely different relationship with their well-meaning but troubled father; Megan MacKendall, a darkly morose woman who still suffers the loss of her cherished father; Devon MacKendall, the virtual clone of his late father, a man-child reluctant to grow up and who struggles to remember the times before Mac's death; and Jillian, watching her siblings with the curious eyes of the clan's youngest.

"So, you got sweaty palms, did you?" Jessica asked, her fingers struggling to unfasten her diamond necklace. "I thought you'd be calling all the shots on that show."

"Don started asking about Zoe. Pisses me off. The interview was supposed to be about the film, not my kids." Dane shrugged out of his jacket.

Jessica went to her husband and slipped her arms around his neck. "You are the film. You are what people want to know about. You, and your exquisitely imperfect family." She kissed the corner of his mouth, creating a small smile there, and then smiled herself. "Besides. There's nothing to tell, right? So what if one daughter's an unwed mother and the other has run off with gypsies. At least she didn't join the circus."

"They're hippies. Cultists. Hell, she might have joined the circus by now. I haven't heard anything from her for two months."

"Are you worried?"

"No. Well, yes, dammit. She's only twenty-one."

"Is this a good time to mention how old you were when you met her mother?"

"I was eighteen. Rita was nineteen. We were both more ... mature than Zoe."

Jessica chuckled. "Yeah, right."

"You'd feel differently if it was Dev who'd taken to the road and didn't call."

Jessica stepped out of her linen skirt. "Yes, I suppose I would. But somehow, I don't think he would ever do that."

It was Dane's turn to laugh. "No, Dev will still be living with us when he's thirty-nine, I'm afraid. In fact, he'll be the one to invite the circus to live with us."

About the Series

StarCrossed Hearts – Book One

Silver screen heroes Dane Pierce and Cory "Mac" MacKendall are as different as cognac and Perrier, and newcomer Jessica Taylor loves them both. Despite his tantalizing green eyes and raw sexuality, Dane is not the man she thinks she needs. It is the solid and devoted - if hot-headed - Mac who wins her hand and heart, and who must endure a lifelong challenge to keep that heart safe from Dane's unending pursuit. From Hollywood soundstage to the Grenadine Islands, **StarCrossed Hearts** makes a journey around the world and through the lives of some very real characters you will not soon forget.

A Hero's Promise – Book Two

If you read **StarCrossed Hearts**, you know that heart-breaking, womanizing Dane Pierce will not find it easy to walk away from the one woman that sets his soul on fire. Promise or no promise, Dane will do everything he can to win back Jessica's love. Now, the heart-stopping sequel you've been waiting for: **A Hero's Promise**, a story of pain and redemption, and a love that survives the very worst of life's challenges.

The Gypsy in Me – Book Three

Their children have grown. Some are his, some are hers; some are half-siblings, others step-brothers and sisters. Growing up the offspring of Hollywood's brightest stars, Jessie, Dane and Mac's kids are each special, each a little neurotic, and each seeking love. The MacKendall and Pierce daughters square off in this next installment to the **StarCrossed series**; who would have thought that history would repeat itself?

To Love a Vagabond:
Devon's Journey – Book Four

He's the son of not two, but three Hollywood megastars. The legacy he's inherited feels more like a ball and chain than a fairytale. Devon MacKendall's life has never been easy, or simple, and when the worst possible tragedy befalls him, he heads for the road in this heart-wrenching installment of the StarCrossed saga. Meeting the elusive Brandy Owens is the last thing he wants, but she just might be the salvation he needs. *Coming 2023!*

Meet Anne Carter

Creating fiction gives one the power to design other lives, filled with romance and adventure, intrigue and passion. My own writing career began in middle school creative writing class, inspiring me to later major in literature. All it took was one teacher' encouragement and I was on my way.

I'm the author of nine published novels, including mystery, romance, paranormal, alternative romance and even a middle grade reader. As for the personal stuff, I'm a Virgo, a procrastinator, like warm better than cold and drink neither Coke nor Pepsi. I was born in the Midwest but migrated to California as a child. My hobbies include doll collecting, photo restoration and writing, of course. My favorite sport is ice hockey, my favorite TV shows include mysteries, romance (Duh!), cooking shows (*Great British Baking Show!*) and crime series that make you think and not count bodies. I am married to my hero of 40+ years and have 3 great kids and two--wait, THREE--delightful grands. Visit me at Beacon Street Books (where I also blog), Facebook, and other fun cyber spots.

Also by Anne Carter

The StarCrossed Romances

StarCrossed Hearts – Book 1

A Hero's Promise – Book 2

The Gypsy in Me – Book 3

To Love a Vagabond – Book 4 (2023)

The Beacon Point Romances

Ever & Always

Point Surrender

Cape Seduction

Angel's Gate

Amoroso Pass (2023)

Paulie & Kate

Unmasking Paulie Bingham

For the Love of Katrina Bingham

www.ingramcontent.com/pod-product-compliance
Lightning Source LLC
Chambersburg PA
CBHW070802180626
46818CB00001B/66
9780615628714